DYING LIGHT

Stuart MacBride has scrubbed toilets offshore, flunked out of university, set up his own graphic design company, got dragged into the heady world of the internet, developed massive applications for the oil industry, drunk heaps of wine and created the perfect recipe for mushroom soup. He lives, just left of the back of beyond, in north-east Scotland with his wife Fiona and enough potatoes to feed an army. The bestselling *Dying Light* is his second novel.

Visit Stuart MacBride's website at
www.stuartmacbride.com

D1492822

By Stuart MacBride

Cold Granite
Dying Light

STUART MACBRIDE

DYING LIGHT

HARPER

Harper
An imprint of HarperCollins*Publishers*
77–85 Fulham Palace Road,
Hammersmith, London W6 8JB

www.harpercollins.co.uk

This paperback edition 2007
1

First published in Great Britain by
HarperCollins*Publishers* 2006

Copyright © Stuart MacBride 2006

Stuart MacBride asserts the moral right to
be identified as the author of this work

A catalogue record for this book is
available from the British Library

ISBN 978-0-00-785560-5

Typeset in Meridien by Palimpsest Book Production Limited,
Grangemouth, Stirlingshire

Printed and bound in Great Britain by
Clays Ltd, St Ives plc

For Fiona
(again)

Without Whom . . .

The truth is a malleable thing, especially when I get my hands on it. So I have to thank the following lovely people for letting me bend their truths, sometimes beyond all recognition: The Procurator Fiscal's Office in Aberdeen for letting me in on how the Scottish Justice System actually works; George Sangster of Grampian Police for an invaluable heap of police procedure and info; and my 'first lady of the morgue' – Ishbel Hunter the Senior APT at Aberdeen Royal Infirmary who is, as always, a star.

I also owe a debt of thanks to Philip Patterson – who isn't just a bloody good agent, but a good friend too – and all at Marjacq Scripts; my wunderkind editorial gurus Jane and Sarah; the brilliant cast and crew at HarperCollins, particularly Amanda, Fiona, Kelly, Joy, Damon, Lucy, Andrea, and everyone else who has done such an excellent job in getting this thing out there; Kelley at St Martin's Press and Ingeborg at Tiden, for their valuable input into this book; and James Oswald for his suggestions and photos of cheese.

I should probably thank the Aberdeen Tourist Board as well, for not having me lynched when the last book came out. If it's any consolation: at least this one's set in summer.

But mostly I have to thank my naughty wife Fiona (or she'll thump me).

1

The street was dark as they entered the boarded-up building: scruffy wee shites in their tatty jeans and hooded tops. Three men and two women, nearly identical with their long hair, pierced ears, pierced noses and pierced God knew what else. Everything about them screamed 'Kill Me!'

He smiled. They would be screaming soon enough.

The squat was halfway down a terrace of abandoned two-storey buildings – dirty granite walls barely lit by the dull streetlights, windows covered with thick plywood. Except for one on the upper floor, where a thin, sick-looking light oozed out through the dirty glass, accompanied by thumping dance music. The rest of the street was deserted, abandoned, condemned like its inhabitants, not a soul to be seen. No one about to watch him work.

Half past eleven and the music got even louder; a pounding rhythm that would easily cover any noise he made. He worked his way around the doorframe, twisting the screwdriver in time with the beat, then stepped back to admire his handiwork – three-inch galvanized woodscrews all the way round the door, holding it solid against the frame, making sure it stayed irrevocably shut. A grin split his face. This would be good. This would be the best one yet.

He slipped the screwdriver back into his pocket, pausing for a moment to stroke the cold, hard shaft. He was hard too, the front of his trousers bulging with barely concealed joy. He always loved this bit, just before the fire started, when everything was in place, when there was no way for them to escape. When death was on its way.

Quietly he pulled three glass bottles and a green plastic petrol can from the holdall at his feet. He spent a happy minute unscrewing the bottles' caps, filling them with petrol and popping the torn rag fuses in place. Then it was back to the screwed-shut front door. Lever open the letter box. Empty the petrol can through the slot, listening to the liquid splash on the bare, wooden floorboards, just audible through the pounding music. A trickle seeped out under the door, dribbling down the front step to form a little pool of hydrocarbons. Perfection.

He closed his eyes, said a little prayer, and dropped a lit match into the puddle at his feet. *Whooooomp*. Blue flame fringed with yellow raced under the door, into the house. Pause, two, three, four: just long enough for the blaze to get going.

Throw a half brick in through the upstairs window, shattering the glass, letting the throbbing music out. Startled swearing from inside. And then the first petrol bomb went in. It hit the floor and exploded, showering the room with burning fuel. The swearing became screaming. He grinned and hurled the remaining bottles into the blaze.

Then it was back to the other side of the road, to lurk in the shadows and watch them burn. Biting his lip, he pulled his erection free. If he was quick he could come and go before anyone arrived.

He needn't have hurried. It was fifteen minutes before anyone raised the alarm and another twelve before the fire brigade turned up.

By then everyone was dead.

2

Rosie Williams died the way she'd lived: ugly. Lying on her back in the cobbled alley, staring up at the orange-grey night sky, the drizzle making her skin sparkle, gently washing the dark red blood from her face. Naked as the day she was born.

PC Jacobs and WPC Buchan were first on the scene. Jacobs nervously shifting from foot to foot on the slick cobbled road, Buchan just swearing. 'Bastard.' She stared down at the pale, broken body. 'So much for a quiet shift!' Dead bodies meant paperwork. A small smile crept onto her face. Dead bodies also meant overtime and Christ knew she could do with some of that.

'I'll call for backup?' PC Steve Jacobs fumbled for his radio and called Control, letting them know the anonymous tip-off was for real.

'*Hud oan a mintie,*' said Control in broad Aberdonian. There was a pause filled with static and then, '*You're goin' ta have ta hold the fort oan yer own for a bit. Everyone's off at this bloody fire.*

I'll get ye a DI soon as one 'comes available.'

'What?' Buchan grabbed the radio off Jacobs, even though it was still attached to his shoulder, dragging him off balance. 'What do you mean, "as soon as one becomes a-bloody-vailable"? This is murder! Not some sodding fire! How the hell does a fire take precedence over—'

The voice of Control cut her off. *'Listen up,'* it said, *'I dinna care what problems you've got at home: you bloody well leave them there. You'll do as you're damn well told and secure the crime scene till I can get a DI to you. And if it takes all bloody night that's how long you wait: understood?'*

Buchan went furious scarlet, before spitting out the words, 'Yes, Sergeant.'

'Right.' And the radio went dead.

Buchan started swearing again. How the hell were they supposed to protect a crime scene with no IB team? It was raining for God's sake; all the forensic evidence would be getting washed away! And where the hell were CID? This was supposed to be a murder enquiry – they didn't even have an SIO!

She grabbed PC Jacobs. 'You want a job?'

He frowned, suspicious. 'What kind of job?'

'We need a Senior Investigating Officer. Your "mate" lives around here doesn't he? Mr Police Bloody Hero?'

Jacobs admitted that yes, he did.

'Right, go wake the bastard up. Let *him* deal with it.'

*   *   *

WPC Watson had the nastiest collection of bras and pants that Logan had ever seen. All of her underwear looked like it had been designed by World War One zeppelin manufacturers on an off day – uniform baggy-grey. Not that he got to see a lot of Jackie's underwear these days, but for a brief spell their shifts were in synch. Logan smiled sleepily and rolled over, the light from the hallway spilling through the open door, illuminating the rumpled bed.

He squinted at the alarm clock: almost two. Still another five hours before he had to report for work and yet another bollocking. Five whole hours.

Click, the light in the hall died. A soft silhouette filled the doorway, having a bit of a scratch as it scuffed its way back into bed. WPC Jackie Watson wrapped her unbroken arm around Logan's chest and settled her head against his shoulder, unfortunately sticking the curly ends of her hair up his nose and into his mouth. Discreetly spitting them out, he kissed the top of her head, feeling the cool length of her body pressed against him. She ran a finger over the inch-long trails of scar tissue that crisscrossed his torso and Logan thought: maybe five hours wasn't so long after all . . .

Things were just getting interesting when the doorbell went.

'Damn it,' mumbled Logan.

'Ignore it, probably just drunks.' The doorbell rang again, more insistent this time. As if the sod on the other end was trying to drill his way into the building with his thumb.

'Bugger off!' Logan shouted into the darkness, causing Jackie to dissolve into a fit of the giggles, but it didn't deter the phantom ringer. Then Logan's mobile phone joined in the noisy predawn chorus. 'Oh for God's sake!' He rolled off, provoking a groan of displeasure, and grabbed the phone from his bedside cabinet. 'WHAT?'

'Hello, sir? DS McRae?' PC Steve Jacobs: the Fabled Naked Swordsman of Old Aberdeen.

Logan let his head slump, face first, into the pillow, still holding the phone to his ear. 'What can I do for you, Constable?' he asked, thinking that this had better be damned important if it was going to distract him from a naked WPC Watson.

'Er . . . sir . . . We've kinda got a body . . . an—'

'I'm *not* on duty.'

WPC Watson made a noise that said, yes he bloody well was, but not one that concerned Grampian Police.

'Aye, but everyone else is off at some fire and we've no SIO, or IB or anything!'

Logan swore into the pillow. 'OK,' he said at last. 'Where are you?'

The doorbell went again.

'Er . . . that was me . . .'

Sodding hell.

Logan grunted his way out of bed and into some clothes, before lurching out of his flat, down the stairs and out the main door, looking rumpled and

7

unshaven. PC Steve, infamous for his striptease rendition of Queen's *A Kind of Magic,* was standing on the top step.

'Sorry, sir,' he said, looking sheepish. 'Across the road: naked woman. Looks like she's been battered to death . . .' And any thoughts Logan had of having fun in the wee small hours disappeared.

At quarter past two on a Tuesday morning the harbour was pretty much deserted. The grey granite buildings looked unnatural and jaundiced in the streetlights, their edges blurred by the drizzle. A huge supply vessel, painted luminous orange, was tied up at the bottom of Marischal Street, its lights bright haloes as Logan and PC Jacobs made their way round the corner to Shore Lane. It was a narrow one-way street at the heart of Aberdeen's red light district: one side a five-storey wall of dirty granite and darkened windows, the other a collection of random-sized buildings. Even at this time of night, the smell was something special. Three days of torrential rain followed by a week of blazing sunshine had left the sewers full of drowned rats, rotting fragrantly. There were sodium lights bolted to the buildings, but most of them were buggered, leaving small islands of yellowed light in a sea of darkness. The cobbles were slick beneath their feet as PC Steve led Logan to a dark pool halfway down, where a WPC crouched over something white sprawled across the lane. The body.

The WPC stood at the sound of their approach, shining her torch full in their faces. 'Oh,' she said, without enthusiasm. 'It's you.' Stepping back, she played her spotlight over the naked corpse.

It was a woman, her face battered and broken, one eye swollen nearly closed, the nose mashed flat, broken cheekbone, broken jaw, missing teeth. She wore a necklace of dark red bruises and nothing else.

She was no spring chicken: the thick white flesh of her thighs rippled with cottage-cheese cellulite; stretch marks making sand dune ripples across her stomach; and in between, short rough stubble: long overdue for another homemade Brazilian wax. A rose and a bleeding dagger were emblazoned on the milk-bottle skin just above her left breast, the tattooed blood refusing to wash away in the rain.

'Jesus, Rosie,' said Logan, dropping to one knee on the cold, wet cobbled street so he could get a better look at her. 'Who the hell did this to you?'

'You know her?' This from the unfriendly-looking WPC. 'You one of her regulars?'

Logan ignored her. 'Rosie Williams. Been working the streets down here for as long as I can remember. God knows how many times she's been done for soliciting.' He reached forward and felt for a pulse on her neck.

'Believe it or not, we already did that,' said the WPC. 'Dead as a doornail.'

The drizzling rain muffled the sound of drunken voices singing and shouting somewhere back along the docks. Logan stood, looking up and down the alley. 'IB? PF? Duty doctor?'

The WPC snorted. 'You must be bloody joking. They're all sodding about at that fire. Much more important than some poor cow who got battered to death.' She folded her arms. 'Wouldn't even send us a proper SIO, so we had to make do with you.'

Logan gritted his teeth. 'You got something to say, *Constable*?' He stepped close enough to smell the stale cigarette smoke on her breath. She stared back at him, her face a thin line of displeasure.

'How's PC Maitland?' she asked, her voice as cold as the corpse at their feet. 'Still alive?'

Logan bit back the reply. He was her senior officer; he had a responsibility to behave like a grown-up. But what he really wanted to do was find one of those greasy, rotting, bloated rats and shove it right up her—

Shouts sounded from the other end of the alley, where it connected with Regent Quay. Three men staggered round the corner, lurching into one another, fumbling with their trousers, laughing as streams of steaming urine splashed against the alley walls. Logan turned back to the smug, defiant WPC. 'Constable,' he said with a thin smile, 'you're supposed to be securing the crime scene. So why can I see three men *pissing all over it*?'

For a moment it looked as if she was going to answer back, then she stormed off up the alley, shouting 'Hoy! You! What the bloody hell do you think you're playing at?'

That left Logan and PC Steve with the battered remains of Rosie Williams. Logan dragged out his mobile phone and called Control, asking for an update on the duty doctor, Identification Bureau, pathologist, Procurator Fiscal and the rest of the circus that was meant to roll up whenever a suspicious death was discovered. No joy: everyone was still tied up at the big fire in Northfield, but DI McPherson would be with them as soon as possible. In the meantime Logan was to stay where he was and try not to get anyone else killed.

An hour later there was still no sign of DI McPherson, or the IB, but the duty doctor had arrived. At least it had stopped raining. The doctor struggled his way into a white paper scene-of-crime suit before trudging down Shore Lane, ducking under the blue 'POLICE' tape WPC Buchan had grudgingly stretched across the alley.

Doc Wilson wasn't at his best at half past three in the morning, a fact he made abundantly clear by dropping his medical bag in a ratty-smelling puddle and swearing a blue streak. The bags under his eyes were family sized, his nose red and raw from a late summer cold.

'Morning, Doc,' said Logan, getting nothing but a grunt in reply as the doctor squatted down over the corpse and felt for a pulse.

'She's deid,' he said, stood, and started back for his car.

'Hold on a minute.' Logan grabbed his arm. 'Is

11

that it? "She's deed?" We know she's dead: care to hazard a guess when and what of?'

The doctor scowled. 'That's no' my job; ask a bloody pathologist.'

Surprised, Logan let go of the old man's arm. 'Rough night?'

Doc Wilson ran a tired hand across his face, making the stubble scritch. 'Sorry. I'm just knackered . . .' He cast a glance over his shoulder at Rosie's naked body and sighed. 'Best guess: blunt trauma. The bruisin's no' that advanced, so circulation must've stopped pretty quickly. Given the lividity I'd say you're lookin' at three, maybe four hours ago.' He stifled a yawn. 'Beaten to death.'

It was twenty past four before anyone else turned up, and by then Doc Wilson was long gone. The sun was already on its way, the sky a soft lemon stain wisped with grey, but Shore Lane remained shrouded in shadow.

The Identification Bureau's filthy white Transit Van reversed up the alley from the dual carriageway, a lone IB technician in white SOC coveralls guiding it in. Both rear doors opened and the ritual fight with the crime scene tent began: wrestling metal poles and blue plastic sheeting up over Rosie Williams's body. A generator roared into life, chugging blue smoke out into the early morning – diesel fumes fighting with the stench of rotting rat – setting a pair of arc lights crackling. The Procurator Fiscal appeared not long after, parking at the far end of the alley where it emptied out onto Regent Quay. She was an attractive blonde in her early forties, looking almost as tired as Logan felt, smelling faintly of smoke. A serious-looking younger woman trailed along behind her: all frizzy hair, wide eyes and clipboard. Logan brought them up to speed as they struggled into a matching set of white paper over suits, then had to go through the whole thing again when the pathologist turned up. Dr Isobel MacAlister: tired, irritable and more than happy to take it out on Logan. Nothing like an ex-girlfriend to take all the fun out of a crime scene. And there was *still* no sign of DI McPherson. Which meant Logan was still responsible if anything went wrong. As if he didn't have enough to worry about. The only upside was that it wouldn't be his problem for long: there was no way they'd leave him in charge of a murder enquiry. Not with his recent track record. Not after he'd almost got PC Maitland killed in a botched raid. No, this case would go to someone who wouldn't screw it up. He checked his watch. Almost five. Still another two hours to go before his day shift was supposed to start and he'd already been at it for half the night.

With a tired sigh, Logan stepped from the cold light of dawn into the SOC tent. It was going to be a long day.

3

Grampian Police Force Headquarters was a seven-storey concrete-and-glass tower block in broad bands of black and grey, hidden down a small road off the east end of Union Street. Topped with a thorny crown of communications antennae and emergency sirens, FHQ wasn't exactly Aberdeen's crowning architectural achievement, but it was home.

Logan grabbed a cup of coffee from the machine and pilfered a bourbon biscuit from the media office. There was no sign of DI McPherson. Not in his office, not in his incident room, not in the canteen, nowhere. Logan tried the dispatch office, but they'd not heard from McPherson since he'd called in from the hospital at quarter to six that morning. Broken leg, fractured wrist and concussion. He'd fallen down two flights of stairs. Logan swore. 'Why didn't someone tell me? I've been waiting on him since half two this morning!' But the dispatcher just shrugged. Wasn't his job to act as a secretary. If Logan was looking for someone to hand the case over to, DI Insch was probably the best bet. Even if he did have that arson attack to look after.

DI Insch's morning briefing was a sombre affair. The inspector perched at the front of the room, dressed in a smart grey suit, his considerable bulk straining its seams. The man just seemed to get larger every year, his round features and shiny bald head making him look like an angry pink egg. There was silence as he told the crowded room that PC Maitland's condition hadn't improved – they'd managed to remove the bullet, but he still hadn't regained consciousness. There was going to be a whip-round for the family.

Next up was a spate of drug-related violence. Some new pushers had moved in, kicking off a mini turf war. Nothing fatal yet, but it was likely to get worse.

Then Logan had to give a five-minute rundown on Rosie Williams's battered body before Insch took over again to talk about the previous night's fire, his voice booming out in the crowded incident room. It had started in one of the older buildings off Kettlebray Crescent: a run-down, boarded-up street of council housing deemed too scabby for human habitation. Number fourteen had been used as a squat for the last couple of months, three men, two women and a nine-month-old baby girl, all of whom had been at home on the night of the fire. Which explained the unmistakable burnt-pork smell when the fire brigade finally managed to break down the door. There were no survivors.

The inspector shifted, making the desk groan as he ferreted about in his trouser pockets. 'I want one team going door-to-door two streets either side of the scene: anything you can get on the squatters, particularly names. I want to know who they were. Team two is going to pick through the surrounding buildings, gardens and waste ground. You,' he said in a merry sing-song, children's-television voice, 'are looking for *clues*. Who was the chef at last night's indoor barbecue? Get me something.'

As the teams filed out of the room, Logan stayed put, trying not to look as tired and hacked-off as he felt.

'Well,' said Insch when the room was emptied, 'what time you off to see Dracula?'

Logan sagged even further into his chair. 'Half eleven.'

Insch swore and shifted his attention to his jacket pockets. 'What kind of a bloody time is that? Why couldn't he drag you in at seven if he was going to chew a strip out your arse? Waste of a bloody morning . . .' A grunt of satisfaction as he finally found what he was looking for: a packet of fizzy dinosaurs. He stuffed one in his mouth and chewed thoughtfully. 'He tell you to bring a Federation rep with you?'

Logan shook his head.

'Well, probably not going to sack you then.' He levered his bulk down from the desk. 'If you've not got the Spanish Inquisition till half eleven, you can go pay your last respects to Rosie Williams. Post mortem's at eight. I've got to do a press conference on this bloody fire. With bastard McPherson off on the sick, *again*, I've got more than enough on my plate without watching the Ice Queen hack up some murdered tart as well. I'm sure you can hold the fort without me. Go on.' He made little shooing gestures. 'You're making the place look untidy.'

Rosie was already washed by the time Logan slumped his way out across the rear car park and down the stairs to the morgue. It was a collection of odd-sized rooms, buried away in the basement of FHQ, not quite part of the building proper. The cutting room was spacious: clean white tiles and stainless steel tables sparkling in the overhead lighting, disinfectant and room freshener fighting a losing battle against the reek of burnt meat. A row of six trolleys sat against the far wall, their occupants sealed in white plastic body-bags. Locking in the freshness.

Logan was only five minutes early, but he was still the only living person there. He let loose a huge yawn and tried to stretch the knots out of his shoulders. No sleep, followed by six hours in a cold, stinking alleyway was beginning to take its toll. Grunting, he slouched over to Rosie's naked body. She lay on one of the glittering cutting tables, beneath the massive extractor hood, ready to give her all one last time. Rosie's skin was even paler than it had been in the alley. Her blood had succumbed to gravity's embrace, slipping slowly through the tissue to pool along her back and the underside of her arms and legs, making her porcelain flesh dark purple and bruised where it touched the table. Poor old Rosie. Her death hadn't even merited front-page treatment, just a sidebar in this morning's *Press and Journal*. 'SIX MURDERED IN ARSON ATTACK!' was the main story.

There was a strange protrusion bumping the skin over her ribcage and Logan was leaning in for a closer look when the door burst open and the pathologist swept in.

'If you're about to get romantic,' said the newcomer with a grin, 'I can come back later.' Dr Dave Fraser, overweight, going on fifty-five, bald head, hairy ears. 'I know you have a thing for the colder lady.' He grinned and Logan couldn't help smiling back. 'Speaking of which: you will be disappointed to hear that Her Imperial Majesty the Ice Queen will not be joining us for this little funfest. Doctor's appointment; not feeling well after last night.' Logan breathed a sigh of relief. He was in no rush to see Isobel again after her foul mood at the crime scene this morning. Doc Fraser pointed at the six trolleys in the corner. 'You can take a peek if you like, while I get set up.'

Against his better judgement, Logan walked across to the collection of trolleys in the corner. Up close the smell was worse: burnt meat and rendered fat. One of the body-bags had been carefully folded up in quarters, the resulting package held in place with silver tape, making it small enough to take a nine-month-old child. Taking a deep breath, Logan picked one of the other bags, standing motionless in the antiseptic room for a moment, wondering if this was really such a good idea, before pulling the zip down. There wasn't much of a face left: nose and eyes gone, the teeth yellow-brown shards poking through scorched-black flesh. The mouth open in a final, silent scream. Logan took one look, gagged, and zipped it back up again. He shuddered his way back to the cutting table.

'Good, isn't it?' asked Dr Fraser, smiling at him from behind his surgical mask. 'Tell you, I did one when they brought them in: all crispy on the outside and raw in the middle. Like every time my wife tries to barbecue.'

Logan closed his eyes and tried not to think about it. 'Shouldn't they be in the fridges, instead of lying out there?'

Dr Fraser nodded. 'Yup, but the winch is buggered, and I'm not doing it: bad back. Brian can shift them when he gets here.'

The aforementioned Brian – the mortuary's senior Anatomical Pathology Technician – arrived bang on eight o'clock, along with the Procurator

Fiscal, her assistant, a police photographer, and the corroborating pathologist: there to make sure Dr Fraser didn't screw up the post mortem and cost them a conviction. He was a cadaverous man with eyes like an unwell fish and a handshake to match. The PF's sidekick was the same one who'd attended the crime scene in the wee small hours, a brand-new substantive depute, two years out of law school and moving up the career ladder. She was dressed in full surgical get-up, complete with mask and hat, her eyes shining with a mixture of fear and excitement. Logan got the distinct impression this was her first time at a real post mortem.

'Everybody ready?' asked Dr Fraser when they'd all clambered into the ubiquitous SOC over suits so as not to contaminate the body.

'Er . . . before we begin,' said the new girl, looking at her boss for permission before continuing. 'I'd like to know where the victim's clothes are: have they been examined?'

Logan shook his head. 'She was naked at the scene. No sign of any clothing. I had two uniforms search the alley and the surrounding ones as well.'

She frowned. 'So whoever killed her took her clothes,' she said, not noticing as Logan and Dr Fraser exchanged a pained look. 'Has she been raped? Is there any sign of recent sexual congress?'

Dr Fraser screwed up his face and Logan could tell he was looking for a polite way to tell her to shut up and sod off. 'We've not got that far yet, but as she was on the game I'd be pretty shocked if we didn't find evidence of recent shagging.' He told Brian to start the tape. 'Now, if you're sitting comfortably, we'll begin.'

Logan tried not to watch too closely as Fraser finished the external examination and went in with the knife – seeing someone's innards getting hauled out in four big chunks and rummaged through always made his stomach churn. From the looks of things the deputy PF's breakfast was doing the post mortem dance too. Her eyes had gone a watery pink and all the colour had drained from the small part of her face on show between the hat and the mask. Nice to see it wasn't just him.

When at last it was all over, and Rosie's brain was floating in a bucket of formalin, Dr Fraser ordered Brian to stop the tape and go put the kettle on. It was time for tea and edited highlights.

They stood in the small office, waiting for the kettle to boil, listening to Dr Fraser translate the medical-speak into English. Rosie Williams had been beaten to death: stripped, punched, kicked, stomped on and strangled. Not necessarily in that order. 'But,' he said, 'she didn't die from manual asphyxiation. Left lung was punctured; the rib severed the vein on the way in so she basically drowned in her own blood. But it would only have been a matter of time before her other injuries killed her anyway. Oh and she was pregnant too. About eight weeks.'

The PF's beeper went off, eliciting a small round

of genteel swearing as she pulled out her mobile phone, couldn't get a signal, and had to go outside. As soon as her boss was gone, the new deputy PF tried to take charge. 'We should get a DNA analysis done on the foetus: we may have to prove a link between the death and the child's father.' Now that there wasn't a butchery exhibition going on under her nose she was a lot more confident. She'd stripped off her surgical gear to reveal a severe black suit with sensible boots. Her long hair was the colour of stale beer, frizzy at the ends, her face pretty in a long-nosed, girl-next-door kind of way, a smattering of freckles marking the recent sunshine. 'What about the sexual assault angle?'

Fraser shook his head. 'Plenty of recent sexual activity – all three entrances – but nothing forced. Signs of lubricant in all orifices, probably spermicidal condoms, but we won't know for sure until we get the lab results back. No semen.'

'Right, Sergeant,' she said, turning to Logan, 'I want you to search the alley for any discarded contraceptives. If we can . . .' she caught sight of Logan's expression and stopped. 'What?'

'Shore Lane is one big open-air knocking shop. There'll be hundreds of used condoms down there, and we've no way of telling how long they've been there for, who was wearing them, or who they've been inside.'

'But the DNA—'

'For DNA to count, first you'd have to prove it'd been inside her, then that it was worn by the killer and not just one of her regulars. Not to mention the whole "was it used at the time of her death" thing. And we don't even know if her attacker had sex with her first.' Something horrible occurred to Logan. 'Or after?' He cast a worried glance at Dr Fraser, but the man shook his head.

'No fear of that,' he said. There had been a nasty case a year ago when little boys were being abducted, strangled and then abused and mutilated. At least this wasn't going to be one of those.

'I see.' She furrowed her neatly trimmed eyebrows. 'I suppose there would also be considerable expense involved in getting DNA extracted from all those contraceptives.'

'Considerable!' said Logan and Dr Fraser at the same time.

'I want them collected anyway,' she said. 'We can store them in deep freeze in case a suspect emerges.'

Logan couldn't see the point, but what did he know? He was just a lowly detective sergeant. Just as long as he didn't have to be the one telling the search teams to rummage about looking for old condoms, preferably filled. 'Will do,' he said.

'OK.' She reached into her immaculate suit and pulled out a slim black wallet, handing each of them a freshly minted business card. 'If anything comes up, day or night, let me know.' And then she was gone.

'Well?' asked Dr Fraser when the morgue door had swung shut. 'What do you think?'

Logan looked down at the card in his hand: 'Rachael Tulloch LL.B, Procurator Fiscal Substantive Depute'. He sighed and stuck it in his top pocket. 'I think I've got enough to worry about.'

Twenty-five minutes past eleven and Logan was getting twitchy. He'd arrived at the offices of Professional Standards early, not wanting to make a bad impression, even though he knew it was *way* too late for that. Inspector Napier didn't like Logan. Had never liked him. Was just itching for a chance to throw him out on his scarred backside. It was twenty to twelve before Logan was finally summoned through to the inspector's lair.

Napier was an unhappy-looking man by nature and had managed to select a career in which his miserable face, thinning ginger hair and hooked nose were a distinct advantage.

The inspector didn't stand as Logan entered, just pointed a fountain pen at an uncomfortable-looking plastic chair on the opposite side of the desk, and went back to scribbling down something in a diary. There was a second, uniformed inspector sitting on the other side of the room with his back to the wall, arms crossed, face closed. He didn't introduce himself as Logan looked nervously about Napier's office. The room echoed the man, everything in its place. Nothing here was without function, nothing frivolous like a photograph of his loved ones. Presuming he had any. Finishing his entry with a grim flourish, Napier looked up and flashed Logan the smallest and most insincere smile in the history of mankind.

'Sergeant,' he said, smoothing out a razor-sharp crease in his tailored black uniform, the buttons winking and shining away in the fluorescent lighting like tiny hypnotists' pocket watches. 'I want you to tell me all about PC Maitland and why he is now lying in Intensive Care.' The inspector settled back in his chair. 'In your own time, Sergeant.'

Logan went through the botched operation, while the silent man in the corner took notes. The anonymous tip-off: someone selling stolen electrical goods from an abandoned warehouse in Dyce. Getting the officers together, fewer than he'd wanted, but all that were available. Piling out to the warehouse in the dead of night when there was supposed to be some big delivery happening. Getting everyone into position. Watching as a grubby blue Transit Van appeared and backed up to the warehouse door. How he'd given the go to storm the building. And then how it had all started to go wrong. How PC Maitland had been shot in the shoulder and fallen from a walkway, twenty feet straight down to the concrete floor below. How someone had set off a smoke grenade and all the bad guys escaped. How, when the smoke cleared, there wasn't a single piece of stolen property in the whole place. How they'd rushed

Maitland to A&E, but the doctors didn't expect him to live.

'I see,' said Napier when Logan had finished. 'And the reason you decided to use an unarmed search team rather than trained firearms officers?'

Logan looked down at his hands. 'Didn't think it was necessary. Our information didn't say anything about weapons. And it was stolen property, small stuff, nothing special. We did a full risk analysis at the briefing . . .'

'And are you taking full responsibility for the entire . . .' he hunted around for the right word, settling on: 'fiasco?'

Logan nodded. There wasn't anything else he could do.

'Then there's the negative publicity,' said Napier. 'An incident like this gathers media interest, much in the same way as a mouldering corpse gathers flies . . .' He produced a copy of the previous day's *Evening Express*. The headline was something innocuous about house prices in Oldmeldrum, but the inspector flicked past that to the centre-page spread and handed it across the desk. To My Mind . . . was a regular column, where the paper got local bigwigs, minor celebrities, ex-police chief inspectors and politicians to bang their gums about something topical. Today it was Councillor Marshall's turn, the column topped with the usual photograph of the man, his rubbery features stretched wide by an oily smile – like a self-satisfied slug.

Police incompetence is on the rise: you only have to look at last week's botched raid for yet more evidence! No arrests and one officer left at death's door. While our brave boys in blue patrolling the streets are doing a sterling job under difficult circumstances, it has become clear that their superiors are unable to manage the proverbial drinks party in a brewery . . .

It went on for most of the page, using Logan's screwed-up warehouse raid as a metaphor for everything that was wrong with the police today. He pushed the paper back across the desk, feeling slightly sick.

Napier pulled a thick file marked 'DS L. McRae' from his in-tray and added Councillor Marshall's article to the pile of newspaper cuttings. 'You have been remarkably lucky not to have been pilloried in the press for your involvement in this, Sergeant, but then I suppose that's what happens when you have friends in low places.' He placed the file neatly back in the tray. 'I wonder if the local media will still love you when PC Maitland dies . . .' Napier looked Logan straight in the eye. 'Well, I will make my recommendations to the Chief Constable. You will no doubt hear in due course what action is to be taken. In the meantime, I'd like you to consider my door always open, should you wish to discuss matters further.' All the sincerity of a divorce lawyer.

Logan said, 'Yes, sir. Thank you, sir.'

This was it: they were going to fire him.

4

Lunchtime, and Logan was still waiting for the axe to fall. He sat at a table in the corner of the canteen, pushing a congealing lump of lasagne around his plate. There was a clatter of dishes and Logan looked up to see WPC Jackie 'Ball Breaker' Watson smiling at him. Bowl of Scotch broth followed by haddock and chips. The plaster cast on her left arm made unloading the tray kind of tricky, but she managed without asking for help. Her curly brown hair was trapped in its regulation bun, just the faintest scraps of make-up on her face, every inch the professional police officer. Not at all like the woman he'd gone to bed with last night, who dissolved into fits of giggles when he blew raspberries on her stomach.

She looked down at the mush on his plate. 'No chips?'

Logan shook his head. 'No.' He sighed. 'Diet, remember?'

Jackie raised an eyebrow. 'So chips are out, but

lasagne's OK is it?' She dug a spoon into her soup and started to eat. 'How was the Crypt Keeper?'

'Oh you know, same as usual: I'm a disgrace to the uniform, bringing the force into disrepute . . .' He tried for a smile, but couldn't quite make it. 'Beginning to think Maitland might just be one cock-up too many. Anyway,' change the subject: 'how about you? How's the arm?'

Jackie shrugged and held it up, the cast covered in biro signatures. 'Itches like a bastard.' She reached over and took his hand, her pale fingertips protruding from the end of the plaster like a hermit crab's legs. 'You can have some of my chips if you like.' That produced a small smile from Logan and he helped himself to one, but his heart wasn't in it.

Jackie made a start on the haddock. 'Don't know why I bothered talking the bloody FMO into letting me come back on light duties: all they'll let me do is file stuff.' Dr McCafferty, the Force Medical Officer, was a dirty old man with a permanent sniff and a thing for women in uniform. There was no way he could refuse Jackie when she turned on the charm. 'Tell you: no bugger here has the faintest clue about alphabetization. The amount of things I've found under "T" when it should be . . .'

But Logan wasn't listening. He was watching DI Insch and Inspector Napier enter the canteen. Neither of them looked particularly happy. Insch hooked a finger in the air and made 'come hither' motions. Jackie gave Logan's hand one last squeeze. 'Screw them,' she said. 'It's just a job.'

Just a job.

They went to the nearest empty office, where Insch closed the door, sat on the edge of a desk, and pulled out a packet of Liquorice Allsorts. He helped himself and offered the packet to Logan, excluding Napier.

The inspector from Professional Standards pretended not to notice. 'Sergeant McRae,' he said, 'I have spoken to the Chief Constable about your situation and you will be pleased to know that I have been able to convince him not to suspend, demote or dismiss you.' It sounded bloody unlikely, but Logan knew better than to say anything. 'However,' Napier picked some imaginary fluff from the sleeve of his immaculate uniform, 'the Chief Constable feels that you have had too much freedom of late, and perhaps require more "immediate supervision".' Insch bristled at that, his eyes like angry black coals in his large pink face. Napier ignored him. 'As such you will be assigned to DI Steel's team. She has a much less demanding caseload than Inspector Insch and will have more time to devote to your "professional development".'

Logan tried not to wince. A transfer to the Screw-Up Squad, that was all he needed. Napier smiled at him coldly. 'I hope you will look upon this as an opportunity to redeem yourself, Sergeant.' Logan mumbled something about giving it his best shot and Napier oozed out of the room, reeking with triumph.

Insch dug a fat finger into the packet of Allsorts and stuffed a black-and-white cube into his mouth, chewing as he put on a reasonable impersonation of Napier's nasal tones: '"I have been able to convince him not to suspend, demote or dismiss you" my arse.' The cube was followed by a coconut wheel. 'Wee bugger will have been in there with the knife. The CC doesn't want to fire you 'cos you're a bona fide police hero. Says so in the papers, so it must be true. And anyway, Napier can do sod all till they've finished the internal investigation. If he thought there was *any* chance of doing you for culpable negligence or gross misconduct you would've been suspended already. You'll be fine. Don't worry about it.'

'But DI Steel?'

Insch shrugged philosophically and munched on a pink aniseed disk. 'Aye, there is that. So you're on the Screw-Up Squad: so what? Get your finger out, don't do anything stupid and you'll be OK.' He paused and thought about it. 'Long as PC Maitland doesn't die, that is.'

DI Insch ran a tight ship. A stickler for punctuality, preparation and professionalism, his briefings were clear and concise. DI Steel's, on the other hand, seemed to be pretty much a shambles. There was no clear agenda and everyone talked at once, while Steel sat by an open window puffing away on an endless chain of cigarettes, scratching her armpit. She wasn't much over forty, but looked a damn sight older. Wrinkles ran rampant over her pointy face, her neck hanging from her sharp chin like a wet sock. Something terrible had happened to her hair, but everyone was too afraid to mention it.

Her team was relatively small – no more than half a dozen CID and a couple of uniforms – so they didn't sit in ordered rows like DI Insch insisted on, just clustered around a handful of chipped tables. They weren't even talking about work; half the room was on 'did you see *EastEnders* last night?' and the other half on what a bloody shambles the last Aberdeen–St Mirren football match was. Logan sat on his own in silence, staring out the window at a crystal-blue sky, wondering where it had all gone wrong.

The door to the briefing room opened and someone in a brand-new suit backed in, carrying a tray of coffee and chocolate biscuits. It went onto the middle table, starting a feeding frenzy, and as the figure straightened up Logan finally recognized him. PC Simon Rennie, now a detective constable. He spotted Logan, smiled, grabbed two coffees and a handful of chocolate biscuits before joining Logan at the window. Grinning as he handed over one of the chipped mugs. He looked awfully pleased with himself.

DI Steel took a sip of coffee, shuddered and lit up another cigarette. 'Right,' she said, her head wreathed in smoke, 'now that DC Rennie has delivered the creosote, we can get started.' Conversation drifted to a halt. 'As you boys and girls can see, we have a couple of new recruits.' She pointed at Logan and DC Rennie, then made them stand so a half-hearted round of applause could be wrung from the rest of her team. 'These two have been selected from the hundreds of keen applicants, desperate to join our ranks.' That got a small scattering of laughter. 'Before we go any further I'd like to give our newest members the standard intro speech.'

That got a groan.

'You are all here for one reason and one reason only,' she said, scratching. 'Like me, you are a fuck-up, and no one else will have you.'

DC Rennie looked affronted: this wasn't what he'd been told! He'd only been a DC for three days, how could he have screwed up?

Steel listened to him with sympathy, before apologizing. 'Sorry, Constable: my mistake. Everyone else is here because they've fucked up; you're here because everyone *expects* you to fuck up.' More laughter. The inspector let it die down before carrying on. 'But just because those bastards think we're worthless, doesn't mean we have to prove them right! We will do a damn good job: we will catch crooks and we *will* get the bastards convicted. Understood?' She glared around the room. 'We are not at home to Mr Fuck-Up.' There was a pause. 'Come on, say it with me: "We are not at home to Mr Fuck-Up".' The response was lacklustre. 'Come on. Once more with feeling: *"We are not at home to Mr Fuck-Up!"*' This time everyone joined in.

Logan snuck a look at the other people in the tiny, untidy room. Who were they kidding? Not only were they at home to Mr Fuck-Up, they'd made up the spare bed and told him to stay for as long as he liked. But DI Steel's speech seemed to have a galvanizing effect on her team. Backs straight and heads held high, they all went through their current assignments and any progress they'd made. Which generally wasn't much. Up at the hospital, an unknown man was showing his willy to anyone daft enough to look; there was a spree of shoplifting going on at the local Ann Summers – naughty lingerie and 'adult' toys; someone was sneaking in and helping themselves to the till at a number of fast-food joints; and two men had beaten the crap out of a bouncer outside Amadeus, the big nightclub down at the beach. When the updates were finished DI Steel told everyone to bugger off outside and play in the sunshine, but she asked Logan to stay behind. 'Mr Police Hero,' she said when they were alone. 'Never thought you'd end up in here. Not like the rest of us no-hopers.'

'PC Maitland,' Logan told her. 'The straw that broke the camel's back.' Other than WPC Jackie Watson, his luck had been nonexistent since Christmas. Since then everything that could go wrong, had.

Steel nodded. Her luck hadn't been much better. She leant forward and whispered conspiratorially into his ear, engulfing his head in a cloud of second-hand cigarette smoke. 'If anyone can work their way out of this crummy team back to the real world, it's you. You're a damn fine officer.' She stepped back and smiled at him, the wrinkles bunching around her eyes. 'Mind you, I say that to all the new recruits. But in your case I mean it.'

Somehow that didn't make him feel any better.

Half an hour later Logan and DI Steel were sat in the back of a newish Vauxhall with DC Rennie driving and a family liaison officer in the passenger seat. Somehow Steel had managed to convince the Chief Constable to give her the Rosie Williams case – probably only because DI Insch was up to his ears and no one else was free, but Logan wasn't about to say so. According to Steel this was her chance to shine again. She and Logan were going to solve the case and get the hell out of the Screw-Up Squad. Let someone else look after the no-hopers for a change.

Rennie slid the car around the bloated bulk of Mount Hooly roundabout, making for Powis. No one said much. Logan was brooding about being transferred to the Screw-Up Squad, Rennie was sulking because the inspector had said he was expected to fuck up, and DI Steel was expending all her effort on not smoking. The family liaison officer had tried to strike up conversation a couple of times, but eventually gave up and descended into a foul mood of her own. Which was a shame, because it was a lovely day outside. Not a cloud in the sky, the granite buildings sparkling in the sunshine, happy smiley people wandering about hand in hand. Enjoying the weather while it lasted. It would be freezing cold and bucketing with rain soon enough.

Rennie swung the car around onto Bedford Road and then left again into Powis. Past a small set of shops: wire mesh over the windows, graffiti over the walls, leading to a long, sweeping, circular road lined with three-storey tenement blocks. They found Rosie's address in a row of boarded-up properties with a yellow Aberdeen City Council van parked outside, the sound of power tools echoing out of the open stairwell next door. Rennie parked out front.

'Right,' said Steel, pulling a packet of cigarettes from her pocket, fingering them, and stuffing them back again, unsmoked. 'What do we have on the next of kin?'

'Two kids, no husband. According to Vice she's currently involved with one Jamie McKinnon,' said the family liaison officer. 'Conflicting reports on whether he's her boyfriend or pimp. Maybe a little of both.'

'Oh aye? Wee Jamie McKinnon? Would've thought "toy boy" was closer to the mark; she's got to be twice his age!' Steel gave a big, snorting sniff, and chewed thoughtfully for a while. 'Come on then,' she said at last. 'Job's not going to do itself.'

They left DC Rennie watching the car, trying not to look like a plainclothes police officer and failing miserably. Rosie's flat was on the middle floor. There was a window set into the stairwell, but it was covered over with a flattened cardboard box parcel-taped into place, shrouding the hallway in gloom. The door was featureless grey with a rusty brass spyhole set into it, a faint glimmer of light shining through from the flat into the murky hall. Taking a deep breath, DI Steel knocked.

No response.

She tried again, harder this time, and Logan could have sworn he heard something being dragged against the other side of the door. The inspector knocked again. And the light in the spy hole went out. 'Come on, Jamie, we know you're in there. Let us in, eh?'

There was a small pause, and then a high-pitched voice said, 'Fuck off. We're no' wantin' any police bastards today, thanks.'

DI Steel squinted at the spy hole. 'Jamie? Come on, stop buggering about. We need to talk to you about Rosie. It's important.'

Another pause. 'What about her?'

'Come on, Jamie, open the door.'

'No. Fuck off.'

The inspector ran a tired hand across her forehead. 'She's dead, Jamie. I'm sorry. Rosie's dead.

We need you to come down and identify her.'

This time the silence stretched out far longer than before. And then the sound of something being dragged away from the door, a chain being undone, a deadbolt being drawn back, and the door being unlocked. It opened to reveal an ugly child wearing an out-of-date Aberdeen Football Club top, tatty jeans and huge sneakers, laced up gangsta-stylie. The haircut was pudding bowl on top and shaved up the sides. Behind him was a tatty dining-room chair. He couldn't have been much more than seven.

'What do you mean, "she's dead"?' Suspicion was written all over his blunt features.

Steel looked down at the kid. 'Is your daddy home?'

The child sneered. 'Jamie's no' my dad, he's just some fuckin' waster Mum's shaggin'. She kicked his arse oot *weeks* ago. Fuck knows who my "daddy" is, 'cos Mum hasn't got a fuckin' clue . . .' He stopped and examined the visitors on his doorstep. 'She really dead?'

Steel nodded. 'I'm sorry, Son, you shouldn't have found out like this . . .'

The kid took a deep breath, bit his bottom lip, and then said, 'Aye, well. Shit happens.' He went to slam the door in their faces, but Steel had her foot wedged firmly against the hinges. In one of the other rooms they could hear a baby start to cry.

The family liaison officer dropped down to the

kid's eye level and said, 'Hello, my name's Alison. Who's looking after you while your mummy's away?'

The kid looked at her, then at Steel, and then back again. 'How fuckin' stupit are you? "Mummy's" no' *away*. "Mummy's" dead.' But the defiant edge to his voice was starting to crumble. 'Understand you stupit cow? She's dead!' In the back room the baby bawled louder and the kid turned and roared a tirade of abuse in its direction, telling it what was going to happen, if it didn't shut up right now! By the time he'd finished there were tears in his eyes.

They left the family liaison officer to call Social Work and have the children taken into care.

Logan was on a serious low by the time they got back to Force Headquarters. Telling the kid that he and his baby sister were off to the children's home had just put the perfect cap on the day. The kicking, the swearing, spitting, threats . . .

At least now they had a suspect. Jamie McKinnon: Rosie Williams's pimp and ex-toy boy. He had prior for assault, possession with intent, breaking and entering, shoplifting, stealing motors. You name it, Jamie had tried it. According to the kid, Rosie had kicked Jamie out for beating her up so badly she couldn't work for a week. DI Steel had Control radio every patrol car in the city. She wanted Jamie brought in, on a voly if possible, in cuffs if not.

'Well,' she said when the call had gone out, 'anything else I should know about?' Logan told her about the new deputy fiscal and her desire to collect used condoms. Steel laughed so hard Logan thought she was going to bring up a lung. 'Rather you than me, Sunshine!' she said, wiping a tear from her eye.

'What's so funny?'

'You telling the search team to go hunting for nearly-new prophylactics! They'll have a fit!'

'How come I have to tell them? You're the one in charge!'

Steel grinned broadly at him, cigarette smoke oozing out between her teeth. 'Delegation, Mr Police Hero. I delegate, you do.' She pointed him at the door. 'Off you go.' Only remembering at the last minute: 'Oh, and while you're at it, you can phone your new condom-loving friend and get an apprehension warrant for Jamie.'

Logan stomped off to the lifts. This was so like DI Steel. He did all the work; she smoked fags and took the credit. Grumbling, he called Rachael Tulloch and told her about Jamie McKinnon. She promised to set up a warrant ASAP. Then Logan called Control and got them to patch him through to the team searching the alley. They weren't happy when he said they had to start collecting every condom they could find. Not happy at all. But by then Logan was past caring. It was nearly five o'clock and he'd been on duty for fourteen and a half hours. The day shift was over. It was time to go home.

5

There was something nasty sitting on Logan's desk when he turned up for work on Wednesday morning. The search team had done as he'd asked, bagging and tagging each and every single used condom they could find in Shore Lane. And there were a hell of a lot of them; little slimy latex tubes oozing their contents out into individual evidence bags, all piled up in his in-tray. Grimacing, Logan scooped them all into a cardboard box, trying not to think about what was making the little bags so cold and clammy.

DI Steel didn't turn up for the morning briefing, so the Screw-Up Squad just sat around their tables, drinking coffee and talking. Today's topic was '*Harry Potter*: seminal moment in world cinema, or a load of old wank? Discuss.' Logan left them to it, taking his box of used condoms down to the morgue where they could be frozen for future analysis. Procurators Fiscal: go figure.

He pushed through the large double doors, onto

the sparkling clean tiled floor of the cutting room. There was no sign of yesterday's rancid-barbecue reek. Instead everything smelled of formalin and pine disinfectant. Standing with her back to the doors was a familiar figure, prodding away at something in a bucket on the dissecting table. Logan's heart sank even further.

'Morning,' he said and she turned to look at him.

Dr Isobel MacAlister, the Ice Queen, Chief Pathologist, ex-girlfriend, fellow victim. Looking a lot better than she had yesterday morning: her neatly bobbed hair held prisoner beneath a green surgical cap, the perfect bow of her lips hidden behind a green surgical mask. She blushed. As usual she was dressed like she'd just stepped off a catwalk: cream linen suit, silk blouse and tan leather boots, with an open white lab coat over the top. Golden jewellery trapped beneath the latex gloves. Obviously not getting ready to hack some poor sod up. 'Good morning,' awkward pause. 'How are you?'

Logan shrugged. 'Same old. You feeling any better?'

For a split second she looked puzzled, and then it clicked. 'Oh, this morning . . .' It was her turn to shrug. 'Just a stomach bug.'

'What, two days on the trot?' he asked. 'No pun intended.'

That almost got a smile. 'Did you want something in particular, or are you just down here for a clip round the ear?'

'Nope, official business . . .' Logan turned and

snuck a peek into Isobel's bucket: a human brain, floating upside down in formalin, the preservative going slightly milky around the grey, whorled surface. Trying not to shudder, he popped his cardboard box up on the table next to the bucket. 'Got a present for you.'

Isobel raised an eyebrow and dug out one of the little plastic evidence bags, holding it up to the light so she could see the slimy contents more clearly. A smile made her eyes sparkle. 'How sweet,' she said, 'used contraceptives. And they say romance is dead . . .' She rummaged about in the box. 'There's got to be a couple of hundred of them in here. You'll go blind.'

It was Logan's turn to blush. 'They're not mine. It's the Rosie Williams case. These are all the condoms we could find in Shore Lane. They're to be stored for DNA analysis.'

Isobel shook her head in disbelief. 'Are you out of your mind? Do you know how long it'll take to analyse the DNA from two hundred used condoms? *It'll cost a fortune!*'

Logan held up his hands. 'Don't look at me; it's that new deputy fiscal.'

Isobel sighed and snatched the box off the cutting table, muttering under her breath. She poured the lot into a large evidence bag, made Logan sign over the chain of evidence, and hurled the condoms into one of the specimen freezers. There wasn't anything to say after that.

* * *

DI Steel rolled in at a quarter to eight, looking as if she'd slept in an ashtray. She yawned her way through a hastily reconvened morning briefing, smoking cigarettes and drinking coffee, before sending them all on their way with the usual benediction about not being at home to Mr Fuck-Up. Everyone except Logan. She had a job for him: they were off to look for Jamie McKinnon.

Outside Force HQ, the sun was shining happily down on Aberdeen from a clear blue sky. The inspector led the way out through the front doors and down onto Queen Street, not bothering to sign out one of the CID pool cars. Instead they wandered up Union Street, enjoying the late summer warmth. When the weather was miserable so was Aberdeen: grey buildings, grey skies, grey streets and grey people, but when the sun appeared everything changed. The Granite City sparkled and its inhabitants abandoned their anoraks, parkas and duffel coats in favour of jeans, T-shirts, and short summery dresses. But when a perky brunette tottered past in a tiny floral skirt and even tinier blouse, her bare stomach tanned a delicate shade of gold, DI Steel didn't even look.

On the other side of the road a blonde, almost wearing a pair of low-slung jeans and a crop top, stopped to wave down a taxi, exposing more flesh in one go than the city had seen all year. Still no comment from the inspector. 'You OK?' asked Logan.

Steel shrugged. 'Rough night. And before you ask: none of your business.'

Fine, thought Logan, sod you then.

Halfway up Union Street the wall of buildings was broken by Union Terrace Gardens, exposing a vista of vivid green all the way across to the glittering façade of His Majesty's Theatre. The gardens were a rectangle of precipice-sided parkland, sinking way below street level. Steep grassy banks on two sides with huge beech trees clinging on precariously. A small bandstand sat at the bottom, sparkling with a fresh coat of paint. And on the far side the floral clock offered its multicoloured blooms to the cloudless sky and warm August sun. Picture-postcard time.

At the corner of Union Terrace a large white-marble statue of King Edward VII held court; his shoulders regally speckled with pigeon droppings. There was a row of benches in a semi-circle behind the king, there so his closest advisors could drink strong cider and lager, straight from the tin, at ten past nine on a Wednesday morning.

They were a fairly mixed bunch: one or two genuine tramps in the regulation filthy suit-trousers, stained vests and crusted sores, others in jeans and tatty leathers, defying the blazing sunshine. Steel cast her eye across the assembled early morning drinkers and pointed at a young woman with pierced ears, nose and lips, heavy black-and-white make-up and lank, pink hair. She was swigging from a tin of Red Stripe.

'Morning, Suzie.' The inspector flicked the last half-inch of her cigarette over the railing. 'How's your wee brother keeping these days?'

On closer inspection the girl wasn't as young as Logan had first thought. Thirty-five if she was a day. That thick layer of white make-up was hiding a multitude of sins, and spots as well. Her face had a rough texture to it, the black-lipped mouth lined like a chicken's bum. When she spoke her accent was broad Aberdonian. 'Havenae seen the manky sod fer weeks.'

'No?' Steel flopped down on the bench next to her, smiling. She draped her arm across the back of the bench so it encircled the woman's shoulders.

Suzie shifted uncomfortably. 'You tryin' tae poof me up?' she asked.

'You should be so bloody lucky. No: I want your wee brother. Where is he?'

'How the fuck should I know?' Suzie took a long swig at her lager. 'Been shaggin' that old whore of his.'

'Funny you should mention that, Suzie, you see, that "old whore" turned up yesterday morning battered to death. And Jamie's no' exactly shy with his fists, is he?'

The girl stiffened. 'Jamie didnae kill nobody.' What the hell was Steel playing at? Logan could see the shutters coming down: they weren't going to get anything out of her now! Steel should have played it cool, pretended it was nothing important, not gone charging in with both bloody feet! No wonder she was in charge of the Screw-Up Squad.

'Tell you what,' said Steel, handing over a dog-eared Grampian Police business card. 'You have a wee think about it and give me a call, OK?' She stood and lit another cigarette, coughing as the smoke worked its way into her lungs.

Suzie told the inspector exactly what she could do with her business card, threw back the last of her lager, and stormed off.

Logan waited until the girl was out of earshot. 'Why did you tell her Rosie was dead? She's never going to tell us where Jamie is now!'

DI Steel's smile became predatory. 'That's where you're wrong, Mr Police Hero. She's going to tell us *exactly* where he is. She just doesn't know it yet.' The inspector stood up on her tiptoes, following Suzie McKinnon's progress up Union Street. 'Come on then, we don't want to lose her.' She marched straight across the street, narrowly missing getting squashed by a bus, with Logan in nervous pursuit. On the other side of the road she clambered into the passenger seat of an illegally parked Vauxhall. DC Rennie was behind the wheel, wearing a pair of trendy sunglasses, and as soon as Logan was ensconced in the back, they were off.

They spotted Suzie easily enough – her black leather get-up and pink hair stood out like a sore thumb amongst all the summer clothes – she crossed the road, just shy of the Music Hall's Doric columns, hurrying off down Crown Street. Rennie kept well back, trying not to look like a kerb crawler. Ten minutes later they were parked opposite a basement flat in Ferryhill. The street wasn't in the best of shapes, a collection of pothole pockmarks and different coloured patches of tarmac making it look like Frankenstein's monster with acne. A rusty old Ford Escort was dying at the kerbside, bleeding oil. A quick PNC check confirmed it belonged to one James Robert McKinnon. Steel smiled at Logan. 'Do you want me to say, "I told you so" now or later?'

The door to the building wasn't locked, so Logan and DI Steel pushed straight through to the stairs leading down to the basement apartment. DC Rennie stayed out front, in case Jamie tried to do a runner.

Down in the mildew-smelling corridor Steel was just about to knock when a thought occurred to her. 'Are you up to this?' she asked Logan. 'What with your Achilles stomach and all.'

'It was nearly two years ago!' he hissed. 'I'm fine.' Liar. The scars on his stomach still hurt when the weather changed, or he bent down too quickly.

DI Steel knocked gently on the door, putting on a Fife accent to ask if Jamie had seen her cat. A key rattled in the lock and a stressed-looking man, wearing a rumpled Burger King uniform, opened the door. Spiky, bleached-blond hair, bloodshot eyes, slightly overweight, podgy nose, daft little beard thing clinging on to the end of his chin for dear life.

'I haven't seen any bloody . . .' His eyes went wide. 'Shite!' And the door was slammed shut. Or would have been if DI Steel didn't have her boot jammed into the gap. She swore as the wood mashed into her foot and Jamie McKinnon bolted back into the flat.

'Ayabastard!' Hopping in the corridor, Steel clutched her injured foot while Logan charged past, through into a grotty hallway. A door at one end of the hall led to the lounge – Suzie was standing in the middle of the room, a fresh tin of Red Stripe in her hand and a shocked expression on her face. No sign of Jamie. Logan spun around to see the door to a filthy little bathroom lying open, and at the far end the door to the kitchen bouncing off the wall and swinging itself shut again.

Cursing, he sprinted for the kitchen. Why couldn't Jamie have made a break for the front, where DC Rennie could have clobbered him one? He burst through the door just in time to see Jamie's backside disappearing through the open kitchen window. The back door was blocked by an ancient washing machine, so Logan had no choice but to clamber through the window after him, and up a small set of steps into the back garden. Jamie was hoofing it hell for leather across the yellowing grass, towards the six-foot-high back wall, where the buildings backed onto the next row of tenements. Gritting his teeth, Logan chased after him.

For once luck was on Logan's side; as Jamie got within lunging distance of the wall his feet tangled in the trailing end of a clothesline. He went down hard, banging his face on a huge, abandoned red plastic fire engine. Swearing, he clasped a hand over his nose – blood welling up between his fingers – and struggled to his feet. Just in time for Logan to tackle him and send them both sprawling to the scabby-yellow grass again.

The impact was enough to set the scar tissue screaming across Logan's stomach, leaving him hissing in pain while Jamie scrambled to his feet and jumped for the back wall. He had one leg over the top when Logan grabbed the other one and yanked him back into the garden. Jamie's chin caught the top of the wall, snapping his head back as he clattered straight down into the rosebush growing at the bottom, breaking the fall with his face, sending pink petals flying.

Breathing hard, Logan jumped on him, twisted Jamie's arm up behind his back and snapped on the handcuffs. As the swearing started, Logan slumped against the wall and tried to convince himself that his stomach didn't hurt anywhere near as much as it really did. When the pain finally settled down, he hauled Jamie to his feet.

Burger King weren't going to be too happy about the state of their uniform. Blood ran freely from Jamie's squashed nose and torn lip, his face a network of thin scratches that oozed red. He looked as if he'd done ten rounds with Mike

Tyson's cat. Swearing, he spat a mouthful of blood out into the rosebush. 'You made me bite my fuckin' tongue!'

'Jesus, Logan,' said Steel when he finally dragged Jamie back into the basement flat. 'I told you to arrest him, not beat the crap out of him.'

Something sly weaselled its way onto Jamie's face. 'Aye, he beat me up! Police brutality! I want my lawyer! I'm gonnae sue you bastards for all you're worth!'

Steel told him to shut his mouth. Suzie was sat on the edge of a tatty settee, worrying at an ever-expanding hole in the cushion with her finger, exposing the plaque-yellow foam rubber. She wouldn't look at anyone.

'You silly bitch.' Jamie spat out another mouthful of blood onto the carpet. 'You led them straight here!'

Suzie just kept on digging.

'Right then, Sunshine.' Steel pulled out a crumpled packet of cigarettes and lit one up, dribbling the smoke contentedly down her nose. 'You don't mind if we take a little peek round your place do you?'

'Yes I fuckin' well do mind!'

Steel's smile got bigger. 'Well tough shite, 'cos I've got a warrant.' She flicked a little nub of grey ash from the end of her fag onto the coffee table. 'Anything you want to tell us before we go a-wandering?' Silence. 'No?' More silence. 'You sure?' Outside a truck rumbled past. 'OK, you're the boss.'

Of course Steel didn't do any of the actual searching herself. Not when she had a detective sergeant and a detective constable to do it for her. They found two small wrappers of heroin, a half-empty box of disposable needles and a lump of cannabis resin the size of a Mars Bar. It was Logan who found the box full of uniforms in the bedroom cupboard.

Back in the lounge he asked Jamie how his career in the fast-food industry was going. Jamie scowled back at him. The nosebleed was drying up, leaving a crust of reddish-brown across the lower half of his face, making his little goatee as spiky as his bleached hair. 'I'm going straight, OK?' he said. 'Keepin' out of trouble.'

'At Burger King?'

'Yes at fuckin' Burger King.'

'Well then,' said Logan, pulling the cardboard box out from behind his back. 'You must be a hardworking little bunny! Flipping all those burgers at Burger King.' He pulled out another uniform. 'McDonald's,' another uniform, 'the Tasty Tattie,' another uniform . . . There were work clothes from half a dozen fast-food places in Aberdeen, each one of them complete with 'HI MY NAME IS' badges, none of which read 'JAMES MCKINNON'.

DI Steel looked confused, so Logan spelt it out for her: 'Jamie's the one been helping himself to tills all over town. Turns up in uniform, no one pays any attention to the new boy. After all: who puts on one of these things for fun? He cleans out the till after the lunchtime rush, and gets changed to do the next place.'

DI Steel dropped her cigarette to the floor, grinding it out against the carpet. 'Aye, very good, Sherlock,' she said, sounding completely unimpressed. 'But we've got bigger fish to fry. James Robert McKinnon, I'm detaining you on suspicion of the murder of Rosie Williams.'

Jamie started shouting that he hadn't killed anyone, but Steel wasn't listening. She just finished reciting his rights then told Rennie to frogmarch the suspect to the car. And all the time, Jamie's sister stared at the carpet, picking at the hole in the settee.

'And, Suzie, thanks for your help,' said Steel with a wink. 'Couldn't have done it without you.'

6

Jamie was booked in at FHQ, given a once-over by the duty doctor and stuck in interview room number three. Where he announced, 'Jesus, it's like a fuckin' oven in here!' He wasn't kidding. Even with the sun cracking the cobbles outside, the radiator was belching out heat. But all the other interview rooms were taken, so they were stuck with it.

Grumbling and sweating, Logan set up the interview tapes: audio and video, then did the introductions: date, time and attendees, and settled back to let DI Steel conduct the interview.

Silence.

Logan cast a glance in Steel's direction. She was looking at him with a puzzled expression. 'Well,' she told him at last, 'get on with it. It's too hot for buggering about.' Bloody typical. Once again he was going to have to do all the work.

With a sigh, Logan pulled out a handful of Rosie's post mortem photographs. 'Tell us about Rosie Williams.'

Jamie scowled at them. 'I'm no' sayin' anything till I've seen a lawyer.'

Steel groaned. 'No' again! How many times do I have to say this? *Under Scottish law you have no right to legal counsel until we've finished with you.* No lawyers. Interview first, lawyer later. Comprende?'

The scowl on Jamie's face didn't shift. 'You're lyin', I've seen the telly. I get a lawyer.'

'No you don't.' Steel peeled off her charcoal-grey jacket, exposing large patches of sweat beneath the arms of her red blouse. 'The telly *lies* to you. It shows you the *English* legal system. Not the same. Up here we do not fuck about waiting for some slimy bastard to help you with your lies. Now get your finger out and tell us why you killed Rosie Williams, so we can all get out of this bastard hothouse.'

'I didn't kill no one!'

'Stop fucking about, Jamie – I'm not in the mood.'

He slumped back in his seat, chewing things over. 'I really don't get a lawyer?'

'No! Now tell us about Rosie Bloody Williams before I pull that stupid-looking chin-warmer off your face, one hair at a time!'

Jamie held up his hands in self-defence. 'OK, OK! We're . . . you know . . . I stayed with her for a bit . . .'

'You were her pimp.'

'We're having fun, you know . . .'

'Fun? Rosie was old enough to be your granny!

She's out there shaggin' for cash, every night, while you're what? Staying home looking after the kids?'

Jamie stared down at his hands. 'Isn't that old.'

'Yes she fucking was! Ugly as hell too!'

'She is not!' Jamie's voice was getting louder with every word. 'She isn't ugly!'

A sly smile blossomed on Steel's face. 'You loved her didn't you?'

Jamie blushed and looked away.

'You did, didn't you? You loved her and she was out there every night, some stranger's dick in her mouth. Screwing them in doorways. Your precious Rosie, out there with—'

'Shut up! Fuckin' shut up!'

'That's why you killed her, isn't it? You were jealous she wasn't all yours. Anyone could have her for the price of a burger.'

'Shut up . . .'

Steel settled back in her chair, scratching vaguely at the damp patch under her left arm. She nodded in Logan's direction and he asked Jamie where he was between eleven o'clock Monday night and two o'clock Tuesday morning.

'I was at home. Asleep.' But there was something in his eyes. 'Suzie'll tell you. She was there.'

DI Steel raised an eyebrow. 'No' in the same bed, I hope.' Jamie just scowled at her. 'We've got Forensics turning your flat upside down: they're going to find her blood, aren't they? You beat her so bad, you must've been clarted in it.' She leaned forwards in her seat, tapping the table with a nicotine-stained finger. 'Wouldn't be the first time you beat her up either, would it? She kicked you out 'cos of it.'

'I didn't mean to hurt her!' The tears were starting.

Steel's smile turned into one of triumph. 'But you did, didn't you? You didn't mean to, but you hurt her really bad. Was it an accident? Come on, Jamie, you'll feel better if you tell us.'

An hour later they still hadn't managed to get anything else out of him. And as Steel said, it was too hot in the interview room to bugger about any longer. So down to the cells went Jamie McKinnon and down to the canteen went Logan and DI Steel. Chilled tins of Irn-Bru all round. 'Christ, that's better,' she said, standing outside on the rear podium two minutes later, surrounded by the patrol and pool cars, drink in one hand, cigarette smouldering away in the other. 'We'll get the PF in to look at the tape. "I never meant to hurt her," my arse, all we need is a couple of witnesses and we're laughing.' She smiled and knocked back a mouthful of Irn-Bru. 'Knew it was about time my luck changed.'

Unfortunately Logan's hadn't. When DI Steel said, 'All we need is a couple of witnesses,' what she actually meant was that Logan had to change shifts and spend the next couple of nights wandering around the docks chatting up prostitutes. The first time in ages that his shift pattern was the same as Jackie's, and the inspector wanted it all changed again. Jackie was going to kill him.

'You're young,' Steel told him when he complained, 'you'll get over it. Better bugger off home after lunch. Get some kip. In the meantime, let's get the PF down here . . .'

The Procurator Fiscal and her new deputy sat through the recording of Jamie McKinnon's interview in silence. The tape was a good start, but it wasn't enough to secure a conviction, for that they'd need some real, hard forensic evidence. 'Speaking of which,' said Rachael Tulloch, deputy PF to the stars, 'how did you get on with those contraceptives?' The Fiscal looked momentarily flustered as Logan explained about the two hundred and thirteen second-hand prophylactics sitting in the morgue's specimen freezers; it looked like this was the first she'd heard of her deputy's *spectacular* plan. At least Rachael had the decency to blush and admit it was a lot more condoms than she'd been anticipating, but now that they had a suspect under arrest, couldn't they match his DNA to them? Prove he was there? The Fiscal went quiet for a minute, considering it, and then agreed it probably couldn't hurt. Logan tried not to groan. Isobel was bound to blame him for all the work she was about to get. He consoled himself with the thought that she didn't like him much anyway.

When he went down to the morgue to break the bad news, Isobel was hunched over her brain-in-a-bucket again. Her reaction to Logan's request for DNA testing was pretty much what he'd been expecting. Only with more swearing.

'Don't look at me,' he said when she paused for breath. 'I told you: it's that new PF. She's mad for used condoms. Could you not just blood test the semen and only DNA match the ones with the same blood group as Jamie McKinnon?'

Reluctantly Isobel agreed that it would be a lot less work. But she still wasn't happy. Grumbling, she dug the condoms out of the freezer, where they'd had just enough time to go hard. For the second time in their lives.

Logan checked his watch and left her to it. If he hurried he could grab lunch with Jackie in the canteen before heading back to the flat to try and get some sleep. Not that he held out much hope: he always had trouble adjusting to the night shift, and usually he had a couple of days off in between to get used to the idea. Sod the diet. He was having chips with his lasagne today. And a pudding.

Though on second thoughts, tapioca probably wasn't the wisest of choices. Looking at it, congealing in the bowl, all white with translucent lumps, all he could think of was Isobel slowly defrosting her condoms down in the morgue. Shuddering he pushed the bowl away.

'Interfering old bitch.' Jackie stabbed her jam sponge with an angry spoon. 'Why did she have to go buggering about with your shifts? If you have to go onto nights today and tomorrow . . .'

She did the arithmetic on her fingers. 'That puts you six days ahead of my bloody shift pattern! It took bloody ages to get the damn things in line!'

'I know, I know. I'll just have to get mine shifted again. Though Christ knows when.'

'And I had plans.'

Logan looked up. 'Oh? We going away somewhere?'

'Not any more we're not, you'll be asleep all bloody Friday.' Stab, stab, stab. 'Tell you I could kill her!'

'Oh-ho, speak of the devil . . .' DI Steel was standing in the doorway to the canteen, craning her neck. Looking for someone. And Logan had a nasty idea who. He was just about to duck down under the table, pretend he'd dropped his fork or something, when she spotted him.

'Oi! Lazarus,' she shouted and Logan winced. Every eye in the place turned to stare. 'You finished?' She didn't wait for him to answer. 'Well, come on then: we've got a shout to go to.'

Jackie leaned over the table and hissed at him, 'I thought you were supposed to be going home to get some sleep!'

It was a Mrs Margaret Hendry who'd found it, out walking her dog, Jack, in Garlogie Woods. Well, technically it had been Jack who'd found it, leaping away into the undergrowth, barking and yipping. Not coming back, no matter how much Margaret shouted. In the end she'd ducked in under the trees after him. It was just off a small clearing, wedged into the roots of a fallen tree: a red suitcase, big enough to take a week's worth of clothes. The smell was appalling: stinking, rotten meat. Jack of course had gone straight to it, and was hanging off the handle, all four little legs off the ground as he tried to scrabble inside. Well, what with the smell and the suitcase, it wasn't difficult to put two and two together. Margaret pulled out her mobile phone and called the police.

The Identification Bureau's dirty white Transit Van was abandoned in the lay-by, just behind a marked patrol car, so Logan had to park their rusty Vauxhall half on the grass verge and hope no one would run into the back of it. DC Rennie spluttered his way out of the back seat, wiping ash from his hair and face – Steel had spent the whole ten-mile journey out from Aberdeen with the passenger window down, the ash from her cigarette spiralling through the car's interior like a mini snowstorm – which was why Logan had elected to drive. He waited until the inspector had shooed Rennie up the path to go find the crime scene, before asking her if this meant he wasn't swapping over onto the night shift.

'Hmm?' Steel looked at him, distracted as she picked three individually wrapped white SOC over suits from a box in the boot of the car. 'No,' she said at last. 'Sorry, but I still need you to go looking for witnesses. We both know Jamie's alibi's a crock of shite. We just have to prove it.'

'Then how come you dragged me out to this?' It came out slightly whiny, but Logan was past caring.

Steel sighed. 'What am I supposed to do? You know why they call it the Screw-Up Squad? The Pish Patrol? The Fuck-Up Factory? 'Cos every bastard that can't find their backside with both hands gets dumped in it. Keep the useless tossers out of the way, where they can't do any damage . . . We only got this call 'cos everyone half-decent was busy.' She smiled, sadly. 'It's a body in a suit-case, Logan, who else am I going to trust to take with me? That bunch of fuckwits I've been lumbered with?' She handed him the protective gear. 'Never mind, you don't have to do a whole shift tonight. Knock off about two. Look on it as a bonus.' Then she patted him on the arm and stomped off up the rutted track into the forest, leaving him to swear quietly in her wake.

They found DC Rennie standing at the side of the track, about half a mile from the main road. There were broken branches and scuffmarks in the carpet of yellow-brown pine needles. 'In there,' he said pointing, obviously proud of himself. Logan gave him the protective gear to carry. As the inspector said: delegation. It was cooler in the woods, the sunlight dappling the ground at their feet, filtered through the canopy of sharp green needles.

It should have been dead quiet beneath the spiky branches, but it wasn't. They could hear a barrage of swearing intermingled with helpful suggestions coming from up ahead. And not long after that, the smell started. It was a rancid, stomach-clenching stench. Gagging slightly, Logan tried breathing through his mouth. The taste was slightly better than the smell, but not by much.

They broke through into a small clearing, where an old pine tree had fallen like a massive wooden domino, taking a handful of smaller trees with it. Now it lay on its side, pointing back towards the track, its roots standing upright like a filthy sunburst, blocking the main attraction from view. The IB team were here, trying to manhandle a scene-of-crime tent over the bottom part of the tree, three of them heaving away at the uncooperative blue material, while another two struggled to get the remainder over the tree's roots. Standing on the other side of the clearing was a middle-aged woman dressed for the outdoors, an excitable Jack Russell terrier on a lead bouncing up and down at her feet. A young uniformed constable snapped to attention as DI Steel approached.

'It's OK,' said Steel, digging out another cigarette, 'you don't have to curtsey.'

Grinning, the constable told them how Mrs Hendry had guided him to the spot and he'd called for the Identification Bureau as soon as he'd seen the case. A duty doctor and pathologist were on their way. As was the Procurator Fiscal.

'Good boy,' said Steel when he'd finished. 'If I was DI Insch, you'd get a sweetie.' Instead she offered him a fag, much to his horror. Surely it wasn't right to smoke at a crime scene. What about contamination? 'Aye, you're probably right,' said Steel, puffing away. They got Mrs Hendry to go through her version of events again. No she hadn't touched anything; well you weren't supposed to, were you? Not when you found a dead body in a suitcase.

Steel waited until Mrs Hendry and her little monster-dog were escorted from the premises before slouching into action.

'Right.' She grabbed a boiler suit from Rennie, leaning on Logan for support as she tucked her trousers into her socks and clambered into it. Once they were all suited up, only their faces showing, she stomped over to where the IB team had almost managed to get the tent erected. The air was thick with flies. 'You lot going to be all bloody day?' she demanded.

A thin man with a dirty-grey moustache scowled at her. 'This isn't easy, you know!'

'Blah, blah, blah. You opened the suitcase yet?' Not bloody likely was the loud reply. You never knew which pathologist you were going to get these days, and if it was that MacAlister woman you'd get your testicles in a jar for messing up her crime scene. So that suitcase was going to stay locked until she, or the duty doctor, got here. Steel stared at the red fabric case. 'Just like Christmas Eve, isn't it?' she said to Logan. 'The present's right there under the tree, you know what's in it, but you're not allowed to open it till Santa's been. Don't suppose a small peek would hurt though, would it . . .' She made for the tent's open door, but Dirty Moustache stopped her on the threshold.

'No,' he told her. 'Not till the pathologist gets here!'

'Oh come on, it's my crime scene! How the hell do you expect me to catch the bastard if you won't let me have a poke about?'

'You can poke about all you like when the pathologist says so. Until then this area will remain sealed. And anyway,' he pointed at the cigarette bobbing away in the corner of the inspector's mouth, 'there's no way you're getting in there with that!'

'Oh for God's sake . . .' And with that DI Steel scuffed off to smoke her fag and sulk in peace. Ten minutes, one and a half cigarettes, later there was a cry of 'Hello?' and the crunch and snap of someone pushing their way through the branches.

It was the new deputy PF, already done up in her scene-of-crime boiler suit, complete with matching blue shoe covers, even though the rest of her party was still in their regular clothes. The real PF followed her, deep in conversation with Dr Isobel MacAlister – the Ice Queen cometh – while Doc Wilson stomped along at the rear of the group, not talking to anyone and scowling at Isobel's back.

The PF gave them a grim smile, asked to be brought up to speed, then suited up and disappeared into the SOC tent, taking Isobel and a reluctant Doc Wilson with her, leaving her deputy to fidget at the entrance to the stinking blue plastic grotto as Dirty Moustache refused to let her into the crime scene. 'You've trailed every bit of grit and dirt and God knows what else in from wherever you got changed!' he said, pointing at her protective suit and booties. 'You'll have to get on a new set.' Blushing furiously she stripped off, revealing a sombre black suit and canary-yellow blouse. The outfit, combined with Rachael's beetroot face and curly red hair, made her look like an angry bee. DI Steel left her to it, dragging Logan with her into the crime scene.

There were hundreds of flies in the SOC tent, buzzing and swooping in the foetid air, making Logan's skin crawl. The sunlight, stronger in the clearing than it had been in the forest proper, made the plastic sheeting glow, tainting everything a sickly blue. Looking a bit like Smurfs in their white over suits, the IB technicians kept a respectful distance from Isobel. Just in case. The video operator went in for a couple of long panning shots before settling down behind her left shoulder so that he could get a good view of the case's contents when it was opened. The photographer flashed away, the sudden *clack* and whine making everything jump into full colour, before fading back to shades of blue. There was a rustle of plastic and Rachael, dressed in a brand-new set of coveralls, poked her head into the stench then joined

Logan and Steel at the back of the tent, looking on as Isobel examined the case.

'It appears to be a mid-range suitcase. Relatively new,' said Isobel, for the benefit of the tape recorder whirring away in her pocket. She tried the catch: it was locked so she made one of the IB team cut the thing out. Telling him, at least seven times, to be careful. At last the lock was sitting in an evidence pouch and Isobel grasped the lid of the suitcase. 'Let's see what we've got . . .'

The smell was instant and overpowering. Logan had thought it was bad before, but with the suitcase opened it was a hundred times worse. The thing was relatively watertight and half-full of viscous, stinking liquid, surrounding what looked like a torso. Two foot long. That meant it was an adult. Logan couldn't see any breasts, so it was probably male. Unless they'd been cut off. The skin was black with hairy mould, slick with slime.

There was a sudden movement at his side as Rachael slapped a hand over her mouth and nose and scrambled out of the tent. Logan couldn't blame her. His stomach was rapidly working its way to the same conclusion.

And then Isobel spoke: 'Son of a bitch . . .'

Logan was almost afraid to ask, 'What?'

She sat back on her heels. 'Literally. This torso.' She pointed at the swollen, rotting lump of meat, crammed into a suitcase and hidden beneath a tree in the middle of a forest in the middle of nowhere. 'It's not human.'

7

There was silence in the tent, broken only by the buzzing of flies. Thick, fat bluebottles that settled on the decomposing torso. Feeding. It was Logan who asked the obvious question, 'What do you mean, "It's not human"?'

'Well, for a start it's completely covered with hair.'

Logan peered into the stinking suitcase. Isobel was right: what he'd taken for black, furry mould, was, in fact, fur. Genuine, bona fide fur. 'If it's not human, what is it?'

Isobel prodded the torso, less careful with it than she would have been with human remains. 'Has to be a dog. Maybe a Labrador? Whatever it is, the SSPCA can deal with it.' She stood, wiping twin trails of slime down the front of her boiler suit.

'But why is it here? Why go to all this trouble to hide a dead dog?'

'You're the detectives, you tell me. Whatever

the motivation, these remains aren't human. Now if you'll excuse me I have *real* work to do.' She swept out.

Logan watched her go, bemused. 'When did this become my fault?' he asked Steel. The inspector just shrugged and buggered off outside for a cigarette, closely followed by the Procurator Fiscal. Logan shook his head. 'Doc? You want to hazard a guess?'

Doc Wilson scowled. 'Oh, I see,' he said, 'it's beneath the great *pathologist* to examine a dead dog, but it's OK for me to do it, is it? I'm a doctor, no' a sodding vet!'

Logan gritted his teeth. 'I just want someone to tell me what the hell is going on! Do you think you could get off your prima donna horse for five bloody minutes and actually help for a change?'

Everyone else in the tent suddenly took an all-consuming interest in their shoes as Logan and the duty doctor scowled at each other. It was Logan who folded first. 'Sorry, Doc.'

Dr Wilson sighed, shrugged, then hunched down in front of the suitcase, beckoning Logan over to join him. As it was no longer a murder enquiry, they didn't have to pussyfoot about with the evidence. Grunting, the doctor dragged the suitcase free from its prison of roots and dumped it on the forest floor, the foul-smelling liquid slopping out onto the fallen needles.

Coughing and spluttering against the stink, Doc Wilson prodded at the hairy torso, turning it over in the suitcase. The underside was saturated with liquid decay. The head, legs and tail had all been cut away, leaving dark purple, swollen flesh behind. 'I'm no pathologist, mind,' he said, 'but it looks like these cuts have been made by some sort of very sharp, medium-length blade. Could be a kitchen knife? Cuts are fairly solid, not a lot of hacking going on. So whoever it was knew what they were doing: slice around the joint then separate the limb from the socket. Very economical.' He turned the body over onto its back again. 'Cut marks around the head are a bit more muddled. No' an easy thing to do, get a head off a body. Tail's just been chopped off . . .' Doc Wilson frowned.

'What?'

He pointed at the base of the torso, where the fur was a mess of fluid and flies. Gingerly, he poked and prodded at the rotting carcass. 'Genital area: multiple stab wounds. Poor little sod's had his bollocks hacked to pieces.' And that was when Logan knew.

Standing back upright, he told the IB team to get going with the bagging and tagging. This was to be treated as a murder scene, even if it was just a dead dog. Puzzled, the bloke with the moustache started to argue, but Logan was having none of it. Everything was to be taken seriously: trace fibres, fingerprints, tissue samples, post mortem, the whole nine yards.

'What's the point?' demanded the moustache. 'It's just a bloody Labrador!'

Logan looked down at the dismembered torso, stuffed in a suitcase, hidden in the woods. 'No,' he said, getting that old familiar sinking feeling. 'It's not just a Labrador. It's a dress-rehearsal.'

DI Steel had Rennie drop Logan off on the way back to the station, so he could get a few hours' sleep before reporting for duty at ten that evening. As they drove off up Marischal Street, Logan cursed his way in through the communal front door and up the stairs to his flat. Neither Steel nor the Procurator Fiscal had been happy to hear his theory about the torso, but they had to agree it looked a hell of a lot like a pre-murder. Someone testing the waters before diving in. So the PF had authorized a full post mortem; Isobel was going to love that, hack up a dirty, rotting Labrador in her nice clean morgue? She'd throw a fit. And then she'd blame him. Grumbling, Logan climbed into the shower, trying to wash off the stench of decaying dog, and half an hour later he was sitting in the lounge, tin of beer in one hand, cheese toastie in the other, watching daytime television, trying to bore himself to sleep.

Jackie had made a big difference to Logan's flat when she moved in – it wasn't half as tidy as it used to be. The woman was chaos with boobs. Nothing in the kitchen made sense any more. Whenever she used anything, it went back in a completely different place to where she'd found it: it had taken him ten minutes just to find the toastie machine. Magazines spilled over the side of the coffee table, newspapers were heaped on the floor, unopened letters mixed with takeaway menus and assorted scraps of paper. Her collection of pigs had also taken up residence: porcelain pigs, pottery pigs, little pink cuddly pigs. They festooned the lounge, gathering dust. But Logan wouldn't have changed it for the world.

Soon he was well into his second tin of beer, the sunlight spilling in through the lounge window, making the room soft and warm. He was actually starting to drift off: sleep washing in and out, like the approaching tide, bringing dismembered corpses with it . . .

Logan sat bolt upright on the couch, eyes bleary and wide, heart hammering in his ears, trying to figure out where he was. The phone went again and he swung round, cursing, grabbing the handset as the dream rotted away. 'Hello?'

A Glaswegian voice boomed happily into Logan's ear. *'Laz, my man. How you doin'?'* Colin Miller, golden-boy reporter on the *Press and Journal*, Aberdeen's main daily newspaper.

'Sleeping. What do you want?'

'Sleepin'? At this time of the day. Been up to a bit of the old afternoon delight with the lovely WPC Watson, eh?' Logan didn't dignify that with an answer. *'Anyway, listen, I got a call from some woman says she found a body in the woods today.'* Christ, thought Logan, that Mrs Hendry didn't waste any time,

72

did she? *'Come on, man, spill the beans! Who is it?'*

Logan frowned. 'You've not spoken to Isobel yet, have you?'

An embarrassed pause and then, *'Aye, well, she's no' answerin' her mobile, and her office phone's on voicemail only.'* In addition to being a golden-boy reporter, Miller was also Isobel's bit of rough, the one who'd taken her fancy when she was finished with Logan. It should have been more than enough reason for him to dislike the pushy wee shite, but for some bizarre reason it wasn't. *'Come on, Laz, spill the beans! Bloody media office's givin' the usual "no comment" bollocks. You was there wasn't you?'*

Sighing, Logan slumped back to his chair. 'All I can say is that we found some remains in Garlogie Woods today. You want more details, you're going to have to go through the media office. Or wait for Isobel to get home.'

'Shite ... C'mon, Laz, give me somethin' to work with here! I've been a good boy, no' printed a thing she's told me without goin' through you first – give us a break, eh?'

Logan couldn't help smiling, it was nice to have the upper hand for a change. If Miller printed a word of what his pathologist girlfriend told him between the sheets without getting the OK from Logan, she was finished. Logan would go straight to Professional Standards and tell them all about Isobel's former "indiscretions" with the media. Her career would be over.

'Tell you what, I'll bring round somethin' tasty for

tea and you and me can have a chat. Maybe I've got something you need to know. We could do a swap, like.'

'What, like last time? No bloody thanks.'

'Look, I'm sorry about that, OK? He told me the place was full of stolen property ...' There was a small pause. *'Listen, you workin' on that big fire?'* Logan said no, but that didn't mean he wasn't interested – after all, a lead on Insch's arson case might help speed his way out of the Screw-Up Squad. *'Perfect, how does eight sound?'*

A rattle of keys in the lock and the front door opened. It was Jackie, back from work and carrying a pizza box from the place up the road, using her plaster cast as a tray. She saw him, and held up a bottle of Shiraz.

'Hold on a minute,' he said, slapping a hand over the mouthpiece. 'Colin Miller wants to come over for tea.'

Jackie snorted. 'Not a bloody chance. Pizza, wine and bed. Maybe all at the same time.' She put the pizza box down on the coffee table and started stripping off her trousers.

Logan smiled. 'Erm ... Sorry, Colin, something's come up. Got to go.'

'Eh? What? What's come up?'

Logan put the phone down.

Yawning, Logan strolled up Marischal Street, making for Force Headquarters. Nine forty-five and the sun was beginning to think about going home for the night. The day's heat slowly leached out of the granite buildings, keeping the temperature up as the evening drifted away. There was a lot to be said for a naked WPC Watson, wine and pizza. And he didn't even have to get all togged up in his work suit either. Tonight was a strictly plainclothes operation.

Force Headquarters was busier than Logan had been expecting; groups of uniformed officers bustling about the place. Big Gary – looking like an overstuffed sofa in an ill-fitting uniform, clutching a Tunnocks Tasty Caramel Wafer in one oversized paw – sat behind the desk taking notes. 'Evenin', Lazarus,' he said, dropping little flakes of chocolate onto the duty roster.

'Evening, Gary, what's with all the rush and scurry?'

'You know there's been all these drugs comin' in? Well, big bust tonight: huge! Half the shift's off to play cops and robbers.' He frowned for a moment and flicked through the chocolate-coated roster. 'How come you're in? Supposed to be on days . . .'

The happy smile slid from Logan's face. 'Night shift today and tomorrow. But I'm only on till two tonight, because I was in most of the day.'

'Bastard . . .' Big Gary scribbled away at the roster with a biro. 'How come no one ever tells me anything? Who decided this?'

'DI Steel.'

Big Gary grunted and ripped a bite out of his wafer. 'Bloody typical.' He shook his head. 'Ever since that Cleaver trial got fucked up . . .' The phone went and so did Big Gary.

After signing in, Logan turned round and went back out the way he'd come in, strolling down Marischal Street, over the bridge and straight past his own front door. The harbour lights were flickering on, picking out a handful of supply vessels, their huge bright-orange hulls glowing as the sun slowly set. The water was already a deep shade of violet, reflecting back the darkening sky. At the bottom of the hill Logan took a left, popping his head around the corner of Shore Lane, seeing if anyone was open for business. It was empty.

Hands in his pockets, he strolled down the quay, visiting every alley, street and parking lot along the way. Most of the working girls he spoke to were helpful enough, once he'd sworn on his mother's grave that he wouldn't arrest them. They knew Rosie, they were in the same line of business, they were sorry she was dead. But not one of them had seen anything.

He was on his second circuit when his phone exploded in a cacophony of bleeps and whistles. Colin Miller again. *'Just a wee call to say you've blown it, man. Press office says the torso's no' human. Just a dog. So yer bargainin' position for info's shot to shite.'*

Logan swore quietly, so much for his ticket out of the Fuck-Up Factory.

'Laz? You still there, man?'

'Yeah, just thinking.' There had to be something he could give Miller . . . and then it dawned on him: he told Miller about his pre-murder theory. *'Bastard, we've gone to sodding press with it as a fuckin' sidebar.'*

'So come on then – spill the beans on the fire.'

'The name "Graham Kennedy" mean anythin' to you? Does a bit of dealin' on the side in Bridge of Don, blow mostly, but harder stuff when he gets his hands on it?' Logan had never heard of him. *'He's one of yer crispy-baked squatters.'* Perfect: rumour had it DI Insch still hadn't identified the bodies. It wasn't much, but it was a start. Logan thanked him and hung up. Today was turning out to be not so bad after all.

By the time he'd worked his way back to Shore Lane it was getting on for half eleven. There'd been no improvement in the streetlight situation since the night before last: the darkness barely punctuated with pools of wan yellow light. At the far end, where the cars would turn off the dual carriageway, a single figure plied her trade. Hands in his pockets, Logan stepped into the alleyway and the heady aroma of decomposing rat; thankfully it wasn't nearly as bad as rotting Labrador. The girl touting for business outside the Shore Porters' warehouse couldn't have been much more than sixteen. If that. She was dressed in a short black skirt, low-cut top, fishnets and black patent-leather high heels. Very classy. Her hair was up in a 1980s-style rock-star perm, her face layered with enough make-up to coat the Forth Bridge. She turned at the sound of Logan's footsteps, watching him warily.

'Evening,' he said, voice nice and neutral. 'You new?'

She looked him up and down. 'What it to you?' Not a local. Her accent was somewhere between Edinburgh and the Ukraine. The words slightly fuzzy round the edges, as if she was on something.

'You here Monday?' he asked. She backed away a couple of steps. 'It's OK,' he said, holding up his hands, 'I just want to talk.'

Her eyes went wide. Left, right, then she ran for it. Logan grabbed her arm and pulled her to a halt.

'You hurting me!' she whined, struggling.

'I just want to ask you a few questions. It's OK—'

A shape stepped out of the shadows. 'No it fuckin' isn't.' Big bloke, dressed in leathers and jeans. Shaved head, goatee beard, fists. 'Let the bitch go, or I'm goin' tae break your fuckin' head open!'

Logan smiled at him. 'No need to get physical. Just a couple of questions and then I'm on my way. You here Monday night as well?'

The man cracked his knuckles and advanced. 'You fuckin' deaf? I told you: let the bitch go!'

Sighing, Logan dug out his wallet and flipped it open, exposing his warrant card. 'Detective Sergeant Logan McRae. Still want to break my head open?' The man froze, looked from Logan's ID to Logan to the struggling girl and back at Logan again. Then legged it.

Logan and the girl watched him disappear – for a big man he moved pretty fast. She stood open-mouthed, forgetting to struggle, before hurling a string of foreign-language abuse after her scarpering pimp. Logan had no idea what the words meant, but the general gist was clear enough. 'Well,' he said, when she'd run out of breath and inspiration, 'it's OK: I'm not going to arrest you. I really do just want to talk.'

She looked him up and down again. 'I talk very good dirty. You want talk dirty?'

'Not that kind of talking. Come on, I'll buy you a drink.'

The Regents Arms was a little bar on Regent Quay with a three am licence. Not the smartest place in Aberdeen: it was dark, dirty, missing an apostrophe, and smelled of spilt beer and old cigarettes. Popular with the kind of people that hung around the docks after sundown. Logan took one look at the clientele and spotted at least three he'd arrested before – bit of aggravated assault, bit of prostitution, bit of breaking and entering – so there was no way he was going to risk using the toilets here. Wander into a small room with only one exit and a bar full of people who'd love to see a policeman with his brains leaking out onto the dirty floor? Might as well smash himself in the face with a claw hammer, save everyone the bother. But no one said anything as he sat the young girl down in a booth and bought her a bottle of Bud. If she was old enough to be selling her body on the streets, she was old enough for a beer.

'So,' he said, 'who was your friend?'

She scowled and hurled another barrage of incomprehensible abuse at her absent protector. When Logan asked what language she was swearing in she told him: 'Lithuanian.' Her name was Kylie Smith – likely bloody story thought Logan – and she'd been in Scotland for almost eight months now. First Edinburgh then Aberdeen. She preferred Edinburgh, but what could she do? She had to go where she was sent. And no she wasn't sixteen, she was nineteen. Logan didn't buy that one either. The pub's lighting was murky, but it was still better than the flickering yellow streetlights in Shore Lane. She was fourteen if she was a day. Like it or not, she'd have to go to the station after this. There was no way he could turn a child that age back out onto the streets. She should still be in school!

Her 'friend' had told her to call him Steve, but Logan wasn't to cause trouble for him, because she had to stay with him, and he'd beat her. Logan just made noncommittal noises and asked Kylie where she'd been Monday night.

'I go with man in suit, he want I do dirty thing, but he pay good. Then I go with other man, smell very bad of chips, skin is all grease. I go with—'

'Sorry, that's not what I meant.' Logan tried not to think of oily fingers pawing away at the schoolgirl. 'What I meant was: where were you getting picked up from?'

'Oh, I understand. Same place today. All night. I make good money.' She nodded. 'Steve bring me breakfast, I do so good. Happy Meal.'

Last of the big spenders. 'Did you know a girl was attacked?'

She nodded again. 'I know.'

'Did you see anything?'

Kylie shook her head. 'She stand there all night, only one man come make fuck with her.'

'What did he look like?'

'It very dark . . .' A frown and then, 'White hair all spike?' She stuck her hands to the side of her head, fingers pointing upwards. 'You know? And beard.' More hand gestures: this time the left, fingers bunched, right on the point of her chin. 'He smell of chips too.'

Logan sat back and smiled. That would be Jamie McKinnon, no doubt fresh from robbing another late-night fast-food joint. Goodbye alibi.

'Did you hear anything they said?'

She shook her head and finished her bottle of beer. 'I go with other man.'

Logan sat back in his seat and looked at her. 'You know someone killed her?'

Kylie sighed, her face suddenly much older than its years. She knew. People got hurt all the time. People died. It was the way the world worked.

'Would you come with me to the station? Look

at some photographs? Make a statement? Just what you've told me?'

She shook her head. 'Steve angry if I not making money.' She rolled up the sleeve of her low-cut blouse, showing him the cluster of cigarette burns in the crook of her elbow. There were needle tracks in amongst the circular scars, just enough to get addiction underway. To make her dependent on 'Steve'.

'What if I told you I could make sure Steve never hurt you ever again?'

Kylie just laughed. That was crazy talk. She wasn't going to come with him, she wasn't going to police station, she wasn't going to cause no trouble for Steve. Thank you for beer and goodbye. Logan insisted, but Kylie was having none of it. She jumped to her feet and made a run for the door.

Logan leapt up to follow, and that was when things started to go wrong. A large man with a tattoo the size of a Rottweiler blocked the exit, just after Kylie charged through the door. He was a good foot shorter than Logan was, but more than made up for it in breadth.

Logan screeched to a halt.

'Lady's no' wantin' your company,' he said, his accent broad Peterhead.

'Look, I need to catch her! She's only fourteen!'

'Oh, like 'em young do you?' Through gritted teeth.

'What? No! I'm a police officer! She . . .' And

82

that's when Logan heard it: the silence. Every conversation in the pub had come to a sudden halt. The only sound in the place was a tatty-looking bandit, bleeping and pinging away to itself.

Fuck . . .

'OK,' he turned around and addressed the bar as a whole, 'I'm looking for whoever killed Rosie Williams. I don't want to cause trouble for anyone else.' More silence. Cold sweat was beginning to run down Logan's back. 'Some bastard beat Rosie to death: strangled her, smashed her face in, broke her ribs. She drowned in her own blood!' Logan turned to face the tattooed thug blocking the door. 'She deserved better than that. Everyone does.'

He was going to get his arse kicked. He could feel it.

The wee muscleman frowned in concentration. The silence stretched. And then he said, 'Go on, bugger off.' He jerked a thumb over his shoulder. 'Mind this, though: it's no' healthy for you in here. Don't come back.'

By the time he was outside there was no sign of Kylie.

Logan didn't know any Lithuanian, so he swore in good old-fashioned Scottish.

8

Logan spent the next few hours going around the car parks and alleys again, but it wasn't any use – the young lady from Lithuania was the only one who'd seen Jamie McKinnon. Everyone else had been too busy making a living in doorways and strangers' cars.

Force Headquarters was like a graveyard when he pushed through the back doors, not a soul to be seen. Except for Big Gary, still sitting behind the desk, with a *Teach Yourself French* book and a packet of chocolate Hobnobs.

'Any news on PC Maitland?' Logan asked, helping himself to a biscuit.

The large man shook his head. 'Far as I know, he's still in intensive care.' His voice dropped to a whisper. 'You know, no' everyone blames you for it, OK? I mean, it's no' your fault they was tooled up. Is it?'

Logan smiled sadly. 'So how come I still feel like shite then?'

''Cos you're no' a heartless wanker, like some of the tubes round here.' He patted Logan's shoulder with a massive hand. 'He'll be fine. Stick some cash in the whip-round: we'll get him a stripper. This'll all blow over. You'll see.' Logan thanked him for his optimism then sodded off to the canteen for a cup of tea and a sandwich, taking both down to Records so he could look at some mugshots while he ate. Searching for a big bloke with a shaved head and a goatee beard: the four-teen-year-old Lithuanian girl's pimp. Clicking his way through ream after ream of bad guys on the computer.

By the time three o'clock arrived, he'd only managed to get through a fraction of FHQ's collec-tion of mugshots. Tomorrow he'd get someone to put together an e-fit identikit picture. Email it round, see if anyone recognized the man. Straightening up with a creak and a yawn, Logan headed back out into the night, wanting to take one last look for Kylie. So much for knocking off at two.

There wasn't a lot of activity down at the docks; Wednesday wasn't really a night for hard drinking so there were fewer drunken idiots staggering out of the nightclubs and strip joints to prowl the streets in search of a cash-based romantic inter-lude. And that meant most of the prostitutes went home too. Now it was just the hard-core left. The women who were the most desperate. Who hadn't had much luck earlier in the night. The ones with varicose veins and no teeth. The ones like Rosie Williams.

Logan walked the docks again, but there were only four working girls still out, three of whom he'd spoken to earlier. The last 'girl' was in her mid to late forties – difficult to tell in the flickering streetlight – dressed in a cheap miniskirt and PVC raincoat, a pair of black plastic kinky boots finishing off the ensemble. Seeing her, Logan wasn't surprised she only came out in the wee small hours, when all her punters would be at their most pissed and least picky. Her face was odd, distorted, lumpy . . . And that's when he realized: someone had beaten the crap out of her recently. That's why her smile was twisted and her face uneven, swollen from the blows. She'd tried to plaster over the bruises with make-up.

She saw Logan staring at her and said, 'You lookin' for a good time?' The words were slurred, slightly lisping – probably missing a couple of teeth. 'Good-lookin' guy like you, *must* be lookin' for a good time . . .' She wiggled her hips at him, winced and opened her PVC raincoat wide, exposing a black lace bustier over white skin covered in bruises. 'See anythin' you like?'

There was no way Logan could answer that honestly. 'Someone give you a going over?'

She shrugged and dragged a packet of cigarettes out of her pocket, sticking one between her swollen lips and lighting it with a petrol-station lighter. 'You a cop?' She looked him up and down. 'Naw, don't bother answerin' that. Course you're a fuckin' cop.' The first good lungful of smoke set off a coughing fit, eyes closed, left arm clutching her ribs as she hacked and grimaced.

'Those things'll kill you.'

She stuck her middle finger up at him and wheezed to a rattling stop, before spitting a dark wad out onto the street. 'I want health advice I'll go to my fuckin' doctor. What do you want? Kickback? Freebie?'

Logan tried not to shudder. 'Rosie Williams,' he said instead. 'Got herself killed night before last. I'm looking for anyone who saw the bastard that did it.'

The woman flinched, wrapping the PVC raincoat tightly around her bruised chest. 'Jesus,' she said. 'Rosie?'

Logan nodded. 'Monday night. You working then?'

She shook her head. 'Naw.' She pulled in another large lungful of smoke. 'Had a bit of an accident couple of nights back.' She gestured at the mess of her face. 'Walked into a door.'

'Must've been a really big door to do all that.'

'Aye. Fuckin' big door.' She lowered her eyes. 'But I wasnae here Monday night. Couldn't fuckin' move Monday, let alone work.' She sighed. 'No' that I'm gonnae do much business lookin' like this . . .' Her voice trailed off into silence, her eyes focused on the past rather than the darkened streets.

'Then why *are* you out here?'

She shrugged. 'Got mouths to feed. You know? And heroin's a fuckin' hungry wee bastard.'

Twenty-two hundred hours: the start of Thursday's night shift. It had been a day for lounging about in bed, only getting up when Jackie came back from work at five. Fish and chips for dinner/breakfast and then back to bed for a bit. This time with company. So it was a pretty happy Logan who sauntered up the street to FHQ at ten to ten. There was an air of doom and gloom about the place as he pushed through the front doors. Sergeant Eric Mitchell was sitting behind the reception desk, engrossed in a copy of the *Evening Express*, the lights reflecting off his ever-expanding bald spot. He looked up, displaying a wide Wyatt Earp-style moustache, and scowled. 'What the hell you looking so damn cheerful about?'

Logan smiled back. 'And good evening to you too, Eric. I am smiling because it has been a lovely day. What's got your moustache in a twist? Big Gary nick all the custard creams?'

Eric just scowled and held up the *Evening Express* so Logan could see the paper's front page with its headline, POLICE RAID WRONG ADDRESS! There was a large photo: dozens of patrol cars, vans and uniformed officers milling about outside a converted church in Tillydrone.

Logan tried not to grin. At least he wasn't the

only one to screw up a raid this month. 'Where were they supposed to be?'

'Kincorth.' Eric slammed the paper back on the desk. 'Silly bastards. Like we don't have enough to worry about!' He poked a sidebar next to the picture. POLICE INCOMPETENCE: CITY COUNCILLOR SPEAKS OUT. 'Wee shite's been gagging for another excuse to make us look like arseholes.' Eric scowled at the little black-and-white photo of Councillor Holier-Than-Thou Marshall doing his usual smug slug impression. Then Eric remembered he had a message for Logan. 'DI Steel says get your arse up to her office, soon as you get in.'

Just like Inspector Napier's lair, DI Steel's office reflected its owner: cramped, untidy and stinking of stale cigarettes. She was sat behind her desk, feet up, cup of coffee in one hand, mobile phone in the other, fag dangling out the corner of her mouth. She waved Logan to take a seat as she pinned the phone between her ear and shoulder, before rummaging about in a desk drawer, coming out with a little black notebook and a pen.

'Course I love you,' she said, the end of the cigarette bobbing up and down, letting loose a half-inch avalanche of ash. 'Yes . . . You know I do . . . No, I'd never do that . . .' She scribbled something awkwardly on the pad and threw it across the desk to Logan. 'You know I do . . . Susan, you're the most important thing in my life . . . Yes . . . Yes . . .'

Logan peered at the spidery scrawl. YOU

IDENTIFIED THAT TART YET? He gave the inspector a puzzled look and she rolled her eyes, waving a hand at him, asking for the pad back.

'Yes, Susan, you know I do . . .' She scribbled another note. LAST NIGHT – THE ONE WHO SAW McKINNON? Logan shook his head and Steel said, 'Damn . . . What? Oh, no, not you, Susan, I dropped something . . . yes . . . uhuh . . .' She demanded the pad back and left Logan a final message: FUCK OFF TO THE CANTEEN. I'LL BE UP IN A BIT.

He was on his second mug of milky tea and halfway through a bacon buttie when DI Steel finally slouched into the canteen. 'Christ, I'm fucking starving,' she said, slumping down on the other side of the table and sighing. 'Right, first things first.' She dragged out a copy of that morning's *Press and Journal* and placed it on the tabletop. 'Care to explain this?' She pointed at the headline: DRY RUN FOR SUITCASE-TORSO MURDERER. Colin Miller had worked his usual magic, weaving Logan's suspicions into a pretty good story. Not surprising he was the newspaper's golden boy.

'I spoke to him last night,' said Logan as he read, groaning at every mention of 'Police Hero Logan "Lazarus" McRae'. Whenever Miller put him in the bloody paper, Angus Robertson – the Mastrick Monster – was always wheeled out to justify Logan's 'hero' status.

'And the reason you screwed over *my* investigation?' Steel's voice was level, cold. Dangerous. But Logan didn't notice.

'Whoever it is, they're counting on the dog being a full, proper, dry run, OK?' he said with a smile. 'So the fact we found the body and released details to the press, means our killer-to-be knows we're on to them. It's one thing to kill a dog and dump it, but it's a hell of a lot more difficult to do it to a human being, especially when you know the police are wise to you.'

'Well,' she said, settling back in her seat, giving Logan the benefit of a hyena smile. 'Sounds like you've got it all figured out, doesn't it?' He nodded and she let the smile grow colder. 'Let's get one thing crystal, Mr Police Hero: this is not a fucking democracy I'm running here. You do *what* I tell you – *when* I tell you, *not whatever you fucking feel like!*' Logan flinched as the inspector hammered on: 'And you know what? This time I actually agree with you, but that does not excuse going to the press behind my fucking back to get your name all over the papers!'

Logan dropped his half-eaten buttie back onto his plate. 'I . . . I'm sorry, I didn't think you'd—'

'No you didn't, did you? But I fucking well do!' She snatched up the fallen buttie and ripped a huge bite out of it. 'I'm getting fucked over enough already,' she mumbled round a mouthful of bacon and bread, 'I don't need you adding to my bloody problems.'

Logan sat quietly in his seat, thinking this was a great way to start a working day: yet another bollocking. 'Sorry,' he said at last.

'Just don't do it again, OK?' DI Steel popped the last of Logan's buttie in her gob and chewed unhappily in silence. 'Right,' she said when she'd finished. 'On a lighter note: I read your report on last night. Result. Or it would have been if you hadn't lost the tart.' She saw the look on Logan's face. 'I know: you did your best. Keep an eye out for her tonight. You can take DC Rennie with you; I've shifted him onto nights as well. Keep him out of trouble.' She stood and ferreted about in her pockets for a packet of rumpled cigarettes. 'Oh, and before I forget: I want to interview McKinnon again tomorrow. See what the bleach-blond, spiky-haired, murdering wee shite has to say for himself after a night in Craiginches.'

'I'm supposed to be off tomorrow! Jackie's got plans, I—'

'For God's sake! A woman's been murdered and all you can think about is getting your leg over?' Logan blushed. 'Look,' said the inspector, 'it's not going to take all day to re-interview Jamie McKinnon. You can see your tasty WPC after, OK?' That, on top of his recent bollocking, just made Logan feel even more guilty.

'Yes, ma'am.'

'Good boy. And while you're about tonight, go see if they've done a post mortem on that bloody dog yet. And don't spend all night in the arms of some prozzie down the docks. I'm not signing off any expense form with "blowjobs" on it.'

*   *   *

DC Rennie looked so much like a plainclothes policeman it was scary. Even in jeans and a leather jacket something about him just screamed 'LOOK AT ME: I'M A POLICEMAN!' Not surprisingly they didn't have a lot of luck speaking to the ladies plying their trade around Aberdeen harbour that night. And their punters weren't stopping either, not with DC Conspicuous hanging around. So all Logan and Rennie got for their night's work was several filthy mouthfuls of abuse.

Come half past twelve they'd been around the neighbourhood half a dozen times. There was still no sign of the fourteen-year-old Lithuanian, or her minder. 'Sod this for a game of soldiers.' DC Rennie slumped back against the railing that separated Regent Quay from the docks proper. 'How many times are we going to go round and round in circles, getting shouted and spat at?' He flinched, and slowly looked up into the sky. Thin raindrops were beginning to fall, making little needle streaks in the streetlights. 'Shite, that's *all* we bloody need.'

Logan had to agree. 'Come on, let's get back to the station.' There wasn't a single tart out tonight he hadn't spoken to yesterday, and he still had an identikit picture to put together *and* a canine post mortem to chase up. They were getting nowhere here.

She smiles at him as he pulls up in his car. Smiles at him, but stays in the doorway. Keeping dry. Lovely fuckin' day this was turning out to be: first

Jason won't eat his Ready Brek, then he's late for school and she's got such a sodding hangover! How's she supposed to deal with Jason's dickhead teacher with a dirty vodka hangover? And then PC Plod and his mate scare off the first nibble she's had all fuckin' night! Should be out there catching fuckin' crooks, not hassling women trying to make a living!

The window buzzes down and he has to lean across the passenger seat to say hello. She always stands on the passenger side. Some dirty bastard drove up, wound down his window and grabbed her tits once. Didn't ask, didn't pay. Just grabbed her nipples like a fuckin' vice, and drove off laughing. There's a lot of sick bastards out there. He asks her how much and she gives him the list. Jacking the prices up a bit, 'cos the car looks new and he's obviously not short of cash. He thinks about it as the rain really starts hammering down . . . Maybe she's hiked the price up too much? Shit. Not like she doesn't need the fuckin' money; Jason goes through shoes like the things were free. She opens her raincoat a little, letting him see the red lace bra she's almost wearing – two sizes too small and uncomfortable as hell, but it always gets the bastards going – and he smiles. Sort of. She keeps herself in good shape, and it shows. So what if her complexion's not the best: she makes up for it where it counts.

'You want to get in?' he asks her. And it's her turn to think about it. After all, that old tart got herself beaten to death a couple of nights ago. But it's a nice car, and it's pissing with rain. And she really, really needs the cash . . . She jumps in. The car has that lovely new, leathery-plastic smell to it, the upholstery clean, the interior spotless, not like that piece of shit she has to drive. This thing must have cost a fortune. She pulls the seatbelt over her breasts, giving him another flash of red lace, and he smiles. He has a nice smile. For a moment the Julia-Roberts-Pretty-Woman-Fantasy flashes through her brain. Just like it does every time she meets a client who's good to her. Doesn't want it too rough, or anything disgusting. He'll look after her and she won't have to fuck strangers for money any more. He tells a joke and she laughs as he puts the car in gear and drives them out into the rainy night. He's really nice, she can tell. She has a sixth sense about that kind of thing.

9

Nearly one in the morning and the morgue was, appropriately, deathly quiet. The only sounds were Logan's shoes squeaking on the tiles and the hum of the overhead lights. The cutting tables sparkled in the middle of the floor, the huge extractor fan set into the ceiling, waiting to whisk away the smell of death. Good job it worked better than the one in Logan's kitchen: that wouldn't whisk away the smell of frying onions, let alone decaying Labrador. 'Hello?' The morgue was supposed to be manned twenty-four hours a day, but as he wandered past the loading bay, the fridges, the cutting room and the viewing suite there wasn't a living soul to be seen. 'Hello?' He finally found someone in the pathologist's office, sitting with her back to the door, feet up on the desk, headphones on, reading a huge Stephen King novel and drinking Lucozade. Logan reached out and tapped the woman on the shoulder. There was a loud shriek; Stephen King and Lucozade went flying as she scrambled to her feet and whirled round. 'FOR FUCK'S SAKE! YOU NEARLY GAVE ME A HEART ATTACK!' Logan winced and she peeled off her headphones. 'Christ!' she said, the metallic *tssshk-tssshk-tssshk* of something loud hissing out of the earpieces. 'I thought you were . . .' then she stopped, clearly not wanting to tell Logan she'd thought the dead had risen up to claim her. Carole Shaw: Deputy Anatomical Pathology Technician, slightly chubby, shortish, early thirties with long curly blonde hair, little round spectacles and a Morticians Do It With Dead Bodies! T-shirt on under an open white lab coat. The latter now stained sticky-orange with ejected Lucozade.

'Good book?' asked Logan innocently.

'Bastard. Nearly sodding wet myself . . .' She bent down and grabbed her book off the floor, cursing as the neon-orange fizzy drink soaked into the pages. 'What the hell do you want?'

'Labrador's torso, brought in for post mortem Wednesday afternoon. Got the results back yet?'

She shuddered. 'Christ, I remember that one. Bloody hell, how come when a rotting, suppurating carcass gets dragged in here for some poor bugger to cut up, it's always yours?'

Logan didn't smile. Last year it had been a little boy and a little girl, neither of them much over four years old. Both of them dead a long time. 'Just lucky I guess,' he said at last.

'Here.' She rummaged through a filing cabinet,

emerging with a slim Manila folder. 'Fido was dismembered with a boning knife: seven-inch single-sided blade – scooped near the handle, straight for most of its length and curved at the tip. They come in most kitchen sets, so nothing distinctive. Find the knife and we'll probably be able to match it, but the carcass is pretty far gone . . . can't guarantee anything.' She flipped through the pages, her lips moving as she skimmed the text. 'Here we go . . . one thing might help: Fido was drugged before he was killed. Amitriptyline: prescription antidepressant. Works a bit like a sedative, so they give it to people who're wound up, anxious, calms them down. We got what looks like minced beef and about half a bottle of the things from the stomach contents. And you do *not* want to know what that smelled like.'

Logan agreed. He didn't. 'What about the suitcase?'

Carole shrugged. 'Pretty standard fare. ASDA in Dyce, Bridge of Don, Garthdee and Portlethen all had them on special a couple of months ago. Sold hundreds of the things.' Logan swore and she nodded. 'Also, fingerprints: bugger all. Same for fibre: clean as a whistle. Whoever did this wasn't keen on getting caught.'

The rest of Logan's night was spent getting together e-fit identikit pictures of the Lithuanian fourteen-year-old and her pimp, then shoving them under the noses of everyone in the station; putting the pictures up on the intranet and briefing pages; emailing them to all the other stations in the area – hoping someone could ID them.

By the time he got back to the flat, the rain had formed an uneasy truce with the early morning sunlight; purple-grey clouds scudding across the sky at a great rate of knots. Jackie was still asleep, curled up under the duvet like an unexploded bomb. She blew up when Logan told her he'd have to go back into work at half eleven to help DI Steel interview Jamie McKinnon. 'What the hell do you mean you've got to go back in? You've just got off night shift! She's already screwed up our whole weekend and now you're going back into work? I had plans! We were going to do things today!'

'I'm sorry, but it's—'

'Don't you bloody "sorry" me, Logan McRae! Why can't you just stand up to the woman and tell her no? You're *supposed* to have time off! It's only a job for Christ's sake!'

'But Rosie Williams—'

'Rosie Williams is dead! She's not going to get any less dead, just because you work more bloody overtime! Is she?' She stormed off to the shower, leaving a deluge of foul language in her wake. Fifteen minutes later she was fighting with the hairdryer, trying to work a comb through her wet hair with the fingers of her broken arm. Swearing and muttering at her reflection in the mirror.

Logan stood in the doorway, watching her angry back, not knowing what to say. Ever since she'd moved in – three months ago – they'd rubbed along fine. It was only recently that he'd started to piss her off. And he couldn't seem to do anything about it. 'Jackie, I'm sorry. There's always tomorrow . . .'

She gave one last tug of the comb, losing it in the long curls of her dark hair, swore, dragged it out and hurled it onto the dressing table, sending jars and tubes of moisturizer clattering. 'Fucking thing!' She stood staring down at the mess. 'I'm going out.' Jacket, keys and gone.

Logan stood alone in the kitchen. Swearing.

The Black Friars was a real-ale pub at the top of Marischal Street, all dark wooden floorboards and beams, split over three levels, following the downward slope of the road. Weekday mornings were usually pretty quiet, just the occasional pensioner washing down the full Scottish breakfast – eggs, sausage, bacon, beans, black pudding, tattie scones, clootie dumpling, mushrooms and toast, all slathered in tomato sauce – with a couple of beers. Logan perched at the end of the lower bar, eating his breakfast and drinking a pint of Dark Island. So what if it was half nine in the morning? He was supposed to be on holiday. With his girlfriend. Who wasn't speaking to him, thanks to DI Bloody Steel and her guilt trip. They could have still been in bed, with nothing to do but laze about playing doctors and nurses. Logan scowled, downed the last of his pint and ordered another.

'Bit early to be gettin' hammered isn't it?'

Logan groaned, put down a forkful of beans, and turned to see Colin Miller, the *Press and Journal*'s golden boy, leaning on the bar next to him. As usual the wee Glaswegian was dressed up to the nines: sharp black suit, silk shirt and tie. He was wide, in a broad-shouldered, muscular kind of way, with a face that took a little getting used to. At least Isobel had tamed down the man's taste for flashy gold jewellery: instead of the three and a half tons of cufflinks, rings, chains and bracelets he used to wear, Colin was restricted to a single silver band on his left pinkie. Like a misplaced wedding ring. But his watch was still big enough to cover the national debt of a small third-world country. He levered himself up on the next barstool and ordered himself a mochachino latte with extra cinnamon.

'What you doing here anyway?' Logan asked. 'Looking for me?'

'Nope, got an appointment: wanted to make sure it was on neutral territory. You know how it goes.' Miller scanned the bar before taking a drink. 'So then, Laz, how've you been, eh? No' seen you for ages, man.'

'Not since you gave me duff information on that bloody warehouse, no.'

Miller shrugged. 'Aye, well, can't be right all the time, eh? My source swore blind it was kosher, like.'

Logan snorted and washed the last of his fried

egg down with a mouthful of beer. 'And who was that, then? No, don't tell me: journalistic integrity, protecting your sources, none of my fucking business, etcetera.'

'Jesus, man, who rattled your fuckin' cage? Did I no' keep your name out the papers, eh? You see one story blamin' you for what happened?' When Logan didn't say anything, Miller just shrugged and took another sip of coffee. 'And I *can* tell you who my source was this time: Graham Kennedy. Remember him? One of the squatters got all burned up in the fire the other night? He was the one told me about that warehouse bein' full of nicked gear, like. No point being anonymous if you're dead.'

Logan groaned. He'd forgotten all about Graham Bloody Kennedy – he still hadn't told DI Insch about him. One more thing he'd screwed up. 'Why the hell didn't you tell me all this on Wednesday?'

'Didnae know you was holdin' a grudge.' He paused, coffee halfway to his lips. 'Oops, gotta dash, that's my half ten appointment turned up.' He pointed through the bar, up the stairs to the middle level, where a dangerous-looking man in an expensive charcoal-grey suit was scowling at an OAP in an Aberdeen Football Club bobble hat.

'Who's the thug?' asked Logan.

'He's no' a thug, Laz, he's a "corporate investment facilitator" and if he hears you callin' him a thug, he'll break your legs. Policeman or no'.' Miller forced a smile. 'If you don't hear from me tomorrow, start dredging the harbour.' He waved, gave a hearty hello, marched up and shook the 'facilitator's' hand, then led him off to a quiet corner. Logan watched them for a while, his breakfast congealing, forgotten on the plate. Miller was smiling a lot, laughing more than was probably necessary. As if he was doing his damnedest not to upset the man in the grey suit. The thug was easily six foot two, short blond hair, square-cut jaw, teeth straight out of a toothpaste commercial. Five minutes later the man handed over a large brown A4 envelope and Miller smiled ingratiatingly, but handled it like it was a dirty nappy. The conversation seemed to be winding to a close, so Logan got up from his seat and wandered over to the specials board, placing himself between their table and the exit, 'accidentally' bumping into the man as he finished shaking Miller's hand and made to leave. The reporter's eyes went wide with alarm as he watched Logan apologize profusely, call the facilitator 'mate' half a dozen times and offer to buy him a drink. The response was a curt: 'Fuck off.' Not shouted. Not emphasized, just quiet, cold and very, very clear. Logan backed away, hands up. Those two words were enough to tell him the guy wasn't from around here. An Edinburgh lad, up on a jolly. The man straightened out his suit, scowled in Logan's direction and left.

Miller stood on tiptoes, watching the grey-suited figure hurry across the road in the rain and jump into the passenger seat of a massive silver

Mercedes. Logan didn't get a good look at the driver – moustache, shoulder-length black hair, suit – before the door slammed shut and the car pulled away. As soon as it disappeared from view Miller ran a hand over his forehead and demanded to know what the fuckin' hell Logan thought he was playing at? 'Did I no' tell you the man would break your fuckin' legs? Are you lookin' to get me disfingered?'

Logan smiled. 'You mean disfigured—'

'I know what I bloody well mean!' Miller pulled up a barstool and ordered a large Macallan whisky, throwing it back in one.

'So,' said Logan, 'you going to tell me what that was all about?'

'Am I fuck. You want to piss in someone's soup? Piss in your own. Mine tastes bad enough as it is.'

Logan watched the reporter storm off, Cuban heels stomping up the stairs two at a time, before turning back to the bar to finish his pint and pay for his half-eaten breakfast.

Quarter past eleven and he was loitering without intent in front of Force Headquarters. He'd tried to speak to DI Insch about Graham Kennedy, but the inspector wasn't in – according to the admin officer he was off buying a big box of Sherbert Dib-Dabs from the cash and carry in Altens. Would Logan like to leave a message? No, he bloody would not. If there was any credit to be had for identifying Graham Kennedy, Logan wanted it. In person. So he slouched about in front instead, waiting for DI Steel. The daylight was pre-autumn amber, turning the grey granite to glittering gold. Up above the clouds were a rolling mass of dark purple and white. The air smelled of rain.

Sure enough, the first light drops started as DI Steel's car purred into the main car park. Cursing and swearing, she struggled with the soft-top, shouting at Logan to get his finger out and help. They got the roof up just before the heavens opened. Logan sat in the passenger seat, looking around. 'Very swish,' he said, as the inspector revved the engine and pulled out onto Queen Street.

'Best mid-life crisis I ever had, buying this thing: it's a bloody babe-magnet . . .' She flicked on the windscreen wipers, squinting at him out of the corner of her eye. 'You been on the piss?'

Logan shrugged. 'Keeping an eye on a friend in the pub. Shifty wee bugger's up to something.'

'Oh aye? Anyone I know?'

He paused for a long moment, before simply saying, 'No.' They cruised up Union Street in silence, the growl of the engine and the drumming of rain on the car's soft roof the only noise. Steel was obviously desperate for Logan to tell her more, but he wasn't going to give her the satisfaction. After all, it was her fault Jackie had stormed out this morning.

The rain sparked off the windscreen, catching the golden sunlight as the traffic crawled past pavements packed with pedestrians. A few were hurrying along under umbrellas, but most of them just marched down the street, resigned to getting wet. Live in the North-east of Scotland for long enough and you stop noticing the rain. Up at the far end of Union Street a rainbow had formed against the lowering clouds.

'Typical fucking Aberdeen,' said the inspector, shoogling about in her seat, trying to get a hand into her trouser pocket. 'Blazing sunshine and pissing with rain. Both at the same time. Don't know why I bothered buying a bloody open-topped sports car.'

Logan smiled. 'Mid-life crisis babe-magnet, remember?'

The inspector nodded sagely, 'Aye, that was it . . . Come on you wee buggers . . .' She was still fighting with her trousers. 'Shite. Hold on to the steering wheel for a minute, OK?' She didn't pause for an answer, just let go of the wheel, unbuckled her seatbelt and dragged out the crumpled remains of a packet of twenty Marlboro Lights, digging one out of the pack before retaking control of the car. 'You don't mind?' she asked, not waiting for an answer before setting the tip glowing. The cramped car interior quickly filled with smoke. Spluttering slightly, Logan wound his window down a crack, letting in the steady hiss of rain hitting the road, buildings, cars and people.

Steel swung off Union Street opposite Marks and Spencer, heading down Market Street. As the harbour drifted past Logan peered around, but Shore Lane was hidden from view by a dirty big supply boat. The clanging and bashing of containers being loaded and unloaded echoed through the rain.

'So what about our hairy friend's post mortem?' the inspector asked as they headed along the north bank of the River Dee, taking the scenic route to Craiginches Prison. He told her about the knife and the suitcase and the antidepressant. Steel just snorted. 'Lot of bloody good that does us.'

'Well, the drugs are prescription only, so—'

'So they might be the *killer's*! Or the killer's wife's, or his mother's, or their neighbour's, or granny's . . .' She wound down the window and flicked the dying remains of her cigarette out into the rainy sunshine. 'Damn things could be Gulf War surplus for all we know. Hell, they might not even have been prescribed locally!' said Steel, swinging around the roundabout onto Queen Mother Bridge. 'What we going to do? Phone up every doctor's office and pharmacy in the country and ask for a list of patients' names and addresses?'

'We could get them to narrow it down a bit; just ask for details of anyone with mental problems who's been prescribed the drug.'

'"Mental problems?"' She laughed. 'If they didn't have mental problems they wouldn't be on anti-bloody-depressants, would they?' She looked across the car at him. 'Jesus, Lazarus, how'd you get to be a DS? They giving out sergeant's stripes free with boxes of Frosties?' Logan just scowled at the dashboard. 'Aye, well,' she smiled at him. 'When we get back to the ranch you can go find one of them tree-hugging wildlife crime officers to chase it up. Dead dog'll be right up their street. We'll start paying attention again if it comes to anything.'

HM Prison Craiginches was segregated from the outside world by twenty-four-foot-high walls, and a small black metal plaque saying, 'PRIVATE PROPERTY KEEP OUT', as if the razor wire wasn't enough of a hint. It was surrounded on three sides by residential streets – the houses festooned with burglar alarms – but on the fourth side there was nothing between the prison's north wall and the River Dee but the dual carriageway to Altens and a very steep bank. DI Steel parked in a bay marked 'STAFF ONLY' and sauntered round to the front door, with Logan slouching along at her heels. Twelve minutes later they were sitting in a shabby little room with a chipped Formica table and creaky plastic seats complete with brown, slug-shaped cigarette burns. There was a tape recorder bolted to the wall, but no video, just the bracket and a couple of loose wires. They sat there for another five minutes, counting the ceiling tiles – twenty-two and a half – before Jamie McKinnon was finally shepherded round the door by a bored-looking prison officer. Logan popped a couple of fresh tapes into the machine and launched into the standard names, dates and location speech.

'So then, Jamie,' said DI Steel when he'd finished. 'How's the food? Good? Or is Dirty Duncan Dundas still wanking into the porridge?' Jamie just shuddered and started picking at the skin around his fingernails, hacking away at it until the quick showed deep pink underneath. It didn't look as if prison agreed with McKinnon; a thin sheen of sweat covered his face and there were dark bags under his eyes. He had a split lip and a bruised cheek. Steel settled back in her seat and grinned at him. 'The reason we're here, my little porridge-muncher, is that there's a *tiny* problem with your alibi: someone saw you and Rosie Williams going at it like knives the night she got herself battered to death! How's about that for wacky coincidence?'

Jamie slowly slumped forward until his face was flat on the tabletop, his arms wrapped over his head.

'You want we should give you a couple of minutes to think up some new lies, Jamie?' asked the inspector.

'I didn't mean to hurt her . . .'

'Aye, we know that,' Steel pulled out her cigarettes and popped one in her mouth without offering them around. 'So why'd you do it then?'

'Been drinking . . . Down the Regents Arms . . . This bloke kept going on how she was nothing but a posh wank. No' even that . . .' He shivered. 'Followed him into the toilets and beat the shite out of him. Talking 'bout Rosie like that. Like she was just a whore . . .'

Steel's reply came out in a cloud of cigarette smoke: 'She *was* a whore, Jamie, sold her arse on the streets for—'

'SHUT UP! SHE WAS NOT A WHORE!' He jerked up and slammed his fists on the table, making it jump. His face was flushed, eyes sparkling and damp.

Logan sighed and stepped in, playing the good cop. 'So you taught him a lesson for insulting your woman. I can understand that. What happened next? Did you go looking for her?'

Jamie nodded, eyes fastening on Logan, ignoring the inspector. 'Yes . . . I wanted to tell her: it has to stop! She has to stay home, look after the kids. No more going out on the streets . . .' He sniffed and wiped his nose on the back of his sleeve.

'What happened when you found her, Jamie?'

He looked down at his picked-at fingers. 'I'd been drinking.'

'We know that, Jamie: what happened?'

'We had this argument . . . She . . . She said she needed the money. Said she couldn't stop.' Jamie laid down another trail of silver on his sleeve. 'I told her I'd support her. I was getting something together, she wouldn't have to worry . . . But she wasn't having any of it: kept going on and on about how I couldn't support her and the kids . . .' He bit his bottom lip. 'So I hit her. Just like that. And she started screaming at me. So I hit her again. Just to make her stop . . .'

Logan let the silence hang for a bit, while DI Steel dribbled smoke down her nose. 'Then what did you do?'

'Threw up in the toilet. Washed the blood off my hands . . . She was lying on the floor, all bruised . . . So I picked her up and put her to bed.'

Steel snarled. 'Put her to bed? That what they're calling it these days? "Putting someone to bed"? What a lovely euphemism for strangling someone in an alleyway! Like fucking poetry that is.'

Jamie ignored her. 'Next day she was covered in bruises. Threw me out. Said she never wanted to see me again. But I never meant to hurt her!'

Logan sat back in his seat and tried not to groan. 'It's *Monday* night we want to know about, Jamie. What happened on Monday night?'

'Went to see her, on the street.' He shrugged. 'Wanted to say I was sorry . . . show her I was making good money . . . You know, from the fast-food jobs? I could take care of her and the kids. I loved her . . . But she wouldn't talk to me: said she had to earn a living . . . didn't want anything to do with me . . . had clients to see. I'd have to pay . . .'

'And did you?'

Jamie hung his head. 'I . . . Yes.'

DI Steel spluttered, sending ash sparking from the end of her fag. 'So you forked out to screw your ex? Jesus, how fucking twisted is that?'

Logan scowled at her. 'Then what happened, Jamie?'

'We did it in a doorway and . . . and I cried and told her I loved her and I was so sorry for what I'd done, but I loved her so much I couldn't stand to see her out there with other men . . .' His red eyes filled with tears. 'I was making good money now, I could do it, we could be together . . .' He wiped his eyes with the same silvered sleeve.

Steel inched forward in her seat, bathing Jamie in a cloud of cigarette smoke. 'She said no though, didn't she? She said no and you hit her. You hit her and you kept hitting her 'cos she wouldn't take a slimy wee shite like you back. You killed her, 'cos it was that or pay for it your whole life. Pay to screw her in alleyways, just like hundreds of other desperate wee fucks.'

'NO! She said she'd think about it! She was going to come back to me! We were going to be a family!' The tears were falling freely now, running down his chubby cheeks, his scarlet nose streaming as sobs shook his body. 'God, she's dead! She's dead!' He crumpled to the tabletop, shoulders heaving.

Logan's voice was soft. 'Did you hit her again, Jamie? Did you kill her?'

He could barely make out the reply. 'I loved her . . .'

10

The ride back from Craiginches was spent with DI Steel smoking and swearing furiously. Now that Jamie McKinnon had admitted to paying for sex with Rosie the night she died, Logan's disappearing Lithuanian witness was worthless. And so was any DNA evidence they got from the hundreds of discarded condoms. Things had been a lot simpler when McKinnon was just denying everything. She pulled up outside Logan's flat and demanded the tapes of the interview. He handed them over and asked if she didn't want him to do the paperwork: taking them into evidence, releasing one copy to Jamie McKinnon's defence lawyer. 'Do I buggery,' was her response. 'Bloody things screw up my investigation.' She took the recordings, turned them upside down and picked a loop of tape free with a nicotine-stained fingernail. Then did 'Flags Of All Nations' with it, sending reels of shiny brown ribbon spooling out into the interior of the car. 'Far as anyone's concerned there was something wrong with the machine OK? No tape was ever made. We forget anything that was said and go back to proving Jamie McKinnon did it.' Logan tried to protest but the inspector was having none of it. 'What?' she demanded. 'We both *know* he did it! It's our job to make sure he doesn't get away with it.'

'What if he didn't do it?'

'Of course he did it! He's got form for beating her up 'cos she was on the game. He goes and pledges his undying love and she makes him fork out for a knee-trembler in an alleyway. Then goes off to shag someone else. He's overcome with rage and kills her. The end.' She shook her head. 'Now get your arse out of my car. I've got things to do.'

Logan spent the rest of the afternoon pottering about the flat. Sulking. So much for the Rosie Williams murder being his ticket out of the Screw-Up Squad. The way DI Steel was going they'd end up with no admissible evidence and a fully compromised case. The woman was a bloody menace. By seven thirty there was still no sign of Jackie, so he went out to the pub and to hell with everyone else. Archibald Simpson's wasn't an option: being just around the corner from Force Headquarters and full of cheap beer, the bar was a regular haunt for off-duty police, and he'd had enough dirty looks about getting PC Maitland shot to last him for one week, thank you very much. So instead he wandered up Union Street to the Howff, sitting on a creaky beige sofa in the farthest corner of the basement-level bar, nursing a pint of Directors and a packet of dry-roasted. Brooding over Jackie and her foul temper. And then another pint. And another. And a burger – smothered in chilli so hot it made his eyes water – and then another pint, getting maudlin. PC Maitland – Logan couldn't even remember his first name. Until the screwed-up raid he'd never worked with the guy, only knew him as the bloke with the moustache who shaved his head for Children In Need one year. Poor bastard. Two pints later and it was time to lurch blearily home, via a chip shop for jumbo-haddock supper; most of which he abandoned, uneaten, in the lounge, before staggering off to bed alone.

Saturday morning started with a hangover. The bathroom cabinet was devoid of massive blue-and-yellow painkillers – the ones Logan had been given after Angus Robertson had performed un-elective surgery on his innards with a six-inch hunting knife – so he had to make do with a handful of aspirin and a mug of strong instant coffee, taking it into the lounge to see what kind of cartoons were on. There was a shape on the couch and his heart sank. Jackie, all wrapped up in the spare duvet, blinking blearily as he froze in the doorway. He hadn't even heard her come in last night. She took one look at him, mumbled, 'Don't want any coffee . . .' and pulled the duvet over her head, shutting him, and the rest of the world, out.

Logan went back to the kitchen, closing the door behind him.

Saturday, their only full day off together, and Jackie still wasn't speaking to him. Obviously she'd rather sleep on the couch than share his bed. What a great bloody weekend *this* was turning out to be. He checked the clock on the microwave. Half past nine. Outside the kitchen window the rain was just coming on again, not the sunshine-and-rainbows rain of yesterday, but the heavy-grey-skies-and-freezing-wind kind of rain. It leached the warmth out of everything, making the city grey and miserable all over again. Matching Logan's mood. He dressed and headed out, meandering up Union Street, taking perverse pleasure in getting cold and wet. 'Playing the martyr' as his mum used to say. And she should know, she was a bloody dab hand at it.

He moped about the shops for a bit: bought a CD by some band he'd heard on the radio last week, two newish crime novels and a couple of DVDs. Trying to take his mind off everything that was wrong and failing miserably. Jackie hated him, Steel was a pain in the arse, PC Maitland was dying . . . He gave up on the shopping and wandered across Union Terrace, down School Hill and onto Broad Street. Drifting inexorably back towards the flat through the rain. At the corner of Marischal College, where the pale grey spines of its elaborate Victorian-Gothic frontage raised their claws to the clay-coloured skies, he stopped.

Straight ahead and it was back to the flat. Turn left and it was a stone's throw to Force Headquarters. It wasn't a tough choice, even if he was supposed to be off. He could always kill some time poking his nose into someone else's investigation. DI Insch was usually good for a . . . Logan screwed up his face and swore; the dead squatter – he *still* hadn't told Insch about Graham Kennedy. Bloody idiot. Miller had given him the name days ago! Sodding DI Steel and her malfunctioning tape recorder act.

The desk sergeant barely spoke to Logan as he squelched in through the front doors and dripped his way across the patterned linoleum of reception.

DI Insch's incident room was carefully orchestrated chaos – phones being manned, information being collated and entered into HOLMES, so the Home Office Large Major Enquiry System could automatically churn out reams and reams of pointless actions at the press of a button. Now and then it came out with something that made all the difference to an investigation, but most of the time: crap. Maps of Aberdeen were stuck up on the walls, coloured pins marking the locations of significant events. The inspector was sitting on a desk at the front of the room, resting one large buttock on the groaning wood while he read through a pile of reports and chewed on a Curly Wurly.

'Afternoon, sir,' said Logan, squelching in, hands

in his pockets, damp underwear beginning to make its presence felt.

Insch looked up from his paperwork, the chocolate-toffee-lattice sticking out of his large, pink face like a DNA-shaped cigar. 'Sergeant.' He nodded and went back to his reports. Two minutes later he handed them to a harassed-looking, cadaverous WPC and told her she was doing a great job, no matter what anyone else said. The admin officer didn't bother to thank him. As she stormed off back to the collating, Insch turned and beckoned Logan over. 'Bit overdressed for bath time aren't you?'

Logan didn't rise to the bait. 'I was wondering how you were getting on with your fatal arson attack.'

Insch frowned, the strip lighting gleaming off his bald, pink head. Suspicious. 'Why?'

'Got a possible ID for one of your victims: Graham Kennedy. Supposed to have been a minor dealer.' That made a smile blossom on the inspector's face.

'Well, well, well. There's a name I've not heard in a while. You—' Insch picked a PC at random and sent him off to phone round the dental practices in Aberdeen. Insch wanted to know who treated Graham Kennedy: dental records, X-rays the whole lot. It was the only way they were going to identify his charred corpse in the morgue. For once luck was actually on their side; the fourth dental practice the PC tried had done a whole heap of fillings on one Graham Kennedy less than eight months ago.

They couriered the X-rays straight over to the morgue and ten minutes later Doc Fraser confirmed the identification: Graham Kennedy was now officially dead. The enquiry finally had somewhere to start.

Insch grabbed PC Steve and told him to go get everything Records had on Graham Kennedy and meet them in the car park, then bellowed for a DS Beattie to get his backside in gear: they were going to break the news to Graham Kennedy's next of kin. And have a bit of a rummage through his things.

'Er, sir,' said Logan, following in the inspector's wake, 'I kinda hoped I could come with you on the shout?'

Insch raised an eyebrow and mashed the lift button with a fat finger. 'Oh aye? And what about DI Steel? You're supposed to be working for her. "More immediate supervision", remember?'

Logan opened and closed his mouth. 'Come on, sir! I didn't ask to be transferred! And anyway, it's my day off. I've—'

'You've got a day off and you want to go on a shout?' Insch looked at him suspiciously. 'You gone mental or something?'

'Please, sir. I need to get out of Steel's team. It's driving me mad! Nothing gets done by the book: even if we do get a result, it's going to be so tainted any defence lawyer worth half a fart will tear it to shreds! If I don't get some sort of success under my belt, I'm going to be stuck there till they fire me, or I go completely off my head.'

Insch shook his head, a small smile on his face. 'I hate to see a grown man beg.' A puffing, bearded detective sergeant appeared at the end of the corridor, dragging on a huge, multicoloured weatherproof jacket. DI Insch waited until he'd run the length of the corridor and come to a screeching halt in front of them, before telling him he wasn't needed after all. He'd be taking DS McRae along instead. Swearing quietly, the bearded bloke slouched back the way he'd come.

The inspector grinned. 'Just like to see the fat wee bugger run for his money,' he said happily. Logan knew better than to say anything about pots and kettles.

As they marched downstairs to the car park, Insch quizzed him on DI Steel's cases, wanting to know everything about the battered prostitute and the Labrador in the suitcase. And by the time they were through all that, a red-faced PC Steve Jacobs was waiting for them by the back door, clutching a small stack of A4 printouts: Graham Kennedy's rap sheet. Insch pointed his key fob at a muck-encrusted Range Rover and plipped open the locks. 'Right,' he said, striding out into the rain, 'PC Jacobs, you can do the honours. DS McRae, in the back, and don't stand on the dog food.'

The inside of Insch's car smelled as if something wet and shaggy had set up residence. There was a big metal grille separating the back seat from the boot and a soggy, black nose was pressed against it as soon as Logan clambered into place, trying not to tread on the jumbo-sized bag of Senior Dog Mix in the foot well. Lucy – the inspector's ancient Springer Spaniel – was pretty, in a manipulative, big-brown-eyed kind of way, but every time it rained she stank like a tramp on a bad day.

'Where to, sir?' asked PC Steve as they cruised slowly up Queen Street.

'Hmm?' The inspector was already immersed in Graham Kennedy's file. 'Oh, Kettlebray Crescent: let's get our esteemed colleague's opinion on the scene of the crime before we go tell Kennedy's granny her wee boy's dead . . . And the car does come with an accelerator, Constable: pedal on the floor, next to the big rectangular one. Try and use it, or we'll be here till bloody Christmas.'

Fourteen Kettlebray Crescent was a mess. Vacant windows stared out at the street, surrounded by dark streaks of soot. The roof was gone, collapsed in on itself as the flames raged through the building. Now faint, rainy daylight filtered into the house's shabby interior. The buildings on either side hadn't fared too badly; the fire brigade had arrived quickly enough to save them. But not the six people who'd been in number fourteen. Insch grabbed an umbrella from the boot and marched off into the fire-ravaged house, leaving Logan and

PC Steve to scurry along behind getting wet. A mobile incident room was abandoned outside the building: a cross between a Portakabin and a caravan, only without the windows. The standard black-and-white checked ribbon ran around the outside, with the SEMPER VIGILO thistle logo in the middle. Like a bow on a grubby, unwanted Christmas present.

They ducked under the blue-and-white POLICE tape stretched across the burnt-out building's garden gate and walked up the path to the front door. It was hanging off its hinges, battered in by the fire brigade as soon as they realized someone was actually in there, but by then it was too late. Logan stopped at the doorframe: there were about two dozen three-inch screws poking through the wood, their shiny steel points grabbing the space where the door should have been. Inside it was like something out of *Better Homes and Infernos*. The walls in the hallway were stripped back to the plaster and lathe, black and covered in soot. 'Er . . . sir?' asked PC Steve, hanging back, peering into the gutted building from the outside. 'Are you sure this is safe?'

The upper floor was missing, leaving the building little more than a burnt-out shell, the ground floor covered in broken slates and charcoaled wooden beams. Rain fell steadily through the gaping hole where the roof used to be, drumming off the inspector's brolly. He stood in a relatively clear patch and pointed up at one of the windows on the upper floor. 'Main bedroom: that's where the petrol bombs came in.'

Logan risked a clamber over the shifting, rain-slicked slates, to peer out into the street beyond. The mud was slowly washing off the inspector's filthy car, the expectant nose of a smelly spaniel pressed against the rear window, looking up at the building where six people had been burned to death. Screaming until their lungs filled with scalding smoke and flame, falling to the floor in agony as their eyes cooked and their flesh crackled . . . Logan shuddered. Did it actually smell of burning people in here, or was it just his imagination? 'You know,' he said, looking away from the window and back into the hollowed-out building, 'I heard it takes twenty minutes for the human brain to die once the flow of blood's stopped . . . all the electrical impulses, firing away to themselves, till there's no charge left . . .' The ruined face, staring up at him out of the body-bag in the morgue: eyes, nose and lips gone. 'Do you think it was like that for them? Already dead, but still feeling themselves burn and cook?'

There was an uncomfortable silence. And then PC Steve said, 'Jesus, sir, morbid much?' Insch had to agree. They picked their way carefully through the debris and back outside; there was nothing else to see here anyway.

Logan stood on the top step, looking up and down the deserted street. 'What did you find when you searched the other buildings?'

'Not a bloody thing.'

Logan nodded and wandered out into the road, slowly turning through three hundred and sixty degrees, taking in the boarded-up houses on both sides of the street. If he was the sick bastard who'd screwed the door shut so that three men, two women and a nine-month-old baby girl would be roasted alive, he'd want to hang about and watch them burn. That would be where the fun was. He crossed the road, trying the door handles, looking for one that wasn't locked . . . Two houses up, something caught his eye, something grey and squishy, trapped in the corner of the doorframe. It was nearly invisible: a disposable tissue, soaked transparent by the rain and slowly disintegrating. He pulled out a small, clear evidence baggie and turned it inside out, using it like a makeshift mitten to scoop up the tissue before flipping the baggie round the right way again, trapping the contents inside. A shadow fell across the doorway.

'What is it?' DI Insch.

Logan risked a sniff at the open evidence bag. 'Unless I'm very much mistaken, it's a wanker-chief. Your man probably stood here to watch the place burn, listen to them scream as they died, tossing himself off to the smell of roasting human flesh.'

Insch wrinkled his nose. 'PC Jacobs was right: you are a morbid bastard.'

11

The woman next door was drunk again. Out in her back garden with the radio blaring Northsound One, staggering about in time to the music, swigging from a bottle of wine, not caring that it was pouring with rain. She just wasn't right in the head, that much had been clear from the moment they'd moved in: her and her strange, pointy-faced boyfriend and their huge black Labrador. He was a lovely dog, a great slobbery lump of affection, but there had been no sign of him for nearly two weeks. The woman said he'd probably run away. That he was an ungrateful bastard and didn't deserve a home.

She said the same thing about her boyfriend.

Shaking her head, Ailsa Cruickshank turned away from the window and finished making the bed. The woman next door didn't care that her dog was missing, so it had been up to Ailsa to make up little laminated posters and fix them to the lampposts and shop windows all over Westhill. Never let it be said that she didn't do her bit.

Outside, the noise got even worse as the woman started singing along with some rap 'song' with the swearwords bleeped out. Only the woman next door wasn't censored like the radio; she roared out the obscenities at the top of her voice. Shuddering, Ailsa went through to the lounge and turned her own television up loud. The woman wasn't right in the head: everyone knew it – she was on tablets. Abusive, drunken, violent; she was every neighbour's worst nightmare. *How were Ailsa and Gavin supposed to start a family with that harpy screeching and yelling next door?* Gavin and the woman were at loggerheads the whole time, arguing over the noise, the language, calling the police . . . Ailsa shook her head sadly, watching as her neighbour slipped on the rain-soaked grass, clanged her head off the whirly washing line and lay there crying for a minute, before swearing and screaming, hurling her wine bottle to explode against the fence. Ailsa shivered: she was going to end up hurting someone; she just knew it.

Union Grove looked a lot more posh than it actually was: a long avenue of granite tenements branching off Holburn Street in the city's west end, lined with parked cars and the occasional tree. Brooding in the rain. The address they had for Graham Kennedy was a top-floor flat in one of the grubbier buildings, the communal front door caked with layers of blue and green blistered paint. The street was empty, except for a trio of small kids standing in a doorway across the road eating crisps, watching the police with interest. A patrol car, Alpha Four Six, was already sitting out front as PC Steve parked Insch's Range Rover half a mile from the kerb, getting an earful from the inspector for his efforts. Blushing furiously he shoogled the car forwards and backwards until the pavement was within walking distance. He was told to stay behind and watch the spaniel.

On the inspector's orders Alpha Four Six had brought a family liaison officer, a nervous young man with a permanently runny nose and two left feet. After a damp handshake he hurried after Insch and Logan into the building, out of the rain, confessing on the way that this was his first case. Insch took pity on the man and gave him a fruit pastille, for which he was obscenely grateful. The stairs up to the top floor were covered in a shabby, threadbare carpet, the walls in peeling flock wallpaper. Everything had that unmistakable, stinging reek of cat piss. Flat number five: brown door, fading brass number screwed to the wood and a plaque bearing the legend 'MR & MRS KENNEDY'.

'Right,' said Insch, offering round the fruit pastilles again, 'this is how it works: we go in, I announce the death.' He pointed the packet of sweets at Logan. 'DS McRae has a bit of a poke about while the family are still in shock.' The pastilles came round to point at Mr Runny Nose. 'You make the tea.' The young man looked as if he was about to complain at being relegated to tea-boy, but Insch cut him off at the pass. 'You'll get to use all that touchy-feely crap they taught you once we've gone. Till then: I take milk, two sugars and DS McRae's just milk. OK?'

The family liaison officer mumbled 'OK' as Logan rang the bell. And then they waited. And waited. And waited . . . Finally a light blossomed in the fanlight above the door. Sounds of shuffling and an old lady's voice saying, 'Who is it?'

'Mrs Kennedy?' Insch held his warrant card up in front of the spy hole. 'Can we come in please?' The chain rattled and the door opened a crack, revealing a weather-beaten face with big glasses and a grey perm. She eyed the policemen on her doorstep with concern. There had been a lot of break-ins in the street over the last couple of years – one old lady had ended up in hospital. The inspector handed her his warrant card and she held it at arm's length, peering at it over the top of her spectacles. The inspector's voice was soft: 'Please, it's important.'

The door closed, there was some rattling and then it opened all the way, exposing a grubby hallway that ran right to left, peppered with seventies-style plywood doors. She led them into a large lounge done up in faded-yellow wallpaper with orange and red roses on it. A pair of rickety couches sat in the middle of a swirly-patterned carpet, wood and fabric groaning alarmingly as Insch sat down and the old lady fussed over a large orange tabby cat the size of a beach ball.

'Mrs Kennedy,' said Insch as the huge cat hopped up onto the coffee table and started licking its bum. 'I'm afraid I have some bad news for you: it's your grandson, Graham. He was one of the people who died in the fire on Monday night. I'm sorry.'

'Oh my God . . .' She clutched at the cat, dragging it away from its ablutions. It sagged into her lap, legs stuck out at right angles, like an over-inflated set of ginger bagpipes.

'Mrs Kennedy, do you know anyone who might have wanted to hurt your grandson?'

She shook her head, her eyes filling up with tears. 'Oh God, Graham . . . You shouldn't have to bury your grandchildren!' The family liaison officer was dispatched to make the tea while Logan surreptitiously excused himself and had a quick look round the flat. It was a big place, shabby, but nothing a couple of coats of paint wouldn't fix. He poked from room to room, peering under beds, into wardrobes and drawers. All the time the muted tones of DI Insch and the sobbing woman leaked through the closed lounge door. Kitchen, bathroom, spare room, Mrs Kennedy's bedroom with its certificates of merit and group photographs of school children . . . Only one of the doors leading off the hallway was locked: from the look of things the stairs up to the attic, but Graham's room was open, the bed made, the clothes all neatly folded and put away, all the socks paired off, not so much as a porn mag under the bed. It didn't fit the image Logan had of Graham

Kennedy from reading his criminal record. Minor assault, breaking and entering, possession with intent . . . Small stuff mostly, but it all added up. He got back to the living room just in time to hear DI Insch say, 'We'll let ourselves out.' Leaving the family liaison officer behind.

They stopped at the communal front door, looking out at the rain drumming on the car roofs. 'Well?' asked Insch.

'Nothing. Place is clean as a whistle. If he kept any gear, he wasn't doing it at granny's house.'

Insch nodded and pulled out the last of the fruit pastilles, munching sadly. 'Poor cow: she raised him pretty much single-handed. Graham's parents died when he was three, then her husband snuffs it a year later.' He sighed. 'That's her whole family gone now.'

'She say anything about what Graham was up to?'

The inspector shook his head. 'Far as she was concerned he was a perfect little angel. Said he only got into trouble because of his friends – who she never approved of. Been leading him astray ever since secondary school.'

'Don't suppose she happens to know their—'

DI Insch held up a notebook with five names scribbled on it. 'Now why didn't I think of that?' He stuffed the notebook back in his pocket. 'Right, back to the station. You're supposed to be off and I've got an investigation to run.'

*   *   *

When Logan finally got back to the flat Jackie wasn't there, just a note pinned to the fridge: GOT EXTENDED NIGHT SHIFT – BACK TOMORROW. No 'LOVE JACKIE', or even 'FOND REGARDS'. So he'd had to fend for himself, which involved a fourteen-inch pizza and two bottles of wine.

Sunday didn't exactly get off to an auspicious start: he woke up alone, mooched about the flat feeling like crap, then microwaved the last two slices of pizza for breakfast. Standing naked in the kitchen, munching on a reheated spicy beef with extra cheese and staring morosely out at the intermittent rain, he had to admit the diet wasn't going too well. His scar-crossed stomach wasn't so much washboard-flat as mangle-bulgy. And feeling more than a little unsettled.

Jackie still wasn't back by half ten, so Logan took off. She didn't want to speak to him? Sod her. He had better things to do with his time than mope about the flat like a bloody lovesick teenager. He just didn't know what those things were. So he went looking for them on the streets of Aberdeen.

There was an Alfred Hitchcock retrospective playing at the Belmont theatre. That would do. A whole day watching Cary Grant getting chased by aeroplanes, Norman Bates peeping on guests in the shower, James Stewart almost falling off rooftops . . . *North by North West* was just reaching its climax when Logan's mobile went off, the bleeping and pinging cutting across the fight on

Mount Rushmore. Angry muttering filled the small theatre as Logan cursed and dragged the phone out of his pocket. His finger was going for the off button when he recognized the number: Detective Inspector Steel. 'Damn.' Apologizing, he hurried down the aisle and out into the corridor, closing the doors behind him before taking the call.

DI Steel brought him up to speed with eight words: Jamie McKinnon. Attempted suicide. Accident and Emergency. Now!

Aberdeen Royal Infirmary was the biggest hospital in the North-east of Scotland, but you wouldn't know that to look at its A&E waiting room. The floor had that nasty, sticky thing going for it, a faint reek of vomit easily discernible through pine disinfectant. A short Asian nurse escorted them through the building to a large public ward, most of which was taken up with elderly men and the smell of boiled cabbage. Jamie McKinnon had been in surgery for a little over an hour, but now he was sitting up in bed, looking groggy, with a big, purple bruise covering one side of his face, the eye swollen almost shut, his top lip split and raw. He flinched as DI Steel plonked herself down on his bed.

'Jamie, Jamie, Jamie,' she said, patting his hand. 'If you missed me, you just had to say. You didn't need to do all this just to get my attention.'

He pulled his hand away and scowled at her with his good eye.

'I'm no' speaking to you. Bugger off.'

Steel smiled at him. 'Prison's done nothing to dull your razor-sharp wit, has it, Jamie my boy?'

Jamie just stared at the far wall.

'So.' Steel bounced up and down on the bed, making the springs squeak. 'Why'd you do it, Jamie? Racked with guilt about killing your woman? Looking for the quick way out? Much better you just talk to me. A lot less painful.' She kept it up for a full ten minutes, teasing him, poking fun, being bitchy about Rosie Williams, the love of his life. Not surprisingly Jamie didn't tell her anything.

Logan – who'd spent the interview cringing with embarrassment at the inspector's crass technique – waited until she'd stomped off for a cigarette, leaving him alone with Jamie McKinnon, before saying anything. 'You know, you don't have to go through this on your own, Jamie. The prison has counsellors. You could—'

'Who the fuck does she think she is?'

'What?'

'Wrinkly old hag, coming in here, treating me like dirt! I'm no' dirt! I'm a fucking human being!'

'I know you are, Jamie.' Logan settled himself down in the spot Steel had vacated. 'Who did the number on your face?'

Jamie raised a hand to his swollen eye, touching the puffy flesh with tender fingers. 'Don't want to talk about it.'

'You sure? Some bastard takes his bad day out on you and you're OK with that?'

A big, shuddering sigh escaped Jamie McKinnon. He slumped further into the pillows. 'Don't know his name. John something or other. He wanted some . . . stuff.' He shrugged. 'You know, but I didn't have any! I'm in prison, for fuck's sake. Where the hell am I going to get smack from? Only he says he knows I've got it and why won't I sell it to him?'

'So he beat you up?'

McKinnon forced a brave smile. 'Didn't beat me up. I fucked him over good . . .' Logan recognized a bare-faced lie when he heard one.

'How come he thought you were holding?'

A shrug, and the forced smile disappeared. 'Don't know.'

Logan settled back and gave him a blank stare, letting the silence grow. Jamie shifted uncomfortably, making the starchy white sheets crackle. 'Look, I know . . . I *used* to know people, OK? I could get hold of things.'

'What kind of things?'

McKinnon looked at him as if he was stupid. 'You bloody well know what kind of things.'

'So this violent scrotum thought your friends would supply you some stuff, even if you were inside?'

A small, humourless laugh and Jamie bit his lip, not hard, but enough to open up the split in it, fresh red oozing up through the yellow-scarlet crust. 'Won't be getting nothing for no one any more . . .'

'No?' Logan had a shrewd idea who Jamie's suppliers had been, and where they were now: filling a collection of body-bags in Isobel's morgue. 'Where you going to get your stuff from now?'

There was a long pause, and then: 'I didn't kill her.'

'I know you say that, Jamie, but there's forensic evidence and witnesses and you've battered her before—'

Jamie sniffed, tears starting. 'I loved her.'

Logan frowned. No matter what Steel said, he was beginning to get the nasty feeling that Jamie might actually be telling the truth. 'Tell me about what happened that night. Right from the start.'

Out in the corridor DI Steel was waiting for him, hands in her pockets, slouching in front of a large oil painting in shades of blue and orange. 'You got any idea what this is supposed to be?' she asked him.

'It's a post-modern representation of the birth of man.' Logan knew all the paintings in the hospital by heart. He'd spent enough time with them, wandering the corridors after dark, IV drip in one hand, walking stick in the other. 'Looks a lot better on morphine.'

Steel shook her head. 'Takes all bloody sorts.' She cast Logan a sly glance. 'So did McKinnon spill his guts then? Come clean to the nice cop?'

'Still maintains he didn't kill her. But from the

sound of things he was a reseller for the kids who got burnt up in that fire Monday night.'

Steel nodded. 'That figures.' She held up McKinnon's hospital chart. Logan hadn't even seen her swipe it. 'Attempted suicide my arse: he swallowed a plastic fork. Every fucker in Craiginches tries it at one time or another. It's not fatal, you get transferred out to hospital for a nice wee low-security holiday. Come visiting time you can get your hands on any substance your loved ones care to bring in. McKinnon's a dealer: he'll be looking for someone to slip him a bundle of something before he goes back inside. Maybe sell some, use the rest himself.' She tossed Jamie's chart into the nearest bin and started for the exit. 'We'll have someone keep an eye on him. See what comes in.'

Logan took one last look at *The Birth of Man* and followed.

The rest of the day was spent getting authorization for a low-key surveillance on Jamie McKinnon, and as usual Logan did all the work. The inspector smoked lots of cigarettes and offered 'helpful suggestions', but it was Logan who had to fight his way through the forest of paperwork. The only bit she'd actually done herself was present the request to the head of CID, who wasn't best pleased. His men were stretched thin enough as it was. The best he could do was get a plainclothes officer to drop by during visiting hours. Provided nothing more important was going on at the time.

That done, DI Steel went off in search of a bottle of wine and a half-dozen red roses. It looked like she was in for a *much* better night than Logan was.

Half eight Sunday evening: Jackie would be up and getting ready for the night shift. The sound of someone murdering the theme tune to *The Flintstones* echoed out of the shower as he let himself in. The singing trailed off into 'da-da, dum-de da-da . . .', the shower juddered to a halt and *The Flintstones* started up again, this time the X-rated version Jackie liked to perform at parties after one too many vodkas.

Logan set the table, complete with tablecloth and candles. Then it was out with the funny-shaped balti dishes his mother had given him for Christmas the year he got out of hospital, and a bottle of white from the fridge. He was just plonking a small bunch of carnations in a dusty vase when someone said, 'What's all this in aid of?' He turned to see Jackie standing in the doorway, wrapped in a Barbie-pink bathrobe, her hair turbaned up in a towel, her broken arm wrapped in a black plastic bag to stop the cast getting soggy.

'This,' he said, making a sweeping gesture to take in the table, 'is a peace offering.' He dug into a plastic bag from the local curry house. 'Chicken jalfrezi, chicken korma, nan bread, poppadums, lime pickle, raita and that red, raw oniony stuff you like.'

She actually smiled at him. 'Thought you weren't speaking to me . . . You know, after Friday . . .' Pause. 'You were out all day yesterday.'

'Thought you'd want to be alone. You spent the night on the couch . . .'

'I . . . I was out on the piss till one in the morning. Didn't want to wake you.'

'Oh . . .'

Silence.

Jackie bit her lip and took a deep breath. 'Look, I'm sorry for storming off, OK? It wasn't you, it was me . . . Well, it wasn't all me, I mean you should've never let that manipulative old bitch talk you into working on your day off, but I suppose it wasn't *all* your fault.' She unpeeled the sticky tape wrapped around the bin-bag, pulling it off to expose the cast on her left forearm. The once pristine-white plaster was now a dirty yellow-grey. 'Ever since I did it, I've been bored out of my head. Filing! Can you believe it? I'm a bloody good police officer, but I'm stuck doing the crappy, shitty, boring, fucking filing.' She picked a fork off the perfectly set table and used it to scratch inside the cast. 'Going out of my bloody mind . . .' Grimace, scratchscratchscratch.

Logan picked a fresh fork out of the drawer. 'I was beginning to think you were fed up with me,' he said.

She stopped scratching for a moment and looked at him. 'Trust me: right now I'm fed up with pretty much everything. But this sodding thing comes off in a couple of weeks, I get to go back to normal duties, everything's fine.'

Logan hoped so. Christ knew he didn't want a repeat of this weekend. Not wanting to spoil the mood he kept his thoughts to himself and dished out the curry.

There wasn't time for a quickie afterwards.

The Monday morning edition of the *Press and Journal* was waiting on Logan's doormat when he finally surfaced sometime after nine. He carried the paper through to the kitchen so he could cover it in toast-crumbs and coffee-circles, getting as far as bite one before glancing at the front page. 'Dirty bastard . . .' The headline explained Colin Miller's private little meeting in the pub on Friday. EDINBURGH DEVELOPER DELIVERS JOBS WINDFALL! Much of the front page was devoted to Miller's gushing praise of the new development: three hundred homes on green belt between Aberdeen and Kingswells. *'McLennan Homes are proud to announce a new development on the outskirts of the small commuter town, bringing jobs and improved amenities to the people of Kingswells!'* Logan snorted: they'd heard that one before. Miller went on to wax rhapsodic about the great things McLennan Homes in general – and its founder in particular – had done in Edinburgh, where the developer had been building *'quality family homes for over a decade!'* Surprisingly enough there was no mention of Malcolm McLennan, AKA Malk the Knife's other business ventures: drugs, prostitution, protection rackets, loan sharking, gun running, and every other variety of criminal enterprise he could get his grubby little paws on.

Logan settled back in his seat and read the article again. No wonder Colin Miller had been so jumpy when he'd seen him in the pub. The reporter had been thrown off the *Scottish Sun* for refusing to complete a series of exposés on Malk the Knife's drug smuggling activities, because two of Malkie's boys had made it quite clear that if he didn't drop the story like the proverbial radioactive tattie, they'd hack off his fingers. And just last Christmas, Malk the Knife had tried, and failed, to bribe his way through the planning regulations and into a lucrative property development deal. Looked like his luck was better second time around.

But the main story of the day wasn't in the *Press and Journal*. It'd be all over the evening news.

12

Sounds were muffled. The mist, thicker here in the forest than out on the road, clung to the trees and bracken, making everything alien and strange. The rain had given up the ghost sometime after midnight, fading to a misty drizzle. Then came the haar, rolling in off the North Sea, smothering the world. The ground beneath her feet was cold and wet as she squelched along the path, the vague outlines of Scots pine, oak, beech and spruce lurking to either side. Dripping. The Tyrebagger Woods were a damn sight creepier today than they'd been yesterday. Anyone could be lurking in the bushes, just around the next bend. Waiting for her . . . Just as well she had Benji to protect her – or would have if the rotten little sod hadn't charged off into the fog at the first opportunity.

'Benji! . . . Bennnnnji?' Something snapped in the forest and she froze. A twig? 'Benji?' Silence. She did a slow pirouette, watching the white-and-grey landscape swim around her. It was deathly quiet. Just like it went in films before something really horrible happened to the blonde bimbo with the big boobs. She smiled at herself. Not that she had any worries on that front, being a flat-chested brunette with a Master's Degree in molecular biology. She was just a bit twitchy because of the job interview. 'Benji! Where are you, you hairy wee shite?' The fog swallowed her calls, not even giving her an echo in return. And yet she was sure there was something . . .

She shook her head and carried on up the track, going the wrong way round the Tyrebagger sculpture trail. A huge disembodied stag's head loomed out of the mist, hanging between the trees like a cross between the more sinister bits of *Watership Down*, Rudolph the red-nosed reindeer, and the dismembered corpse of a bright-yellow Ford Escort. Whenever she saw the thing she couldn't help smiling. But not this time. This time there was something primitive about it. Something pagan. Something predatory. Shivering, she hurried past, calling out for Benji again. Why the hell did he have to pick today to go AWOL? It wasn't as if she could spend all morning looking for him! Her interview was at half eleven. This was just supposed to be a little walk in the woods to calm her nerves. Not tramp about like a bastard in the fog looking for a stupid bloody spaniel. 'BENJI!'

That cracking sound again. She froze. 'Hello?' Silence. 'Is . . .' She was going to hate herself for saying it: 'Is anybody there?' Might as well pop on a pair of stiletto heels and a push-up bra then sit back and wait for the axe murderer.

Silence.

Not so much as a whisper. The only sound was the pounding of her heart. This was ridiculous; just because some woman was beaten to death last week didn't mean there was someone lurking in the woods . . . Waiting for her . . .

Crack! The breath caught in her throat. There *was* someone out there! Fight or flight, fight or flight? FLIGHT: sprinting hell-for-leather up the barely visible path, splashing through puddles and mud. Just wanting to get back to the car park alive. Trees whipped past on either side of the track, their trunks and branches distorted by the mist into wild-killer shapes. Someone was coming after her: she could hear him, crashing through the bushes behind her, getting closer.

Past the poetry trees at a sprint, up the hill, the wet ground treacherous beneath her feet. One foot caught on a tree root and she went sprawling on the gritty mud, fire lancing across her palms and knees as the skin broke. She cried out in pain, but the bastard chasing her didn't care. There was just time to scream before a dark shape launched itself out of the mist. And slavered all over her with a huge, wet tongue.

'Benji!' She pulled herself to her knees and swore and swore and swore while Benji danced and skittered around her, hunkering down on his forelegs and wiggling his ridiculous stumpy tail in the air. And then he stopped, stood stock-still and charged off into the woods again. 'Bastard fucking dog!' Both her palms dripped with neon-red blood, the scrapes peppered with little black flecks of dirt. Her trousers were ripped open, exposing a similar story about the knees. And her head hurt like hell. With trembling fingers she reached up and gingerly touched a tender spot above her left eyebrow, wincing. More blood. 'That's just fucking marvellous!' So much for making a good impression. She'd have to cancel, or turn up at the job interview looking like she'd been beaten up. 'You *BASTARD* dog!'

Benji was barking from somewhere up the track. Bloody animal had probably found something filthy to roll in. Limping, she followed the sound into the fog-shrouded woods, all thoughts of a sinister attacker forgotten.

The lights of Alpha Two Zero cut solid blue bars through the fog. It sat in one of the Tyrebagger car parks, empty, the radio chattering away schizophrenically to itself, as WPC Buchan and PC Steve picked their way into the woods. Looking for the body.

They'd got the call about twenty minutes ago: young woman's body found battered to death, stripped naked in the woods. According to the dispatcher, the person who called it in wasn't that coherent, just kept yammering on about death and the mist and trees. And something about buying sun? WPC Buchan wasn't in the mood for this. Not after yet another fight with Robert, coming home stinking of cheap perfume and stale sweat – what was she, stupid? She stomped along the muddy path, hands in her pockets and a scowl on her face as PC Steve played Earnest Police Officer Number One, keeping up a running commentary as he swept the foggy undergrowth with a huge torch. She trailed along behind, watching him roam from bush to bush on either side of the path. He had a nice arse, even if he was a bit of a mummy's boy. She could . . . A faint smile drifted across her face as she thought about all the things she could do to PC Steve Jacobs. God knew it would be a damn sight more fun than the crap she'd have to go home to tonight.

They clambered up a small hill, the ground slippery beneath their feet. Just past the summit was one of those wooden post things, with a Perspex notice incorporated into it. She flipped it out, reading about how some woman called Matthews had sculpted a group of European bison resting in the primeval forest, out of chicken-wire, moss, wool, and bits of old metal. The usual heritage-slash-council-slash-art-grant-crap. WPC Buchan let the sign fall back into the post and stared into the woods where a barely visible track wound its way into the trees. 'Buying sun . . .' Without saying another word, WPC Buchan stepped off the muddy path and followed the track into the mist.

She could hear PC Steve babbling away to himself, his voice gradually trailing off as she moved away and the fog swallowed him whole.

The ground rose beneath her feet as the track gave way to forest loam. It was like twilight here, shadows of skeletal trees lurking in the mist. Quiet as a shallow grave. And then she heard it: a faint sobbing. WPC Buchan stopped dead in her tracks. 'Hello?' She clambered to the crest of a small rise and stepped out onto an area of flat ground. 'Can you hear me?'

Still nothing.

'Oh for fuck's sake . . .' She pulled out her torch, even though she knew it probably wasn't going to do her the slightest bit of good. The fog would just bounce the light back, but the torch's weight felt comforting in her hand. The sort of thing you could crack someone's skull open with. Forward into the fog and WHAT THE FUCK WAS THAT? They loomed out of the mist, cadaverous beasts, partially rotted. Grazing on the scrub-grass between the fog-shrouded trees.

It was the sculptures: bison resting in the primeval forest. WPC Buchan might not know much about art, but she knew what gave her the fucking willies, and these things took the hairy biscuit. The sobbing was louder now, coming from somewhere near the biggest mouldering animal, the fog clearly visible through holes in its carcass. 'Hello?' She clicked on the torch and suddenly the world went white. Two unnatural green eyes flashed in the opaque mass and a low growl split the silence like a rusty knife. 'Aw shite . . .' The eyes came closer and she moved her free hand very slowly to the bulky utility belt at her waist, easing the tiny canister of pepper spray out of its pouch. 'Nice doggy?' A face full of that stuff would have anything rolling over and playing dead.

The thing that stalked out of the fog was a spaniel, but without any of the usual happy-go-lucky exuberance. The dog's lips were curled back, exposing teeth like daggers, its muzzle smothered in gore. She pointed the canister at it, prayed, and sprayed. Suddenly the growling stopped. There was a moment of silence, then yelping exploded from the animal as it staggered around, trying to get away from the searing pain. WPC Buchan didn't resist the urge to give the dog a good kick in the ribs as she picked her way past.

The sobbing was coming from behind the rotting bison. It was a woman – mid twenties from the look of her clothes – face, hands and knees sticky with plum-coloured blood. Silly cow wasn't dead after all. It was just another stupid hoax call. WPC Buchan slipped the pepper spray back into its holster. 'Are you OK?' she asked. The woman didn't answer. Not directly. Instead she extended a grubby, bloodstained hand and pointed to one of the sculpturally rotting bison. It lay slumped on the ground, as if it had been trying to get up when death came to call. WPC Buchan turned her torch on it, illuminating the statue in all its decomposing glory. There was something white sprawled alongside it, blending into the fog.

'Oh fuck . . .' Grabbing the radio off her shoulder, she called Control. They'd found the second body.

DI Steel turned up on Logan's doorstep in a suit that looked almost new. She'd even threatened her hair with a brush: it hadn't made much difference, but it was the thought that counted. 'Mr Police Hero,' she said, picking a fresh cigarette from an almost empty packet, not seeming to care that one was already smouldering away between her lined lips. 'Got some good news for you! They've found another dead tart!' Soon they were roaring out of Aberdeen on the Inverurie road, past the airport and up the hill to the Tyrebagger Woods. It wasn't far, less than fifteen minutes from the centre of town the way the inspector drove.

Logan sat in the passenger seat of Steel's little sports car, trying to stay calm as they hurtled through the rolling fog. 'So tell me again how this is good news . . .'

'Two dead prostitutes, both stripped naked and battered to death. This isn't just a murder enquiry any more: we've got ourselves a bona fide serial killer!'

Logan risked a peek: a huge grin split the inspector's face, a half-inch of cigarette butt making the car's interior almost as foggy as the world outside. She winked at him. 'Think about it, Laz:

this is our ticket out of the Fuck-Up Factory! We've already got Jamie McKinnon in custody, all we need to do is tie him to both bodies and we're laughing. No more crappy cases no one else wants, no more getting lumbered with every halfwit and reject in the force. You and me: back doing *real* police work!' They almost missed the turning in the fog, a twisting ribbon of tarmac that snaked away into the shrouded forest. Steel followed it until the slow-motion blue strobe of a patrol car's lights marked the entrance to the car park. She pulled up between the filthy hulk of the Identification Bureau's Transit and a flashy Mercedes. That would be Isobel's. Logan groaned. Just what he needed. All around them the forest was dense and silent, wrapped in a thick blanket of white. There wasn't a breath of wind as DI Steel popped the boot, swapping her surprisingly clean shoes for a tatty old pair of Wellingtons. And then they headed up the path.

'What do we know about the victim?' asked Logan as the inspector wheezed up the hill beside him.

'Bugger all.' She stopped and lit the last fag in her packet from the smouldering remains of the one in her mouth, before flicking the tiny butt off into the mist. 'Dispatch said, "naked and beaten"; I said, "mine!"'

'Then how do you know she was a prostitute?'

'Handbag full of condoms. No ID, but loads and loads of condoms. Could have been an erotic balloon modeller I suppose, but my money's on tart.'

'What if it's not?'

'What if it's not what?'

'A serial killer. What if this wasn't McKinnon? What if it's a copycat?'

DI Steel shrugged. 'We'll burn that bridge when we come to it.'

The crime scene wasn't hard to find, even in the smothering fog. The clack-flash-whine of the IB photographer's camera lit up the area like sheathed lightning. An enthusiastic cordon of blue POLICE tape was wound between the trees and they ducked under it, making for the noise and lights. Suddenly, out of the mist, loomed the shapes of decaying animal carcasses. Off to one side, the Identification Bureau had abandoned the traditional SOC tent – it was too big to fit between the trees, so they'd rigged up a bivouac by draping the blue plastic sheeting over the branches and a web of POLICE tape.

Logan and Steel struggled into a set of white paper coveralls, complete with booties. The IB had erected a walkway of tea-tray-sized rectangles with short metal legs, which wound its way across the clearing towards a cluster of people, preventing the attending personnel from treading all over the crime scene. Steel and Logan clanged their way along it, three inches off the ground, making for the body. An IB photographer hovered on the periphery, camera flashing away as the Chief

Pathologist peered and prodded at the remains of a young woman. The victim was lying on her side, one arm stretched up over her head, her legs like open scissors on the damp, black forest floor. As Logan watched, one of the Identification Bureau technicians asked Isobel if it was OK for him to bag the hands. She nodded and he wrapped clear evidence pouches over the bloodstained fingers, just in case there was any trace evidence under the victim's nails. Logan was surprised to see they'd done the same thing to her head . . . and then he realized it was a large, blue freezer bag. That would be an original crime scene feature. Her whole body was covered with weals and bashes, but the skin was like porcelain, a thick line of dark purple marking low tide along the length of her body where the blood had pooled after death.

Isobel sat back on her haunches, snapped off her latex gloves and handed them to the first person she clapped eyes on. Her face had a haggard look, as if she wasn't sleeping, the dark circles under her eyes still visible through her make-up. She stayed there for a moment, staring at the plastic bag over the victim's head. 'Get her down to the morgue,' she said at last. While one of the IB techs pulled out a phone and dialled a local firm of funeral directors to pick up the body, Isobel wearily stuffed things back into her medical bag.

'What's the story?' asked Logan, and she jumped.

'Oh . . . it's you.' She didn't exactly sound

pleased. 'If you're looking for wild speculation you're out of luck. Until I get the bag off the victim's head I can't tell if she was beaten to death like the other one, or suffocated.'

'How about time of death?'

Isobel looked around at the still, silent forest. 'Difficult to say. Rigor mortis has come and gone . . . cold, wet weather . . . I'd say you're looking at about three days. What with all the rain we've had there's not going to be a lot of trace evidence.' She pointed at the stain of dark purple blood that ran in a straight line down the victim's body – from the tips of her outstretched fingers to her foot – congealed haemoglobin, trapped in the two inches of flesh closest to the forest floor. 'Looking at the lividity, I'd say she was either killed here, or the killer dumped the body within the first couple of hours. We'll take some soil samples. See how much blood and other body fluids we get out of the ground.' She straightened up and stifled a yawn. 'Off the record, I'd say he took her out here, got her to strip off and then beat her to death.'

Logan looked down at the body sprawled across the carpet of pine needles. 'He would have stripped her after death.'

Isobel favoured him with one of her withering glances. 'Ever tried to undress a dead body?' she asked him. 'Much easier to get her to strip under the pretence of having sex.'

He didn't take his eyes off the dead girl. 'Three

days ago puts this at Friday night. It was pissing down. No way she'd come all the way out here in the pouring rain and take off all her clothes for a quickie. That's shagging in doorways territory. Back of cars. Not the middle of the forest . . .'

Isobel bristled. 'Well, I'm sure *you* know best, Sergeant. Now, if you'll excuse me, I have to prepare for the post mortem.' She swept out, gripping her medical case like she was about to cause it a permanent injury. And wishing it was Logan's scrotum. DI Steel waited until she'd disappeared from view before slapping Logan on the shoulder. 'You used to shag that?' she asked, admiringly. 'Christ, your poor wee dick must've got frostbite!'

Logan ignored her. The crime scene looked relatively clean, but you never knew your luck. He pulled out his mobile phone and told Control to send every open-search-area-trained officer they had. And a police search advisor as well – to carve the forest up into grids and organize the teams. After all, there was no point keeping a dog and barking yourself, as DI Steel liked to say. And while they were at it, a mobile incident room wouldn't go amiss either.

DI Steel watched him with approval on her wrinkly face. 'Right,' she said when he'd hung up. 'Get the troops mustered in the main car park. Fingertip search between there and where the body was discovered. And while we're at it, better get a six-hundred-yard cordon set up around the crime scene. Every tree, every bush, every fucking rabbit burrow: I want it gone through with a fine-toothed comb. And I want to speak to the woman who found the body.'

He must have looked surprised, because the inspector threw a predatory smile in his direction. 'And remember,' she said, 'we are not at home to Mr Fuck-Up.'

Logan hoped to God she was right.

13

By the time the Deputy Procurator Fiscal arrived, the search was underway. The fog-smothered car park was stuffed to the gunnels with patrol cars and police transports, all of them in need of a good wash. She pulled up at the far end, blocking in a small sports car. This was it: the big one. Two dead women in just over a week, both stripped and badly beaten; it was either a serial killer or one hell of a coincidence. Smiling grimly, she headed up the hill, following the intermittent lightshow of police torches through the thick mist. A serial killer for her very first case. OK, technically it was the PF's case, but she was assisting, holding the fort until the Fiscal got here. And Rachael Tulloch couldn't have hoped for a better chance to shine. The investigation would draw a lot of publicity, and publicity meant promotion. Provided no one screwed up and let the bastard get away, that was. She stomped past a cordon of uniformed constables, all done up in bright yellow reflective vests, poking and prodding their way methodically through the undergrowth. It all looked extremely efficient. Probably that Detective Inspector Insch. Everyone in the Aberdeen office had a lot of respect for the man, not like some of the DIs she could mention.

There was no sign of Insch when she got to the top of the hill, but most of the activity in the clearing was centred on a shortish figure in an SOC boiler suit with a fag hanging out of the corner of her mouth. Rachael's heart sank. If this was still DI Steel's case there was no chance it was *ever* going to be a success. She'd not done a lot of work with the inspector – just the Rosie Williams case, and that dog's torso in the woods – but so far she wasn't impressed. And she'd heard all about how the inspector had screwed up the Gerald Cleaver trial just last year – a known paedophile with a track record of violent abuse going back years, nearly twenty victims prepared to testify, and Steel *still* couldn't get a conviction. They were doomed . . . But that didn't mean Rachael Tulloch wasn't going to do her job properly.

Straightening her shoulders, she struggled into a white paper boiler suit, marched up to DI Steel and demanded an update. And shouldn't she put that cigarette out? This was a crime scene after all! The inspector raised an eyebrow and stared at her, leaving a gap that was far longer than strictly necessary before asking if there was something rammed up Rachael's arse. Because if not, the inspector's size six Wellington boots could be. Rachael was too stunned to speak.

'Listen up, Curly-top,' said Steel, flicking a small flurry of ash from the end of her cigarette, her voice cool and level. 'I am having a fag because we have already searched every square inch of this clearing. I am a detective inspector with Grampian Police, not some fucking numptie for you to order about. Understand?' DI Steel turned and dismissed the clump of constables surrounding her with an amiable, 'You lot bugger off back to your jobs. I want this whole forest turned upside down. *And I mean the whole forest!* No skipping bits. Rabbit holes, streams, bushes, nettles, badgers' bum holes: everything gets searched.' They yes-ma'amed their way off into the fog, leaving DI Steel and a blushing deputy procurator fiscal alone in the middle of the clearing, surrounded by sculptures that reeked of death.

'You want to start over again?' asked the inspector.

Logan walked on his own through the fog, following the squelchy path, checking up on the search teams. The whole thing was pretty much a waste of time, crawling about in the damp grass looking for clues that weren't there. Other than the victim's handbag – currently undergoing every test the IB could think of – the immediate scene had turned up empty. It didn't help that the only place they might have found something concrete, the car park, was now covered in SOC vehicles, minibuses and patrol cars. Any trace evidence ground into the mud and gravel by countless police tyres and size nine boots. The search teams might get lucky and find something else the killer had missed, but Logan doubted it: pick up the girl, park the car, force her out into the rain, beat her to death and strip her corpse. The end. Whoever it was, he didn't go traipsing about the forest in the middle of the night, scattering clues about like some demented evidence fairy.

Logan picked his way across a slippery bridge and headed uphill. The last search team was on the south side of the forest, working their way back towards where the body was discovered. Pointless it might be, but DI Steel wanted this one done by the book. Maybe there was hope for her yet?

The team was working its way down a steep slope when he found them, prodding the under-growth with sticks and poles, going through the motions. A familiar face scowled at him as he struggled up the track – that grumpy cow from last Monday night, the one who'd had a go at him for PC Maitland getting shot. And working next to her was someone he hadn't expected to see: WPC Jackie Watson prodding about in a holly bush, using her plaster cast to hold back a spiny-leaf-covered branch as she jabbed away with a pole. She didn't look too happy either. He pulled her to one side. 'What the hell are you doing out here?'

'Relax,' she smiled. 'I'm not really here. Right now I'm collating the division crime statistics for the year to date: says so on the roster, so it must be true.'

'Jackie, you can't do this! You're supposed to be on light duties, not operational! If the inspector finds out you'll be for it!'

'Steel? She couldn't give a toss. Look, I just wanted to be out of the office for a bit, OK? Do some real bloody police work for a change, instead of shuffling bits of paper about.' Jackie threw a glance over her shoulder; a goldfish-faced sergeant was coming their way, all fake suntan, puffing cheeks and ping-pong eyes. 'Now bugger off, before you get us into trouble.'

'Is there a problem?' asked the sergeant. Logan took one last look in WPC Watson's direction and said that no, there wasn't, how was the search going? Sergeant Fish-Face wrinkled his nose. 'We're miles away from the crime scene and there's no way in hell anyone would cart a body all the way through this, when he could just drag it a fraction of the distance up from the car park. It's a complete waste of everyone's time.'

Logan made soothing noises, it was important to be thorough, everyone appreciated his team's efforts, blah, blah, blah . . . The grumpy WPC had been hanging back as Logan and Sergeant Goldfish talked, ignoring the line as it moved slowly away into the mist. 'What the hell are we *doing* out here?' she demanded, her face like a skelped arse.

Logan only had time to open his mouth before the sergeant roared, 'You're here because you're supposed to be a bloody police officer. Now get your backside back to work before I kick it from here to Peterhead!'

She scowled at Logan like it was his fault she'd been yelled at, then turned on her heel and started stabbing the nearest bush with all the venom she could muster, muttering obscenities under her breath as she caught up with the rest of the search team, rejoining the line next to WPC Jackie Watson. Thirty seconds later Jackie cast a glower back in his direction and Logan sighed. The bloody woman was probably telling Jackie what an utter shit he was. And from the expression on Jackie's face it looked as if she agreed. So much for getting back on an even keel. Their curry-fuelled truce had lasted a whole day.

Enough was enough: Logan was going to— A sudden scream pierced the fog, before being quickly swallowed by the trees and mist. There was silence for a heartbeat and then everyone exploded into action. Logan scrambled down the hill, towards the search team, Sergeant Goldfish hot on his heels, making for the source of the scream. They slithered to a halt at the top of a nearly vertical slope punctuated with deep beds of stinging nettle and spiky gorse. Halfway down, just visible through the swirling fog, was a WPC, lying on her back in the middle of a massive clump of nettles. Her shirt and jumper had been pulled up to her shoulders as she'd careered down the slope, exposing white skin already starting to go red with nettle stings. She was swearing a blue streak. 'Are you OK?' called Sergeant Fish-Face.

More swearing.

With a start Logan realized Jackie was standing at the lip of the slope, looking down at the thrashing figure as the woman stung herself more and more thoroughly with every flailing attempt to rise. 'WPC Buchan,' said Jackie, pointing. 'Guess she must've slipped . . .' She smiled.

Five minutes later they'd extricated Buchan from the nettle-infested slope. Puffing, wheezing, scratching and swearing, she clambered back up, looking daggers at WPC Watson the whole way. She was lurid-red from the under-wire of her bra right down to the waistband of her trousers. Everything in between was swollen and lumpy and itchy and stinging and she couldn't even pull down her blouse and jumper because it just made it hurt more and . . . and . . . Sergeant Fish-Face sent her home. As she limped down the trail, arms out to the sides so as not to touch the painful red rash that circled her torso, the sergeant confided in Logan that it couldn't have happened to a nicer person. Jackie just winked at him.

'You didn't have anything to do with that, did you?' he asked when they were alone again.

She grinned. 'Nobody calls my man names and gets away with it.'

Logan left them to it, smiling all the way down the hill, back to the main path. It was ten to one, according to his watch. If he and DI Steel hurried they could get back to FHQ and grab a bite to eat before Isobel launched into the post mortem at half past. He took a shortcut, labouring up the hill at the side of the track, making for the clearing and its menacing sculptures. As he crested the rise the fog took on a golden glow. A single shaft of sunlight had pierced the white gloom, spotlighting the edge of the clearing where two men in black suits were manhandling a blue plastic body-bag into a brushed metal coffin, ready for its trip to the morgue. DI Steel was talking to the Procurator Fiscal, pointing at things and nodding seriously as the Fiscal replied. Logan waited on the periphery while they went over the details of the crime scene. Someone coughed beside him and Logan turned to see the new deputy PF standing in full SOC costume, her curly hair escaping from the elastic around the hood, framing her face. Her green eyes glittered above the mask. 'How's the search coming?' she asked. Logan told her, leaving out the bad language and WPC Buchan's fall. Rachael nodded as he finished, as if she'd been expecting this all along. 'I see . . .' A long pause to convey deep thought. 'What did you make of the handbag?'

'Why did he leave it behind you mean?' He paused, thinking about it. 'Two options: one, he's leaving us a message – something in the bag, or *removed* from the bag, is supposed to tell us something; option two – it was a mistake. Maybe she threw it at him and he couldn't find it again in the dark, after he'd finished with her. Or she dropped it running away . . .' He shrugged. 'Difficult to tell with only two bodies what is and isn't part of the pattern.'

'*Only* two bodies? Jesus.' Rachael looked out at the crime scene, the rotting bison, the little metal walkway, the cordons of POLICE tape. 'How many more of these do we need?' He was about to answer that when DI Steel beckoned him over and he had to go through the whole search update all over again: no one had found anything.

'It was always a long shot,' Steel told the Fiscal, 'after all this time out in the open and the rain, but I'm not taking any chances.' She squared her shoulders and raised her pointy chin, stretching out the sagging skin beneath it. 'There's a killer out there and we're going to catch the bastard.'

Logan tried not to gag. That was the cheesiest thing he'd heard all week. But the PF seemed impressed. She too struck a determined pose, asked them to keep her posted – if there was anything she could do, etc. – and left them to it, taking her deputy with her. Rachael looking back over her shoulder, her emerald-green eyes meeting Logan's for a moment, then she was gone. He watched her disappear into the fog, before speaking. 'Laid it on a bit thick, didn't you?'

Steel shrugged and pulled an empty cigarette packet from her pocket, shaking it and peering inside as if that would somehow magically make some fags appear. 'Position we're in, we need all the friends we can get. Now the PF and Madame Frizzy-Hair go back and tell the Chief Constable we're not fucking this whole thing up. That we're doing things by the book.' She smiled and crumpled the empty pack in her hand. 'Things are starting to go our way, I can feel it in my water.'

'Of course, you realize this means Jamie McKinnon isn't a serial killer,' he said, watching as the funeral directors carried the coffin out of the clearing. 'If the victim was killed three days ago that's Friday night – Jamie was banged up in Craiginches.'

Steel sighed. 'I know, but a girl can dream, can't she?'

Half past one on the dot and the morgue at Force Headquarters was getting crowded. In addition to Isobel, her assistant Brian, DI Steel and Logan, the Deputy Procurator Fiscal was here with her boss, and the corroborating pathologist – Doc Fraser, an IB photographer, the detective chief superintendent in charge of CID, the Deputy and Assistant Chief Constables. It was like a who's who of Aberdeen law enforcement, all of them worried about the possibility of another serial killer preying on the city. Knowing it would turn into a political nightmare as soon as the media found out. Even God himself had turned up; the Chief Constable being given pride of place at the head of the table. Logan wondered if he'd be saying grace before Isobel started carving.

Logan could almost smell the anticipation in the room as Isobel began her external examin-ation of the body on the slab. According to her instructions the Identification Bureau techies, who'd picked over the body for trace evidence under her assistant's watchful eye, had positioned the victim exactly as she'd been on the forest floor: lying on her side, legs scissored out on the shiny, stainless steel surface, one arm up over her head. The thick purple line of pooled blood marked horizontal with spirit-level accuracy. They'd removed the blue plastic freezer bag from her head, exposing her battered face and bloodshot, bulging eyes. As if she was staring indignantly at the people gathered around the dissecting table. Something about the tableau made Logan shiver. This wasn't like a normal post mortem, where the body was laid out on its back, all washed clean and clinically dead. Somehow, with the body arranged as it had been discovered, it was as if they were all voyeurs at the last, intimate moment of the victim's existence. As if this was part of the killer's performance. The final scene for this bruised and brutalized actor. Logan shivered again. PC Steve was right: he really was turning into a morbid bastard.

Three hours later Isobel's audience was pale, quiet and slightly shaky, standing in an otherwise empty briefing room on the second floor. A passing uniform had been dispatched to fetch coffee, not the plastic crap from the vending machine, but proper coffee reserved for high-powered meetings and special occasions. The Chief Constable reckoned they all needed it, and Logan wasn't about to disagree.

Isobel was in the corner with Doc Fraser, a

modest smile on her face as he complimented her on a first-rate post mortem. Very thorough. Very revealing. Someone behind Logan muttered, 'Jesus, did she have tae peel the poor cow's face off?' Up at the front of the room, the Chief Constable finished saying something to the Procurator Fiscal and they both laughed. The new deputy fiscal managed a dutiful smile, but she was still green about the gills. When the laughter had subsided the DCC ping-ping-pinged a spoon off the side of his china cup and everyone fell silent. It was time to post mortem the post mortem. Isobel walked them through the sequence of events as she saw them, illustrating the salient points on the whiteboard with diagrams of fractured skull and ribs and limbs. Like some demonic game of Pictionary.

'Cause of death was asphyxiation,' she said, drawing a red circle about the head of the body she'd drawn on the board, 'partly due to the plastic bag secured over the victim's head and partially due to pneumothorax: the right lung punctured by the ends of the fourth and fifth ribs. Her ribcage filled with air and collapsed the lung. Cyanosis would have been rapid and fatal.' Then Steel asked the question they were all dying to know: was this the same MO as the one used on Rosie Williams? Had the same man killed them both? Isobel's smile was condescending. 'Well, Inspector, I'm sure you're aware that there is a *great* deal of supposition involved in—'

But Steel wasn't having any of it. 'Just yes or no.'

Isobel stiffened. 'Possibly. That's all I can say at this point.'

The inspector wasn't impressed. 'Possibly?'

'Well obviously the first victim didn't have a bag over her head . . . I'd have to go over the post mortem notes—'

DI Steel waved a hand in Isobel's general direction, cutting her off. 'Then I suggest you go do that, right now. We need to know if we're looking for one deranged maniac or two.' When Isobel didn't move she added, 'Unless you've got something more important to do, that is?'

Bristling, Isobel placed her china cup down on the nearest table, nodded at the Chief Constable, grabbed Brian, and swept from the room, promising to have a report on the inspector's desk within the hour. There was a moment's silence, everyone looking from DI Steel, to the doors closing in Isobel's wake, and back to the inspector again. Steel smiled grimly. 'I'm not taking any chances with this,' she told the assembled great and good. 'There are lives at stake.'

And then the questions started: Inspector, what do you plan to do? What will we tell the press? How many men do you need? DI Steel kept a straight face, but Logan could see she was doing a victory lap inside. She was back.

14

The press conference was held at five thirty, set up in a rush so there would be time to get it on the Six O'Clock News. The Chief Constable, his deputy, DI Steel and an attractive blonde woman from the press office faced the media from behind a row of flat-pack tables draped with the Grampian Police logo. Steel had somehow managed to tame her feral hair; that and the newish suit made her look like a competent and determined police officer, rather than her usual cross between a tramp and a startled Cairn Terrier. Logan stood at the back of the conference room, behind the sea of cameras and journalists, as the Chief Constable told the world they'd found the body of a woman in the Tyrebagger Woods . . . Isobel had been true to her word – her report was on DI Steel's desk in under an hour. There were only small differences between the two killings, this was probably the work of the same man.

As soon as the CC's statement was finished

every hand in the place shot up: 'Is this the work of a serial killer?' 'Have you any suspects?' 'What about the man already in custody?' 'Have you identified the victim yet?' 'Why have you put DI Steel in charge of the investigation?'

The Chief Constable leaned forward and told the assembled crowd, 'Inspector Steel has my complete confidence.'

'Sarah Thornburn, Sky News. After the inspector's performance on the Gerald Cleaver trial, is that wise?'

Logan could see DI Steel bristling, but she managed to keep her mouth shut as the CC once more told everyone what a solid, dependable and experienced officer she was and how she had his complete confidence. Absolute and complete confidence. Logan grimaced: that was what Prime Ministers always said when someone high up in the government was caught with their hand in the till, or someone else's knickers. Right before they were, regrettably, let go. There were more questions, but Logan wasn't really listening. Instead he let his eyes drift over the assembled journalists and pundits, looking for a wee Glaswegian in an expensive suit . . . Colin Miller was sitting between a chisel-jawed woman from BBC News and a saggy man from the *Daily Record*, scribbling away furiously into a palmtop computer, not bothering to stick his hand up and ask questions. As soon as the CC stood, indicating that the press conference was at an end, Miller was out of there.

Logan caught up to him in the car park. 'What,' he asked, 'you not speaking to me any more?'

'Hmm?' Miller looked up, saw Logan and started walking again. 'Got things tae do . . .' He fumbled in his trouser pocket and pulled out his car keys.

Logan frowned. 'You all right?'

Miller marched straight up to his fancy-looking dark grey Mercedes. 'Don't have time for this . . .'

Logan grabbed his shoulder. 'What's got into you?'

'Me? What's got into me? Well, let's have a fuckin' think about that one shall we? Every fuckin' thing! OK? I've had enough!' He wrenched the car door open and threw himself in behind the wheel. 'Every fuckin' bastard in the whole fuckin' . . .' The engine growled into life and he slammed the door, twisted the wheel and put his foot down. Logan stood in the car park, watching as the car screeched to a halt at the junction before roaring off into the traffic, disappearing in the mist. 'Something I said?'

Tuesday morning started at quarter past seven with the flat's phone blaring out its electronic warble – on and on and on . . . Logan peeled open an eye, grumbled and curled back up under the duvet. The answering machine could take care of it. Today he was supposed to be starting on the back shift. Three days of working from two in the afternoon through till midnight. Technically he should have started yesterday, but after putting in a full day

170

with the search team, DI Steel had given him time off for good behaviour. So today he was going to stay in bed until Jackie came home, share a bit of breakfast and invite her back to bed for some under-the-duvet fun. He smiled and wriggled deeper beneath the covers as the answering machine in the lounge dealt with the call.

Maybe he and Jackie could – an explosion of electronic bleeps, whistles and buzzing as Logan's mobile went mad. 'Oh for God's sake!' He poked a hand out of the tiny cave he'd made with the duvet, fumbled about blindly on the bedside cabinet, grabbed the phone and dragged it into the warmth with him. 'What?'

'Where the hell are you?'

Logan groaned: it was DI Steel. 'Do you know what time it is?'

'Yes. Where the hell are you?'

'In bed! I'm—'

'In bed?' The inspector put on a sleazy voice. *'What you wearing?'*

'A frown. I'm on the back shift today, you said—'

'Stop buggering about. We've got a serial killer out there knocking off tarts – get your backside in gear!'

Logan closed his eyes and counted to ten while the inspector banged on about a sense of duty and how shift patterns were for the weak. 'OK, OK!' he said at last. 'I'm coming in. Give me half an hour.' He hung up, swore, sprawled out on the bed limbs akimbo, scowled at the blind, swore some more, got up, stubbed his toe on one of Jackie's boots, swore, and limped his way off into the bathroom for a shower.

When he finally made it into Force HQ DI Steel's briefing was in full swing. There were a lot more people here than usual – the Screw-Up Squad had been supplemented with some real police officers for a change. Unlike the normal rambling shambles, everyone was in ordered rows, uniform and CID sitting to attention as the inspector took them through the events of the last twenty-four hours. The handbag discovered at the scene was covered with fingerprints, but they all belonged to the newly identified victim: Michelle Wood. That was the woman whose face had been peeled off yesterday, so Isobel could get a good look at the damage to the underlying musculature and bones. Logan shuddered at the memory. What with that and the arson victims last week he was spoilt for choice when it came to nightmares.

He tuned back in just as DI Steel was setting up the various teams and doling out their assignments. She wrapped the briefing up and sent them on their way with a rousing chorus of 'We are not at home to Mr Fuck-Up!'

When there was no one left except Logan, she cracked open a window and sparked up a cigarette with trembling hands, inhaling like a suffocating man. She closed her eyes, sighed happily then lurched into a rattling cough. 'Jesus, I've been bursting for a fag!' She took another deep drag, shuddering in pleasure as the nicotine and smoke filled her lungs. When she breathed out it hung around her head like her own private fog bank. 'You see the papers?' she asked. Logan said no, so she dug a copy of that morning's P&J from the bin and tossed it over. SHORE LANE STALKER STRIKES AGAIN! right across the front page, BY COLIN MILLER. It wasn't his best work. 'I suppose,' she said as Logan read, 'I'd better go tell Michelle's dad she's dead . . .' Sigh. 'You know, you wouldn't think it to see her on the slab, but she was a pretty girl when she was little. Before spots and boys and underaged drinking. I brought her in about a dozen times when she was younger: shoplifting. Baby clothes, food, shoes, booze, stuff like that . . .' her voice trailed off. 'Arrested her all those times and I didn't even recognize her, not with her face all smashed up like that. Only ID'd her this morning when the prints on the handbag came back . . . She was only twenty-four. Poor wee bitch.'

'She been on the game long?'

The inspector shook her head. 'Not that I can tell. No arrests for soliciting on her record. Not even a warning.'

Logan didn't say anything, but he couldn't help thinking of the woman he'd spoken to down the docks: the one with the PVC raincoat, black lace bustier and all the bruises. The minute she realized he was a policeman she'd offered him a bribe, or a free ride on the venereal express. Maybe there was a reason Michelle Wood hadn't received so much as a caution. Maybe one of Aberdeen's fine, upstanding boys in blue had been getting freebies.

'Right.' Steel dropped her cigarette butt and ground it into the carpet with a scuffed shoe. 'While I'm gone I want you to make sure everything's up and running properly. I don't trust any of these bastards to get it right.'

Logan was surprised. 'You don't want me to come with you?'

She shook her head. 'Her dad's going to have enough to deal with without a house full of bloody policemen.'

Logan was on his way down to the incident room when a familiar, hawk-nosed, ginger-haired bastard stuck his head out into the corridor and asked for a moment of his time. Inspector Napier smiled like a scar as Logan settled uncomfortably into the rickety plastic chair in front of the desk. 'So, Sergeant McRae.' The inspector leaned back in his seat and smiled his post-surgery smile again. 'I take it you are familiar with the nature of the case now being headed up by DI Steel?' Logan carefully admitted that he was, wondering where this was going. 'Well,' said Napier, 'I'm sure I don't have to tell you the importance of a quick and decisive result. One that will stand up in court. You see,' he picked up a silver pen, slowly twisting it back and forth in his fingers, 'I know that you have . . . "friends" in the media. These people will try to protect you should things go wrong.' The smile became colder. 'It might be wise for you to ensure that they do not use Inspector Steel as a scapegoat.' Significant pause. 'In the interests of teamwork.'

An uncomfortable silence filled the space between them.

'What if it's her fault?'

Napier waved a hand, as if shooing a troublesome fly. 'Are you aware of the fable about the fox and the chicken? The chicken burns down the farmer's barn and blames the fox. The farmer shoots the fox and then eats the chicken . . .' He pointed the silver pen at Logan's chest making it clear who the poultry was in this scenario. The inspector's chilly, unsettling smile disappeared. 'I will supply the sage and onion.'

15

Their new incident room – courtesy of the Chief
Constable the minute this became a serial case –
was huge, the walls covered with maps of
Aberdeen and scribbled-on whiteboards. The
middle of the room was taken up with phones
and computers, the monitors flickering in the overhead light as uniformed officers took calls and
entered the details into HOLMES. There was
already a huge stack of automatically generated
actions waiting for him, so Logan pulled up a chair
and started working his way through the lot;
sorting them into two piles he called 'To Do' and
'Bollocks'. The system's greatest strength was that
it would churn its way through endless reams of
data, automatically picking out connections and
patterns. Its greatest weakness was that it
frequently didn't have a sodding clue what it was
doing. He was just finishing when DI Steel finally
got back from speaking to Michelle Wood's father.

'How did it go?'

The inspector shrugged and started flicking half-heartedly through Logan's pile of 'Bollocks', turfing them one after the other into the bin. 'How do you think it went? Telling some poor bastard his daughter's been battered to death by a psycho, and her naked body was abandoned in the fucking woods for three days before someone fell over it in the fog . . . oh and by the way, your little girl was fucking strangers for money.' She sighed and ran a hand over her face. 'Sorry, been a shitty week.' Logan handed her the 'To Do' pile and she whittled that one down too; there weren't many actions left by the time she was finished. She palmed them off on the admin officer, telling him to get them cleared by the end of the day.

'Right,' she said as the man grumbled away to get the personnel organized. 'Plan of action?'

'Well, what do you want to do about Jamie McKinnon?'

'Leave him where he is, we've still got plenty tying him to Rosie's murder.' Steel pulled out a packet of king-size cigarettes and started fiddling with the silver paper insert. 'If we get someone else in the frame for both tarts we'll do McKinnon for the fast-food jobs instead. But if anyone asks, we're dealing with the killings like they're part of the same pattern.'

'OK.' Logan grabbed a magic marker and started drawing up a rough map of the docks on one of the whiteboards. 'Rosie Williams was found here . . .' He drew a blue circle on Shore Lane.

'Do we know if Michelle Wood worked the docks?'

'Who knows?'

'If she did, then we've got a hunting ground. We put in some surveillance: unmarked cars . . .' He picked up a green pen and started putting 'X'es where a rusty Vauxhall could be parked without attracting too much attention.

'What bloody good are unmarked cars going to do us?' asked Steel, corkscrewing a finger into her ear. 'Dirty bastards pick up women down there the whole time. How're we going to spot our man: pull them all over and ask?' She dropped her voice an octave and put on a broad east London accent. '"Excuse me, sir, 'ave you picked up this tart wiv the intention of beatin' 'er to death, or just givin' 'er a serious knobbin'?"' She smiled pityingly at him. 'Good plan: I can see that working.'

Logan scowled at her. *If you'll let me finish.* We get a couple of WPCs done up as bait and they do the rounds. If someone tries to take them anywhere we've got them wired for sound: the unmarked cars follow and we catch the guy in the act. What do you think?'

Steel wrinkled her nose and took a good look at Logan's crude diagram. 'Don't think it stands a chance in hell, but what have we got to lose?' she said at last. 'Go pick yourself out a couple of WPCs. Remember, this bloke did Rosie Williams and Michelle Wood so he can't be all that fussy. I want a couple of pugglers.' Logan said he'd see what he could do.

*   *   *

It was the perfect day for drying towels: sun shining, light breeze and no midges. Ailsa smiled, taking pleasure from the simple domesticity of it all. Gavin had promised to come home from work on time for a change. So tonight was going to be special: she was still ovulating after all.

She pulled the last towel from the basket and pegged it up on the line. All done. And then she caught the tell-tale, clinging stench of cigarette smoke, drifting through the fence from next door's garden. It was the pointy-faced boyfriend, his features bruised and battered. Again. Why he stayed with that horrible, drunken, abusive, *violent* woman Ailsa just couldn't understand. Surely any sane man would have left her the first time she broke his nose. Or the second. Or third . . .

The boyfriend was smoking with his head back against the metal whirly washing thing. Wincing as he breathed out, one hand flinching over his ribs, unaware that Ailsa was watching him. He finished his cigarette and flicked the butt out into the knee-deep grass where it disappeared among the weeds.

A loud shout from inside the house and the boyfriend jumped. In that moment his eyes caught Ailsa's and she knew he was every bit as trapped by this horrible harridan as she and Gavin were. She was like a mincing machine for the soul, grinding them up until nothing was left but a bloody pulp. Shoulders slumped in defeat, the boyfriend turned and limped into the house.

Ailsa watched him go with a shudder. There, but for the grace of God . . .

While the inspector was off on yet another extended fag break, Logan trolled through Michelle Wood's post mortem report. The killer had managed to snap one of her legs, both arms, and almost all of her ribs. Internal organs ruptured, probably caused by her attacker stamping on her stomach. Head battered repeatedly with fists, feet, a rock . . . Someone had really gone to town on her. Logan sighed, looking at a crime scene photograph: a big, full-colour eight-by-ten glossy of Michelle's plastic-bag-smothered head. There was no doubt about it: their boy was getting better at it. Every attack worse than the last, until . . .

Logan swore. How the hell could he have missed it? He shouted for DC Rennie. 'Grab your notebook: I want you to find out who patrols the docks, someone who knows the layout and the girls, we—'

'Excuse me, sir?' It was PC Steve. He hung his head round the door and smiled uncertainly in Logan's direction. 'DI Insch wants to see you.'

Logan groaned, wondering what he'd done wrong now. 'OK,' he told Rennie, 'you go: get me a name. I want to speak to them.' Then he remembered the Aberdonian pimp and the Lithuanian teenager. 'And show those identikit pictures round again – someone *must* know who they are.'

There was a new corkboard on the wall of DI Insch's incident room, divided up into six sections – each square taken up by a name, a face and a post mortem photograph. The small head in the bottom right corner was connected to the blackened face above it with a thin red ribbon. The inspector stood in front of the board with his skeletal admin officer, pointing at things while she took notes in longhand. Insch glanced up, saw Logan and called him over, dismissing the woman with a couple of fizzy cola bottles.

'What can I do for you, sir?'

'This lot.' Insch tapped a photograph of a human head that looked like a side of barbecued pork. 'Remember we got that list of Graham Kennedy's school chums?' He stuffed a handful of the sweets into his mouth, mumbling as he chewed. 'Graham you know, but this is Ewan, Mark, Janette and Lucy.' Poking the post mortem photos one by one, leaving behind little sparkling fingerprints. 'All identified by their dental records. According to the hospital the wee girl,' he didn't poke her picture, 'belonged to Lucy. Gemma . . . poor wee sod.' Sigh. 'Anyway, we got five names from Graham's granny: one, two three, four. One missing.'

'So, who wasn't on the menu that night?'

'Karl Pearson. Twenty-four. Lives with his mum and dad in Kingswells, or he did until about three weeks ago. They got a call from him looking for some money Wednesday before last, but that was it. Haven't heard from him since.' He pulled a holiday snap from his inside pocket showing a lumpy young man with a broken nose and a single eyebrow stretched across his face. He looked like the kind of person who would quite happily start a fight at a football match, just for the hell of it.

Logan studied the picture for a minute. 'You think he's the torch?'

Insch nodded. 'Been in trouble a couple of times for burning things that weren't his. Neighbours' sheds, an abandoned caravan, that pitch-and-putt hut down at the beach.'

'That was him?'

'The very man. I've put out a lookout request, but I also have a couple of addresses.' An evil smile split the inspector's huge, bald head. 'Thought you might fancy the exercise.'

'What about your DS, you know, the bearded one?'

'What, Beattie?' DI Insch stuck his hands in his pockets, making the already groaning material bulge alarmingly. 'Bugger that. Lazy sod couldn't catch clap in a Dundee whorehouse, let alone crooks.'

'I'm supposed to be helping DI Steel, she—'

'Already OK'd it with me. You're not needed till the operation tonight. Grab your coat.'

'But—'

Insch dropped his voice, laying a huge ham-like hand on Logan's shoulder. 'Thought you wanted off the Screw-Up Squad: this is your chance.' He turned and lumbered out of the room, grabbing PC Steve by the collar on his way past. Logan hesitated, looking from the inspector to the photo gallery of death. Bloody DI Steel, trading him off to Insch without even consulting him! Muttering obscenities, Logan followed on behind.

The first address for Karl Pearson was no use, neither were numbers two, three or four. No one had seen him in ages. Four down, two to go. Address number five was halfway up a block of flats in Seaton – down where the River Don meets the sea – one of a set of four seventeen-storey buildings with spectacular views out over the water. Lovely on a clear summer's day and bloody freezing in the dead of winter, when the wind roared in off the North Sea, fresh from the Norwegian fjords. Logan and Insch headed inside, leaving PC Steve downstairs to watch the front door.

Sixth floor, corner apartment. Insch marched straight up to Karl Pearson's alleged flat and did his policeman's knock, putting his weight behind it. Making the door boom and rattle as if God himself had come to announce judgment day.

No response.

Insch launched into his wrath-of-God routine again and a door cracked open down the hall. The occupant took one look at the huge man pounding on the corner flat's door and hurried back inside.

'Think they'll call the police?' asked Logan.

'Doubt it, but just in case . . .' Insch dragged out

his mobile phone and called Headquarters, letting them know that the thug trying to break into the corner flat was him, so not to bother sending out a squad car. While he was doing that, Logan squatted down and peered in through the letterbox. A small hallway decorated with Aberdeen Football Club posters and pages torn from *FHM* magazine – half-naked women and footballers: an adolescent boy's dream – coats hanging on a set of hooks, mirror on the other side, scabby-looking golf clubs leaning in the corner, a little mudslide of junk mail on the mat. There was a door at the far end, slightly ajar, leading into what looked like a kitchen. Four more doors led off the little corridor, but only one of them was open and Logan couldn't really see into the room. He was about to give up when suddenly he got the feeling someone was staring at him . . . And then his eyes drifted to the hall mirror again. Someone *was* staring at him through the reflected lounge door, only Logan was pretty sure they couldn't actually see him. They couldn't see anything, not with their throat lying wide open like that, dark brown blood covering everything.

He sat back on his heels and let the letterbox flap snap shut.

'You still on the phone to HQ?' he asked Insch.

'Aye.'

'Better tell them to call off the search: we've found Karl Pearson.'

16

The Identification Bureau were delighted to have an indoor corpse for a change, it meant they didn't have to fight with that bloody SOC tent. Karl Pearson's lounge was decorated in much the same way as the hall, with posters and magazine pages, only the naked ladies in here were a lot more hard-core. The IB team had put down their little metal walkway and then proceeded to cover the whole place in black fingerprint powder; empty the flat's vacuum cleaner into an evidence bag; take samples of blood – not difficult, considering how much of it there was in the lounge; argue about whether or not one of the naked women – pictured playing with a variety of battery-operated devices – was Detective Sergeant Beattie's wife; photographed everything and stood quietly by as Doc Wilson pronounced the naked man tied to a dining-room chair with his throat cut dead. 'Amazing the things these doctors can diagnose nowadays,' said Insch, leaning against the far wall. He was wearing the biggest set of white paper coveralls the IB boys had, but it was fighting a losing battle against the inspector's huge frame. 'Care to hazard a guess at time of death?'

Doc Wilson favoured Insch with a withering glance. 'No,' he said, snapping his medical bag shut. 'What is it with you people? You always want a bloody time of death off the poor bloody GP! You know what? I haven't got a bloody clue. OK? Satisfied? You want a time of death? Ask a fucking pathologist.' He straightened up and made for the door, pausing on the threshold to run an appraising eye over the inspector's straining SOC suit. 'Tell you what, I'll give you a time of death, free of charge. Eighteen months if you don't do something about your bloody weight.' And he was out of there before Insch could do much more than go beetroot red and splutter.

Logan groaned; that was all they needed, Doc Bloody Wilson lighting the blue touch paper and running like buggery. Leaving the rest of them to deal with the explosion. 'Don't pay any attention to him,' he tried. 'Wilson's had a weasel up his arse all week. He's just being a wanker for the sake of it.'

Insch turned a baleful eye on Logan. 'You tell that bastard, if I ever see him at one of my crime scenes again, I will personally make sure he ends up in the FUCKING MORGUE!' Everyone else in the room went very quiet. 'I WILL FUCKING WELL DECLARE DEATH ON HIM!' Spittle flew from Insch's mouth. Logan had seen him angry plenty of times, but never anything like this. Trembling with the effort, Insch walked quietly into the kitchen and slammed the door behind him so hard every loose object in the flat rattled. From the apartment upstairs came the sound of a television being turned up.

'Jesus,' whispered the IB cameraman. 'Touched a nerve, or what?'

DI Insch was still sulking in the kitchen when the duty pathologist arrived: Doc Fraser this time, rather than Isobel, much to Logan's relief. Fraser agreed with the duty doctor's diagnosis: Karl Pearson was indeed dead. Logan could go ahead and call the funeral directors to come pick up the body. The post mortem would be at three. And now that the formalities were out of the way, Logan was free to examine the victim without upsetting anyone. Just as long as he didn't actually touch anything.

Karl Pearson: twenty-four, naked, tied to a chair and very, very dead. His throat was sliced nearly all the way through, his head hanging to one side; eyes wide open in surprise, staring vacantly out into the hall. The left ear was missing a large chunk, from the lobe right up to the tip, leaving a crescent moon of skin behind. Deep weals ran parallel along his cheeks from his open mouth round the back of his head. It looked as if he'd been wearing some sort of bondage gag, the little round buckle holes imprinted on the waxy flesh.

Karl's arms were secured behind his back, attached to the chair's legs by a set of plastic cable ties. The hands were crusted in more blood, making detail difficult to pick out, but one thing was abundantly clear: several of Karl's fingers were a lot shorter than they should have been. Some ended at the second joint, others had been taken off at the knuckle, some in between: bone and cartilage showing through the stumps like boiled fish eyes. The severed ends were lying underneath the chair, the nails ripped out. Karl's chest – where it wasn't covered with blood from the gaping neck wound – was speckled with cigarette burns and his right nipple was missing. Karl's legs were splayed wide open, giving Logan an excellent view of his bollocks. Those were either pubic hairs, or staples, Logan couldn't decide which, and he wasn't going to get any closer to find out. The pale, hairy legs were also covered in little burns, the knees lumpen and misshapen. It looked like someone had taken a hammer to his feet.

'What do you think?'

Logan turned to see the deputy PF standing on her own in the doorway, trying to look casual in the standard-issue boiler suit while completely avoiding eye contact with the blood-caked, naked body. There was no sign of the IB team, who were probably poking through the rest of the flat, giving the kitchen a wide berth until DI Insch calmed down a bit. 'Well,' said Logan, 'if he knew anything, he'll have talked.'

Rachael risked a glance at Karl Pearson's body. 'Tortured for information?'

'Probably drugs-related. Karl had form for dealing and we know there's a new crew in town. Looks like they play rough.'

Rachael worked her way around to the far side of the lounge, staring out of the window at the sun-kissed North Sea. Keeping well away from Karl Pearson. 'How the hell do you torture someone in a block of flats and not get caught? Surely someone must have heard something! He's in here getting . . . getting *that* done to him and no one called 999?'

'Well, if it was me I'd gag him, tie him to the chair and *then* torture him. Stub out some cigarettes, rip out some fingernails, break some toes . . . Then, when he's finished screaming behind the gag, pop it off and start asking questions. By now he knows you mean business. You put the gag back in and you go to work again. Slice off an ear, hack off a couple of fingers: *really* make him suffer. Ask your questions again. See if you get the same answers twice. Then do it all one last time, just to be safe.' He sighed. 'Long as you keep the gag in while you're working, no one's going to hear a thing . . . Except maybe the hammering.' She was silent. 'You OK?'

Rachael shuddered. 'You know what it's like: never really seen anything on this . . .' she waved at Karl's tortured body, 'this *scale* before. Not in the flesh. I mean we get to see a lot of photographs when we're doing the cases in court, but . . .' She flapped her hands again.

'But it's not the same.' Logan nodded. Outside the window a seagull swept past on the breeze, its white body caught in a beam of sunshine, fluorescing against the deep, clay-blue sea.

'What the hell's wrong with this place?' she asked, staring out at the clouds scudding across the eggshell sky. 'You'd think a quiet little city like Aberdeen would be safe . . . You ever look at the statistics? According to the Scottish Office, we murder more people here, per million head of population, than the whole of England and Wales combined. How about that?' She leaned her head against the glass. 'And if that's not bad enough, we've got twenty-six times as many attempted murders as we have successful ones! Really makes you proud.'

Logan joined her at the window. 'Really? Twenty-six times?'

Rachael nodded. 'Twenty-six times.'

He shook his head. 'Wow . . . We must be *really* crap! How could we miss so many times? I blame the parents.'

She actually cracked a smile.

'Anyway.' Logan wandered back to the tortured body in the middle of the room. 'My guess is that our parochial wee drugs war has just stepped up a notch. We're going to start seeing a whole lot more of this kind of thing.' He stared down at Karl Pearson's sliced-off ear and realized he was starving. According to his watch it was already two thirty. The post mortem on Karl Pearson was due to kick off at three; that left him thirty minutes to get something to eat and get back to the station.

A clunk at the front door and the Procurator Fiscal stuck her head into the lounge, sweeping the crime scene with a practised eye before frowning, marching straight past the body and peering at Karl's homemade wallpaper. 'Isn't this DS Beattie's wife?'

Karl Pearson's post mortem seemed to take forever, and by half five Logan had to excuse himself, claiming a prior engagement – making sure DI Steel had everything in place for the surveillance operation this evening. Knowing her, she'd be expecting him to do all the legwork. And anyway, the only bit of real news from Doc Fraser's dissection of the tortured body was the collection of fresh needle marks in Karl's upper bicep. Logan was willing to bet the blood work would come back with traces of narcotics. Not enough for Karl to get high, just enough to stop him from going into shock. Maybe even enough to act as a reward if he told the truth. Something to make the pain go away.

Upstairs, DI Steel's incident room was nearly as dead as Karl Pearson. The occasional phone rang, but nothing much was going on. The inspector was lounging against a computer terminal, picking her teeth and reading an *Evening Express*. Yes, of course she'd done the paperwork, and had it signed by the Detective Chief Superintendent himself, no less. Which meant they couldn't screw this one up; if they did everyone and their dog would be lining up to tear a chunk out of their arses. And let's face it, if DI Steel didn't get results from the stakeout, what the hell else could she do? It wasn't as if leads were easy to come by on this bloody case. Somehow two dead prostitutes hadn't captured the attention of the public, not even with the words 'Serial Killer' attached. They'd barely received a call all day.

'How about we stage a reconstruction?' Logan asked. 'Get it on the news?'

Steel smiled at him in a disturbingly motherly kind of way. 'What a great idea! We'll get someone to dress up as a murdered prostitute and get someone else to be the killer, enticing her into his car. Then we'll ask for anyone who was hanging around the docks at that time of night to come forward with any information they have.' There was something sarcastic coming, Logan could feel it. 'Can you imagine the avalanche of calls we'll get? All those public-spirited pimps, whores and kerb-crawlers! "Yes officer, I was down the docks that night lookin' for a prostitute and I saw a nasty man pick up the tart who got killed . . ." I'd better get some more uniforms to answer the phones. We'll be swamped!'

'Fine,' said Logan. 'Be like that.'

Steel grinned at him. 'Never mind, Mr Police

Hero, if it all goes tits-up tonight I'll think about it. If nothing else it'll make the Chief Constable think we're doing something. Now why don't you go pick out a couple of nice, ugly WPCs to be our hookers? Tell them there's a bottle of vodka in it for them, if they don't wind up stripped and beaten to death.'

Half past eight and the briefing was winding to a close. DI Steel had laid out the ground rules, walked everyone through the plan – including the Detective Chief Superintendent who gave a five-minute inspirational speech on the risks and rewards of this kind of operation – and detailed the four teams. Team one was the smallest: WPCs Davidson and Menzies, the inspector's fake prostitutes, neither of whom would win a beauty contest anytime soon. They were already dressed up for their role tonight: short skirts, push-up bras, three inches of make-up and hair like a home perm gone bad. Each one wearing a transmitter/receiver, a secondary backup set – just in case – and a hand-held GPS tracker sewn into their formidable underwear. If anything happened they weren't going to disappear off the face of the earth. Not to mention the tiny canisters of CS gas they both carried. Team two was eight plainclothes officers, two per car. They'd park in the places Logan had identified, where they could keep an eye on Davidson and Menzies plying their trade. Team three was by far the largest, three marked patrol cars, two unmarked CID pool cars, and half a dozen uniforms in the back of an unmarked dark blue Transit Van, lurking on the streets leading to and from the red light district all kitted out with video surveillance equipment and ready to roll as soon as the word was given. Team four would stay at the station and keep all the communication channels open. Relay the messages. Make sure everyone was where they were supposed to be and, in the cases of WPCs Davidson and Menzies, still alive. It was a big operation; lots of manpower, expensive, but the Detective Chief Superintendent assured them all that the Chief Constable was behind them one hundred percent. Steel had sanction for the next five nights, but the DCS was sure they'd get a result *long* before that. Logan, well aware of just how many holes there were in the plan, kept his mouth shut.

DC Rennie cornered him as the briefing broke up and everyone headed off to their assigned positions. 'I've got that bloke you were looking for.' Logan obviously looked puzzled, because Rennie felt obliged to explain. 'The one who's patrolling the docks at the moment? You wanted me to track him down?'

'Right, right. Where is he?'

'Comes in at ten: PC Robert Taylor. Been doing tom patrol for about two years. I left a message with Control that you wanted to speak to him.' Rennie smiled, as if he was waiting for a sweetie. Logan didn't give him one.

'What about the e-fit pictures?'

'No one recognized the girl but a couple of CID thought the bloke might be called Duncan or Richard or something.'

Logan frowned. The Lithuanian girl had said her pimp was called Steve. 'No last name?'

'Nada.'

'Shite.'

'Aye.'

The operation started at nine pm on the dot, much to Logan's surprise. He and the inspector were sat in a rusty old Vauxhall, just inside the gates at the bottom of Marischal Street leading out onto the docks at Regent Quay. They'd parked far enough back not to arouse suspicion if spotted from the street, but with a direct line of sight – through the high fence of grey, cast-iron spikes that enclosed the docks – all the way down Shore Lane, to where WPC Menzies was trolling for business. The inspector even had the good sense to keep one hand cupped over the end of her cigarette so the glowing orange tip wouldn't give them away. One by one the other teams checked in, and last but not least, the bait. Or the Ugly Sisters as DI Steel insisted on calling them. Not surprisingly she'd named it 'Operation Cinderella'. Logan was amazed she didn't get punched on the nose more often.

'Are you sure this is going to work?' he asked as WPC Menzies finished complaining that the wind was whistlin' right up her arse in this bloody short skirt.

'No,' said Steel, puffing away, the smoke oozing out through the car's windows. 'But it's all we've got right now. If we don't put a watch on the docks and some other poor tart goes missing we'll be crucified. And anyway, it's your bloody plan, so don't start, OK?'

'But what if someone goes missing while we're here?'

Steel shuddered. 'Don't even fucking think about that!'

'But all we're doing is watching two WPCs done up as pros. What if one of the real tarts gets in our man's car? How're we going to know? He could be anybody!'

'I know, I know.' She pulled the last gasp from her cigarette and chucked the tiny glowing nub out the window. 'It's a shite plan, but what else can we do? Rosie Williams got herself killed Monday last, Michelle Wood got it on Friday. Four days.' She counted them off on her fingers. 'Saturday, Sunday, Monday, Tuesday. That's tonight. If he sticks to his pattern another one's going missing today or tomorrow.'

'If he hasn't already got one and we just don't know about it yet.'

Steel scowled at him. 'Am I missing something, Sergeant? Are you making helpful suggestions here, or just bumping your bloody gums?' Logan kept his mouth shut. 'Aye,' said the inspector, 'thought as much.' An uncomfortable silence.

Logan sat staring out at the street, thinking. 'Had an interesting chat with Inspector Napier this morning,' he said at last.

'Oh aye?' Suspicious.

'Yeah. He said you have to come out of this case smelling of roses or I'm for the chop.'

'"The chop?" That doesn't sound like Napier. Thought he was more of a "De blood is de life, hah, hah, haaah!" kind of guy,' she said in a dreadful Transylvanian accent.

'Well he dressed it up in an allegorical story about a farmer, a fox and a chicken, but that was what he meant.'

'Which one were you?'

'The chicken.'

'Nice.' She was grinning.

'How come you've got him looking out for you?'

The grin didn't falter as the inspector dug out another cigarette and lit it. 'Let's just say that Napier and I have an understanding, and leave it at that.' Of course Logan didn't want to leave it at that, but Steel had no intention of telling him anything more, so they sat in silence again.

After what felt like hours, WPC Menzies' voice crackled out of the speaker, *'Car comin'!'* A set of headlights sparked at the far end of Shore Lane. Static and rustling from the radio, and Logan pulled out the night-vision goggles, struggling with the focus until he had a good, close-up view of the entrance to the one-way alley. WPC Menzies with her hands on her hips, chest out, leaned forward to peer in the driver-side window. *'Hey, darlin','* she said suggestively, *'lookin' for a good time?'* Logan couldn't get a good look at the man behind the wheel: Menzies had picked one of the few working streetlights to stand under, and the reflection bounced right off the windshield, hiding the driver's face. Some muffled conversation, too distorted to make out – she seemed to have got the tiny microphone caught up in the lace of her bra and every time she moved it scratched against the pickup, overwhelming everything with a grating hiss. *'How about you an' me ... AYA BASTARD!'* Steel sat bolt upright in her seat. The suspect's car roared into life. Through the night-vision goggles Logan could see WPC Menzies clutching at her left breast. She bent down, disappearing from sight as DI Steel grabbed up the radio and shouted 'Go-go-go!' And then Menzies was back up again, hurling something at the departing car. A loud bang and the car screeched to a halt on the cobbles. The driver had his door open in a flash and was out, staring at the smashed rear windscreen. He was too busy storming back up the alley to notice the two unmarked CID pool cars skidding to a halt at each end of Shore Lane, blocking it off.

Logan could hear the man shouting at WPC Menzies, the words picked up loud and clear, even over the bra-crackling. *'You filthy bitch!'* He drew back a fist, but Menzies didn't give him time to use it. Instead she floored him with a single, round-house kick. She wasn't on the division's kick-boxing team for nothing. By the time Logan and Steel arrived he was cuffed, lying prostrate on the filthy cobbled street in a pool of darkness, screaming blue murder and demanding a lawyer while Menzies held him down.

'Ah, Jesus . . . Stitch . . .' The inspector, bent double from the effort of running the three hundred yards from where they'd parked the car, clutched at her side and grimaced. 'Menzies,' she asked through gritted teeth, 'you OK?'

The WPC growled at the handcuffed, swearing figure. 'Bastard grabbed my fucking nipple: nearly tore the damn thing off!' She peeled down the top of her indomitable bra to show the inspector, but Steel told her it was OK, she had two of her own and didn't need to see anyone else's right now. As soon as there was any threat of WPC Menzies getting her breasts out, Logan made himself scarce, choosing to examine the man's car instead. It was a dowdy MPV thing, lots of seats and boot-space, with a sticker saying 'MUM'S TAXI' in what was left of the back window. There was a lump of rust-crusted metal sitting in the middle of a dog's bed, surrounded by tiny cubes of broken safety glass. Logan dug out his mobile phone and called Force Headquarters for a PNC check on the vehicle's registration.

Somehow DI Steel thought a cigarette would help her get her breath back. Coughing and spluttering, she dragged Logan away from the car and told Menzies to get the suspect on his feet. In the darkness of the alley it was difficult to make out his face; the fact that he was filthy from being pinned to the alley floor didn't help. 'Name,' demanded the inspector, taking the cigarette from her mouth so she could spit something dark and nasty out onto the cobbles.

The man's eyes darted left and right. ' . . . Simon McDonald.'

The inspector frowned, head on one side like a cat examining a juicy hamster. 'How come you look familiar, Simon? Have I done you for something?'

'I have *never* been in trouble with the police!'

Logan's phone went: Control, telling him that there was no vehicle of that make and registration in the system. Was he sure he'd got the number right? Logan walked back to the car and squatted down by the back bumper. Now he looked closely, there was something dodgy about the registration: it didn't reflect the torchlight. Someone had taped a bit of laminated paper over the top of it. From a distance, in the dark, it was pretty convincing, but up close it had obviously been produced on someone's home computer with a colour printer. He peeled off the fake number plate and gave Control the real registration hidden underneath, a grin spreading across his face as he heard the result. He swaggered back to where the inspector was giving WPC Menzies' attacker a hard time, questioning him on his whereabouts last Monday and Friday nights. Logan waited until she'd finished before asking, 'Don't you know it's an offence to give a false name to the police, *Mr Marshall*? Not to mention driving with falsified number plates.'

The suspect flinched and DI Steel grabbed him by the lapels and dragged him under one of the few working streetlights, letting out a low whistle as she finally recognized him: Councillor Andrew Marshall, chief spokesman for the Grampian-Police-Are-Useless-Tossers brigade. An obscene smile ripped across Steel's face, like a fire in a nunnery.

'Well, well, well, a member of the city council, as I live and breathe,' she said with obvious relish. 'You are well and truly fucked!'

Councillor Marshall spluttered, panic and indignation fighting for control. 'You have *no right* to treat me like this!'

'No?' DI Steel winked at him. 'Indecent assault, resisting arrest, giving a false name, driving with false number plates . . . Think we'll find anything else incriminating when we search your car?' The councillor suddenly wouldn't meet her eyes and she nodded. 'Thought as much. Think you and me need to have a little chat, don't you?'

DI Steel wrapped an arm around the shivering man's shoulders and led him away.

17

DI Steel didn't want anyone else present while she 'interviewed' Councillor Marshall, didn't even want to take him into the station until she'd had a chance to talk to him. In private as it were. So Logan was sent off to swear the rest of the team to secrecy and search the councillor's car, discovering a number of scary-looking marital aids and a couple of specialist magazines so hard-core the pictures made his eyes water. But he'd collected the lot, sealing them away in clear plastic evidence pouches, not wanting to touch anything he'd found.

Steel had commandeered Logan's pool car, parking it further down the docks where she could talk to Councillor Marshall without being disturbed. Now the only signs of life inside the rusty Vauxhall were the fiery-orange tip of the inspector's cigarette and the smoke slowly curling its way out of the open car window. Logan, on the other hand, sat in the councillor's people carrier, bundled up against the cold wind whistling in through the ruined back window. He'd driven it out from the alley to the harbour's entrance, where he could keep one eye on the Vauxhall and the other on Shore Lane.

There wasn't much business being done tonight. The presence of multiple plainclothes police officers had pushed the genuine working girls into the surrounding streets, leaving Shore Lane completely under WPC Menzies' dominion. WPC Davidson had performed a similar trick on James Street, doing more to clear prostitution from Aberdeen's red light district than months and months of community policing. So there was the answer: you want to cut down on the sex trade, don't bother with initiatives and public awareness campaigns, just put a couple of unattractive WPCs out there selling their wares on the streets, and back them up with about two dozen plainclothes CID pimps. Problem solved.

Logan turned up his collar and shivered. Summer was in the process of buggering off and autumn wasn't going to hang about for long. It was going to be another cold, wet end of year. Still, he thought, at least he wasn't done up in stockings, suspenders and a push-up bra that would put Hannibal Lecter off his sausages. Right on cue, WPC Menzies reported in, complaining about the cold and her sore nipple and wishing death and hellfire on every slimy wee bastard out trolling the docks at this time of night. Did they really have another four and a half hours of this to go?

At long last the inspector's passenger door cracked open and a hunched, cowed figure stepped out. He turned and said something before marching, head down, towards the harbour gates and his damaged car. Logan jumped out and held the driver's door open for him, grinning. The man crawled sheepishly in behind the wheel and started the engine, almost squealing in terror as Logan called out a cheery, 'Drive safely, Councillor!'

Eyes darting and fearful, the man raced away from the scene of his disgrace as fast as the speed limit would allow. Logan stood there, waving, until the car disappeared from view, then picked up the bagful of seized pornographic material and hurried over to the waiting, smoke-filled Vauxhall. 'Christ, it's freezing out there!' he said, cranking the heaters up and wringing his hands over the vent. 'You get much out of Mr Marshall?' DI Steel didn't answer, just asked him what he'd found when he'd searched the councillor's car. Logan held up the plastic bag and started digging evidence pouches out of it, listing the things off as he went, finishing with the pièce de résistance: a huge red rubber phallus with separate power/motion control, covered with spines and nobbles. Steel set them twitching, vibrating and rotating by playing with the dials and buttons. The whole thing buzzed and throbbed in its clear plastic evidence pouch,

like some sort of malevolent insect larva struggling to get free.

'Classy,' said Steel, reading the device's name
off the side: 'THE ANAL ADVENTURER. Fun for all the
family.' She pushed another button and the end
started to pulse and judder. 'Jesus.' She nearly
dropped it. 'It's alive! ALIVE!' Grinning she clicked
the thing off and threw it over her shoulder into
the back of the car. 'So nothing illegal then, just
hella-dodgy?'

Logan agreed. 'What about you? You get
anything out of our friend on the council?'

'Yup.' Steel's smile was almost as obscene as
the huge, battery-operated rubber willy now lying
on the back seat, but she didn't say any more.

'Going to share?' Logan asked at last.

'Nope.'

Half past eleven came and went without much
happening. By the time midnight was sounding
on the St Nicholas Kirk bells WPC Menzies had
only been propositioned three times, including
Councillor Marshall. WPC Davidson hadn't fared
much better either, netting a total of four. Not one
of the blokes looked like a good fit for the killer,
but they'd been detained anyway. Tomorrow
morning someone would check out their alibis for
the Monday and Friday nights. Logan didn't hold
out much hope.

Stifling a yawn, he asked DI Steel if she wanted
him to pick up something to eat while they were

waiting? After all, they'd been on duty since about eight yesterday morning . . .

'Eight?' She snorted. 'I started at seven. Mind you, had a couple hours' kip in the afternoon. Makes the world of difference.'

Logan looked at her. 'I wouldn't know. I was at a crime scene with DI Insch for most of the morning and then in a post mortem till half five.'

Steel frowned at him. 'What the hell did you do that for? You knew we were going to be out here all night!'

'You told Insch I'd help him!'

'Did I?' The inspector shrugged. 'Ah well, never mind.' She dug a hand into her jacket pocket, coming out with a stained neoprene wallet from which she extracted a twenty. 'Go make yourself useful. White pudding supper with extra salt and vinegar . . . oh, and a pickled egg. And some tomato sauce if they've got it. And get something for yourself, if it'll wipe that skelped-arse expression off your face.'

Logan had to concentrate very hard on not slamming the car door. He marched up Marischal Street to the Castlegate, grumbling all the way. The sooner they caught this bastard the better. After that he could go back to working for Insch, or DI McPherson. Anyone other than DI Bloody Steel.

This close to midnight the streets were still pretty busy, taxis mostly. Taxis, buses and drunkards. People going on from the pubs to the casinos, or nightclubs, or specialist venues boasting erotic dancing. There was a pool of fresh vomit sitting in the middle of the pavement at the top of the street, steaming gently, and Logan picked his way around it, trying not to get too close to the green-looking young man staggering about next to it. In defiance of the weather the silly sod was dressed in a pair of jeans and a short-sleeved Aberdeen Football Club top, the shiny red material streaked with regurgitated curry.

There was a chip shop not too far down George Street and he placed Steel's order, getting himself a jumbo haddock with pickled onions and a couple of tins of Irn-Bru, munching on the burning-hot chips as he walked back down to the docks. The AFC vomiter was gone, but a group of giggling girlies dressed in miniskirts, cropped tops and high heels filled the void by hurling abuse at passers-by. They staggered across the pedestrian crossing from the other side of the road, swigging at bottles of Bacardi Breezer, asking Logan for some of his chips, and calling him a 'miserable cunt' at the top of their lungs when he refused. Sighing Logan kept on going, over the crest and down the hill. The haddock was good, fresh and flaky and moist and, shit: that was his phone. He juggled his fish supper out of the way, wiping his greasy fingers on the paper it came wrapped in, before pulling the noisy clanging mobile out into the cold night air.

'Hello? This DS McRae?' A man's voice. Logan admitted that it was. 'Right, right, got a message you wanted to speak to me. PC Taylor?'

Logan had to think for a moment. 'Constable Taylor,' he said at last, trying to fold the paper back over the top of his chips to keep the heat in. 'You patrol the docks, don't you? Shore Lane, Regent Quay, that kind of thing?'

'Aye.'

'I'm looking for a young girl, fourteen to sixteen, been working Shore Lane. Lithuanian, not been in town long, pretty, hair like something out of an old rock video. Said her name was Kylie Smith. I want her and/or her pimp.'

Silence for a moment and then, 'Doesn't ring any bells, but I can ask around.'

'Good. Next: woman, Caucasian, mid-forties, PVC raincoat, black lace top, long boots. Short permed blonde hair. Looks like a regular. Recently had the crap beaten out of her – I need to speak to her urgently.'

The answer was immediate this time. 'Sounds like Agnes Walker, Skanky Agnes to her friends. On some sort of methadone programme I think.'

'You got a home address?' PC Taylor didn't have it on him, but he'd find out. Logan thanked him and hung up. DI Steel's chips were still fairly warm by the time Logan made it back to the car. She wolfed the lot without a word while Logan skoofed his way through a tin of Irn-Bru.

'Right,' said Steel, sooking the last of the salt

208

off her fingers and settling down in her seat. 'Back to the grindstone.' She was snoring within fifteen minutes.

Logan sighed. It was going to be a long night.

Around about half two he roused the inspector. His back was beginning to ache from sitting in the car all night watching nothing happen. While Steel blinked, yawned and lit up yet another cigarette, Logan stepped out into the darkness to stretch his legs, breath misting about his head, caught beneath the harbour's arc lights. A massive blue-and-green supply vessel was docked behind them, the windows dark and empty, reflecting back the silent cityscape. Distant sounds of clanging came from around the docks, the spark and flash of welding on a Russian boat, its red paintwork streaked with rust and grime. The clatter of a ship's door slamming shut. The whine of a crane. Drunken singing.

Hands rammed deep in his pockets, Logan set off on a lap of the streets that made up Aberdeen's red light district. The nightclubs would be chucking out soon, one final upsurge in business for the working girls, a drunken knee-trembler in a filthy doorway, or a once in a lifetime opportunity to be battered to death and abandoned in a ditch somewhere. And it wasn't as if the police had any idea where, when or even *if* the killer would strike again. Tonight, tomorrow, the day after . . . And suppose he did strike, how would they know? If he didn't take the bait, grabbed one of the real working girls instead of Operation Cinderella's ugly sisters, Grampian Police wouldn't find out until the body turned up. Then there would be hell to pay. Logan scowled at the darkened alleys leading off the road, picturing the headlines: LOCAL WOMAN SNATCHED WHILE POLICE LOOK ON!, or SERIAL KILLER STRIKES UNDER POLICE NOSES!, or even just DS MCRAE SCREWS UP AGAIN!!! *'It was my plan,' said disgraced former Police Hero, Logan (Lazarus) McRae. 'It was a sack of s***, but I made them go through with it anyway. All we had to do was watch the streets, and we couldn't even manage that. He snatched her and we couldn't do a b***** thing.' Grampian Police gave notice today of DS McRae's immediate suspension . . .*

He turned left off Commerce Street, just shy of a tiny corporation car park – little more than a triangle of tarmac with a pay-and-display machine – empty now but for an unmarked Transit Van full of policemen. He resisted the urge to give them a wave. The wind was beginning to get up, freezing cold gusts that leached the feeling from his cheeks and made his ears sting. He wandered past the tile shop and the mini business park, peering down the side streets as he went. There weren't many girls left on the game tonight. Either frightened off by the cold or the huge police presence. Maybe the killer would be too? Maybe he couldn't get it up if there was an army of constables and CID watching. Or maybe his dick shrivelled up in the cold and no amount of pounding some poor cow's skull in with a rock would help. Whatever it was,

Logan got the feeling their man wasn't going to show tonight. This had all been one huge waste of time.

She's been standing on this street corner for ages, and it's *bloody freezing*. Shifting from foot to foot, trying to get some sort of circulation going, she cups her hands to her mouth and blows. Breath comes out in a fog, momentarily warming her fingertips, but even that small relief is soon whipped away in the icy wind. 'Fuckit,' she says to herself under her breath. If she didn't need the money so much . . . By all rights she should be at home tonight, curled up in front of the fire with a bottle of vodka and something nice on the telly. But that would be asking for too much, wouldn't it? God forbid Joe should get off his arse and go to work for a change. No: *much* better he should raid the fucking housekeeping and bugger off with the money for the electric. What the hell were they supposed to do with no bloody electricity? The sodding card meter was already down to its last flicker. So Joe goes out on the piss and she has to go out on the game. In the freezing cold. Just so they can have enough fucking electricity to see by. 'Selfish fuckhead.' He hadn't even left her enough for a packet of fags. She'd had to beg some off Joanna. She scrunched up her face and scowled at the deserted street. Enough was enough. The lazy bastard had to go. It wasn't as if he was even good to her. No, it was always demands and complaints and . . . A car. She pulled herself upright and tried for a smile as it slowed down. It was a nice car, one of those new ones they were advertising on the telly. Whoever it was, they weren't short of a bob or two. She wriggled her bra down, getting as much cleavage on show as possible.

Maybe tonight wouldn't be such a let down after all.

18

The sun was already well on its way up the sky when Logan finally slouched into work at half past nine. Yesterday's shift had been way too long: eight am on the Tuesday right round to five am on the Wednesday. Twenty-two hours straight. By the time he was climbing the stairs to his flat things had started to get a little strange. His hands left vapour trails when he moved them, and his eyes made whooooooshing sounds. Showered and barely shaved, Logan groaned his way up to DI Steel's incident room, just catching the end of an update meeting with the head of CID.

Apparently every single person they'd detained last night had a cast-iron alibi for the Monday and Friday – surprisingly enough there was no mention of Councillor Marshall or his Anal Adventurer. Whoever the killer was, they hadn't caught him. When the DCS had gone, and the rest of the team was dispersed to perform the myriad tasks DI Steel had thought up for them, the inspector cornered

Logan and told him he looked like warmed-up shit.

'Thanks a heap,' he said, rubbing his tired face. 'I've had about two hours' sleep in the last day and a half.'

Steel stood up straight and peered down her nose at him. 'So have I, but you don't see me slouching in here looking like a zombie's armpit.' Which wasn't entirely true. Whatever magic the inspector had performed on her wild hair yesterday, it'd worn off. The suit was still new, if a little more creased than it had been, but the top of her head looked like a frightened mongoose.

Logan stared at her in disbelief. 'You spent half the stakeout asleep! I watched the bloody alleyway while you were snoring your head off!'

The inspector grinned at him, completely unabashed. 'Aye? Well, privilege of rank and all that shite. Come on, I'll buy you a nice bacon roll on the way.'

'On the way where?' But she was already gone.

For some reason DI Steel's assertion that shifts were for the weak didn't extend to DC Rennie: he wouldn't be in until later – so Logan had to pick up a CID pool car and drive them to the hospital, expending all his concentration on not crashing into anything. By the time they were sat at the traffic lights on Westburn Road, the lush green jungle of Victoria Park on one side, the wide-open spaces of Westburn Park on the other, Steel was onto her second post-bacon-buttie cigarette.

'You're no' still sulking are you?' she asked as the lights changed and they inched forward.

'I'm not sulking, I'm tired.'

'Aye?' The inspector eyed him sceptically. 'How come you've no' asked why we're going up the hospital then?'

Logan sighed. 'We're going to see Jamie McKinnon.'

Steel nodded. 'Aye. Want to guess why?'

'Not really, no.'

'Suit yourself.'

The ward was fairly quiet when they arrived, most of the beds were full, their occupants sitting on their own, engrossed in the morning paper or staring morosely out of the window. Jamie McKinnon had been moved to a bed in the far corner and was lying on his side with his back to the door, hiding under the blankets.

Steel plonked herself down on the end of the bed and gave him a cheery, 'Jamie, my wee porridge-muncher, how's it hanging?' The man in the next bed harrumphed and ruffled his *Press and Journal*.

'Come on, Jamie, don't be rude: you've got visitors! I even brought grapes.' Steel pulled a tube of sweets from her pocket and tossed them onto the bedspread. 'Well, wine gums, but it's the thought that counts, eh?'

Jamie McKinnon rolled over and scowled at her with his one good eye. For some reason his bruised face wasn't healing much. If anything it was worse than before. 'Go fuck yourself.'

'Ah, Jamie, Jamie, Jamie . . . if only I had time. We found this *huge* dildo last night, but between you and me, it's a bastard on the batteries.' She picked up the wine gums. 'You wanting these or not?'

He snatched them out of her hand and glowered. 'Nothing happened.'

'No . . . ?' Steel faded off into silence, looking over her shoulder at Logan standing at the foot of the bed. 'For God's sake get yourself a chair, you look like an undertaker standing there with your face like that.' Grumbling Logan did as he was told, dragging an orange plastic seat over from the next bed. He was just about to sit down when Steel told him to draw the curtains round the bed.

'There we go,' she said when he'd closed them off from the rest of the ward. 'Much more cosy. Now, Sunshine.' She poked Jamie in the shoulder. 'A nice nurse told me you had some visitors last night. And that when they were gone, you pressed your little "help me" button and she had to get your hand X-rayed.' Logan's eyes darted to Jamie's left hand. All four of the fingers were splinted together, wrapped in white gauze bandage.

'I . . . fell.'

'You fell.' Steel nodded. 'You fell and managed to break four fingers.'

'That's right.'

'Hit your eye on the way down too?' Steel pointed at the swollen mass of bruised flesh.

'I fell, OK? I fell on my face and I put my hand out to stop myself and I banged my fingers.'

'You sure?'

Jamie suddenly found the packet of wine gums very interesting; he fumbled awkwardly at the wrapper with his splinted fingers before giving up and trying with his other hand.

Logan had a bash at being the good cop. 'Who were they, Jamie? The people who came to see you last night?'

Jamie shrugged, never taking his eyes off the packet in his hands. 'Just some people I know. You know, friends, like . . .'

The inspector snorted. 'Bollocks. Tell you what, Jamie, I think your visitors were trying to pass you controlled substances. So, just to be on the safe side, I'm going to call a nice man from the Drugs Squad and get him to perform a full body-cavity search on you. Would you like that?' She smiled. 'Would you? Nice big hairy man's hand all the way up your backside looking for a package of fun? Mmm? Big, big hairy hands?'

'They didn't give me nothing, OK? They wanted to, but I wouldn't take it.'

DI Steel's smile softened. 'I wish I could believe you, Jamie, I really do. But you're going to need to give me more information than that. I want their names.'

'I don't know their names!'

Steel shook her head, then mimed pulling on an elbow-length rubber glove, complete with sound effects. Jamie's eyes darted from the inspector to Logan. 'I don't know! They wouldn't tell me! Please!'

'What did they want?'

'They said I had to use them as suppliers. I told them I wasn't doing that kind of stuff any more, I was going straight . . .' He held up his hand so Logan could see the bruises in between the fingers where the bandages didn't quite meet. 'Then they did this.'

Logan winced. 'Why didn't you call for help?'

Jamie laughed painfully. 'Think I didn't want to? Big fucker had me pinned to the bed, stuffed a rag in my mouth while his fucking friend giggled and snapped my fingers. Couldn't even scream.'

'And no one saw anything?'

'They pulled the curtains.'

'You could have said something afterwards.'

Jamie raised his undamaged hand to his swollen eye, touching the puffy flesh with a wince. 'Said they'd be back. Said they knew where I lived. Said they could have a lot of fun with my sister if I fucked things up for them.'

Steel listened to all this with a thoughtful look on her face. When she was finally certain that they weren't going to get anything more out of Jamie McKinnon she hopped off the bed and motioned for Logan to follow. 'Thanks for that, Jamie. Oh, and you'll be sad to know that some other tart got herself beaten to death on Friday night.' At that Jamie sat up straight in bed. 'Nah.'

Steel shook her head. 'Don't get your hopes up, we're treating them as separate incidents. You're still going down for what you did to Rosie. See, we got the lab results back this morning: Rosie was up the stick with your kid. You knew that. Couldn't stand the thought of your baby inside her getting poked by strangers' dicks every night.' All the blood drained from Jamie's face and the inspector grinned. 'You have fun now.'

Jamie was in tears as they pushed their way out of the ward, Steel making the call to her friend on the Drugs Squad to set up Jamie's full body-cavity search.

Ailsa stood at the kitchen sink washing the breakfast things in hot soapy water. Normally she would have done the washing up straight after breakfast, but she was a bit behind today. Gavin had bought her a dishwasher, he was good like that, but somehow it seemed so wasteful to put it on just for a couple of plates, and she couldn't bear the thought of the breakfast dishes festering in there all day, so she always did them by hand, staring out of the kitchen window through the fence, watching the schoolchildren troop across the grass and in through the doors. Praying that one day, she'd have one of her own . . . But it was late and they were all gone now, leaving the playground empty and silent, waiting for the morning break to come. She sighed and scrubbed dried-on egg off the good plates.

Gavin had been in a foul mood last night. He'd had to work late *yet again* – even though he'd promised – and when he finally got home the horrible woman next door was out in the garden. Staggering about, screaming and swearing at her boyfriend. Gavin had dumped his briefcase in the hall and marched right round there to give them a piece of his mind. She had never, ever, heard her husband use language like that before. But it didn't make any difference to the harpy next door: she just started shouting and swearing at Gavin instead. Then she got violent! Screaming obscenities and swinging punches . . . Gavin came in with the beginnings of a black eye. He called the police, not that it ever did any good. After that he didn't want to eat the supper she'd made for him, preferring instead to drink a huge amount of whisky. And even though the schedule they'd got from the doctor said they had to try every night while she was ovulating, he said he couldn't. Not after a long day in the office and the fight. He was going to have another drink and watch the television. So Ailsa had gone to bed alone.

That horrible woman next door had ruined everything . . .

With a sigh, Ailsa stacked the last mug on the draining board. The noise next door was getting worse again, the yelling, the foul language, the sound of something breaking. Then the pointy-faced boyfriend limped out into the back garden, covering his head with his hands as a beer bottle sailed out through the French windows. The horrible woman lurched out after it, drunk at half past ten in the morning, swigging from another bottle. The boyfriend tried to get out of the way, but she grabbed him by the collar and punched him in the face! She was going to beat him up again: right there in the back garden, where everyone could see!

He staggered back, blood streaming from his crooked nose and she tried to swing for him again, missing, collapsing on the grass. Crying. The boyfriend turned and ran into the house, screaming that he was leaving her, that he'd had enough, slamming the door behind him.

Ailsa never saw him again.

The horrible woman rolled over onto her back, like a beached whale in jogging pants, and started to snore. Ailsa shuddered – maybe she should call the police?

But she didn't. Instead she picked up the dish-towel and started to dry.

The nurse who'd seen to Jamie McKinnon's fingers wasn't exactly the most attractive woman ever to don a blue uniform: bobbed brown hair, squinty nose, pointy ears and thinnish lips, but DI Steel was smitten from the outset. She perched on the edge of the nurse's desk, giving the young woman her undivided attention while she told them all about Jamie McKinnon's visitors last night. Two men, both neatly dressed in suits. One with really nice teeth and short blond hair, the other with shoulder-length black hair and a moustache.

A little warning bell went off in the back of Logan's head. 'They didn't have Edinburgh accents by any chance, did they?'

They did.

Steel protested, but eventually Logan managed to drag her away from the nurses' station and up to the hospital's security office, where a lone guard kept an eye on a bank of CCTV monitors. He was dressed in the standard turd-brown uniform with brass buttons and yellow trimmings that looked disturbingly like chunks of sweet corn. It took a little persuasion, but eventually he showed them last night's tapes. There wasn't a camera in Jamie McKinnon's ward, but there *was* one in the corridor not far from it. Logan ran through the tape, watching the fast-forward flicker of motion as the machine played back yesterday evening. The system was only set up to record an image every couple of seconds and the doctors, nurses and civilians jerked past in a strange stop-motion ballet. Two large figures twitched into view, drifting along the corridor to disappear suddenly outside Jamie's ward. The timestamp at the bottom of the screen said ten seventeen. Regular visiting hours ended at eight. When they re-emerged the time-stamp said ten thirty-one. Fourteen minutes of dislocating Jamie McKinnon's fingers and threatening his family. Logan hit the pause button. Now the figures were walking towards the camera he had a good view of their faces. The picture quality wasn't great, but it was good enough: the bloke in the suit with the short blond hair was the same 'corporate investment facilitator' Miller had met for breakfast in the pub. And the man at his side was a dead ringer for the driver who'd been waiting in the car outside while Miller agreed to write a puff piece on McLennan Homes' latest business venture. 'And we have a winner.'

'What?' Steel was slouched in her chair, not really paying attention to the screen, or to the clockwork animation people on it.

'This one,' said Logan, poking the screen with his finger. 'Works for Malcolm McLennan.'

It was DI Steel's turn to swear. 'You sure?'

'Yup. So anything your mate digs out of Jamie McKinnon's arse belongs to Malk the Knife.'

19

Eleven o'clock and they were back in the car again, heading for the HQ of Aberdeen's main local newspaper. DI Steel sat in the passenger seat, worrying away at her thumbnail, her expression conflicted.

Jamie McKinnon was being kept under close supervision, not even toilet breaks allowed, until Steel's mate from the Drugs Squad turned up with his long rubber glove. She was determined to pin something on the two thugs from down south. The trouble would be getting any sort of case together. Somehow Logan didn't see Jamie McKinnon having the balls to stand up in court and say, 'Yes, Your Honour, those are the men that forced six kilos of heroin up my backside.' Not if he didn't want to end up filling a shallow grave out in the Grampian hills somewhere. But you never knew your luck.

Logan took the car up across Anderson Drive and onto the Lang Stracht. The *Press and Journal* – local news since 1748 – shared a squat, concrete, sprawling box of a building with its sister paper, the *Evening Express*, on a small industrial estate packed with car dealerships and warehouses. Inside it was all one huge, open-plan office. It always amazed Logan that the place was so quiet, just the ever-present *hummmmm* of the air-conditioning and the odd muffled conversation overlaying the soft, plastic clickity-clack of people typing on word processors. Colin Miller, however, was hunched over his computer, hammering away at the keyboard as if it had recently called his mother a schemie whore. The desks around him were packed with piles of paper, mugs of congealing coffee and bespectacled journalists. Every head within an eight-desk radius snapped up as Logan tapped Miller on the shoulder and asked for a quiet word.

'Oh, for fuck's sake! Can you no' see I'm busy?'

'Colin,' said Logan in a low, friendly voice. 'Trust me on this; you want to have a wee chat with us. And it'll be *much* nicer if we have it over an early lunch in the nearest pub than down at the station. OK?'

Miller looked from Logan to the article flickering away on his screen – something about a bake sale in Stonehaven, if Logan wasn't mistaken – before hammering Ctrl-Alt-Delete, locking his computer. 'Come on then.' Miller stood and grabbed his jacket from the back of the chair. 'You bastards is buyin'.'

They didn't go into the nearest pub – according

to Miller the place would be hoachin' with nosey-bastard journalists and if there was any chance of a story coming out of this, he wasn't going to share it with anyone – so instead he made Logan drive them into the centre of town, dumping the car back at Force HQ so they could make the two-minute walk to the Moonfish Café on Correction Wynd. On the other side of the narrow, sunken alley a huge granite wall, at least twenty-foot tall, held back the dirt and graves of the 'Dead Centre' – St Nicholas Kirk – the sky an icy blue, trapped between the looming church spire and the twisted willows. They were halfway through ordering when Steel jiggled about in her seat, then dragged out her mobile phone. 'Got it on vibrate,' she said with a wink. 'Hello? What? No, I'm in a restaurant . . . Yes . . . Susan! No, that's not . . . Look I know you're upset . . . but . . .' Swearing she stood, grabbed her jacket off the back of the chair and marched outside. 'Susan, it's not *like* that . . .'

'So,' said Logan as the inspector stomped back and forth on the other side of the restaurant's front window – a freshly lit cigarette leaving wild smoke trails in the wake of her gesticulating hand, 'Isobel feeling any better?'

The reporter looked alarmed. 'Better?'

'Doc Fraser said she'd been sick.'

'Oh, right. Aye . . .' Shrug. 'Summer cold or somethin', no' sleepin' much, you know?' An awkward silence settled onto the table, followed by complimentary slices of freshly baked bread.

They helped themselves, making small talk about Aberdeen's chances in the coming match with Celtic, waiting for the inspector to finish what looked like a very loud argument.

Eventually the door banged open and Steel marched in, threw herself into her chair and scowled at the specials board.

'So whit's this all about?' asked Miller as they waited for their sea bass in crayfish butter.

'You know fine what it's about,' said Steel, turning her scowl on him instead. 'You had breakfast with some wee shite-bag from Edinburgh last week. I want to know who he is. And I want to know right bloody now!'

Miller raised an eyebrow and took a contemplative sip of his Sauvignon Blanc, eyeing up DI Steel over the top of his glass, taking in the saggy neck, pointed features, wrinkles, escaped-loony hair, and nicotine-stained teeth. 'Jesus, Laz,' he said at last, 'I think your mum's coming on to me.'

Logan tried not to smile. 'We think your "corporate investment facilitator" assaulted someone in hospital yesterday, maybe even forced him to accept drugs for resale.'

Miller groaned and took another swig of his wine, draining half the glass. 'I don't know anythin', OK?' He pushed his chair out and stood. 'I'll get a taxi back tae the paper—'

Logan grabbed his arm. 'Look, we're not going to involve you, OK? We just need a bit of info.

Far as anyone else is concerned, you didn't tell us anything.'

'Aye, damn right I didn't.' The reporter cast a significant glance at DI Steel. 'And I'm not goin' tae either.'

The inspector scowled. 'Listen up, you soap-dodging Weegie bastard: if you like I can drag you into the station and *force* you to make a statement. Understand?'

'Oh aye? And how the hell do you think you're goin' tae do that, Grandma? I don't have to tell you shite if I don't want to. You want to go get a court order, you get off your wrinkly, stinky old arse and get one.'

Steel was up on her feet, leaning over the table, teeth bared. 'Who the fuck do you think you are?'

'Me?' Miller smacked himself in the chest with a fist. 'I'm the free-fuckin'-press, that's who I am. Want to see your haggard old face splashed all over the paper? I'll screw your career over in a fuckin' heartbeat!'

That was all Logan needed – if Steel got pilloried in the P&J, Napier's sage-and-onion threat would stuff Logan out of a job. 'Inspector,' he said, placing a hand over her trembling, tobacco-yellowed fist. 'Why don't you leave me to speak to Mr Miller? I'm sure you've got much more important—' But Colin Miller wasn't hanging around. He grabbed his coat off the stand and barged out of the restaurant, slamming the door behind him, rattling the glass.

Steel stared after him. 'If you need me,' she said, 'I'll be back at the ranch.' And she too was gone. Logan let his head sink forward until it was resting on the tabletop, the beginnings of a headache sidling up behind his eyes. The woman was a nightmare: all they needed to do was sit down and have a quiet word with the reporter, sound him out, get a name and take it from there. Instead of which, she goes out of her way to piss him off.

'Er . . . excuse me?'

Logan peeled an eye open to see a blue apron hovering at his shoulder. Further up there was a pretty brunette attached to it, balancing three large plates. She smiled uncertainly down at him. 'Sea bass?'

Back at Force Headquarters, DI Steel was in deep conversation with the Assistant Chief Constable when Logan pushed through the incident room's door. He left them to it – not feeling up to polite conversation, having made a good attempt at eating all three portions of fish out of sheer bloody-mindedness. Brooding as he chewed.

'Jesus, sir: you OK? You look like sh . . . erm . . . dreadful.' DC Rennie was trying to get into the room bearing a tray covered with coffee and chocolate biscuits. Logan didn't reply, just helped himself to a mug of mid-brown slurry on his way to the desk he was sharing with the admin officer. One side of the desk was covered in orderly stacks of paper and an ancient-looking computer, the other side belonged to Logan; an expanse of bare Formica with a brand-new yellow Post-it note bang slap in the middle. He picked it up, trying to decipher the biro scrawl. It looked like AOPEN WULHIR and an address that could have been SANITTFILD DRIVE, or SUNITHFIULD DRIVE. DC Rennie came past with the biscuits, took one look at the note and said, 'Smithfield Drive? I had a great aunt lived there when I was wee. Nice old lady: loved *Coronation Street*.' He offered Logan a Jaffa Cake. 'Didn't miss a single episode till they carted her off to the crematorium. They played the theme tune as she went through the curtains.'

Logan stuck the note under the constable's nose. 'What about that bit?' he said, pointing at AOPEN WULHIR.

Rennie squinted. 'Looks like "Agnes Walker" to me . . . Oh, is that Skanky Agnes? I did her once: drunk and disorderly down the docks. Puked all over the back of the van, dirty cow.'

That sounded about right. 'You busy?' he asked. Rennie shook his head. All he'd done that morning was file paperwork and get the teas in.

They picked out one of the newer CID pool cars, Rennie driving as Logan slumped in the passenger seat. It was warm in the car, the sunlight seeping in through the windshield – a soporific blanket that wrapped itself around him adding to the effects of a large lunch. He drifted off, not quite asleep, but not quite awake either as Rennie drove them through the centre of town, dribbling on and on about how someone from *Home and Away* was in *EastEnders* now, playing someone else's uncle. Logan tuned him out, head lolling against the window, letting the city's summer streets slide by as Rennie took them past Victoria Park and up Westburn Road. The lights were against them at the junction to the hospital and Logan felt a pang of guilt: he'd still not been to see PC Maitland. Not paid his respects to the nearly dead . . . Red, amber, green and they were on their way again, leaving the hospital behind.

Smithfield Drive was on the other side of North Anderson Drive, overlooking the dual carriageway where it dipped down the final hill and died at the Haudagain Roundabout. The buildings were standard Aberdeen City Council fare, no different to the other schemes of rectangular granite slabs all over the city. Skanky Agnes's building was a two-storey block of four flats, hiding behind a front garden that groaned under the weight of gnomes, wishing wells and ornamental trellis smothered in vivid-yellow climbing roses. Not exactly what Logan had been expecting. Agnes's flat was top right, behind a pristine red front door with the name 'SAUNDERS' on it. He stifled a yawn and got Rennie to lean on the doorbell. It took two more goes before the red door opened and a creased face blinked out at them. Early thirties; bleached-blonde curly hair, flat on one side and

231

sticking up on the other; black-and-gold kimono clutched half-heartedly closed at the waist, exposing an expanse of cleavage at the top end, and a pair of sturdy legs at the other. Mascara smudged around both eyes on a hardened, but still attractive, professional face. Definitely not Skanky Agnes. 'What fuckin' time you call this?' Rennie told her it was twenty to two. 'Oh for fuck's sake . . .' A yawn, big enough to take a full-grown cat. 'What is it with you police bastards? Can you no' let a body sleep?'

Rennie bristled, obviously a little flustered at being ID'd as a copper so easily. 'What makes you think I'm not a Jehovah's Witness?'

She sighed, looked him up and down once more, then pulled the kimono a little tighter, hiding the cleavage, but exposing a dangerous amount of upper thigh. 'Christ, you're not, are you?'

'No, but I could have been.'

The woman laughed and released her grip on the kimono, causing it to fall back into exactly the same position it had occupied in the first place, only more open. 'Aye. That'll be shinin'. You got copper written all over you. What you want?'

'Ms?'

'Saunders.'

'Right, Ms Saunders, we're looking for Agnes Walker. We understand she lives here?'

The woman's eyes narrowed. 'Why?'

'We . . . er . . . that is . . .' Rennie passed a

panicked look back at Logan, who hadn't actually told the constable what they were doing here.

'We want to speak to her about an assault that happened two weeks ago.'

Ms Saunders shifted her attention from Rennie to Logan as he told her that Agnes wasn't in any trouble, they wanted to find out who beat her up, so they could stop him from doing it again.

The woman folded her arms, making the hem of her kimono rise a good four inches. 'And how come you're suddenly so bloody interested in Agnes's welfare? Eh? Where the hell were you when he was beatin' the shite out of her?' She squared her shoulders. 'Come to think of it, how come it's taken you this long to take a bloody interest?'

Logan had to admit she had a point. 'She told me it was an accident.'

'An accident?' She snorted. 'Are you kiddin' me? You see the state of her? That was no accident, some bastard tried to strangle the poor cow! Four days she was laid up in her bed, pissing blood half the time. Sheets were in a hell of a mess.'

'Did she tell you who did it?'

'She didn't know. She did, I'd've been round there in a shot with a pair of rusty shears, cut the bastard's prick right off!'

Logan peered over her shoulder into the darkened flat. 'Look, can we talk about this inside—'

'No you fuckin' don't: I don't do freebies. And definitely no threesomes!'

'I'm not looking for a "freebie", OK? And neither is he,' Logan jerked a thumb in Rennie's direction. It was difficult not to notice that the constable was spending an inordinate amount of time staring at the flesh appearing beneath the woman's slipping kimono. 'Give us a description – did Agnes tell you what her attacker looked like?'

She shrugged. 'Medium height, brownish hair, ordinary looking.' When Logan didn't say anything, just stood there silently, she sighed again. 'Look, I don't know, OK? Said he had a flashy motor, one of them big BMWs. That's all I can remember. You want any more, you'll have to ask her yourself.'

'I will. Where is she?'

'No idea.'

A man's voice echoed out from inside the flat – hoarse, deep and sounding of Fraserburgh: 'Whit is it?' She turned and shouted back, 'It's nothin'. Start on yer own, I'll be in in a minute,' before turning back to Logan. 'She didn't come back this morning.'

The man's voice again, 'Are you fuckin' comin' or what?' and Ms Saunders sighed. 'In a fuckin' minute!' She stuck out her hand to Logan. 'Give us your card. She'll call you when she gets back, and if she doesn't, I will. Wee shite did that to her deserves all he gets.' And as soon as Logan handed over his Grampian Police business card the door was slammed in their faces.

234

'So,' said Rennie on the way back to the car. 'You want to tell me what that was all about?'

'Agnes Walker had the crap beaten out of her about twelve days ago. Four days later, give or take, Rosie Williams is beaten to death. Four days after *that* it's Michelle Wood's turn.'

'So?' Rennie plipped the locks and clambered in behind the wheel.

'What if Rosie Williams wasn't the guy's first?' said Logan, getting into the passenger seat. 'Suppose he's been out there hunting before, only victim number one puts up a fight and he can't finish the job. He learns from his mistakes and out he goes again. He tries Rosie, and she's not as strong as the first one, or maybe he's just better prepared this time: he kicks and punches her till she's dead. Four days later he's back again. He did Rosie right there in the street; anyone could come along – too risky. This time he snatches his victim. Instead of killing her at the scene, he takes her away somewhere quiet and secluded where he can enjoy himself a bit more. Less chance of discovery.' Rennie did a three-point turn and headed back towards Anderson Drive as Logan fought with the seatbelt. 'The more he does it, the better he gets. So far, Skanky Agnes is the only one who's seen him and lived. Soon as we're back at FHQ get a lookout request out for her. We need to know what he looks like.'

Rennie whistled, waiting for his turn at the roundabout onto the dual carriageway. 'So that *definitely* puts the kybosh on Jamie McKinnon killing Rosie . . .'

'If it's the same man.'

The car lurched onto the roundabout as Rennie floored it, nipping out before an articulated lorry could flatten them. He drove straight across the Drive, heading back into town. 'You think it's the same man, don't you?'

Logan shrugged. 'Either that or it's a huge bloody coincidence . . .' He watched the houses on Rosehill Drive go by for a moment, before coming to a conclusion. 'Change of plan: drop me off at the Journals. I've got to see a man about some drugs.'

20

As Rennie pulled away from the P&J's concrete bunker, Logan called Colin Miller on his mobile. 'Colin, it's me.' Silence from the other end of the phone. 'Look, Colin, I know Steel can be an arse at times, but . . .' He couldn't actually think of an excuse for the inspector's behaviour, so he settled for, 'But I could really do with your help.'

'I'm busy.'

'Five minutes. I'm outside. Come on, we can go for a walk in the sunshine . . .'

A deep sigh. 'OK, OK – if I do, will you promise tae leave me alone?'

'Scout's honour.' Ten minutes later Miller appeared, dressed in his shirtsleeves, jacket slung casually over one shoulder. They walked up the Lang Stracht, sun on their faces, bus fumes in their lungs. 'So, you want to tell me about your friends from down south?'

Miller sighed. 'You know the bloody answer to that.' He glanced back at the bulky, grey P&J

building as it slowly disappeared from sight. 'Everythin's fucked.' He shook his head. 'I was on tae a nice wee gig here, know what I mean? All the front page stories I wanted, nice car, good woman . . .' He trailed off as he remembered he was talking to Isobel's ex-lover. 'Aye, well . . . you know. Now these fuckers are screwin' it all up.'

'I saw your piece on McLennan Homes.'

'Piece of shite, *that* was. Can you believe I had tae beg tae get that on the front page?' He gave a bitter smile. 'Everyone thinks I've lost it, Laz.'

'What they do, threaten you?'

Miller looked up at him, brow furrowed. 'What, Malkie's lads? Oh, just your basic how hard would it be to type with no fingers? Tellin' me whit a lovely home I have and how pretty Isobel is, what a shame it'd be if somethin' happened to her face . . . So I published, and now I'm damned: stuck doin' shitey wee pieces on fairs and bloody bake sales.'

'If it makes you feel any better, last night they broke a guy's fingers in hospital. Smacked him around a bit. Probably forced him to hide a couple of condoms of coke up his arse. So he probably had a worse day than you.' Miller almost smiled; it was the first time in ages Logan had seen him without a scowl on his face. 'Look, you need these guys to go away – I can do that if you help me. I'll keep you out of it. I just need to know who they are, where they're staying, anything you've got.'

They walked along in silence for a while, heading back towards the newspaper building. Up above, the pure blue of the sky was beginning to fade, a long, low purple band of cloud coming in off the sea. 'Brendan Sutherland,' said Miller at last, 'known as "Chib" to his pals, on account of him stabbin' folk, like.'

'"Chib"? What is he, west-coast mafia?'

Miller laughed, short and sharp. 'Naw, he's a wannabe Weegie. An Edinburgh tosspot with delusions of grandeur. Only trouble is, as you know, he's a fuckin' huge tosspot. When he turned up first time, I did me some diggin'. Wee shite's got himself a *big* reputation. Doesn't play in the shallow end of the cesspit. Malk the Knife likes tae keep Chib for breakin' in new territories. Fixin' stuff. Gettin' rid of people Malkie doesn't want anyone to find.'

Logan wasn't surprised Miller had been bricking it in the pub the other morning. 'What about the other one, his driver?'

Miller shook his head. 'No idea. Soon as I saw Chib's résumé I stopped askin' questions. Someone slaps my knob in a blender, I'm no' playin' with the buttons.'

'Does Isobel know?'

The reporter blushed. 'I . . . er . . . You're no' to tell her, OK? I don't want her upset. No' now.'

'If this Chib bloke's threatening both of you, she's got a right to know!'

'You don't fuckin' tell her! Promise me! I'll sort it out.'

'How? How the hell can you sort this out? If Chib's here to carve up Aberdeen for Malk the Knife, he's not leaving any time soon!'

A crafty light glimmered in Miller's eye. 'Unless something happens to him . . .'

'Don't even start. What you going to do? Hit him over the head and bury the body in your back garden?'

Miller grinned. 'I've got a mate with a pig farm up by Fyvie. They'd love a bite of prime Edinburgh bampot . . .' He thought about it for a minute then shrugged. 'Give us a day. I'll get you an address. But for Christ's sake don't let him find out where you got it, OK?'

'OK.' They walked back to the P&J offices, Miller promising to phone as soon as he found out anything. And while they were on the subject, Logan asked for a little favour. 'I want you to lay off DI Steel.'

'Bollocks to that. I'm no' taking shite like that from a manky wee bitch—'

'If you screw her over in the paper, Professional Standards will have my arse. I don't know why, but they've got a thing for her. She goes down, I do too. And if I go down, I can't help you.'

Miller swore. 'OK, OK: hands off the saggy-faced old cow. I get it. I don't shaft her and you don't tell Isobel about these Edinburgh bastards. Deal?' They shook on it, then the reporter shifted uncomfortably from foot to foot, looking as if he was gearing himself up for something. 'Er . . . Laz, you know I'm stuck doin' this shitey bake-sale crap? Well, any chance of . . . you know . . . You got anything I can use? Somethin' about them dead prostitutes, like? Or anything else? I'm fuckin' dyin' here!'

Logan was about to say he'd see what he could do when his phone rang. It was Steel; telling him to get over to the hospital. Jamie McKinnon had just failed his rectal exam.

Aberdeen Royal Infirmary wasn't far, just over the lights at Anderson Drive and down the hill a bit, so Logan made his excuses and walked. By the time he got there the thin band of cloud had grown until it covered half the sky, battleship grey and ominous purple. He ducked into the hospital's lobby as the first tentative specks of rain stuttered against the automatic doors.

The ARI front lobby was an open-plan space with pictures and comfortable seating that always made his skin crawl. He hurried across the infirmary's coat of arms and made his way to Jamie McKinnon's ward. Only Jamie wasn't there any more. A knackered nurse in a bloodstained uniform told Logan he'd been moved to a private room on the third floor. It didn't take him long to find it.

DI Steel was already there, along with a tall bloke from the Drugs Squad. Logan was introduced and got as far as shaking the man's hand before remembering where it had just been. It was a huge hand, engulfing Logan's own, and he had a sudden pang of sympathy for Jamie McKinnon – who was now lying curled up on the bed like a spanked child, face to the wall. That must have hurt! Councillor Marshall would have been delighted.

'Go on,' said Steel to her large friend. 'Show him what you found.'

The man gave a cold smile and held up a stainless steel kidney dish with two slimy, lumpy packages in it, each one no more than four inches long, looking like a pair of small mealie puddings. 'Rough guess, I'd say you're looking at about a quarter-kilo of crack,' he said. 'No way this much cocaine is for personal use: this is for dealing. Don't see that much of it up here. Your boy must be looking to start a trend.'

Steel sank down on the bed, next to Jamie's foetal form, patting him on the thigh. 'So, Jamie, you want to tell us all about your mates from down south now, or shall I just go ahead and add "possession with intent to supply" to your list of charges?' But Jamie had had enough of the long arm of the law for one day. He kept his face to the wall, curled up in a ball, silent.

Half past four. Ailsa Cruickshank picked up the phone and called Gavin's office. It was Norman who answered, far too young to be an account manager and a terrible flirt. Blushing, Ailsa asked him if she could talk to her husband. There was a moment's silence on the other end of the phone, as if Norman was thinking about something. And then, *'Ailsa, what does a fine, hot babe like you want to be speaking to an old fart like that for?'*

'I need him to pick up some things for tea,' she said, embarrassed and thrilled to be called a 'hot babe'.

'Hold on a minute, OK, sexy?' There was muffled conversation at the other end. *'Sorry, Ailsa, my kitten, I'm afraid the old stinker's out with a customer. Probably won't be back till late. Sorry, love, you know how it goes here: customer comes first and all that. But if you're lonely, I could always come over and keep you warm?'* Smiling, she told him it was OK and hung up. Norman was simply dreadful! Full of compliments and naughty suggestions, just like Gavin had been, before all the tests had taken the spark out of things. Four years of trying for children. Four years of medical evaluations and ovulation cycles . . . Anyway, it didn't matter. Things would be back to normal soon. Life had a way of working things out. It always did.

With a brave smile she picked the keys to their new car off the table. She'd just have to go to the supermarket herself. Gavin always liked steak for his birthday tea, maybe she'd make it tonight as well. Just for a treat.

Next door the music started booming.

The stakeout operation started again at ten on the dot: same team, same cars, same positions. Thick raindrops had given way to a fine drizzle before petering out, leaving the alleyway rife with puddles and slick cobblestones. High above, the clouds were low and dark, reflecting back the orange-yellow glow of the streetlights. Down in Shore Lane that was pretty much the only illumination there was. Three of the remaining lights had died, leaving only one sulphurous lamp for WPC Menzies to strut her stuff beneath.

Logan had parked the pool car in the same place as before and while the inspector called round all the positions on her radio – making sure everyone was in place – he reclined his seat and shut his eyes, determined that tonight was going to be *his* turn to catch up on sleep. Since leaving the hospital he'd requested Brendan 'Chib' Sutherland's record from Lothian and Borders Police, chased up the lookout call on Agnes Walker – still no sign of her yet – and filled in the paperwork to get Jamie McKinnon charged for the drugs he was packing. As soon as McKinnon got out of hospital he was going to go straight to court and then back to Craiginches. Logan couldn't help but feel sorry for the guy: it wasn't as if he'd had much say in the matter when Chib decided to ram a quarter-kilo of crack cocaine inside him.

Logan wriggled in the driver's seat, trying to get comfortable without standing on the pedals or banging his knees on the steering wheel. It was the same car from yesterday – no one had even bothered to chuck the chip papers in the bin. They were still lying on the back seat, along with all the items seized from Councillor Marshall's car. Logan had half expected them to get signed into evidence, but for that to happen some sort of charge would have to be pressed, and the inspector flat-out refused to do it. Christ alone knew what sort of dodgy deal she'd done with Marshall to keep the man out of court and out of the papers.

He was just about asleep when the sound of snoring drifted across from the passenger seat. The inspector had beaten him to it. Grumbling, Logan pulled his seat upright again and sat staring morosely at the darkened alley: one of them had to stay awake in case something happened. It was going to be another long night.

Five to midnight and Logan was sent out to fetch the inspector's chips. Again. At least it wasn't raining any more and, to be honest, he was grateful for an excuse to get out of the car and stretch his legs. The inspector had been making sounds like a tractor from one end and a leaky inner tube from the other, all night.

Instead of heading straight up Marischal Street to the chip shop he cut right along Regent Quay, intending to make a left onto Commerce Street like last time, then keep on going till he could nip across the roundabout and in round the back of the Castlegate. At least it would keep him away from Steel and her noisome backside for an extra ten minutes.

There were a lot more people on the streets

tonight, most of them drunk; lurching, staggering and singing away to themselves in a mixture of broken English and Russian. One of the big boats must be in.

WPC Davidson was standing at the corner of Mearns Street – dressed in a vast upholstered bra and tiger-print miniskirt, with a duffel coat over the top. She got into character as soon as she saw him coming, shouting out, 'Oi, Big Boy, you looking fer a good time, darlin'? I'll bile yer tatties and champit yer neeps! Whoooooarrrrr!' ending with an embarrassingly graphic display of breast-clutching and hip-thrusting as he walked past laughing.

'Couldn't afford you, Mrs Davidson: too classy for me.'

She gave him a farewell two-finger salute and went back to picking her teeth. He took a left at the corner, leaving the Quay for Commerce Street, walking out into the road to avoid a huge puddle of black, oil-skimmed water.

It wasn't the prettiest end of town by any stretch of the imagination. Unloved, utilitarian buildings in uniform grey, interspersed with modern units in plastic and corrugated steel. Welders and tool-rental places rubbed shoulders with ships' chandlers, prowled after dark by late-night drunkards and drugged-up hookers. One of the latter was negotiating with two of the former in the mouth of a tiny, darkened alleyway. Logan kept walking, trying to ignore the exchange, but hearing it nonetheless: 'Come on,' said a big, unsteady bloke, slurring. 'You . . . you can do both of us for that, can't ye, darlin'? Aaatha same time like? Yer man Steve says you're the best . . . aaatha same time?'

His mate, barely able to stand, shouted, 'Am no' takin' sloppy fuckin' seconds!'

'Shuthafuckup – I know that! Did I no' just say she had tae do us aaatha same time?' Belch. Two steps backward, one step forward. 'Which end you want?'

'Cost more, both at same time. More!' Slavic accent.

Logan froze: it was her.

'More?' It was Fat Boy again, undoing his trousers and letting them fall round his ankles. 'C'moan, amma sex god! You should be payin' me!' He lurched forward, tripped over his trousers and fell in a heap on the cobbles. His friend immediately commenced pissing himself with laughter.

Logan stepped into the alley. The friend was now doubled up, as Fat Boy tried valiantly to scrabble to his feet – vast, white, hairy arse first. 'Kylie' watched all this with unfocused indifference, scratching away at the crook of her left arm, the one with the cigarette burns and needle tracks. Logan walked right up to her. She stared through his shoulder for a moment, before swaying her eyes up to his face and smiling. 'You want make fuck now? You police: I do for free . . .'

'Why don't you and me go for a walk and a chat?'

She grinned. 'I talk dirty good!'

'Yeah, I know: you told me that before, remember?' He took hold of her arm and steered her back towards the street, provoking a cry of protest from the bloke with his trousers round his ankles. Apparently Logan was jumping the queue. 'She's fourteen,' Logan replied, 'and I'm CID. Want to see me arresting you for child abuse?' The big man yanked his trousers up and mumbled something about having kids himself and wasn't it terrible and he never meant anything by it and he *really* didn't know she was fourteen . . .

Beneath the streetlights Logan got his first good look at her. Sometime in the last week she'd managed to break her nose. 'What happened to your face?'

Kylie shrugged. 'Steve – he get angry. I tell him rain bad for business, but he say I not make enough money.'

'You look like you haven't eaten for a week.'

She shook her head, staggering a little as they walked up the side of the Citadel and into the Castlegate. 'I eat Happy Meal. Steve good to me.'

Yeah, thought Logan, good old 'Steve'. 'Come on, I'll buy you some chips.'

The queue was longer than usual, the drunk and the not-so-drunk waiting patiently for their turn to order smoked sausage supper and a mealie pudding, beneath the silent, flickering glare of a television set up above the till. Logan and Kylie slowly shuffled their way around the little chicane in the middle of the shop to encourage orderly queuing, with the Lithuanian explaining why Edinburgh chip shops were much better than the ones in Aberdeen because they did salt and sauce, not just salt and vinegar. They'd finally made it as far as the long stainless-steel-and-glass bunker – where the deep-fried bits and pieces went to die – when Kylie pointed up at the silent TV screen and squealed with delight. 'I make fuck with him!'

Blushing, but unable to help himself, Logan looked up to see the smug, slimy face of Councillor Andrew Marshall. 'You sure?' he hissed, not wanting to draw any more attention than they already had.

She nodded. 'At private party, when I come Aberdeen first, him and bald friend both at same time. "Spit roast", is right? When bald man in mouth and other man is up—'

Logan didn't need to hear any more; given the Councillor's taste in magazines it was pretty clear where he would have been. He paid for their chips and walked her across the road to eat them. She was so engrossed she didn't even notice they'd walked all the way around the Arts Centre and were heading up the ramp onto the rear podium. In fact it wasn't until Alpha Six Two honked its horn to get past that she suddenly realized where she was: Grampian Police Force Headquarters. Screaming curses in Lithuanian she hurled her remaining chips at Logan and turned to run, but he grabbed her by the scruff of the neck and dragged her, kicking and screaming, into the building.

Half an hour later Logan jumped into DI Steel's CID pool car and handed the inspector a white pudding supper, with the obligatory pickled egg.

'Where the hell have you been? I've been waiting bloody ages!'

Logan grinned and sank down in the driver's seat. 'Oh, here and there.'

'What?' she said, chewing suspiciously on a handful of chips. 'What's so damn funny?'

'I just picked up a prostitute.'

'Oh aye?' She picked up her white pudding and ripped a bite out of it, chewing round the words. 'What's the matter, WPC Watson not dirty enough for you, 'cos I can—'

He didn't let her finish. 'A fourteen-year-old Lithuanian prostitute to be precise. Called Kylie.' This got a blank look. 'Saw Jamie McKinnon having sex with Rosie Williams the night she was murdered?'

Steel groaned and shovelled in another handful of chips. 'What fucking good is that to me?' Bits of chewed potato were falling onto her blouse. 'Bastard already admitted shagging her. And if it was the same guy who killed Rosie and Michelle Wood, then it doesn't matter *who* saw McKinnon there.'

'But just in case – it puts him at the scene. We

don't have any evidence remember? You destroyed . . .' He stopped when he saw the expression on the inspector's face. 'I mean, the tape machine wasn't working.'

'And you'd better fucking remember that.'

'There's something else, if you're interested?' He smiled and let the question hang as Steel took another huge bite out of her white pudding. As if she was trying to castrate the thing. 'This fourteen-year-old girl says Councillor Marshall's shagged her up the arse while she was sucking someone else's dick.'

There was a sudden explosion of half-chewed white pudding coating the inside of the windscreen while DI Steel choked.

Logan winked. 'Thought you'd like that.'

21

Thursday started much like any other day, unfortunately. Not enough sleep and what little he'd managed to grab after Operation Cinderella packed up for the night was riddled with dreams of dead children, damp and rotten, the flesh falling from their bones as they skipped and danced through his flat, their eyes like runny-yolked eggs. No wonder he felt dreadful. He was definitely going to check up on PC Maitland today. Pop past and see how he was doing. Offload a bit of the guilt.

DI Steel was in the incident room, speaking to DI Insch and fiddling with a pack of cigarettes. Logan was too tired to bother listening in, so he slouched over to his desk instead and tried to figure out what he was going to do about Steel. She'd told him in no uncertain terms that he was to have nothing more to do with Kylie – she'd be taking over the underage sex thing personally. And if he breathed a word of it to anyone she'd have his balls.

There was a plastic bag full of videotapes sitting on Logan's desk, each one bearing a sticky label with 'OPERATION CINDERELLA NIGHT 2' scribbled on it, and next to that a big Manila folder: the criminal records of one Chib Sutherland. Sighing, Logan got himself a mug of coffee and started to read.

Chib was every bit as lovely as Colin Miller had implied. Most of his formative years were spent in borstal for knifing some attendant at the children's home he was staying in, then on to a serious life of violent crime. Right up to the time he started working for that great philanthropist, Malcolm McLennan – AKA Malk the Knife. He'd taken the boy in and moulded him in his own image: a vicious wee thug who wouldn't get caught any more. According to Lothian and Borders he was in the frame for at least eight murders, though there was never enough hard evidence to do him for any of them. But people had gone missing, never to be seen again. Then there were the bodies that *had* been found, battered and mutilated. Everyone knew Chib was responsible; there just wasn't any way to prove it. Not when any witnesses were so conveniently struck down with amnesia, or a cricket bat.

'Hoy, Lazarus.' Logan looked up to see DI Steel hovering over the desk, smiling at him with yellowed teeth. 'Good news,' she said, 'in a crappy sort of way. Seems like the big boys down south have decided to lend little old Grampian Police a helping hand. Isn't that just fucking swell?' When Logan didn't answer she slapped a couple of sheets of A4 on top of the report he was reading. 'They've sent us up a preliminary psychological offender profile! Wow! According to Insch, you've already worked with the specky-four-eyed git who wrote it, so guess what?' The inspector beamed and punched him on the shoulder. 'You have "experience". I want to know what all the shite in that report means, and – more importantly – if any of it's worth the paper it's written on. And don't take too long: Mr Clinical Psychologist is on his way up the road as we speak. I want some sort of synopsis before he gets here at eleven.' Logan tried not to groan. Instead he poked the plastic bag full of videotapes and asked the inspector what she expected him to do with them all. 'I don't bloody care, do I,' she said. 'Take them home and record over them if you like, it's not like we're ever going to watch the bloody things anyway.' She stopped, halfway to the door. 'Oh, and don't forget what we talked about last night.' The threat was implicit: *tell anyone and you're screwed*.

Dr Bushel was exactly as Logan remembered: arrogant, self-satisfied, balding and immaculately dressed. The strip lights sparkled off his little round glasses as he stood at the front of the briefing room taking a select group of Grampian's finest through his psychological profile for their potential serial killer. There wasn't anything here that Logan hadn't already told DI Steel after reading the report, but it was all new to the Assistant Chief Constable, the deputy CC, and the head of CID. The killer would be white, male, in his mid to late twenties, have intimacy issues, and have used a prostitute before, but found it a humiliating experience. The beating was a sign of his hatred towards women, the intensity of his rage acting as a pointer to buried conflict with his mother. He would have a menial job, but be articulate enough to lure Michelle Wood into his car. Socially adequate. He took his victims' clothes, not as a trophy, but because he wanted to humiliate them. And possibly for some sort of masturbatory fantasy. He would strike again.

Once the doctor had finished his presentation, DI Steel started asking the questions Logan had raised in private earlier, framing each one as if she was pulling it out of the blue, thinking on her feet. Putting on a show for the senior brass while Logan sat and fumed in disgust.

Dr Bushel hummed and hawed and speculated and theorized, but it all sounded like bollocks to Logan. The man had come up with a vague outline based on next to no evidence, having never seen either of the crime scenes at first hand. Logan couldn't see how any of it was going to help them actually catch the killer.

The ACC thanked Dr Bushel for his time and invited him to a special lunch with the Chief Constable later. When they were all gone, DI Steel slouched in her seat and blew a long, wet raspberry. 'Did you ever hear so much shite in your life? "He will strike again!" Course he bloody will, he's got away with it twice, what's he going to do, call it quits and take up needlepoint instead?' She shook her head, scratching away at her left armpit. 'And I'll bet Bushel gets paid *twice* as much as we do. Specky git.'

Logan scowled. 'So how come you played up to it then?'

'Ah . . . politics, Sergeant. When the top brass hand you a turd, you polish it and say, "my, what a lovely jobbie!" That way they are impressed by your intellect, perception and ability. If you don't, all you've got is a handful of shit. Come on, we've got more important things to do than sod about here. We've a killer to catch.'

It was just after lunch when Logan finally got a result from his lookout request on Skanky Agnes, though it wasn't the one he'd been hoping for. A WPC, over at Aberdeen Royal Infirmary visiting her mother in intensive care, had spotted Agnes Walker lying on a bed in the corner, tubes going in and out of every orifice. She'd been mainlining heroin while pissed out of her face on supermarket vodka – the perfect recipe for an overdose. An unemployed receptionist discovered her slumped in the ladies' toilets at the Trinity shopping centre. She lapsed into cardiac arrest in the ambulance and had been in a coma ever since. DI Steel sent a WPC up to sit by her bedside, just in case she made a miraculous recovery and decided to give them a description of whoever had beaten her up. They weren't holding their breath.

So instead of charging off to save the day, Logan was stuck wading through the list of known sex offenders in an attempt to match one of them to Dr Bushel's ridiculously vague offender profile. It was too noisy in the incident room, so Logan grabbed his piles of paperwork and went looking for somewhere quieter. All the other offices were busy, but interview room four was free. He annexed it, flicking the switch that changed the light outside from green to red: INTERVIEW IN PROGRESS, before spreading out the files and printouts on the battered tabletop. Trying to find a killer in amongst the rapists, paedophiles and flashers. Even with the window open it was too hot in here – Logan loosened his tie, yawned, rested his elbows on the table and propped his head up with his hands. Slowly the words started blurring into each other. Blink. Rapist. Blink. Rapist. Nod . . . blink. Paedophile. Yawn. Blink, blink . . . darkness.

'Mmmphf . . . ?' Logan snapped upright, eyes wide and dilated, what the hell was – he dragged his mobile out, wiping the small trail of drool from the side of his mouth with his other hand. Blink, blink. The clock on the interview-room wall said seven minutes past five: he'd been asleep for three whole hours. 'Hello?' trying not to sound like he'd just woken up. It was DI Insch.

Mrs Kennedy's lounge was a disaster area: chairs and tables overturned, paintings slashed, photo frames smashed, china poodles reduced to glittering shards on the carpet. Mrs Kennedy sat in a ruptured armchair, fat orange cat clutched to her bosom like a security blanket. It eyed the detectives standing in the middle of the room with evil distrust, yellow eyes narrowed to slits, ears back.

'Honestly,' said the old lady, shaking. 'I don't want to cause any fuss, I'm fine. Really . . .' She'd been out at the time, but the downstairs neighbour had heard the destruction and called 999. They couldn't bear to think of poor old Mrs Kennedy lying up there in a pool of blood, battered to death! They were basically well meaning, but no bloody help whatsoever. They didn't see anything, didn't peer out the spy hole in their door to watch the bad guys come down the stairs. Didn't even look out the window to see if they got into a waiting car, or a bus, or a taxi, or clambered aboard a passing elephant. They were scared someone would see them looking. It was a pain in the arse, but Logan could understand their reticence. They were in their seventies, why risk being seen by violent thugs who might come back and get them? Instead they'd kept their heads down and called the police. It was still more than a lot of people would do.

Whoever the vandals were, they'd done a pretty good job of bankrupting Mrs Kennedy's insurance company. The lounge, kitchen, and both bedrooms had been thoroughly trashed. But there was something odd in the lounge, something that seemed a bit out of place amidst all the devastation. Smack bang in the middle of the far wall the words 'STOP NOW' had been scrawled in dripping, fluorescent orange paint. 'Any idea what it is they want you to stop doing?' asked Logan, pointing at the bright, spray-painted letters.

Mrs Kennedy shook her head and hugged the cat even tighter, causing it to wriggle. 'I . . . I help organize a youth club for local youngsters? Up at the school? We have football matches and jumble sales . . .'

'Hmm,' said Insch. 'Well unless you're caught in the middle of a turf war between the Boy Scouts and the Girl Guides, I think we can rule that out. Anything else?'

'I still tutor some children. Since I had to retire I sometimes think it's the only thing that keeps me going.'

'Oh aye?' Insch was poking about in the remains of a large china dog with his shoe. 'Piano? French?'

'Chemistry. I was a chemistry teacher for thirty-six years.' She smiled, eyes misty with recollection. 'I taught thousands and thousands of children in my time.' She sighed. 'And now all I have is this . . .' DI Insch made his excuses as the tears started, but Logan decided to do the decent thing and make her a cup of tea. The kettle was dented, but otherwise functional, so he set it to boil and went hunting for some teabags. They were scattered all over the floor by the upended bin, mingling with broken eggshells, potato peelings and other debris. He found one that didn't look too unhygienic – after all it was going to get boiling water poured over it – and plopped it in a mug that still had its handle attached. While the bag was stewing, Logan rummaged about, looking for milk and sugar. He found it in the fridge: a large, clear plastic bag of something that looked like fresh herbs, only not so wholesome.

The sound of footsteps crunching on debris and Logan spun around to see Mrs Kennedy standing there, *sans* cat. Hands clenching and unclenching, she watched aghast as he stood up, holding the bag of 'herbs'. Logan popped open the zip-lock top and took a tentative sniff at the contents.

'I . . . I can explain . . .' she said, voice low, eyes darting down the hall where a uniformed PC was writing down details of the damage on a large clipboard. 'It's for my arthritis . . .' She held up her trembling hands. 'And my sciatica.'

'Where do you get it from?'

'I . . . an ex-pupil of mine. He said it had helped his father. He brings me some every now and then.'

'There's a lot here,' he said, shaking the bag. 'All for your own use?'

'Please believe me.' The tears were starting again. 'It makes the pain go away: I never meant to break the law!'

Logan stood watching her as thick tears rolled down her cheeks, a thin dribble of snot starting on its way south from her nose. She fumbled a handkerchief from her pocket and he stared at her hands: swollen joints, squint fingers, just like his grandmother's had been for the last fifteen years of her life. 'OK,' he said at last, popping the bag back in the fridge and closing the door. 'I won't tell anyone if you don't.' He let himself out. STOP NOW: a funny thing to scrawl on an old lady's wall. Esoteric. Probably made perfect sense to whatever drug-addled halfwit scrawled it up there. But still . . .

The sky was a dirty dove-grey as Logan stepped out of the front door. The white and orange of the patrol car had attracted the same audience as last time: a trio of small children, all watching the policemen with awe. It must be just like having the telly come to life, right outside your house. Who knew what sort of exciting things you could see . . .

Logan crossed the road and walked up the steps to the little cluster of kids, dropping down on his haunches so he wouldn't tower over them. Two little boys, four or fiveish with snotty noses, wide blue eyes and bowl haircuts, and a little girl in a stroller. She couldn't have been more than two and a bit: frizzy blonde hair done up in pigtails, teddy bear clutched in one hand, sucking her thumb and looking up at Logan like he was a hundred feet tall. 'Hello,' he said, in his best non-threatening voice, 'my name's Logan. I'm a policeman.' He pulled out his warrant card and let one of the bowl haircuts handle it with grubby fingers. 'Were you here earlier?'

The little girl pulled her thumb out, a long trail of spittle stretching from lips to finger before falling onto teddy's nose. 'Man.'

'Did you see a man?'

She pointed a dribble-covered finger at him. 'Man.' Then held the bear up, so he could see that she'd chewed most of the fur off one ear, and said 'Man' again. Logan's smile began to falter. Maybe this wasn't such a good idea after all.

DI Insch sat behind the wheel of his filthy Range Rover, peering out through the windscreen as the first flecks of moisture gave way to a steady down-pour. 'So much for a sodding barbecue tonight,' he said as Logan leapt into the passenger seat and out of the rain. 'How'd you get on with the Grampian Police Fan Club?'

Logan sighed and tried to wipe sticky finger-prints off his warrant card. 'Tom's doggy did "big ones" in daddy's slippers last night and had to sleep in the toilet. Other than that: bugger all.' He glanced up at the building and saw Mrs Kennedy's scared face staring down from the kitchen window. Probably terrified he was going to tell the inspector her dirty little secret. He turned to see the three children staring at him as well.

'Do you think it's odd the same kids are always hanging around?'

Now it was Insch's turn to stare at him. 'Ever occur to you that they might actually *live* here?'

'OK, point taken.' Logan pulled on his seatbelt. 'So how come you dragged me over here to see this?' he asked as the inspector did a three-point turn on Union Grove and headed back towards the Holburn Street junction. 'Come to that: what are *you* doing here? Breaking and entering not a job for uniform?'

Insch shrugged and told Logan to look in the glove compartment, which revealed an old packet of sherbet lemons, the yellow lozenges gluey from sitting in the car for God knew how long. The inspector clutched the bag to the steering wheel with one hand while he dug about in the sticky packet with the other, eventually emerging with a lump of three or four, all welded together. He stuffed them in his mouth and sucked his fingers clean, before offering the bag to Logan, who politely declined. 'I suppose,' said Insch around a mouthful of boiled sweets as he forced his way into the stream of traffic, 'I was thinking there might be a connection – you know, with her grandson dying in the fire. And we've still got bugger all to go on with Karl Pearson. Someone tortures the hell out of the ugly wee toe-rag and all we can do is cart him off to the morgue and carve him up some more.' He sighed and Logan got the distinct impression that once again Grampian Police's left hand didn't know if the right one was scratching its elbow or picking its arse.

'Did DI Steel not tell you about Brendan "Chib" Sutherland?'

Insch said that no, she hadn't, so Logan filled him in on the way back to the station, including Colin Miller's promise to find an address for the Edinburgh hoodlum.

'How come we've got to rely on that Weegie shitebag? No, on second thoughts, don't tell me. I don't want to know. But when you get that address, you tell me. I'm not leaving that daft old cow . . .' He threw a swift glance at Logan and harrumphed. 'I mean, DI Steel has enough on her plate right now. I wouldn't want her to be distracted going after something that wasn't directly related to her investigation.'

Logan grinned and kept his mouth shut.

That night's stakeout operation was nearly cancelled. The rain had steadily built in tempo until it was chucking it down, bouncing off the pavements and swallowing the gutters. Faint light flickered overhead, followed by a pause: one, two, three, four – thunder boomed out across the blackened skies. 'Four miles away,' said the inspector, settling back in her seat with one of Councillor Marshall's specialist insertion magazines.

Logan shook his head. 'It's less than a mile. Sound travels at seven hundred and fifty miles an hour, so that means . . .' he trailed off into silence. Steel was glowering at him.

'Four miles away!' she said again and went back to looking at the dirty pictures by the light of the glove compartment. Occasionally saying things like, 'Jesus, that's not natural!' and, 'Ouch!' and once or twice, 'Hmmm . . .' Logan scrunched down in the driver's seat and peered out through the windscreen. WPC Menzies was swearing and grumbling down at the other end of Shore Lane, shifting from one stiletto-heeled foot to the other, trying to keep warm. In the interests of health and safety, she was wearing a long fur coat from the lost-and-found store over her whore outfit tonight. Clutching an umbrella.

Her voice crackled through the radio. *'This is ridiculous! Nae bastard's going tae come oot here in this pishin' weather!'* Sounds of agreement immediately came through from WPC Davidson: it was nearly midnight and they'd not had a single bite. This was a waste of everyone's time. Logan had to agree they had a point. But the inspector was not for turning, they'd been given sanction to keep this going for five nights and she was damned if they were giving up before then. In the end everyone settled back into unhappy perseverance. Steel snored, WPCs Menzies and Davidson whinged and moaned, Logan brooded. This was such a stupid idea – twenty-six police men and women, sitting in the dark, waiting for some sicko to abduct an unattractive WPC wouldn't prove anything. He might as well strip down to his underpants and run around the docks in the rain for all the good it would do.

DI Steel had settled into a steady buzz-saw-in-a-washing-machine drone, one of Councillor Marshall's dirty magazines open in her lap, spot-lit by the open glove compartment, exposing something Logan did not want to see. He leaned over the inspector and snapped the glove compartment shut.

'Umn, scrrrrrrnch, emph?' Steel cracked open an eye and peered blearily at him leaning across her. 'Dirty wee shite. I'm no' fuckin' . . .' She drifted to a halt and yawned, the motion ending with a small burp. 'What time is it?'

'Half twelve,' said Logan, rolling the window down, letting some fresh air into the car, bringing the steady roar of torrential rain with it. Steel gave another yawn, stretching and groaning in the passenger seat as Logan finally decided to take the plunge: 'Why don't you want Councillor Marshall prosecuted?'

'Hmm?' She peeled the plastic wrapper off a pack of twenty cigarettes, throwing it over her shoulder into the rubbish-tip back seat. ''Cos you can catch more flies with shite than vinegar. You look out there,' she said, setting a lighter to the end of her cigarette, 'and you see guilty or not guilty, yeah? Black or white. Well sometimes it's no' that clear cut—'

'He was paying a fourteen-year-old girl for sex!'

'Didn't know she was fourteen though, did he?'

He couldn't believe what he was hearing, 'Does it *matter*?'

'See – there you go again, black or white. It pays to have people in your debt, Logan, especially people who . . .' She stopped, peering out into the night. There was a figure walking down Marischal Street, dressed in a featureless ankle-length raincoat buttoned all the way up to the neck. Bald as a coot, clutching an umbrella, the black surface shrouded in mist as the rain hurled itself towards the ground. Detective Inspector Insch.

'Hoy, hoy,' said Steel, 'it's Uncle Fester.'

DI Insch marched slowly across the road and around the car to Logan's side. Something congealed in Logan's innards as he looked up into the inspector's impassive face. Insch's voice was like a graveyard. 'It's Constable Maitland,' he said, and suddenly Logan could hear each and every drop of rain. 'He's dead.'

22

Flames reached up to the sky, devouring wood and plastic, paper and flesh. The blaze crackled and sparked in the rainy night – the downpour doing nothing to quench its hunger. He'd put *way* too much petrol through the letterbox for that. His very own makeshift crematorium.

The location was perfect: a little winding road down by the river in the south of the city. High stone walls on one side – keeping the lowlife out of some sort of hotel grounds – scattered, detached houses on the other. Secluded enough to stop the alarm being raised too soon, and with plenty of cover for him to hide in and watch the place burn. And even if someone did raise the alarm, the fire engines were busy elsewhere.

He knew he shouldn't be here. Not so soon after the other fire. He knew he would get in trouble for this one, but he just couldn't help himself. Standing in the shadows, on the other side of the road, he grimaced, pounding away at his erection as the upstairs windows exploded outwards in a shower of glass.

God, this was beautiful.

The screaming had lasted for ten whole minutes. Four petrol bombs in through the bedroom windows. Someone had even braved the inferno in the hallway, hammering frantically against the front door, not knowing he'd screwed it shut, just like the one round the back. He bit his bottom lip, imagining their flesh crackling and popping in the heat. Flames raging downstairs, flames raging upstairs. Nowhere to run. All they could do was die. He grunted and shuddered . . . squeezing tighter, trying to make it last, but it was too late. He threw back his head and moaned in ecstasy as the roof finally gave way, sending an eruption of orange and white sparks spiralling up into the night. Then the fire brigade arrived – charging about with their ladders and their hoses, but it was far too late for the family of four charring away beneath the burning rubble.

He really shouldn't have burned the house; he was bound to get in trouble.

But right now, he just didn't care.

Seven forty-five, Friday morning, tired, bleary and hung-over. It hadn't been a good night for Logan; DI Steel had sent him home early, where he'd made friends with a bottle of twelve-year-old single malt whisky. Getting drunk and maudlin and thoroughly depressed. One minute PC Maitland was lying there in his persistent vegetative state, and the next he was gone. DI Insch had told Logan not to worry: it was dreadful, but these things happened. It wasn't his fault. It would all blow over. And when the inspector had gone, marching back up the road in the rain, DI Steel told him that Insch was talking bollocks. This was a perfect opportunity for the slimy bastards to crawl out of the woodwork and stab him in the back.

The summons from Inspector Napier had been waiting for him when he got into work first thing this morning.

So here he was, sitting outside Professional Standards, feeling sick, stomach churning away as he waited for Napier to call him into the Office of Doom. Right on cue the inspector stuck his pointy face around the door and beckoned Logan inside. This time the room was crowded. In addition to Logan, Napier and the silent, unnamed inspector in the corner, Big Gary was sitting in one of the uncomfortable visitors' chairs, his huge frame making the plastic buckle alarmingly. He looked up and nodded as Logan entered. This was it then. He was in real trouble this time.

'Sergeant McRae,' said Napier, settling down behind his pristine desk. 'As you can see, I have asked your Federation representative to attend this meeting.' He threw a cold smile in Big Gary's direction. 'But before we start I'd just like to say how saddened we all are at the news of PC Maitland's untimely death. He was a good officer and will be greatly missed by his colleagues and friends. Our thoughts and prayers go out to his wife and . . .' Napier peered down at a sheet of paper on his desktop. 'Daughter.'

And then Logan had to go through the bungled raid again, while Napier nodded gravely and Big Gary took notes. 'Of course,' said Napier when Logan had finished, 'you realize that we have been lucky with the timing of this.' He held up a copy of that morning's *Press and Journal*. The headline FATAL FIRE KILLS FOUR! was stretched across the front page above a photo of a ruined house, still burning in the darkness with fire engines clustered outside. 'This arson story has far more public appeal. Also, the papers didn't get wind of Constable Maitland's untimely death until after their second editions had run. Naturally we can expect "prominent citizens" like Councillor Marshall . . .' the name came out sounding like a disease from Napier's lips, 'to make their feelings known on the subject.'

Logan suppressed a groan. That pompous, slimy wee pervert would have a field day.

'Of course, the internal enquiry now has to take into account the fact that an officer *died* during the operation you organized, resourced and led,' said Napier, probably loving every minute of this. 'If you are found to have been negligent, you can expect a reduction in rank and possible expulsion from the force. Criminal charges cannot be ruled out.'

Big Gary sat forward in his beleaguered plastic seat and frowned. 'I think it's a wee bit premature to be talking about criminal charges, don't you? Sergeant McRae's no' been found guilty of anything.' The silent inspector in the corner twitched.

Napier held up his hands. 'Of course, of course. I apologize. Your Federation representative is quite correct: innocent until proven guilty and so forth.' He stood and opened the door. 'A date for the enquiry will be set later today. Please feel free to drop in should you wish to discuss things further.'

Interview room number six was vacant, so Big Gary commandeered it, dragging Logan in for a pep talk. Screw Napier. Logan hadn't done anything wrong, had he? No. So there was nothing to worry about: the internal enquiry would come back negative, they'd all have a big touchy-feely lessons-learned exercise, and everyone would get on with their lives. Everyone, thought Logan, except for Constable Maitland.

When Big Gary was gone, Logan slumped back in his chair and scowled at the ceiling tiles. Bloody Napier and his bloody witch hunt, as if he didn't already feel guilty enough about Maitland being dead! Any excuse to belittle, or threaten, or condescend and there was Napier, ready to stick the knife in and twist. And where the hell did he get off telling Logan to make sure Steel wasn't screwed over by the press? Bloody Steel and her bloody sarcasm and her bloody 'everything's not black and white' like he was some sort of school kid! Protect *her* from the press? It'd be Logan getting a roasting off that smug, sanctimonious, child-molesting pervert Marshall, not DI Steel. No, *she* had him eating out of the palm of her nicotine-stained hand . . . Fine, you know what: two could play at that game. Logan yanked his phone out, dialled Control, and asked for a contact number for Councillor Andrew Marshall. It took him three minutes to get past Marshall's personal assistant, but finally the man's familiar voice oiled imperiously out of the phone, *'Is this important? I have a chamber meeting in five minutes.'*

Logan smiled. 'Just a quick question, Councillor: does the name "Kylie" mean anything to you?' There was silence on the other end of the phone. 'No? Young Lithuanian prostitute, claims to have been sexually intimate with you and a friend of yours last month. At the same time.'

A bit of stammering, and then, *'Sexually intimate?'*

'Well, the exact term she used was "spit roast". I believe you took the back end?'

'I . . . I don't know what you're talking about.'

'We've got her in custody: she identified your picture. Did you know she was only fourteen?'

'Oh God . . .' There was a long pause. *'What do you want? Money? That's it isn't it – it's what you people* always *want! Why can't you all just leave me alone?'*

Logan smiled. He'd always suspected DI Steel

was on the take. 'So someone's already black-mailing you for having anal sex with a fourteen-year-old girl?'

'Oh God this is a nightmare . . . I never knew she was fourteen till he told me afterwards! I swear! I wouldn't have touched her if I'd known!' He was starting to panic.

The smile froze on Logan's face. 'Till *he* told you? Who's *he*?'

'It . . . I . . . I don't know his name. I just got a letter and a photo of me . . . of the three of us . . . together. I didn't know she was fourteen!' He was getting louder and louder, and Logan wondered if Marshall had been bright enough to close his office door, other-wise the whole council would know about his little 'indiscretion' by lunchtime.

'I want your friend's name, Councillor, the one on the other end of your underaged rotisserie.'

A pause, then another gulp. *'He . . . You're going to blackmail him as well, aren't you?'*

'I want his name.'

It was John Nicholas, the council's Chief Greenbelt Development Planner. Feeling pretty pleased with himself, Logan hung up. An under-aged Lithuanian prostitute up from Edinburgh has sex with the guy responsible for deciding what can and can't be built outside the city, photos are taken, threats are made, and all of a sudden Malk the Knife's property development company has permission to put up a stack of new homes on greenbelt? If it was a coincidence it was a bloody unlikely one. And as Brendan 'Chib' Sutherland was Malkie's fixer, he was probably responsible for McLennan Homes' sudden turn of good luck. Something else to ask him about, presuming Colin Miller ever managed to dig up an address.

It didn't take long for the news of PC Maitland's death to get out – the first call from the media came at nine on the dot, putting an end to Logan's good mood. The press office issued a statement that was much the same as Napier's: PC Maitland was a fine officer and would be missed by his colleagues, blah, blah, blah. By the time PC Steve stuck his head around the incident-room door and asked if Logan had a minute, almost every news organization in the country had been on the phone.

'Been another fire,' said PC Steve, holding up a copy of the P&J.

'I know, Napier showed me this morning.'

PC Steve raised an eyebrow. 'You seen Dracula? How come . . .' and then he ground to a halt as he remembered. Maitland's death was all over the station. Coming into work this morning had been like walking into a silent movie; all conversation stopped as soon as Logan entered a room. 'Aye, well,' said the constable, blushing slightly. 'Inspector Insch wants you to join him up at the scene. Says you're to come do your morbid bit.'

Logan didn't bother clearing it with Steel first.

* * *

The scene of the fire wasn't hard to spot amongst the restrained bucolic splendour of Inchgarth Road. The rain had drifted away, leaving the trees and bushes a verdant green, glowing in the warm, golden light of a hazy sun. Down here, the city fought an awkward battle with the countryside, allotments and farmland mingling with council housing estates and expensive private homes. Gritty, soot-coloured dirt made a slick across the road surface, clogging the drain and leaving a shallow lake on the tarmac. What was left of the house hulked at the end of a short gravel drive, one end wall caved in, spilling bricks and mortar across the debris. A dirty white Transit Van was parked next to a scorched rose bush, along with a grimy police pod, people in white paper boiler suits drifting back and forth, taking samples and photographs. It was cramped in the pod, but there was just enough room for Logan and Steve to change into their scene-of-crime outfits while someone boiled the kettle for a brunch Pot Noodle. And then it was back out into the garden.

The firemen had battered the front door down, which can't have been an easy task: the frame was peppered with three-inch wood screws, just like last time. That was all they needed, another serial nut job. The part-glazed door lay on its back in the middle of the hall, half buried under a pile of broken roof tiles and charcoaled timbers.

Inside, the upper floor was gone, just the occasional beam marking the level where a whole family had died. The remaining walls were blackened and scorched. Rubble filled the corridor along with the twisted remains of the staircase.

Insch was in what would have been the lounge, dressed in a straining white paper over suit, balancing on top of a mound of rubble while a man in grimy overalls and a fire brigade hard hat poked about with a long pole. Teetering over fallen bricks and lumps of charred wood, Logan joined the inspector. 'You wanted to see me, sir?'

'Did I?' Insch frowned. 'Oh, yes. Family of four: mother, father and two little girls. Fire investigators say petrol was poured in through the letterbox, followed by petrol bombs through the windows. Sound familiar? Whoever did it made four hoax calls from a stolen mobile phone, every one of them on the other side of the city. By the time the fire brigade got here it was all they could do to stop it spreading next door.' He shook his head and picked his way down the mound of debris to the blasted remains of the front window. 'Poor bastards didn't have a chance. I was beginning to think the last fire – the squat – was drugs-related, but this feels more . . . I don't know, personal, if that makes sense.' He sighed and ran a hand across his round, red features. 'I can't get it to match up. That's why I want you to take a look: fresh pair of eyes.'

Logan nodded. 'They found the bodies?'

'Bits of them . . . Seems the girls' bedroom was above the kitchen. When the roof caved in, the whole lot collapsed. Best guess the mother and father were in there with them. We won't know till we get the room emptied.'

Logan picked his way through the remains of the house, moving from room to room, taking in the devastation. There wasn't much left he could recognize, everything had burnt or melted, the only thing even vaguely intact was the battered front door, still lying where it had fallen, the paintwork blistered and peeling, the glass panes cracked and nearly opaque with soot. He stood staring down at it – the only thing to survive a fire that claimed four lives. There was a little brass plaque on the door, just above the letterbox, and he squatted down, brushing away the dirt and debris until he could read it: ANDREW, WENDY, JOANNA & MOLLY LAWSON. The only thing missing was REST IN PEACE. He was just turning to leave, when he thought he saw something through the door's firedamaged glass. Heart hammering in his ears, he wrapped his hands round the edge of the door and pulled, the wood creaking and groaning as it came free of the debris, sending roof tiles clattering to the brick-strewn floor. Underneath, part buried in bits of ceiling, was a burnt human face, features gone, ochre teeth the only really identifiable feature, the skull flattened on one side by a chunk of fallen masonry. Logan's hung-over stomach lurched.

When he called for help, DI Insch came lumbering through, took one look at what Logan was pointing at, frowned, then the swearing started. 'Every bastard and their dog's been through here!' He shouted for the bloke from the fire brigade, demanding to know why the hell no one had found this sooner? While they were arguing over whose responsibility it was to make sure people didn't go traipsing over dead bodies, Logan lurched across the threshold and out into the real world again.

The sun was still shining, but the air was full of the stench of burning meat and roasting timbers. Closing his eyes, Logan tried to take a deep breath. He wasn't going to be sick, he wasn't going to be sick – charred women and children, battered prostitutes, the skinned face of a young woman, rotting animal carcasses, Maitland . . . He *was* going to be sick. Logan managed a few slow steps in the direction of the garden wall before abandoning all pretence and sprinting for the safety of a large purple buddleia, ripping his mask aside, falling to his knees and retching behind the bush. When there wasn't even any bile left, his stomach aching from the effort, he shivered to his feet, wiping the strings of bitter spit from his mouth with the sleeve of his jumpsuit. Please God let no one have seen him puking in the bushes . . . He cast a quick glance around, but everyone was going about their business, getting on with the job like he was supposed to be.

Standing on the flattened grass, looking up at the ruined building, he tried not to think about the faces of the dead. The fire at the squat, where six people died, had been a spectator sport, he was sure of it. One man out there in a darkness all his own, turning human beings into charred corpses while he played with himself in the shadows. He would want a good view of proceedings. Preferably close enough to hear their flesh pop and sizzle. Logan started a tour of the garden, looking for the perfect position from which to watch a family of four burn, somewhere that wouldn't become a trap if the fire brigade turned up earlier than expected. There wasn't one. He did a slow three hundred and sixty degree turn. There was a hotel driveway across the road, the entrance marked by rusting lanterns set into the eight-foot-high stone wall. It would be the only place with a really good line of sight.

Still dressed in his white boiler suit, surgical gloves and booties, he sloshed through the puddle of soot-coloured water and into the hotel's grounds. You *could* lurk behind the granite posts, peering round the corner and hoping no one looked in your direction while you were busy having a wank, but that would probably spoil the romantic atmosphere . . . There was a huge rhododendron bush six feet in from the entrance. Perfect: if anyone looked, all they'd see were leaves and shadow. Logan walked through the wet grass to the rhododendron, peering under the fringe of dark green, waxy leaves. The flower heads were dying back, their delicate scarlet blooms battered away by last night's rain, lying like flecks of blood on the grass. There was a clear footprint in the mud, just inside the bush.

The manager of the hotel was a little concerned about the effect a blue plastic scene-of-crime marquee was having on his guests. It was bad enough that the road had been blocked off since last night, but to have a bunch of people wandering around the hotel grounds like something off the television was just . . . Well, he wasn't quite sure what it was, but he did send a nice young man out with a huge thermos of tea, another of coffee and a platter of Danish pastries. Much to DI Insch's delight.

Things were looking up. The leaves hadn't just kept their arsonist dry while he played with himself, they'd also helped preserve any evidence he'd left at the scene. In addition to the footprint, they'd also discovered another disposable paper handkerchief, smelling of semen. And the Identification Bureau were swarming all over the inside of the rhododendron, looking for fibres, traces, fingerprints, anything.

Insch was happily finishing off a third pastry from the tray when a patrol car pulled up outside the burnt-out shell opposite and a familiar bald-headed clinical psychologist stepped out. Hands behind his back, he strolled around the house's garden, peering at things.

'Oh joy,' said Insch, brushing the crumbs from

his chin. 'You want to deal with Professor Patronizing, or shall I?' In the end they both sloshed back over the road. They found Dr Bushel squatting over a large white plastic sheet with four open body-bags laid out on it. There were bits of person arranged in each. A scorched femur, a blackened clavicle, the body they'd discovered under the front door, a lump of burnt meat that had once been a child's torso . . . Logan's empty stomach gave a warning lurch. The doctor smiled up at them as they approached, the sunlight glinting off his little round glasses.

'Inspector, Sergeant, nice to see you again,' he said, pulling himself to his feet. 'Lucky I was here, don't you think? The Chief Constable has asked me to produce a profile of your arsonist. It will take a little while to write up, but I can certainly give you the gist of it now, if you're interested?' Clearly a rhetorical question. 'The psychological pathology of the offender is very clearly one of hatred. The preparation, screwing the door shut, pouring in the petrol, making sure no one can escape – always directed towards families. Did you notice?' Insch told him that the first group of victims weren't a family. Just a bunch of squatters living together. Dr Bushel smiled indulgently. 'Ah, yes, Inspector,' he said, 'but they were still a family unit: living together, bringing up a child. I think the offender has a deep-seated rage against his family and is acting upon that when he does these things.' He nodded modestly to himself, as if someone had just congratulated him for his brilliant deduction. 'And look at the front door: *screwed* shut. It's a sublimated act of penetration. He possibly has some form of erectile dysfunction – I haven't decided on that one yet – but the very choice of the *screws* is significant, don't you think? The connotation is very sexually charged. Hence the evidence of masturbation you found at the first scene.' He shrugged again. 'It wouldn't surprise me if you discovered something similar here as well, you just have to know where to look . . .' Dr Bushel turned slowly in place, peering over at the allotments. 'I deduce he would have—'

'Rhododendron bush,' said Insch, hooking a thumb over his shoulder at the hotel grounds. 'DS McRae already deducted it. But thanks anyway.'

Flustered, Dr Bushel pulled off his spectacles and gave them a thorough polish. 'Ah, yes . . . Well done, very good.'

'All right,' said Insch, hands in his pockets, 'that's enough effusive praise for one day, we don't want DS McRae to get a swollen head.' Not that there was much chance of that happening today, thought Logan as he watched Dr Bushel clamber back into the patrol car, heading back to Force Headquarters. Not with Maitland's death hanging over him. As the car pulled away, Insch peeled back the hood of his boiler suit, exposing an expanse of sweaty bald head. 'God, it's bloody roasting in here.' He unzipped the suit to the waist and leaned back against the wall. A sudden grin split his face. 'Think you stole Dr Smartarse's thunder there . . .' He stopped. 'What? You've got a face like my mother-in-law's arse.'

Logan watched an IB technician carefully place a turnip-sized lump of charcoal in one of the children's body-bags, where a head would have gone. Joanna or Molly? He closed his eyes, not wanting to see any more. 'Maitland.'

'Ah yes, PC Maitland . . .'

'I kept meaning to go see him, but . . .' Sigh. 'You know what it's like – something always came up.' He scrubbed his tired face with tired hands, the latex gloves making squeaking noises on his skin. 'I can't believe I didn't go to see him, even once.'

Insch laid a huge hand on Logan's shoulder. 'No point beating yourself up about it now. What's done is done. He's dead and you have to think about your career. You're a good copper, Logan. Don't let the bastards guilt-trip you into throwing it all away over this.'

23

PC Steve drove him back to Force Headquarters, trying to cover the uncomfortable silence with small talk. Logan clicked the radio on, but Steve didn't take the hint, just went on and on about the weather and the last film he'd seen and wasn't it great all the women were out in these skimpy tops? Something bland and poppy juddered to a halt, the song followed by a Northsound DJ Logan didn't recognize, then a couple more songs, and then it was the news. '*Dozens of Kingswells residents stormed the council chambers today, interrupting business in protest against the decision to grant McLennan Homes planning permission for three hundred new houses . . .*'

'Bloody criminal, isn't it?' said PC Steve, abandoning his current topic: the alleged extra-curricular activities of Detective Sergeant Beattie's wife. 'They should all be shot, that planning department. My dad tried for planning permission for a single house, yeah? Just the one – and they turn him down. But up pops this McLennan Homes lot, wanting to put *three hundred* of the bastards on greenbelt and it's all: "Yes sir, Mr McLennan sir, and can I polish your knob for you while you wait?" Makes you sick.' Logan didn't tell Steve his dad would have a much better chance of building his house if he took photos of the Chief Greenbelt Development Planner with his dick in a fourteen-year-old girl.

The next piece was on a new dress shop in Inverurie winning some sort of big fashion thing – PC Steve had nothing to add to that one – and then it was on to the main news story of the day: fatal fire kills four! But it was the last piece before the weather that made Logan's heart sink. *'Today colleagues and friends paid tribute to Constable Trevor Maitland, the officer tragically shot during an operation to recover stolen property earlier this month.'* The announcer's voice was replaced by a tearful woman telling the world how her Trevor was a wonderful husband and father. Then someone else saying, *'Unlike a lot o' folk, Trev niver wanted ta be CID. Could'a done the job no bother, but he wanted ta stay in uniform, oot on the streets, like, helping people. That wis Trev all over.'* And finally, the voice of doom – at least as far as Grampian Police were concerned – Councillor Andrew I'm-A-Dirty-Dirty-Bastard Marshall. *'It is important at a time like this to remember all the good that Officer Maitland and his colleagues do every day on the streets of Aberdeen. I'm sure I speak for everyone when I say that we are all thinking of his family during this difficult time.'* And that was it. No accusations of incompetence or any of his usual anti-police rants. If Logan had been driving he would've crashed the car in shock.

'Bloody hell,' said PC Steve, staring aghast at the radio. 'Did Councillor Slug-Face just say what I think he said? Did he just miss a chance to rub our noses in the shi—'

'Watch where you're going!' Logan grabbed onto the dashboard as PC Steve slammed his foot on the brake and swerved back into his own lane.

It was a little after one when Steve dropped him off at FHQ – he still had time to get something to eat in the canteen before the afternoon collapsed in on him like a ton of bricks. He'd got as far as punching the first two digits of the entry code into the keypad that opened the internal door, when Sergeant Eric Mitchell appeared behind the big glass barrier that topped the reception desk, and called out, 'Sergeant! Sergeant McRae, can you assist?' Logan turned to see what was up, his heart sinking as he saw who was sitting in one of the nasty purple chairs set against the far wall: expensive suit, slim briefcase, a pair of half-moon spectacles on the end of his nose and a superior expression on his face: Sandy Moir-Farquharson, AKA Sandy the Snake, AKA Hissing Sid, AKA Anything Else Derogatory They Could Think Of At The Time. This was all Logan needed; a perfect way to crown off the whole bloody month. Hell, the whole year. Sandy Moir-

Farquharson: the nasty little shite who'd defended Angus Robertson, the Mastrick Monster. Who'd tried to convince the world that Robertson was the real victim here, rather than the fifteen women he'd raped and murdered. That it was Grampian Police in general, and Logan in particular, who were to blame. And he'd nearly succeeded.

Moir-Farquharson was halfway out of his chair before Eric pointed to the other bank of seats, the ones by the front window. An attractive woman sat snivelling beneath the plaque commemorating the force's dead from World Wars I and II, wringing a handkerchief like she was trying to strangle the thing. Sandy the Snake got as far as, 'I was here first,' before Logan showed the woman into a small room off the reception area, closing the door in the lawyer's face. She was pretty, even with the puffy eyes: long bleached-blonde hair, slightly upturned nose – with a drip hanging from the end of it – full lips concealing a slight overbite, and a figure that would have had DC Rennie dribbling. 'Now, Miss . . . ?'

'Mrs. Mrs Cruickshank. It's my husband Gavin, he's not been home since Wednesday morning!' She bit her lower lip, the tears welling up in her bloodshot green eyes. 'I don't . . . I don't know what to do!'

'Have you reported him missing?'

She nodded, handkerchief clasped over her scarlet nose, shuddering for breath. 'They . . . they told me they *couldn't do anything*!' Mrs Cruickshank buried her head in her hands and cried and cried and cried. Logan gave her a couple of minutes to see if she'd pull herself together, before offering to fetch her a cup of tea and excusing himself, feeling like a shit for running out on her. As soon as Logan stepped out into the reception area, Sandy the Snake was on his feet again, this time making it all the way to, 'DS McRae, I must insist that—' Logan dismissed him with a gesture and asked Eric to see if he could dig out the missing person report on a Mr Gavin Cruickshank. And a cup of tea for Mrs Cruickshank as well. He turned from the reception desk to find Hissing Sid standing directly in front of him. At six foot two the lawyer was just tall enough to look down his squint nose at Logan. 'I am here about my client, Mr James McKinnon. *Sergeant*, I insist that you allow me access!'

Arrogant fuck. Logan glowered up at the man, getting angrier by the second. Who the hell did he think he was, coming in here and throwing his bloody weight around? 'You insist all you want: I am currently busy with a distraught member of the public. You want access to your client? Try the hospital – visiting hours are two thirty to five.' He pushed past Mr Moir-Farquharson and started back towards the interview room. A firm hand grabbed his shoulder.

'I insist you—'

Logan didn't look round, scared that if he did he'd end up smacking the bastard. 'Get your damn

hand off me, before I break your bloody fingers.'
His voice low and clear, the words squeezed out
between gritted teeth. Just begging for an excuse
to vent some of the shite that had filled his every
day for the last six months on this smarmy, stuck-
up, sleazy lawyer *bastard*. Moir-Farquharson
flinched back as if burnt, snatching his hand away.

Silence.

The door to reception banged open and a
ragged-arsed man lurched in, breaking the
moment. Dressed in a tatty AFC tracksuit from
three seasons ago, with a beard that looked more
like mould than hair, he made a concerted stagger
for the centre section of the reception desk,
pounded on the wooden top and shouted, 'Ah've
hud ma script nicked!'

The missing persons form arrived on a tray with
two mugs of hot, milky tea and a folded note from
Sergeant Eric Mitchell suggesting that Logan might
like to finish up his interview sharpish and get
the hell out of the station and not come back for
the rest of the day. Slippery Sandy the Snake was
making a formal complaint.

Trying not to look as if he was hurrying the
process along, Logan went through the background
of the case with Gavin Cruickshank's distraught
wife. How they were both desperate for a baby and
had been trying for months. How she'd given up
her job so she'd be less stressed and more fertile.
How Gavin had to work late most nights these days.

About his battles with the next-door neighbour. The last time she'd seen her husband he'd been going out the front door, a pair of sunglasses hiding a black eye – courtesy of the harridan next door – still furious . . . and that was Wednesday morning. She hadn't heard from him since. 'I phoned the office, but . . . but they said he was out with a client and wouldn't be back till late.' Her eyes were desperate. 'He always comes home! Always!'

'So, when he didn't you phoned the police?' said Logan, scanning the report for the date she'd reported her husband missing: half past seven, Thursday morning.

She nodded, sending tears dripping into her congealing tea. 'Sometimes he doesn't get back till four or five, if he has to go to the casino, or one of those . . .' she blushed, '*clubs*, so I went to bed. When he wasn't back by six I tried his mobile, but it said to leave a message. I tried again and again and . . . then I called the police.'

Logan nodded, trying to concentrate on her story and failing. Why on earth did he have to threaten Hissing Sid? As if the enquiry into PC Maitland's death wasn't going to be painful enough without adding a formal complaint to the pile . . . Suddenly Logan realized that Mrs Cruickshank had just finished saying something and was looking at him expectantly. 'Hmmm . . .' he said, putting on a frown of concentration, no idea at all what she'd just asked him. 'In what way?'

'Well.' She scooted her chair closer to the table.

'What if she's done something to him? She's *dangerous*!'

'Dangerous . . . I see . . .' No he didn't: he wasn't any the wiser. He'd just have to bite the bullet and admit that he hadn't been listen—

'That woman next door has been nothing but trouble since she moved in! She hit him! Gave him a black eye! He reported it . . .' The tears started again. 'You have to find him!' Logan promised her he'd do his best and escorted her to the front door. There was no sign of Sandy the Snake in reception – probably off complaining to the Chief Constable in person – so he made himself scarce, grabbing one of the CID pool cars. Not really caring where he went just as long as he was far away from FHQ before anyone noticed he was gone. To be on the safe side, he switched off his mobile phone as well. What he needed was something to keep his mind off things. Something to make him feel useful, even if he was only marking time until the summons back to headquarters for another ear-bashing. And maybe a bit of getting fired. According to Mrs Cruickshank, her husband worked for an oil-service company based in the Kirkhill Industrial Estate, hiring lifting gear out to the drilling rigs and platforms. OK, so it was only a missing persons job, but at least he'd be doing something.

ScotiaLift occupied a featureless two-storey rectangle with a small car park in front and a gated enclosure out the back stacked with brightly coloured lifting equipment. The car park boasted a Porsche, a huge BMW four-wheel-drive thing, a soft-top Audi – none of which looked more than a couple of months old and all of which had personalized number plates – and a six-foot-tall sign with the company's logo rendered in layers of shiny plastic. Logan parked his filthy, dented CID pool car next to the Porsche, severely lowering the tone of the place, and let himself into the building's reception.

Aberdeen had a long and proud history of hiring attractive young ladies to sit behind reception desks and ScotiaLift was no exception. She smiled brightly as Logan entered. 'Can I help you?' The smile faltered as he proffered his warrant card and told her he was there to ask some questions about the disappearance of a Mr Gavin Cruickshank. She looked from the card to Logan and back again, worry making little creases at the corners of her eyes.

'I know,' he said, 'it's a dreadful photo. I need to speak to Mr Cruickshank's colleagues and anyone else who might have seen him on Wednesday.'

'But he didn't come in on Wednesday!'

Logan frowned. 'Are you sure?'

The woman nodded and tapped the reception desk with a painted fingernail. 'I would have seen him.' Logan turned and took a quick look around the reception area. It wasn't huge and the front door was directly opposite where the woman sat.

She was right: if he'd come in the front she would have seen him.

'There isn't a back way?'

She nodded, pointing off through an open door to the left of the desk. 'Round the side, but it opens into the yard and the gate's kept locked. Well, unless there's equipment getting moved. Everyone parks out front – I'd've seen his car.'

'In that case,' asked Logan, 'how come when Mrs Cruickshank phoned on the Wednesday afternoon she was told her husband was out with a customer?'

A slight blush. 'I don't know.'

Logan let the silence hang for a minute, hoping she'd leap in and say something more. But she didn't. Instead she took an all-consuming interest in the phones, as if willing them to ring and give her an excuse not to speak to him any more, cheeks turning redder by the minute. 'OK,' he said at last, breaking the uncomfortable silence, 'then I'll need to speak to everyone who worked with him.'

She found him an empty office on the first floor, Gavin's: an untidy room with a girlie calendar hanging on the back of the door, another one on the far wall, two computers and a huge desk that looked as if it hadn't been cleared since the last ice age. But it did have a lovely view of the car park. One by one, all of ScotiaLift's employees were called into Logan's commandeered office, from the yardsman to the managing director, sitting on the other side of the messy desk and telling Logan what a great guy Gavin Cruickshank was and how it wasn't like him to just disappear like that. None of them admitted to speaking to Gavin's wife on the phone and telling her he'd just popped out to see a client. Logan was getting ready to leave when a flashy two-seater sports car pulled up out front. He watched from his first-floor window as a tanned man in his early twenties hopped out, pointed his key fob at the car and plipped on the alarm, before swaggering towards the building and disappearing from view. Thirty seconds later the same tanned face popped around the door to Logan's office and grinned at him.

'Evenin', squire, understand you're looking for me?' Spiky blond hair, linen suit, no tie, Armani sunglasses, faint Dundee accent.

'That depends. You speak to Gavin Cruickshank's wife on Wednesday?'

'The lovely Ailsa?' The grin grew even wider as the man peeled off his jacket and hung it on a hook by the door. 'Guilty as charged. One of these days she's going to wise up and dump that tosser husband of hers.' He gave Logan a wink. 'You ever met her? Knockers like melons, sexy as hell. Never believe she used to be the size of a house. Must go like a fucking bunny . . .' He sighed, happy with his fantasy.

'Wednesday afternoon: why did you tell her Gavin was out with a client?'

'Hmm? Oh, 'cos he was.'

'Funny. Everyone else says he didn't turn up for work that day.'

Pause. Fidget. And then the smile was back. 'You got me, it's a fair cop. He didn't show up Wednesday morning.'

'So why did you lie to her?'

'Well, you see, it's kinda like this: sometimes he doesn't come in till later. Sometimes he doesn't come into the office at all. Gav brings in a lot of business, so he can get away with murder round here.'

'So how did you know he was with a client? Did you speak to him?'

'Not as such, no. But he sent me a text message.'

'When was this?'

'Dunno, mid morning I think. Said he wouldn't be in till later, didn't say when.'

'So you assumed he was with a client?'

'Ah . . .' The smile flickered on and off as he settled into the chair behind the messy desk and switched on one of the computers. 'Not really, no. You see, Gav is what we call a "cheating bastard". Here . . .' He dug about in the piles of paper, coming out with a glossy photograph of a topless Gavin Cruickshank, surrounded by a gaggle of T-shirt-stretching blondes and brunettes bearing the legend Hooters. One of them was squeezing his tanned chest, her hand almost covering a black tattoo. They had Hooters emblazoned on their chests; he had Ailsa on his. 'Got that taken when we was in Houston for the last offshore technology

296

conference. He knobbed three of them in four days. Not that his poor bloody wife has any idea. She still thinks he's Mister Shiny.' He shook his head. 'Unbe-fucking-lievable isn't it? I mean if you could go home and screw someone like Ailsa, why the hell would you need anyone else? But there you are: he's an arsehole.'

'So when he sent you a text saying he wouldn't be in until later, you thought . . .'

'That he was off getting his knob sucked by some lovely young thing? Yeah. Wouldn't be the first time.'

'Any idea who?'

'Well, you met Janet on reception? He's been poking her off and on for a bit. I think he's been giving one of your lot's wife a good seeing to. Detective Sergeant something or other. And he's been seeing this pole-dancer at Secret Service, you know, the titty bar on Windmill Brae? Hayley . . .' An envious grin. ''Cording to him she does some of the filthiest things with a carrot you ever seen! Criminal. Hey, maybe she's got a pimp or something and he's done for Gav? Or maybe they've just run off together. Silly bastard's talked about it often enough . . .' And the grin became a leer. 'I could console his poor, sexy, abandoned wife! Give her a shoulder to cry on and a knob to bounce on. Jesus, that would be sweet.'

Back outside in the sunshine Logan stood in the car park, looking up at the building Mr Gavin

Cruickshank ran his empire of extramarital sex from. Four women – how did he have the energy? Logan had enough trouble with one.

24

Logan's phone started ringing pretty much the moment he switched it back on – a harsh cacophony of bings, squeaks and whistles that made his stomach clench. But it was only Colin Miller; the reporter had managed to track down an address for Brendan 'Chib' Sutherland. According to Miller's sources, Chib and his mate with the long hair and 'tache were staying in an exclusive little development on the western edge of Mannofield. Logan got the feeling there was something else, something the reporter wasn't telling him, but no amount of prompting, cajoling or questioning would get him to spill the beans. So in the end Logan just had to thank Miller for the info. Whatever it was, he'd probably find out soon enough. *'So, Laz . . . you got anythin' for me? You know, quid pro quo, like?'* Logan thought about it. DI Steel wanted to let Councillor Marshall get away with abusing a fourteen-year-old, wanted everyone to look the other way, had told him in *no* uncertain terms to keep his nose out of it? No problem, he'd let the *Press and Journal* do it for him. So Logan told Miller all about Councillor Marshall, the Chief Greenbelt Development Planner, and the fourteen-year-old Lithuanian prostitute. Miller nearly exploded with delight. *'Holy shit, that's fantastic! Talk about caught with your pants down!'* Pause. *'You sure I can use this?'* Logan told him to go ahead and knock himself out, then hung up. It was the first time in ages he'd actually got some job satisfaction.

Logan turned the car back towards FHQ – he'd managed to spend a whole four and a quarter hours away from the office, but like it or not, he'd have to go back in to do something about Chib and his greasy-looking mate.

Sergeant Mitchell was having a sly fag on the back podium as Logan slid the pool car into one of the vacant parking spots. 'What the hell you doing back here?' he shouted, not bothering to take the cigarette from his mouth. 'Thought I told you to make yourself scarce?'

'I take it Napier's been looking for me.'

'Surprisingly enough, no.' He oozed smoke out through his nose, where it became entangled in the hairs of his moustache, leaving it smouldering. 'The lovely Count Nosferatu has been away with the Chief Constable all day, on what is being politely referred to as "a jolly".' Logan nodded gloomily. It just meant the bollocking was postponed until tomorrow. 'But one of them Wildlife Crime Officers came past about your dog in a suitcase.'

'Yeah?' He'd forgotten all about handing the investigation over, what with the fires and all the dead prostitutes. 'Any luck?'

'How the hell should I know?'

'Wonderful, *thanks*, Eric.'

'You're welcome.' Sergeant Mitchell took a deep drag and tried for a smoke-ring, failing miserably. 'By the way: Social Work've been round, that wee whore of yours is really only thirteen.' He raised his cigarette in salute. 'Fuckin' proud moment for Aberdonians everywhere . . .' and suddenly Eric looked all of his forty-one years. 'Oh and DI Steel wants to see you as well. *And before you ask:* no idea. You'll have to ask her yourself.'

DI Steel's incident room was slowly fumbling its way back into chaos, as time and the inspector's natural flair for entropy took hold. The back shift were manning the phones and pushing paper about; not that there was a lot going on at the moment. Dr Bushel's profile for the prostitute killer – or 'The Shore Lane Stalker' as the papers were calling him – wasn't being released to the media, but it was stuck up·on the wall next to the post mortem photographs. There was no sign of Steel.

Three fresh yellow Post-it notes lurked in the middle of Logan's desk along with yet another plastic bag of videotapes from Operation

Cinderella. Logan stuffed them, unwatched, in the cupboard with all the others. The first Post-it was from Steel, telling him that the labs had finally got their finger out and come back with an analysis of the items retrieved from Jamie McKinnon's bumhole: crack cocaine. No surprise there, but he was to call her. Note number two was from the Wildlife Crime Officer: he'd been through all the reports of missing black Labradors but none of them were likely candidates for the torso in the woods. And note number three was from an inspector whose name Logan didn't recognize saying that he was to phone as soon as he got in. As long as it was before five. Which it wasn't. So Logan went off to look for DI Steel instead. She was in the canteen, polishing off a ham and cheese sandwich.

'You wanted to see me?' said Logan, dropping himself into a seat on the other side of the table, eyeing Steel suspiciously.

'Mmmmphhh . . .' She chewed, forced a big wedge of sandwich into the side of her mouth and mumbled something about leaving him a note.

'I got a possible address for our Edinburgh pushers.'

A predatory smile slunk its way onto the inspector's face. ''Bout bloody time too,' she said, washing down the last of her sandwich with a skoof of Irn-Bru. 'Right, let's get a search and apprehension warrant. I want to take the bastards tonight, before they have a chance to do someone else.'

'What about Insch?'

Steel frowned. 'What about him?'

'Well, we think that maybe these guys might have something to do with Karl Pearson. You know, the man we found tortured to death with his throat cut?'

'And?'

'Don't you think we should *tell* him about—'

'Bugger that: this is our collar. Insch can have his turn when we've finished doing them for the drugs.' She settled back in her seat and started digging between her rear molars with a fingernail. 'This is our chance to shine, Lazarus. We tell Insch and he'll take the whole thing over. If there's any credit going on this one, I want it. Insch doesn't need it.' And that was it, end of discussion. She wouldn't even let him tell the Drugs Squad.

It took the best part of an hour to organize the warrants, identify a team and get them together so the inspector could take them through the compulsory pre-operation briefing. Nine firearms-trained officers and a handful of uniform for backup. There was a good mixture of men and women, all of them straight-faced and deadly serious, listening intently as Steel filled them in on Chib Sutherland's colourful background. Much to Logan's surprise, DC Simon Rennie had turned out to be firearms qualified – personally he wouldn't have trusted him with a water pistol, but according to the computer he'd passed with flying colours. He sat right at the front of the room, his usual not-so-plain-clothes replaced by the black SAS-style kit worn by the rest of the firearms team. As soon as the inspector had finished Rennie stuck his hand up. 'You sure they're going to be armed, ma'am?'

Steel shook her head. 'Haven't got a bloody clue, but I'm no' taking any chances. No one is to go into that house without a gun and a bullet-proof vest. Understand? I want everyone in the address accounted for, face-down in the lounge, with hands cuffed behind their backs before anyone unarmed goes in. OK? We clear on that?' Sigh. 'What is it, Rennie?'

'Do we know how many of them there's meant to be?'

'We're expecting at least two of them, maybe more. Possibly armed. That's why I want the place turned upside down. I do *not* want some bugger jumping out the linen closet with a machete while we're all having a cup of tea and scratching our arses!' She stood, hands thrust into pockets. 'What we need to . . . What?' Rennie had his hand up again.

'Do we know if they've got a dog?'

'No we don't know if they've got a bloody dog! If I knew they had a bloody dog, do you no' think I would've told you?' Rennie went red and apologized. 'Right,' said the inspector, dragging a bashed packet of cigarettes from her trouser pocket. 'I want you all geared up and ready to roll in fifteen minutes.'

Twenty minutes later, Steel's new firearms team was installed in the back of an unmarked van and heading off to Mannofield. 'Operation High Noon', as the inspector had tactfully named it, was underway. A pair of patrol cars took a more circuitous route to the target address, keeping a low profile so as not to attract too much attention. Logan and Steel followed in the inspector's mid-life-crisis-mobile, detouring past Athol House in Guild Street so Logan could jump out and pick up the warrants while Steel loitered on the double yellows outside. The Procurator Fiscal's office was on the fifth floor, but her deputy was waiting for him in reception, a buff folder in one hand, a mug of coffee in the other. Her frizzy hair was pulled back from her head in a ponytail that still managed to come down to her shoulder blades, her dark green suit wrinkled after a long day in the office. There were faint purple circles under her eyes. She gave him the folder, but kept the coffee. 'Thanks,' said Logan, riffling through the paperwork, making sure all the bits were signed where they were supposed to be.

'Er . . . Sergeant McRae,' she said, 'I understand there's a possibility your visitors from Edinburgh might be responsible for torturing Karl Pearson. That true?'

'Hmm? Oh. It's possible, but we've not got anything linking them yet, it's all just supposition really. Thanks for getting these together so quickly, Ms Tulloch, I really appreciate it.'

She smiled. 'Not a problem. And it's "Miss Tulloch", not "Ms". You can call me Rachael.'

Logan smiled back. 'In that case, I'm Logan.' He stuck out his hand. 'Pleased to meet you, Rachael.' Outside someone leaned on a car horn, the loud braying *breeeeeeeeep*, clearly audible through the building's doors. 'That'll be the inspector. Gotta dash. Thanks again.' And he was back outside, just in time to be consumed in a cloud of blue diesel smoke from a passing bus.

Steel was hanging out the car window, cigarette jammed between her lips, puffing away for all she was worth. 'Come on! We haven't got all bloody day.' The inspector cut across town, avoiding the traffic on Union Street, sticking to residential back streets, the pale granite buildings rouged with orange and gold as the sun began its slow, downward slip into twilight.

'Did you know,' said Logan as the inspector finally pulled the car to a halt, across the road and three houses down from where Chib and his mate were supposed to be staying, 'that we murder more people, per million head of population, in Aberdeen than the whole of England and Wales combined?'

Steel cranked on the handbrake, and looked at him as if he'd written the words KNOB END across his forehead with indelible marker. 'Don't be daft: they kill more people in bloody Manchester in a month than we do all sodding year! Who the hell told you that rubbish?'

'Rachael, and it's not that daft if you think about it, it's averaged over the—'

'Who the hell is "Rachael"?' She cracked open the driver-side window and fumbled in her pockets for the ubiquitous pack of crumpled cigarettes.

'The new deputy fiscal, she—'

'Thought you were knobbing WPC Watson, in-between prostitutes that is.' She snorted and lit up, letting the smoke ooze out into the evening air. 'Better watch that, or she'll have your bollocks for earrings. Watson can be a right vindictive cow when she puts her mind to it.'

'What? No!' Logan stared at the inspector in horror. 'Nothing's going on! Who said anything was going on?'

Steel held up her hands, head wreathed in smoke. 'I'm just saying: watch your step, OK? I mean, I like you and all that – for a man you're less of a fuckwit than most of your species – but still . . .' She stared out the window. 'Look, there are some things in this life you can't take for granted. Trust me on this – it's *way* too easy to put the job first, forget what's really important.' Steel sighed. 'Just don't screw it up, OK?' For once Logan got the feeling she wasn't being sarcastic, which was ironic as she was the one dragging him into work the whole time, pissing Jackie off.

They sat in silence for a minute. Then the radio crackled into life – DC Rennie saying the van was in position. Logan watched as it pulled up outside the house, blocking the large, silver Mercedes in the driveway. 'About bloody time,' the inspector muttered, then grabbed the handset and shouted into it, 'What the hell took you so long?'

'Well ... er ... We had to make a toilet break ...'

'Oh for God's sake.' She slumped in her seat, took the fag out of the corner of her mouth and boinged her head off the steering wheel.

'Inspector?'

'Rennie, I swear to God, I'd come over there and ram my boot up your backside if your shoulders weren't in the bloody way. Now get going!' The sound of muffled conversation crackled out of the speakers and Logan saw the rear doors of the van pop open. Two black-clad officers in full bullet-proof get-up, with chunky black helmets, Heckler and Koch MP5 machine pistols, and the lower half of their faces obscured with black scarves, scurried up the garden path. They skidded to a halt, either side of the front door, and made clenched fist gestures back at the van. Another pair of armed officers leapt from the vehicle and sprinted across to join them, guns at the ready. All very Hollywood. They were followed by a big-boned WPC with a battering ram and a pronounced limp. There was no sign of movement from the house.

'Echo three sixer, we are in position.'

Steel frowned and picked up the radio handset. 'What the hell is "Echo three sixer" when it's at home?'

'Er ... it's PCs Littlejohn, MacInnes, Clarkson, and WPC Caldwell. We're round the back.'

'Well, why didn't you bloody well say so? Right, listen up you lot: I want this done nice and cleanly. No shots fired if we don't have to – Rennie, I mean you – if no one gets hurt, first round's on me, OK?' She took her thumb off the transmit button and grinned at Logan. 'I love this bit.' Click. 'GO GO GO!'

The battering ram smashed the front door off its hinges and the large WPC jumped to the side as her colleagues charged past, guns at the ready.

Steel watched them disappear into the house and smiled. That was it. There was nothing to do now but wait for the team to go through every room in the house and give the all clear. She dug the cigarette packet back out again and shoogled it in Logan's direction. He politely declined the offer. 'No? You sure? Ah well, takes all sorts,' she said, lighting up. 'While we've got a minute, I wanted to speak to you about a little visit I had today from an old mate.' A couple of folded sheets of A4 appeared from the inspector's inside pocket. She handed them over. 'You've had papers served on you.'

Logan's heart sank. Professional Standards strikes again. Even though he'd been expecting this all afternoon, it still came as a kick in the testicles. 'I see . . .'

'Sandy the Snake!' Steel shook her head. 'What, you forgot to pack your brain this morning? Like you're no' in enough fuckin' trouble?'

'I . . . he grabbed me. I just wanted . . .' He didn't

really know what he wanted. 'I was pissed off, and he was being an arrogant bastard and I was trying to deal with a misper . . . I was this close to popping him one.'

Steel nodded sagely. 'I see. Well, I can understand that. You remember when he got his nose broken last year? I've still got that on video – Insch made me a copy.' She smiled. 'He's got it as a screen-saver on his computer at home. Bang, right on the nose . . .' The inspector drifted off into happy reminiscence, before sighing her way back to the present. 'Anyway, the really great thing about that was he couldn't touch any of us for it. We got to watch and enjoy, and no one got hurt – other than Hissing Sid. No one got fired, or demoted.' Logan nodded gloomily and Steel reached out to pat him on the arm. 'You've done a very stupid thing, Sergeant. But I'll see what I can do.'

25

Not one shot was fired. According to DC Rennie, Chib Sutherland and his hairy friend had been sitting calmly at the dining-room table, finishing off their microwaved ready meals. They didn't shout, or fight back, or do anything, just calmly assumed the position – legs spread, hands flat on the tabletop. Rennie and his colleagues had searched the rest of the house, but there were no signs of any weapons, drugs, stolen goods, or anything else that would justify smashing their front door in with a battering ram.

'So,' said the inspector, stepping through into the lounge, where Chib and his mate were lying face-down on the carpet, a pair of armed officers standing over them with Glock 9mm pistols trained on the backs of their heads. 'They give you any trouble?'

Chib raised his head from the blue tufted Wilton, his face perfectly calm and impassive. 'My friend and I have done nothing wrong. We are cooperating with the police.'

'Aye? I thought you two was supposed to be hard men? What happened to you'll-never-take-me-alive-copper?'

'My friend and I have no reason to cause trouble. We have done nothing wrong.' There was no sign of menace in his voice, not like when he'd told Logan to fuck off in the pub.

'Whatever. Rennie, get these two back to the station. Separate cars. I want them processed and in different interview rooms by the time I get there. OK?' Rennie snapped off a salute and dragged Chib to his feet. The man was a good three inches taller than Rennie, but he allowed himself to be led from the room without any hint of a struggle. Just before he reached the door his eyes met Logan's and there was a momentary flash of recognition, swiftly replaced by a calm poker face.

The big WPC who'd hefted the battering ram followed suit with Chib's mate. In addition to the large moustache, the man now had a beautiful black eye. The WPC led him out to one of the waiting patrol cars, leaving Logan and Steel alone in the lounge. The inspector treated her armpit to a thoughtful scratch. 'Come on,' she said. 'Let's go have a poke about. See if we can't find something Rennie and his idiots missed.' The bedrooms looked as if they'd been caught in a tornado, all the drawers yanked out, beds stripped, wardrobes emptied. It was the same in the bathroom, and up in the attic the team had taken up the fibre-glass insulation, leaving the plasterboard visible between the rough timber joists. They'd even taken the top off the cold-water tank. Logan and Steel finished their tour of the premises in the garage, where a large chest freezer was stuck against the far wall. 'Aha!' The inspector strode across to it and wrenched the lid open. It was nearly empty, just a couple of packets of fish fingers and some bags of frozen peas. None of the usual mass of unidentifiable random meat that filled every other chest freezer Logan had ever seen. With a triumphant gleam in her eye, Steel pulled out a packet boasting: PURE COD FILLET WRAPPED IN CRISPY BREADCRUMBS!, opened the flap at the end and tipped out a half-dozen pasty-orange blocks of processed fish onto the palm of her hand. 'Shite,' she said, peering into the now empty packet. She stuffed the fish fingers back in the box and tried the same trick with the remaining cartons. All contained exactly what they claimed to. Swearing, DI Steel wiped her hands clean on the trousers of her off-grey suit, leaving two smears of defrosting orange breadcrumbs.

'Not fond of fish fingers then?' asked Logan innocently.

'Don't take the piss. I once found a whole freezer full of cannabis resin, all done up as packets of Weight Watchers chicken vindaloo.' She scowled, poked about in the frozen peas, then slammed the lid shut. 'Get onto the Drugs Squad. Tell them to take the damn place apart if they have to, but I want some sodding evidence!'

Logan made the call, but he was pretty sure they wouldn't find anything. Chib and his quiet buddy had been way too damn calm for there to be anything incriminating on the premises. They left a uniformed officer to guard the house and drove back to FHQ via the Burger King on Union Street. The clock on the dashboard said five past three, so Logan checked his own watch: nine seventeen. Chib and his mate had been in custody for nearly half an hour. 'We're going to have to get a shift on,' he said. 'Only got another five and a bit hours before we have to charge them or let them go.'

'Let them go my arse, those two are guilty as . . . bloody hell, mayonnaise . . .' She wiped at the front of her blouse, smearing the glob of shiny white into the black material. 'Look like fuckin' Monica Lewinski . . . Anyway, we've got them on camera at the hospital. Jamie'll cop to them forcing that crack up his bum, or we'll do him for dealing.' She rubbed at her blouse again. 'You got any napkins?'

Up in interview room number five there was a disturbingly calm and relaxed atmosphere. Brendan 'Chib' Sutherland sat on the other side of the interview table, wearing a white paper boiler suit while his own clothes were being examined for forensic evidence. He'd been photographed, DNA sampled and had his fingerprints taken by the LiveScan AFR machine. Right now the national computer database was being scanned for a match.

Even though they already knew who he was. 'So then,' said Steel, settling a plastic cup of nasty coffee in front of Chib. 'How come you're no' bleating for a lawyer?'

Chib smiled at her, picked up the coffee, sniffed it, and put it back on the chipped tabletop, untouched. 'Would it do any good?'

'No.' She turned to look at Logan, who was still fighting with the cellophane wrapping on a pair of blank videotapes. 'You know,' she said, 'it bugs the tits off me when they ask for a lawyer all the time, but when somebody doesn't it's kinda disappointing.'

Logan grunted, clunked the switch to set the audio and visual records running, and read out the standard pre-interview data. Then they settled down in silence for a minute, each side weighing up the other. And then Steel started in with the questions: where did Chib get the crack from? Why did they choose Jamie as their mule?

'I don't understand.' Chib put on a puzzled expression. 'Has this McKenzie made a complaint of some kind?'

'Not McKenzie, *McKinnon*, as well you know, you arrogant wee shite. You attacked him while he was lying in a hospital bed, broke four of his fingers and stuffed condoms filled with crack cocaine up his arse.'

Chib chuckled in a good-natured sort of way. 'No, I'm sorry, you must be mistaking me for someone else.'

'We got you on the hospital security tapes, doing it.' Steel settled back in her seat and grinned. 'Now you can face the charges on your own, take the fall, play the big man . . . But you'd be going down for a long, long time.'

The big man shook his head sadly. 'Inspector, I have *never* forced anything up anyone's backside against their will.' He smiled disarmingly. 'And we both know that there isn't a tape of this horrible crime being committed by me, because I'm not guilty of anything.'

Steel snorted. 'Don't come it, Sunshine; you're guilty as sin. Your mate the child molester's being interviewed as we speak—'

'He's not a child molester.' Chib's voice took on the same ominous timbre it had in the pub.

'No?' Steel sniffed and paused for a bit of a chew. 'Long hair, moustache: looks like a child molester to me. Anyway, you think he isn't going to roll over on you? He'll spill his guts and you'll take the fall for the whole lot: drug trafficking, assault, resisting arrest—'

'I did no such thing!' He leant forward in his seat, hands on the tabletop, still secured together with the cuffs. 'As soon as the police officers identified themselves my companion and I complied fully with their instructions.'

Steel puckered her lips, making her face look even more pointy. 'You and your mate can comply with my sharny arse—' There was a knock on the interview-room door and DC Rennie stuck his head round and asked if he could speak to the inspector for a moment. 'Aye,' said Steel, picking herself up from the squeaky plastic seat, 'hud on a minute. Interview suspended at . . . what is it, nine thirty-seven?'

Silence settled back into the room as the inspector stepped outside with DC Rennie. Chib sat back in his chair, relaxing. 'You know,' he said to Logan once the tapes were stopped. 'You really look dreadful. But then I suppose that's what happens when one gets into the habit of drinking before lunchtime.'

'What?'

'Don't you remember? We met in that pub last week? You barged into me and then called me "mate" about seven hundred times. Wanted to buy me a drink . . .' He settled further back into his chair and treated Logan to his best smile. 'I was really rather flattered. Constable . . . ?'

'McRae. Detective Sergeant.'

'McRae, eh? McRae, McRae, McRae, McRae.' A frown. 'Not *Lazarus* McRae? The one in all the papers last year? Caught that kiddie fiddler?' Logan admitted that it was. Chib smiled in admiration. 'Well, well, well, as I live and breathe, a real life police hero. If there's one thing I simply can't stand, it's paedophiles. Prison's too good for them. But I know I'm preaching to the choir on that one, eh?' He winked.

Logan scowled. 'It was an accident.'

The large man from Edinburgh nodded sagely.

'Right, an *accident*. I get you. Mum's the word.'
There then followed a very uncomfortable silence.

'So,' said Logan eventually, 'heard from Kylie lately?'

The smile froze on Chib's face. 'Who?'

'You know: Lithuanian, thirteen, bad perm, selling herself on street corners? Ring any bells?'

'I have no idea what you're talking about.'

'Oh, come on, you must remember Kylie: you used her to get that planning permission for Malk the Knife's new houses?'

Chib frowned, making a big show of thinking about it. 'You know, I think I would remember doing something like that. Must be another case of mistaken identity.'

'What did you do? Sell her on to "Steve" when you were finished with her? Or is he working for you too? All part of one big, happy criminal family?'

The thug cocked his head to one side and smiled at Logan. 'You do have a very active imagination, Sergeant. I would almost say—' The door clattered open and DI Steel hooked a thumb in Logan's direction, wanting him to join her in the corridor.

'It's that bloody prostitute-watch of yours,' she said, prodding him in the stomach with a nicotine-stained finger, ignoring the resulting grimace. 'The whole bloody team's sitting about like spare pricks, waiting for someone to brief them.' Logan groaned; he could see what was coming. 'I,' said Steel, 'am too busy with Twinkle Toes in there and his mate, to pish about all night on the off chance some dozy bastard's going to play Grab-A-Prozzie. Operation Cinderella was your idea: you deal with it.' She pointed an imperious finger down the corridor towards the stairs. 'And if you do catch the Shore Lane Stalker, make sure you don't arrest him till I turn up. I need the brownie points.' She turned her back on him and headed back into the interview room, closing the door behind her.

Operation Cinderella had been running long enough for the novelty to wear off. The top brass didn't bother turning up to the briefings any more, and neither did middle management, so it was just DS Logan McRae and a roomful of bored police men and women. This was the second-last night they'd have a full contingent of officers, after tomorrow their five-day sanction would be up. The operation wouldn't be cancelled – there was too much danger of another woman going missing, turning this into a public relations nightmare – but the manpower would be severely restricted from Sunday night on. Just enough to keep the thing ticking over for appearance's sake, with as little impact on the overtime bill as possible.

Logan gave the room the standard speech, leaving out the inspector's 'We are not at home to Mr Fuck-Up' bit. As Steel wasn't in charge tonight, Logan was making some changes: for WPCs Menzies and Davidson, their minders and a skeleton crew working the video surveillance gear, it was business as usual; everyone else was to change into their civilian clothes and do the rounds. Speak to the working girls. See if anyone hadn't turned up for work recently. If anyone was missing. It looked like their boy was more or less on a four-day cycle, that meant he'd probably have another one under his belt by now. And it might be a sack of shite, but everyone was to read through Dr Bushel's half-baked psychological profile again. See if any of the girls, or their pimps, had seen, or screwed, anyone that fitted the doctor's loose description.

They parked the CID pool car in the usual position down at the docks. Only this time Rennie was stuck behind the wheel while Logan slouched in the passenger seat. If there was any sleeping to be done – and Logan was determined there would be – he'd be the one doing it. Privilege of rank as DI Steel liked to say. They hadn't been in position for long before the world started to come and go in slow-motion flashes. His eyelids stayed down for longer each time until his chin sank towards his chest.

The night passed in a blur, people came and went, but Logan didn't recognize any of them. The car was cold and uncomfortable and Rennie wouldn't shut up about his top ten best episodes of *Coronation Street*. When Logan finally got back to the flat, it was all he could do to take off his clothes and fall into the empty bed. 'Sleep, sleep,

sleep . . .' Darkness. Then a soft hand on his shoulder and the warmth of a naked body against his. Gentle lips caressing the side of his neck, a hand making lazy circles amongst the scars on his stomach. Then lower, the kissing becoming more intense. And then she was on top, her long hair spiralling down across his face and chest, grunting and moaning as Jackie sat up in bed next to him and asked what all the noise was about. *Click* and the bedside light came on, exposing Rachael Tulloch in all her naked glory, straddling him. 'Oh,' said Jackie, 'that's all right then. I thought it was mice.' Logan tried to explain, but she just rolled over and went back to sleep while Rachael buried his face in her pale breasts. And then the door opened and his mother was standing there holding a frying pan, dressed like Henry the Eighth. 'Sir!' Her voice was hissing and urgent. 'I think they've found something.'

'Hmmmmmphf?' Logan sat bolt upright in the passenger seat, banging his head off the car roof. DC Rennie was looking at him with concern on his face.

'You OK?'

Logan scrubbed a hand across his eyes, slumped back in his seat and swore. 'First bloody dream in ages that doesn't feature dead bodies and you wake me up! Bastard!'

'Sorry, sir, but I thought you'd want to know – Caldwell says she's got a lead on a missing prostitute.'

Logan shook his head, trying to banish the last remnants of the dream, the smell of Rachael's naked body still fresh in his nostrils. This was all DI Steel's fault! If she hadn't said anything about him screwing around he wouldn't be having dirty dreams featuring the Deputy Procurator Fiscal. He'd have been having his usual nightmares about rotting children, battered women and charred corpses. At least he wouldn't have this weird sense of guilt. 'What do you mean they've got a lead?' And the smell of Rachael was gone.

26

'Her name's Joanna,' said WPC Caldwell, jerking her thumb over her shoulder at a girl who couldn't have been much more than sixteen and was having difficulty standing upright. 'Says she usually meets up with this older woman before the start of their shift. You know, drink strong cider and cheap vodka. Get nice and numb.' The WPC sniffed and glanced back at the staggering prostitute, probably thinking she was old enough to be the girl's mother. 'Only "Holly" didn't turn up for work tonight. Or last night either.'

Logan nodded. It was a long shot. Holly had probably taken a couple of days off, or was up in the infirmary getting a dose seen to, but you never knew. Joanna had the sunken cheeks and lazy eyes of someone on more than just alcohol. A plague of purple love bites infected either side of her neck, her breasts wobbling at the top of a grubby, petrol-blue basque, the left nipple poking through a hole in the lace. Black miniskirt and high-heeled ankle boots. She'd thrown a thread-bare maroon coat over the top of the ensemble. Very stylish: if you were into authentic diseased-junkie chic. 'Joanna?'

She looked up at him and smiled, hungrily. 'You looking for a good time?'

'No. No I'm not.' And even if he was there was no way in hell he'd be looking for it with her. 'I want to speak to you about your friend Holly.'

Joanna screwed up her face and spat a glob onto the cobbled street. 'Cow hasn't showed up for days! Owes me a pack of fags.' The shifty look was back. 'And fifty quid as well.'

'When did you last see her?'

She shrugged, and dug her hands into her over-coat pockets. 'Dunno . . . What day is it today?' Logan told her it was Friday and she counted back-wards on her fingers, taking two attempts to come to the conclusion, 'Tuesday night. That's when she begged the fags off me.' Tuesday night: four days after Michelle Wood was killed. Joanna leaned forward, exposing more of her chest than Logan wanted to see. 'She's no' been back since. No sign of her! Supposed to meet up for a wee drink before . . . you know, before we go out.' A car slowed down, then the driver caught sight of all the people hanging about beneath the streetlight and speeded up again. 'Aw, *fuck*!' Joanna stomped a high-heeled foot and stared after the departing car. 'He was totally going to stop! You bastards have to piss off and leave me alone, or I'll never make any money!'

'Soon as you give us a last name for Holly, and an address too.'

Joanna gazed down the empty street, where the car's tail-lights were just disappearing from view. She licked her lips, then looked back at Logan, that hungry glint in her eyes again. 'It'll cost you.'

In the end Logan had to cover Holly's alleged debt: fifty quid and a packet of fags. The address was for a council flat in Froghall, an area of Aberdeen with a less than spotless reputation. There was no guarantee that Holly from Froghall was actually missing, but it wasn't worth taking the risk. He called FHQ and asked them to send a squad car round to the address. If she opened the door dressed in a rubber nun's outfit then at least they'd know she wasn't dead. He settled back into the passenger seat of the CID car to wait for the report, drifting in and out of sleep while Rennie kept watch on WPC Menzies down the far end of Shore Lane.

He surfaced just after one, stiff and sore from sleeping in the car. According to Rennie, the streets had been pretty quiet. Business wasn't exactly booming in Aberdeen's red light district. Logan yawned; thank God he finally had a day off tomorrow – there was no way he could keep this up much longer. He tried to work the crick out of his neck, before radioing round to check in with the rest of the team. Rennie had been right, it'd been a quiet night to begin with, but now it was completely dead.

Control called in at half past one: Alpha Two Zero had been to the address in Froghall but no one was home. Provided nothing more important came up, they were going to try again later, but Logan wasn't to hold his breath. Operation Cinderella was taking a big bite out of the night-shift as it was. There was a whole city out there that needed patrolling.

By two o'clock in the morning, Davidson and Menzies were playing Eye Spy over their concealed radios, while the rest of the team played If-You-Had-To-Or-Die, picking names like Saddam Hussein, the Queen, Ann Widdecombe, Homer Simpson, Oprah Winfrey, and in one instance, DI Insch. Not surprisingly, more people were prepared to die rather than sleep with him. Finally Logan called the operation to a halt and sent everyone back to FHQ.

He left DC Rennie to park the car and headed up to Steel's incident room. No sign of her, she was *still* interviewing Chib and his friend. Logan checked his watch; they had less than an hour and a bit before the pair of them would have to be formally charged, or released. A bored-looking constable was slouched against the wall outside interview room number three, reading a copy of the *Evening Express* and muttering under his breath. 'Mornin', sir,' he said when he saw Logan coming up the corridor. 'You lookin' for the inspector?'

'Yeah, she in there?' Logan pointed at the door over the man's shoulder.

'Nope, just that Chib bloke. Inspector's in number two with the other one.'

'You know if he's copped to anything?'

'Doubt it: this one's said bugger all the whole night. Been like watching paint dry.'

No surprise there. Logan couldn't see someone with Chib's reputation breaking down and confessing all his sins. He knocked on the door to number two, letting himself in without waiting for a reply. DI Steel was slouched back in her seat, arms folded, scowling at the man on the other side of the table. He was wearing one of the IB's paper boiler suits, but looked comfortable in it, as if he was at a pyjama party for alien abductees. A WPC stood in the corner, looking every bit as bored as the officer outside in the corridor. It seemed Chib's friend wasn't much of a talker either. There was a Manila folder sitting on the tabletop in front of the inspector and Logan helped himself to it, flicking through the sheets as Steel carried on her silent war of attrition.

According to the file the suspect had been identified as one Greg Campbell from Edinburgh. There wasn't much on him: when he was wee he'd served some time in the same borstal as Chib, after that there was a bit of breaking and entering, resetting – flogging stolen car stereos down the pubs by the Edinburgh docks – and when he was seventeen he got into a pub fight and glassed someone.

But since then he'd been relatively clean. Or at least he hadn't been caught, which was a different thing entirely. If Greg was hanging out with Chib, he was working for Malk the Knife. And Malkie didn't hire choirboys. Not unless he thought he could rent them out to 'discerning' priests.

Suddenly DI Steel rocked forwards and slammed her hands down on the tabletop, making the whole thing jump. But Greg Campbell didn't so much as flinch, just sat there with a misty, faraway look in his eyes. 'Enough!' Steel stuck her finger in Greg's face. 'You don't want to talk? Fine.' She turned and glowered at the bored-looking WPC. 'Constable, take this sack of shit down to the cells. Charge him: assault, possession with intent to supply . . . Looking like a child molester.'

For the first time a flicker of emotion showed in Greg Campbell's face. 'I am not a child molester.'

'Jesus Christ on a moped!' Steel struck a dramatic pose. 'It talks!'

'I am not a child molester.' His voice was low and soft, not threatening, or angry, just matter of fact.

'Sure you are; long hair and a moustache equals child molester in anyone's book.' Steel leant over the table, her face inches from Greg's. 'That why you're up here? Eh? Come to indulge your sick little self? Get some wee kiddies hooked on crack cocaine, so you can have your wicked way with them?' She winked. 'Come on, Greggy, you can tell your Auntie Roberta: what you doing up here?'

Greg took a deep breath, closed his eyes and said, 'I have done nothing wrong. I am cooperating with the police.' He settled back into his fuzzy gaze, and nothing Steel tried could get him to talk again. She eventually gave up and ordered the WPC to take him back to the cells.

As soon as Greg Campbell was gone Steel exploded, cursing, swearing, snatching the Manila folder out of Logan's hands and hurling it against the far wall, where it spilled open, scattering its contents across the stinky room. Logan just crossed his arms and sat on the edge of the table, waiting for the tantrum to pass. Eventually she ran out of steam, the torrent of foul language fading to a trickle and then drying up entirely. 'Christ,' she said, slumping down in one of the plastic chairs. 'I needed that – wee shite was doing my head in. Fuckin' bursting for a fag.' She pulled out a packet and lit one up, sticking two fingers up at the big No Smoking sign screwed to the wall next to the door. Then she saw the little red light winking away on the video camera, swore again and mashed her finger down on the stop button. 'Damn. Now I'm gonna have to screw about with the tape to get rid of the evidence. Smoking in the workplace, what *would* the Scottish Executive say?' She rubbed a tired hand across her face, moving the skin around.

'So, you didn't get anything out of Tweedledee then?'

Steel laughed, a short barking sound borne on

wings of second-hand smoke. 'That wee outburst you witnessed was the most he'd said all bloody night. Beginning to think the bastard was mute.'

'You touched a nerve with that child molester thing though.'

'All the bloody good it did.' She slumped back against the wall and puffed her cigarette down to a tiny stump, grinding the remains to death beneath her shoe. 'Come on, let's go tell Mr Sutherland some dirty, stinking lies.'

Brendan 'Chib' Sutherland looked somewhat the worse for wear. Five and a bit hours in captivity had left him with bags under his eyes and a peach-coloured fuzz on his chin. He made a big show of yawning and stretching as DI Steel settled down on the other side of the table. She was grinning like a Halloween lantern. 'Sergeant McRae, do the honours, would you?' and Logan went through the usual rigmarole of getting the tapes in place and performing the introductions: Chib Sutherland, DI Steel, DS McRae and the bored PC from the corridor. Then Steel bounced up and down in her seat, like an excited schoolgirl. 'Chib, Chib, Chibbity, Chib-Chib-Chib . . . Guess what a wee birdie just telt us!' She gripped the edge of the desk and leaned forward. 'Go on, guess. No, you'll *never* guess, but try anyway!' Silence. 'OK.' The inspector gave a big leering wink. 'I'll give you a clue. We've been talking to your mate, Greg the Kiddie Fiddler, and he's been telling us all sorts of funny stories about you, two condoms full of crack cocaine and Jamie McKinnon's backside!'

Chib's face was like a stone. 'He's not a bloody child molester. I won't tell you again.'

'Poor old Chib, here you are looking after your mate's best interests and all the time he's been through there fitting you up. 'Cording to him, you did the whole lot: you broke Jamie's fingers and then you forced some crack-filled condoms up between his plump little bum cheeks.' She stuck a finger in the side of her mouth and flicked it out with a loud pop. 'Says you really enjoyed doing it too. That you're into that kind of thing . . .' Chib's face was getting darker and darker, like a storm gathering. Steel beamed. 'Oh! Oh – I know! I've got some magazines you'd *love*! Took them off someone who's into it too, but just between you and me, I think it's a bit rude to stuff things up someone else's bum, unless you've at least bought them dinner first.'

'I have done nothing wrong, I am cooperating with the police.' Chib's voice was trembling with the effort of staying calm and level. The vein in his forehead throbbing in time to the clenching of his jaw.

Steel scooted her chair closer to the table. 'So, how come it was crack then? Did you no' know heroin was the drug du jour up here? You trying to start a new trend?'

'I have done nothing wrong. I am cooper- ating—'

'With the police.' Steel finished for him. 'Yeah, we've heard it before. Your mate the paedophile trotted it out at least a dozen times before he turned on you.'

'HE IS NOT A BLOODY PAEDOPHILE!' Chib was halfway out of his seat before the PC grabbed him by the shoulders and pushed him back down.

'Chibbly.' The inspector smiled at him. 'You don't want to go getting yourself all riled up like that, could cause yourself an injury. Now why don't you tell us *your* side of the story, eh? Do a bit of damage limitation. 'Cos as it stands, when we go into court later today and tell the nice sheriff what's been going on, you're gonna be screwed. Right now, your buddy goes free and you go down. I ask you: is that fair?'

Chib glowered at DI Steel and said, 'I have done nothing wrong. I am cooperating with the police.' After that, his lips were sealed.

27

The sunshine was somehow thinner today, as if it knew autumn was on the way. Logan and Jackie wandered along Union Street, fighting their way in and out of the stream of Saturday-morning shoppers. So far the day had consisted of a much needed lie-in, a late breakfast and a long shower. Jackie had unplugged the phone and made Logan switch off his mobile – they were going to have a day off, just like normal people did. They stopped off pretty much at random: a couple of bottles of wine, a CD, some chocolate, and then off into the Trinity Centre where Logan had to hang about while Jackie tried on clothes. *Just* what he wanted to do on his day off. He slumped against the wall, along with all the other afflicted husbands and boyfriends whose womenfolk had decided it would be fun to go shopping.

While Jackie was in the changing room with an armful of blouses and trousers, he clicked his phone back on to see if anyone was looking for him. There was a message from Colin Miller sounding depressed. Logan wandered off to the periphery of the changing area, far enough to not be overheard by the motley collection of bored men, but still close enough to keep an eye on Jackie's shopping, and called him back. 'What can I do for you, Colin?'

'Hey, Laz.' Sigh. 'Wonderin' if you've got anythin' for me?'

'What, again? What happened to the Lithuanian spit roast?'

'Bugger all, that's what happened to it. I went and spoke to the guy in Plannin': says they threatened to go to the press with pictures of him and Marshall with their dicks in that wee girl if he didn't push through the plannin' permission for Malk the Knife's houses.' Another sigh. 'Can you see the headline? HOUSING HOOD HIRES TEENAGE TART TO PERVERT PLANNING! exclusive . . . I can't publish anythin': they'll kill me.'

Logan was about to admit that Miller had a point when Jackie stuck her head round the corner of the changing room, searching the collection of bored men for him. He had just enough time to throw Miller a hurried goodbye and switch the phone off again before she saw him. As soon as she did he was handed a pile of clothes and told to find the same things in a size fourteen. As he rummaged through the summer tops, Logan wondered why on earth he'd agreed to come on this expedition; probably because Jackie had made the gesture of a full Scottish breakfast this morning

– a peace offering, like the curry he'd bought last week – and he was still feeling guilty for having that dream about Deputy PF Rachael Tulloch. And her pale breasts . . .

An hour later they'd got as far as Marks and Spencer's underwear department – no doubt to buy some more World War I army surplus industrial-strength bras and pants – before Logan got the chance to secretly turn his mobile on again, intending to call Miller back and see what else the reporter had got out of Councillor Marshall's friend. The screen lit up with about a dozen messages, all from DI Steel. Call her back, or ignore her? It *was* his day off after all. He called her back.

'Where the hell have you been? I've been calling all bloody morning!'

'I'm on my day off,' said Logan, eyes darting across the rows of underwired bras, making sure Jackie was still in the fitting room.

'Don't be so bloody wet; we've got a missing tart to find!'

'We don't even know she's missing.'

'Aye, well that's where you're wrong. Got a warrant to force entry this morning. Found the boyfriend passed out in a pool of vomit – he's no' seen her for about a week.'

'Maybe she's gone away for a bit?'

'Aye, right, and my arse squirts perfume. Get back here: we need to come up with a plan.'

'I'm on my day off!' He turned and scowled at

a line of scarlet thongs. 'Can this not wait until tomorrow?'

'*No it bloody can't.*'

Jackie could tell he'd done something stupid the moment she stepped out of the changing room. 'You're going in, aren't you? That bitch called and you're going in.' Logan nodded and she screwed her face up, counting to ten. 'Right, I want you back at the flat by seven *at the latest* – we're having dinner. If you're late I'll kill you. And then I'll kill her. Understood?'

Logan kissed her on the cheek. 'Thanks.'

'Aye, well, just you make sure you solve this bloody case and get shot of the rancid old cow for good.'

The rancid old cow was standing in front of the incident-room whiteboards, a magic marker in one hand and a cup of milky coffee in the other. There was a new picture on the board – though this time it wasn't paired off with one from the associated post mortem – and DI Steel stared at it, tapping the pen off her cigarette-yellowed teeth. The new girl was in her late thirties: frizzy bleached-blonde hair, brown eyes – one slightly off centre, wide nose, cleft chin and one of those fake-looking beauty spots. Like a greasy black mole. Not the prettiest. Right up their killer's alley. DI Steel turned suddenly and caught Logan standing behind her. 'Jesus,' she said with a start, 'what you doing sneaking up on me like that for? You want to give me a heart attack?'

Chance would be a fine thing. 'This Holly?' he asked, pointing at the new face.

'Yup. Probably lying battered and dead in a ditch by now, but at least we know who we're looking for. I've got three search teams out.' She counted them off on her fingers, 'Hazlehead, Garlogie and Tyrebagger – where we found the last one.'

Logan nodded. 'Think he'll go back to the same place twice?'

'Stake my left boob on it, but just in case I want the other two given the once over. And if we don't find anything we expand the search: get some more bodies in and work our way through every bit of woodland from here to Inverurie.' Logan shuddered to think just how much effort that would take.

'So what do you want me to do then?' he asked. 'Sounds like you've got it all under control.'

Steel opened her mouth and then closed it again. 'Buggered if I can remember,' she said at last. 'Oh, aye: that woman with the missing husband's phoned about a million times today, and you've got to go see Complaints and Discipline. Here.' She passed him a hand-scrawled note. 'If you hurry you'll just catch him.'

Logan sat in the small reception area outside Professional Standards scowling at the note, trying to get some sense out of its random collection of squiggles. He could strangle DI Steel! Dragging him in on his day off, *again*, just so that smug bastard Napier could tell him he was going to be fired. Hooray! What a great way to spend the day. It would serve them all right if he just marched straight in there, slammed his warrant card down on the table and told Count Nosferatu where he could shove it. The job and the warrant card both, right up his sanctimonious ar—

'Ah, Sergeant, if you'd like to step inside . . .' It wasn't Napier, it was the other one, the quiet one who always sat in the corner taking notes. The quiet man settled himself down into one of the nasty visitor chairs and motioned for Logan to do the same. There was no sign of Napier.

'I take it you know why you're here?' said the inspector, pulling out a copy of Sandy the Snake's complaint. 'Mr Moir-Farquharson alleges that you were abusive and threatened him when he visited the station yesterday. That you said you would, and I quote, "break his bloody fingers". Is that correct?' Logan nodded and kept his mouth shut. 'I see,' said the inspector, scribbling something down on his copy of the form. 'And were there any witnesses to this incident?'

Sigh. 'No. We were alone in the reception area.'

'Really?' The inspector sat forward in his chair. 'Mr Moir-Farquharson says that a member of the public was also present. A Mr . . .' he flicked through his notes. 'Mr Milne who'd come in to report a theft?'

'Milne?' Logan frowned. 'What, Manky Milne?

He turned up, ranting about having his script nicked, same as he does every Friday. Thinks if he reports his dihydrochloride stolen he can get more from the drugs rehabilitation scheme. But he's just selling them on to buy heroin. Makes up the difference with a bit of housebreaking.'

'I see . . . so not a reliable witness then.'

'Last time he was in court the judge called him a barefaced liar with the morals of a plague rat. And anyway, he didn't arrive till after.'

The inspector smiled. 'Excellent. In that case it will be down to Mr Moir-Farquharson's word against yours. Especially if this Milne character wasn't even present at the time of the alleged incident . . . Excellent, excellent . . . Well, thank you for your time, Sergeant. I'm sure you have much more important things to be getting on with.' And that was it: Logan was shown out of the office, given a handshake and sent on his way.

He stood on his own in the empty corridor, the sound of damp shoes squeaking on the drab, dirty-olive floor from somewhere round the corner. 'What the hell was that all about?' This just didn't make any sense. It actually felt like the inspector was trying to help . . . Maybe he was having some good luck for a change? If so he'd better make use of it, before it disappeared again. Logan commandeered a couple of uniforms, an office, and three portable video units. They were going to go through the footage shot by Operation Cinderella on the night Holly McEwan went missing.

28

DI Steel squinted at the video monitor. 'So what am I supposed to be looking at again?' Logan hit rewind and the car that had been sweeping towards the camera went into reverse. He hit play and it swooped forward again. A brand-new Audi. The picture was a little ropey, but it was clear enough to make out the figure in the passenger seat. She was caught in the glow of a streetlight: frizzy bleached-blonde hair, squint nose, cleft chin, half a ton of make-up and a black beauty spot on the left cheek.

'Holly McEwan,' said Logan, tapping the screen. 'This was taken by the video surveillance unit in the van. You can't really make out all of the number plate, but if you look over here . . .' He pointed at the next monitor, where a view along Regent Quay flickered and jiggled. He pressed play and the image settled down to show the same brand-new Audi stop at the junction before disappearing onto Virginia Street. He rewound the tape and hit pause again. This time the car's number plate was clearly visible.

'You sure this is the same car?' asked Steel, pressing her nose against the glass.

'Positive: the partial registration from the other tape matches this one and so does the time stamp. But just in case, I've asked the lab to see if they can't get a better image of the first number plate.'

'Ya wee beauty!' Steel grinned, showing off a row of yellow teeth. 'All we need to do now is—'

Logan held up a piece of paper. 'Vehicle registration, name and address.'

'Sergeant, if you were a woman: I'd kiss you.'

The Bridge of Don was a sprawl of housing developments on the north of the city, growing over the years like a Mandelbrot fractal of cul-de-sacs in tan brick. Neil Ritchie owned a four-bedroom, two-storey detached villa on the very edge of the development, its large back garden studded with mature trees marking the boundary between the city and fields of oilseed rape. Around the front of the property Logan and DI Steel sat in a reasonably clean CID car, with DC Rennie in the back. There was no brand-new Audi sitting on the driveway – just a little, dark blue Renault Clio and a huge motorbike – but there was a double garage sitting at the end of the lock-block drive. Steel pulled out her mobile and punched in Neil Ritchie's phone number. There was a pause, and then DI Steel said in a broad Aberdonian accent, 'Hullo, is iss Mistur Ritchie? . . . Fit? . . . Aye, aye, aye . . . Noo, I ken he wis askin' fer a pucklie chuckies, but ah canna deliver em imarra . . . A pucklie chuckies . . . Chuckies . . . Aye, d'yis want tae pit im oan?' She clasped one hand over the mouthpiece and smiled like a crocodile. 'Bastard's in. Let's do it.' She opened the car door and stepped out into the cloudy afternoon, closely followed by Logan and Rennie.

Logan spoke into a radio handset and told the other team it was all systems go as Steel strode up the drive to the front door. She gave the nod and Rennie leant on the doorbell. 'Hullo?' she said into the phone clamped to her ear. 'Is iss Mistur Ritchie?'

From the other side of the door they could hear a man's voice: 'Damn, can you hold on a minute? That's the front door . . .' It opened revealing a man in his early thirties holding a cordless phone. He was all dressed up in a set of expensive biker's leathers, a little heavy around the middle, with a face that no one would think to look twice at. Not ugly, just forgettable. Exactly the sort of face you'd want for picking up prostitutes and beating the life out of them. He smiled at Rennie and pointed at the phone. 'Be with you in just a minute . . .' He turned his attention back to the call. 'Now, who did you say was calling?'

'It's the police,' said Steel, 'we've come to have a little chat.'

The man looked at the phone, then at the inspector, then said, 'Sorry?' into the mouthpiece.

Steel smiled at him and snapped her phone shut. 'Mr Neil Ritchie? Want to let us in, or would you prefer us to drag you down to the station, kicking and screaming?'

'What? I'm just on my way out, I—'

'Not any more you're not.' She whipped out the warrant and pointed at Rennie. 'Make sure there's not a dead tart lying on the kitchen floor, there's a good boy.'

Inside, the house was opulent. Expensive-looking Turkish rugs on polished hardwood floors, the pale cream walls festooned with vivid water-colours and photographs, the whole thing looking suspiciously like it had been professionally designed. There was a woman sitting in the spacious lounge reading a Val McDermid, a cup of what smelled like peppermint tea sitting on the Moorish coffee table beside her. She looked up and frowned as DC Rennie marched past her into the kitchen. 'Neil? Who is that man? Is there something wrong?'

Neil stood, wringing his hands in front of the fireplace. 'It's some sort of dreadful mistake!'

DI Steel sidled up and threw a chummy arm around him. 'That's right: just a mistake. I'm sure you didn't mean to pick up those prostitutes, strip them naked and beat them to death. Now why don't we all have a nice cup of tea and you can tell us *all* about it.'

The woman was out of her seat in a flash. *'Prostitutes?* Neil? What prostitutes? What the hell have you been up to?' She clutched her book to her chest, tears welling up in her eyes. 'You promised me! You promised you wouldn't do that again!'

'I . . . I didn't! I swear to you! I didn't do anything!'

'You know,' said Steel, patting the man on the shoulder, 'you'd be surprised how often we hear that in our line of work. Where were you last Wednesday morning at a quarter to three?'

'I . . . I was at home, asleep.'

'And Mrs Ritchie here can confirm that, can she?'

He looked imploringly at his wife, but she collapsed back onto the sofa, staring at him in horror. 'Oh my God! I was away at my mother's all week! He's been here on his own! It's you isn't it? That man in the papers!'

'Suzanne – it's not what it looks like, I swear! I didn't do anything!'

'I see.' The inspector smiled. 'And tell me, Mr Ritchie, where's that nice new car of yours?'

'What? It's in the garage . . . I didn't do anything!'

'Well, we'll let the forensic team decide that, eh? Now, how about you come down to the station voluntarily, and we can sort this whole thing out? How does that sound?'

His eyes darted left and right, but Logan was

blocking the doorway and there were policemen in the back garden. 'I . . . I want to speak to my lawyer first.'

Steel tutted and shook her head sadly. 'Sorry, that's not the way it works. You can come with us voluntarily, or in cuffs, but either way, you're coming with us.'

Back at the station, Mr Ritchie was stuck in interview room number five, with a nice cup of decaffeinated brown sludge and a glowering PC. The IB team had found bleached-blonde hair on the passenger seat of Ritchie's new car that looked a lot like the samples they'd taken from Holly McEwan's flat. Down in the incident room, DI Steel was busy fidgeting with her bra strap while Logan pinned up everything they could find on Neil Ritchie: thirty-four; married – no children; working as a hydrocarbon accountant for one of the major oil companies. The only blemishes on his police record were two warnings for kerb crawling, both more than four years old. Other than that he was Mr Squeaky Clean. He'd even organized a 'teddy bear scramble' in aid of the Archie Foundation – a local charity that raised money for sick children. So the IB were going through his home computer, looking for internet kiddie porn.

'Right,' said the inspector when Logan was done. 'Let's go see what he has to say for himself. You can play good cop if you like?'

'What? No, I can't.'

'You want to be nasty? No offence, but you're not exactly—'

'No, I mean I can't do the interview.' This was the bit Logan had been dreading. It was already twenty past six – an interview would take hours and Jackie had been quite explicit about what would happen if he wasn't back at the flat by seven.

'You're kidding me! We've got the bastard by the balls, and you don't want to be in at the kill?'

'I do. I do want to. But I can't. I have to get home.'

'Ahh.' Steel nodded sagely. 'You're on a promise and you think getting your leg over is more important. I understand. Fine . . .' She crossed her arms and stuck her nose in the air. 'I'll take DC Rennie in with me. Be good experience for him, breaking a case like this. You go get laid.'

'It's not like that, I—'

'By the way, did you speak to Complaints and Discipline this morning?'

'What?' Logan frowned, thrown by the sudden change of tack. Complaints and Discipline was what Professional Standards used to be called, before they'd changed their name to appear more cuddly and approachable. 'Er . . . yes. I did.'

'Going to let you off with a caution, are they?'

'Well, it was kinda weird, they were talking like it might even get thrown out. No charges.'

All expression fell from the inspector's face.

'Aye, well don't say I never do anything nice for you.' She turned on her heel and stomped off. Logan almost made it as far as the front door before an out-of-breath PC Steve grabbed him, sounding like he'd just sprinted all the way from Dundee.

'Sorry, sir . . .' Puff, pant. 'But DI Insch wants to see you, right away!'

Logan checked his watch: he still had thirty-five minutes, enough time to go home via a florist and pick up something for Jackie, so she'd know he appreciated the armistice. A few more minutes here probably wouldn't hurt.

Up in the main incident room DI Insch had parked himself on a desk at the epicentre of organized chaos, one large buttock resting on the top, the other hanging over the edge as he listened to a report from the bearded detective sergeant he'd tormented earlier. DS Beattie, he of the porn-star wife. Insch glanced up from the report to stuff another cola bottle into his mouth, saw Logan walking in with PC Steve and told Beattie to go do something else for ten minutes. 'Sergeant,' he said, fixing Logan with a cool gaze. 'Join me in my office.'

Detective Inspector Insch's office was bigger than Steel's: enough space to fit a large, tidy desk, a computer, three filing cabinets, a huge weeping fig, and a couple of comfy chairs. But Logan wasn't offered a seat – as soon as he was inside the door was slammed shut and Insch demanded to know what the blue fucking hell Logan thought he was playing at?

'Sir?' He took a step back, bumping into a wastepaper basket overflowing with sweetie wrappers, sending an empty packet of Gummi Bears fluttering to the dirty carpet tiles.

'You had those bastards in here last night and you DIDN'T TELL ME!'

Logan held up his hands. 'Who? Who did . . .' and then it dawned on him. 'What, Chib Sutherland and his mate?'

Insch was getting redder and redder. 'You bloody well knew I wanted to speak to them, but did you call me and let me know you had them in custody? No: I had to hear it when I came in this afternoon. *After* they'd been released on bail!'

'They got bail?' Bloody typical, you could murder your granny with a tattie peeler these days and still not get remanded in custody.

'Of course they got bail!' The inspector's face had gone past red, heading into a dangerous shade of purple, spittle flying from his lips as he yelled. 'You tried to do them for a piddling little drugs charge! I wanted them for suspected murder. MURDER! Understand? Not just a couple of condoms of heroin!'

'It was crack cocaine . . .' He regretted the words as soon as they were out of his mouth.

Insch jabbed a sausage-like finger into Logan's chest. 'I don't care if they were filled with C-Four explosive and rammed up the Duke of Edinburgh's

348

backside: I wanted to speak to them!' He took a deep breath then settled back onto his desk, crossing his huge arms and scowling. 'Come on then, let's hear it: your *brilliant* excuse.'

'DI Steel told me not to.' He might feel shitty for landing the inspector in it, but it was hardly his fault. He'd tried to get her to involve Insch at the outset. 'I told her you should be informed about the operation and she refused.'

Insch's eyes narrowed, until they were little angry black pearls, glittering dangerously in his flushed, piggy face. 'Is that so . . .' He stood, flexing his shoulders, making his shirt bulge alarmingly. 'If you'll excuse me, Sergeant, I have some business to attend to.'

The sky was low and grey above the opulent granite buildings of Rubislaw Den as Colin Miller heaved himself out of the car, dragged the laptop from behind the driver's seat and plipped on the alarm. It had been yet another shitty day. Not so long ago he'd been a proper journalist. Used to win awards. And now look at him; reduced to writing crappy human interest stories, and all because of that lousy puff piece on Malk the Knife's bloody housing development. Bad enough Malkie sends his psychopaths up to lean on him to produce the thing in the first place, but now the paper didn't trust him to write about anything more challenging than bloody knitting fairs and sheep dogs. And the one good story he had, the one that would save him from all this shite, was the one story he couldn't publish.

Colin stood up straight and glowered at the looming clouds. He should quit: write a book. Something gory with lots of death, blood and sex in it. The paper could stick their human-bastard-interest stories. He'd be out there drinking champagne and eating fucking caviar! He didn't need the P&J, it needed him . . .

He sighed, slumping slightly, feeling the weight of his new responsibilities. Who was he kidding, he couldn't afford to lose his job. Not now there was—

'Well, well, well, if it isn't ace paperboy, Colin Miller.' Edinburgh accent, deep voice, right behind him.

Colin spun around to see Brendan 'Chib' Sutherland leaning casually against a big silver Mercedes. Oh Christ, what now? 'Er . . . Mr Sutherland, nice to see you again . . . ?'

Chib shook his head sadly. 'I don't think so, Colin. I don't think it's going to be very nice at all. Shall we go for a little ride? We can take my car.'

'I . . . er . . .' He took a couple of steps back, clutching the laptop bag like a shield, and bumped into a solid mass. It was Chib's mate, standing right behind him. 'I can't, I have—'

Chib held up a finger. 'I insist.'

A large pair of hands wrapped around Colin's upper arms and forced him into the back of the waiting car. Slithering over the leather seats to the far side, he scrabbled for the handle, but nothing happened – the child lock was on. He turned to see Chib slide onto the back seat with him, closing the door with a solid clunk. 'Now then,' said the man he'd called a wannabe Weegie, pulling a pair of poultry shears from his coat pocket. The curved blades glinted in the grey evening light. 'My associate is going to drive us somewhere nice and quiet, where we can be alone. I need to ask you some questions and you'll need to scream.'

Six forty and Logan was legging it away from HQ – Marks and Spencer for a bunch of scarlet roses, back along Union Street, stopping off at Oddbins for the second time that day: sparkling Chardonnay from the chiller cabinet. Then hell for leather round the corner and down Marischal Street, getting to the flat's communal front door with thirty seconds to spare. Puffing and wheezing, he let himself in, clambered up the stairs, and got into the flat just after the stroke of seven.

Silence.

Somehow he'd been expecting soft candlelight, romantic music, the smell of something nice simmering away on the stove. He did a quick tour of the flat, but it was cold and empty. 'Bastard.' He stuck the fizzy in the fridge, the roses in a dusty vase and the heating to ON. It clunked, pinged and rattled as he stripped off and clambered into the shower. Running around like an idiot had left him pouring with sweat. He could hear the phone ringing while he fought with the shampoo bottle, but let the machine pick it up. Whatever it was, it could wait. And that's when the thought occurred to him that it might be DI Steel, calling to thank him for landing her in it with Insch. Screwing her over. After all she'd done for him – which would have been laughable yesterday, but that was before Professional Standards had bent over backwards to play down the complaint from Sandy the Snake. Why couldn't he have come up with a nice convincing lie? Something that would have defused DI Insch, but kept Steel out of it. He groaned. She was going to kill him.

By the time he'd climbed out of the shower and into some clean clothes the flat was warming up nicely, but there was still no sign of Jackie. She clattered in fifteen minutes later, swearing under her breath and struggling with half a dozen carrier bags. 'Ever tried shopping in town with your arm in a cast? Don't, it's a bastarding nightmare.' She froze, staring past him at the vase on the kitchen table. 'You bought flowers?'

'And champagne. Well, not champagne-champagne: it's Australian, but it's supposed to be good.'

Jackie smiled. 'You know, Mr McRae, sometimes you're not so bad.' She dumped all her bags on the carpet, wrapped her arms round his neck – accidentally bashing him one on the head with her plaster cast – and planted a big, soggy kiss on

352

his lips. Logan worked his way through the buttons on her blouse, opening it wide to expose—

'What the hell is this?' He took a step back and stared in horror at the huge, industrial lace construct that imprisoned Jackie's chest. 'I thought you were going to buy some new bras and pants: this thing looks like the Forth Rail Bridge!'

'This,' she said, snapping the bra strap with pride, 'is the Triumph Doreen: best-selling bra in the world. Get used to it.'

Logan flinched. 'Are you seriously going to be wearing this?'

'Hey, I'm running after some scumbag: you want my boobs bouncing up and down like watermelons in a sock, getting all saggy? You want me to have saggy boobs? That what you want?' Logan had to admit that no, he didn't. Trying not to think about the Bra From Hell, he pulled her close and kissed her.

Jackie closed her eyes, leaning into him, enjoying the heat of their bodies pressed against each other, unaware that Logan's gaze had strayed to the little red light flashing away on the answering machine. The winking, baleful eye of a guilty conscience.

29

The woods were deep and dark, the faint slivers of sky visible between the trees fading from tarnished silver to graveyard black in the dying light. A cough rattled feebly in the small clearing, a wet, sick sound that finished in a dribble of blood. With a small start, Colin Miller realized it was him. He'd been somewhere . . . somewhere dark and warm, but now he was back. Cramp in his legs, cramp in his shoulders, numb everywhere else. He'd stand up in a minute. Just as soon as the feeling died down. Just as soon as his shoulders and legs stopped hurting. Just as soon as . . . darkness.

Sparks of white and yellow exploded through his head, shoving him back, tipping the lawn chair over, sending him crashing backwards into the leaves, his arms and legs still strapped to the seat. Unable to move. And then the real pain starts, not the cramp – that's nothing, this is like fire! Like someone's taking a blowtorch to his hands. Burning his hands! He opened his mouth and screamed.

'Evening, handsome. Nice to see you're awake.' A pause, filled with Colin Miller's screams, then, 'Pick him up, will you, Greg? And see if you can't get him to shut up.'

Large hands grabbed the front of Colin's shirt, dragging him up until the lawn chair was back on its feet. He screamed again, but something hard smacked into his cheek and the taste of fresh blood filled his mouth. The cry faded to a whimper.

A face loomed out of the growing darkness: cropped white hair, perfect teeth, eyes like holes carved in marble. 'There we go! That wasn't so bad now, was it?' Miller didn't answer and the bastard from Edinburgh just shrugged. 'OK, Greg, you can untie his hands.'

Oh God, his hands! Someone fumbled with the cable ties holding his wrists to the back of the chair, and then they were free . . . He pulled his hands round to see how badly they'd been burned. And screamed again as it all came flooding back. The searing pain of flesh parting, the noise of bones and cartilage snapping apart.

'Oh Christ, again with the bloody screaming?'

This time Greg didn't need to be told, just balled up a fist and smashed it into Miller's face. He crashed sideways to the ground, still attached to the chair by his ankles, sprawling out on the forest floor, staring at his ruined hands. Sobbing.

'Now then, Colin, there's just two more items on the agenda before we're finished here. First one is this . . .' Chib dropped down and stuck a photo into Colin's face. Blocking his view of the stumps. It was from Miller's wallet: Isobel, standing on the balcony of a hotel in Spain. There was a smudge of blood in the top left corner, where Chib's latex glove had touched it. 'Good-looking woman. Now, Colin, if I even *think* you've been hanging about with the police again, I'm going to finish the job on you, and then I'm going to make her very, very ugly.' He took the photo back, kissed it and slipped it into his inside pocket. 'Item number two is just a wee matter of tidying things up.' Something hard and cold bounced off Colin's face, then another one, and another and another. Chunks of fingers, each a single bone long, raining down from the sky. 'I want you to eat them.'

Miller stared, trembling, at the pale cylinders lying in the dirt. Four of them were just the tips – fingernail to first joint; three were the middle section; two were from the base – still trailing the tendon that was supposed to lie across the knuckle. Nine little bits of piggies go to market. 'I . . . I can't!' He sobbed. 'Oh please God, I can't . . .'

Chib smiled down indulgently. 'Now now, let's have less of that. You eat them up like a good boy and we can all go home.'

Colin reached out with fumbling hands. Trying to pick up the pieces of his own fingers, the remaining digits slick with blood. Feeling the bile rise again. 'Oh fuckin' God, my hands . . . my fuckin' hands . . .'

'I'm running out of patience, Colin. Either you

eat them, or I snip off another joint and make you eat that as well.' He waggled the poultry shears in the reporter's face, the stainless steel clarted with blood. 'The longer you mess me about, the less fingers you got.'

Two bits: a tip and a middle section lying in the palm of his shaking, blood-clotted hand, their flesh cold and white. The ends dark red-black, bone and cartilage showing through. 'Oh God . . . They could . . . they could put them back on! They could stitch them back on!' A hand grabbed the hair on top of his head and pulled it round until he was looking up at Chib Sutherland's smiling face.

'You know what: maybe they could.' The smile grew wider. 'I'm a reasonable man. Why don't you pick three bits to keep? That's a whole finger's worth! Call it a gesture of good faith. Can't say fairer than that, can I?'

Tears were streaming down Colin's face, making streaks in the dirt and blood. 'I can't . . .' Voice small and broken. Then a shriek as Chib grabbed his left hand by the wrist and pulled it up, opening the shears wide and clamping them around the top joint of the index finger.

'Now you choose your three bits, then you eat the rest of your fucking fingers. Understand?'

Crying like a frightened child, Colin picked up the remains of his butchered hands and did as he was told.

30

'You wee beauty!' DI Steel stood by the window in her office, having a sly fag, reading the preliminary forensic report on the hair samples from Neil Ritchie's brand-new Audi. They were a perfect match for the ones taken from a hairbrush in Holly McEwan's flat. She turned and beamed at Logan as he entered the room, technically an hour and a half late for work, but as he'd worked the two days he was supposed to be off he didn't think it would matter that much. And anyway, he wanted to put off seeing the inspector for as long as possible. That winking red light – when he'd finally plucked up the courage to find out what it was at half past four this morning – turned out to be a recorded voice telling him his phone number had won a Caribbean cruise, five thousand pounds cash, or a certificate as the world's most gullible bumhole. He hadn't called them back.

Steel waved him over and shot him a grin. 'Lazarus, just the man I've been waiting for all my life . . .' She paused and checked her watch. 'Well, since seven am anyway. Still, never mind,' she said. 'You're here now.'

Logan frowned. This wasn't exactly the welcome he'd been expecting. Why hadn't the inspector ripped a chunk out of his backside yet? 'Er . . .' Change the subject. 'What did you charge Ritchie with?' With no body it would be hard getting a conviction.

'Nothing yet. Get this: *he's still on a voly!* He's no' even been detained yet!' Her face lit up like the Stonehaven Christmas lights. 'How cool is that?' The six-hours detainment rule wouldn't start until Ritchie was formally detained. He was still here voluntarily; as it was, they could keep him as long as they liked. Or at least until he asked to leave. 'Spent most of last night blubberin' about how he hadn't done nothing and it's all some dreadful mistake.' She grinned. 'Had that pompous tosspot Bushel interview him, doing his criminal psychiatrist bit. Four-eyed git was so excited he nearly wet himself – Ritchie fits the profile to a tee: absent mother, domineering father who liked to shag prozzies, miserable childhood, blah, blah, blah, nobody loved him. The usual stuff.'

'Wait a minute – the profile said he's supposed to have a menial job; Ritchie's a hydrocarbon accountant!'

'So what? Profiling's hardly an exact science, is it? Anyway, the forensic evidence ties him to Holly McEwan – the PF agrees, Ritchie's our man.'

'What about Michelle Wood and Rosie Williams?'

'Don't complicate things. We've still got Jamie McKinnon if we can't do Ritchie for all three tarts. In the meantime . . .' She rummaged about in the mess of paperwork that covered her desk, coming out with an address. 'Ritchie claims he didn't have his shiny new car when Holly went missing. Probably bollocks, but I want it checked out. And take Rennie with you: he's getting right on my tits this morning.'

Wellington Executive Motors was a single-storey glass box, lined inside and out with top-of-the-range motorcars that cost more than Logan's two-bedroom flat. The showroom sat on Crawpeel Road, in Altens – an industrial estate on the coast road south out of Aberdeen, packed with oil-service companies. Here and there huge architectural monstrosities in steel and glass loomed over the yards and warehouses – major oil companies making sure everyone knew who was boss. But this early on a Sunday morning, Wellington Motors was the only place open.

Still worrying about why DI Steel hadn't chewed him out for landing her in it to Insch, Logan had barely heard a word Rennie said on the way across town from FHQ. Which was probably just as well; today the detective constable was on his high horse about some sub plot in *Coronation Street* being identical to one in *Brookside* years ago.

He was *still* banging on about it as they pushed through the glass doors onto the showroom's dark, rubber flooring. The whole place smelled of new car and freshly brewed coffee, Vivaldi emanating discreetly from hidden speakers.

'Good morning, gentlemen.' They turned to find a saleswoman smiling at them with all her teeth. 'Welcome to Wellington *Executive* Motors.' She indicated the showroom with a sweeping gesture, just in case they didn't already know where they were. 'I'd be delighted to assist you in selecting a model to test drive, but while we do: cappuccino? Biscotti?' Logan asked for the manager and her smile faltered, before scrambling back into place. 'Is there anything *I* could help you with?' No, there wasn't. 'Well, er . . . Mr Robinson's with a customer at the moment. Can I offer you something while you wait? Cappuccino? Biscotti?'

Mr Robinson was a round and jovial man with a light grey comb over and a neatly trimmed beard, all smiles and handshakes until he found out Logan and Rennie were policemen. Then it was all pensive horror, wringing hands and, 'Has something happened?'

Logan put on his best disarming smile. 'Nothing like that, sir, I need to talk to you about a car you sold to one Neil Ritchie last week. Brand new—'

'Audi. Yes, Audi. Executive model, air-conditioning, sunroof, satellite navigation, power—'

'When did he pick it up?'

Mr Robinson spluttered. 'I . . . No, no, it's out

of the question. I couldn't discuss a client's details, Wellington Executive Motors values our—'

'It's important.'

'I'm sorry, but I'm sure you would need some sort of warrant—'

Logan pulled out two sheets of folded paper from his pocket and held them up. 'I *have* a warrant.' No he didn't – it was just a printout of the e-fit pictures of Kylie and her pimp, but Robinson didn't know that. The fat man blanched and Logan hid the pages away again, just in case he asked to see them. 'According to the car's registration papers he bought the car last Monday. When did he pick it up?'

With much harrumphing and muttering the showroom manager explained that *unfortunately* Mr Ritchie was *regrettably* unable to collect his vehicle on the Monday due to an *inopportune* incident with a seagull, requiring the bonnet to be resprayed. Logan cursed under his breath – that meant Ritchie wasn't the one who— 'However,' Robinson smiled with pride, 'we *were* able to drop the vehicle off at Mr Ritchie's home on Tuesday, along with a complimentary bottle of Veuve Clicquot to compensate him for the delay.' Holly McEwan didn't go missing until after eleven on Tuesday night – Ritchie would have had plenty of time to take delivery of the car, pick her up, transport her out to the Tyrebagger Woods and batter her to death. Which meant Ritchie was back in the shit again.

'We'll need to take a statement from whoever dropped off the car.'

The manager peered out through the showroom's glass wall, pointing at a bland man in a grey suit talking to an overweight woman in a bright yellow cardigan. 'I'm afraid he's with a customer at the moment. But while you wait – cappuccino? Biscotti?'

They had their coffee and biscuits by the front door, looking out at the forecourt as the first wisps of rain started to fall, speckling all the expensive metal parked outside. The man in the grey suit escorted his becardiganed customer inside to the sales desk, fawned over her a little, complimented her on her *excellent* taste as she put down a staggeringly large deposit on a new BMW, and escorted her back to her own car with one of the company umbrellas. Rennie cornered him as soon as he returned. Yes he'd delivered Mr Ritchie's car – drove it round there on the Tuesday after work. Apparently some seagull had done a monster crap on the bonnet, then danced about on it for a while. Made a hell of a mess of the paintwork. Logan let the constable take the statement while he went back to worrying about DI Steel. Maybe she was doing it to punish him, holding off on taking her revenge, letting him stew . . . To be honest that didn't sound much like Steel; a swift knee in the bollocks was more her style.

The glass doors opened and he looked up to see a familiar figure striding into the showroom, chatting amiably to a frumpy-looking woman. Councillor Marshall's face fell when he saw Logan standing by the window. The saleswoman cut through the ranks of expensive cars like a shark, smiling and calling out how nice it was to see the Councillor again, and wasn't Mrs Marshall looking lovely today? Which was a blatant lie – she was in her mid fifties with a figure that wouldn't quit . . . spreading. Her voice was like a dentist's drill as she told the sales-shark that they were looking to replace their people carrier after it had had a small accident, weren't they, Andrew? God only knew what her original hair colour had been when she was younger, but now it was fire-engine orange and permed to within an inch of its life. Logan could see why the councillor was so keen to trade up for a newer model. He was loath to admit it, but maybe Steel was right, maybe it wasn't as simple as 'guilty' or 'not guilty'. Maybe this was one of those times when the unique verdict allowable under Scottish law applied – 'not proven'.

'Well?' asked Steel when they got back to FHQ. She was sitting behind her paper-strewn desk, feet up on a pile of interview transcripts, her suit jacket thrown over the back of the chair so everyone could see she hadn't bothered to iron her blouse.

'Car was delivered on the Tuesday after the showroom shut at six, so he would have had it by half six, quarter to seven at the latest.'

'Excellent. You get a statement?'

'Yup.'

'Good, you can type it up while Rennie gets the coffees in.'

Rennie pouted. 'Again? How come I always have to get—'

'Chain of command, Constable.' She winked at him. 'And you always manage to scrounge up chocolate biscuits.' Rennie was obviously about to protest some more, so Steel told him to get a bloody move on, shouting, 'And wash the mugs this time!' after him as he muttered, mumbled and grumbled his way down the corridor. When he was gone she opened the window and told Logan to close the door while she had a fag. The smoke drifted out into the grey Sunday morning – disappearing against the charcoal skies. 'So,' said the inspector, picking a loose hair of tobacco from her lip, 'you got something to say to me?'

Here it comes. He took a deep breath and apologized for landing her in it with DI Insch. The inspector listened to him without saying a word, smoking silently like a smouldering volcano. 'Actually,' she said when he'd finished, 'I was talking about Complaints and Discipline. I put a good word in for you and they let you off without so much as a spanking. I didn't know about the DI Insch thing.'

Logan tried not to wince. Why couldn't he have kept his bloody mouth shut? 'I didn't mean to cause trouble. I—'

'Doesn't really matter what you *meant* to do, does it, Sergeant? It's what you actually did that counts. Even a moron like you should know that.'

Logan bristled. 'At least I didn't tell him about Councillor Marshall!'

'Well that's really *big* of you—'

'You're damn right it is! What would Professional Standards do if they found out you've been blackmailing him?'

Steel froze, her eyes cold and hard. 'I *beg* your pardon?'

It was too late to back out now: 'Keeping his "little indiscretions" secret must've cost him a fortune.'

She stared at him, the muscles in her jaw clenching and unclenching. 'I've no' taken a bloody penny off the man. You want to know what my "price" is? Do you? He's no' allowed to fuck us over in the papers, or give out fucking quotes about how Grampian Police are all a shower of shite! *Nothing* else.'

Oh God, that explained Marshall's sudden change of heart. He opened his mouth to apologize, but Steel got there first. 'Now I think I'd like you to get the fuck out of my sight, before I do something you're going to regret.'

DI Insch was sitting in his usual spot when Logan slunk into the arson incident room. A new pin board had been set up over by the windows, this one covered with photos of Karl Pearson. One of him smiling at a football match, and a montage of what was left of him in a sixth-floor flat in Seaton. 'Er, sir,' said Logan, trying not to look at the graphic, Technicolor close-ups of Karl's stapled testicles, 'can I speak to you about DI Steel?' Insch's face darkened, but Logan charged on. 'I was wondering what you did yesterday . . . About the interview suspects being released?'

'None of your damned business, that's what I did about it.' He dug out a crumpled packet of Fizzy Fish and started throwing the yellow shapes into his mouth, one after another, chewing angrily. 'She's caught her serial killer and can do no wrong in the eyes of our beloved bloody Detective Chief Superintendent.'

'Oh.' What a surprise, Steel had obviously taken all the credit for tracking down Neil Ritchie. 'So are you going to bring them in? Chib and his friend?'

'On what grounds? That they're from Edinburgh and look a bit dodgy? Think the PF'll give me a warrant with no bloody evidence?' He scowled and finished off the packet, crushing it in one huge fist before throwing it at the nearest wastepaper basket. 'I've already had Dr "I'm-So-Sodding-Clever" Bushel in here twice this morning wanting to do up a profile on whoever killed Karl. Little attention-seeking, glory-hunting, four-eyed . . .' He snarled. 'Apparently the Chief Constable is *delighted* someone so knowledgeable and special is "assisting" poor thick old DI Insch. How? How does writing rubbish about the fires being a sexual thing help us catch the bastard doing it? What am I supposed to do with that? Put an ad in the personal columns? "Looking for white, male GSOH, mid twenties – into setting fire to people's houses, with them inside, and masturbating while they burn – for long-term commitment at Her Majesty's pleasure. Genuine psychos only; no time wasters." Can really see *that* working.' Scowl. 'Oh, and before I forget: we got the DNA results back on your wankerchiefs – both the same. I've got them running a search through the database, see if we can find some sort of match, but there's a dirty big backlog because of that serial rape case in Dundee.'

'What about the MO? It's pretty distinctive.'

'What a great suggestion, Sergeant. I hadn't thought to run a search on something as bloody obvious as that.' He gave Logan a withering glance. 'You think I sailed up the River Don on a used condom? Course I bloody checked. Three other fatal fires where the entrances were screwed shut – Lothian and Borders sent up the investigation reports.'

'They got any idea who did it?'

Insch gave him that same look again. 'I don't know, I forgot to ask. Why, do you think it might be important?'

'OK, OK, there's no need to bite my head off; only trying to help.'

Insch rummaged around in his suit pockets, but

came up empty handed. He sighed. 'I know. I'm just pissed off because nothing's bloody happening. We've got someone out there burning people to death, and I haven't got a clue how to stop him.' The inspector hauled himself off the edge of the desk. 'Anyone asks, I'm off to the shops. There's a big bag of sherbet lemons out there with my name on it.'

Logan watched the inspector go. So much for hiding out with DI Insch until Steel calmed down a bit. Maybe it would be best to make himself scarce. He signed for a CID pool car and headed out into the late morning traffic just as the first specks of rain started to fall. Logan clicked the radio over to Northsound Two, the music fighting a losing battle against the *wheeeeeek-whonnnnnnnnk* of the car's windscreen wipers. He drove about more or less at random, trying to figure out what he was going to do for the rest of the day. With Steel pissed off, the murdered prostitute case was pretty much off limits. There wasn't anything he could do about Chib Sutherland and his mate – even if they could pressure Jamie McKinnon into making a statement about the forced insertion of drugs, he wasn't going to stand up in court and testify against two of Malk the Knife's goons. Might as well wrap his willy up in smoky bacon and dance naked in a cage full of rabid Rottweilers. So it was the missing person case or nothing. At least it'd keep him busy. He'd already spoken to the wife and the colleagues, which left the pole-dancer and the neighbour. The strip joint was closer.

Just off Union Street there was a steep cobbled alley, descending rapidly until it disappeared, three storeys down, under Bridge Street. Windmill Brae, home to nightclubs, bars and Friday-night fist-fights. Secret Service was near the bottom of the hill, with not-so-discreet boards in the windows – silhouettes of naked women – protecting the public from seeing anything raunchy going on inside. Logan parked outside on the double yellows. The front door was open, a mop and bucket standing in the space between the narrow pavement and the kiosk where you could buy your ticket. The water in the bucket swirled with disinfectant, trying to overcome the overpowering reek of last night's vomit.

Inside it was pretty much what he'd been expecting: a long, dark room on three levels, bar on one side, dancing stage with four metal poles and floor-to-ceiling mirrors on the other. Just to make sure you didn't miss anything. Little round tables filled the remaining space, the chairs upturned on top so that a spotty youth could work a floor polisher in between them. The loud *wub-wub-wub* of the machine punctuated with the occa-sional clang as it bounced off one of the tables' central supports. A large man appeared behind the bar, clutching a bottle of detergent, yelling over the noise, 'How many times I have to tell you to go easy with that thing? It's no' a fuckin' race car!' Then he noticed Logan standing in the doorway and scowled. 'We're closed.'

'I can see that.' Logan pulled out his warrant card. 'DS McRae. You've got a dancer called Hayley working here?'

The man didn't move. 'Why – what's she done?'

Logan crossed the still wet floor and leant on the bar. 'She's not done anything. I just want to know when you last saw her.'

'Depends, doesn't it?'

'On what?'

'On why you want to know.'

He pulled out a copy of the photo Mrs Cruickshank had submitted with her missing person report. 'This man's been missing since Wednesday afternoon. Someone told me he and Hayley were an item. I need to find out if she knows where he's gone.'

'Ha, you'll be fuckin' lucky. Didn't show up for her shift Wednesday night. Hasn't been in since.'

'Wednesday?'

'Aye. She does it every couple of months, disappears off to Ibiza, or some other tourist trap, soon as she's got enough cash from the tips. Gets them last-minute deals off the internet and buggers off without a word. First we know of it's when the fuckin' postcard arrives.'

'So it's not unusual for her to just go away like this?'

'Sometimes one of the other daft cows here goes with her, sometimes she takes a bloke, depends who she's shagging at the time.'

Logan proffered the photo again. 'You recognize him?'

The man squinted at the picture. 'Aye: Gav. In here most nights when Hayley's dancin'. She's been doing him for a couple of months.'

Logan took the picture back. It was beginning to sound like Gavin Cruickshank was an even bigger bastard than he'd thought – sodding off to Ibiza with a pole-dancer. 'You got an address for Hayley?'

'Let's see that warrant card again.' Logan handed it over, and the man squinted at it for a while. 'OK,' he said at last, digging about under the bar and coming up with a box of postcards. 'Just had these printed. You know, showing off the best girls. Going to hand them out in the pubs at closing time, get the punters all hot and bothered for a lap dance.' He flipped the top card over, scribbling an address and telephone number on the back, before passing it across the bar. The photo showed a very attractive woman in her mid twenties, striking brown eyes, sexy smile, long black hair, black leather bikini, knee-length kinky boots, a small diamond crucifix hanging from her pierced belly button. First Ailsa, then the ScotiaLift receptionist and now this. How the hell did Gavin Cruickshank do it?

The man grinned. 'Fuckin' tasty, eh? You wouldn't kick that out of bed for fartin'.'

Logan gave him a business card. 'Call me if she gets in touch, OK?'

Outside, the rain was getting heavier and Logan had to make a run for the car. According to the scribbled address, Hayley lived in a flat down the bottom of Seaforth Road. He didn't expect it to amount to much, but he drove over there anyway, the traffic creeping along in the downpour. The radio burbled away to itself as Logan navigated the drenched streets, wondering if last night meant things were finally starting to go right with Jackie again. It had been a good evening – good food, good wine, and afterwards had been pretty damn good as well. The news came on and Logan turned the radio up, listening to reports of a car crash in Torry, another protest being scheduled for Monday's planning meeting, and the main story of the day: someone was 'assisting the police with their enquiries' into the murder of a number of prostitutes. And lo and behold, there was Councillor Marshall on the radio, telling the world what a great job Grampian Police was doing and how we could all sleep safely in our beds again. A little bit of DI Steel's blackmail went a long way.

Hayley's flat was on the second floor of a three-storey granite tenement block. From her front room she'd have a great view of the sprawling Trinity Cemetery with Pittodrie Stadium – home to the intermittently disastrous Aberdeen Football Club – lurking in the background, drab and dreary in the rain. Lovely.

He clambered out of the car and rang the door-bell. No answer, not that he'd really been expecting one. So he tried the neighbouring flats; no one had seen Hayley since Wednesday morning. Later this afternoon he'd put in a call to the local airport, see if they had any record of her and Gavin buggering off to sunny climes in the last week. And if that didn't turn anything up there was always Inverness, Edinburgh, Glasgow, Prestwick . . .

Wherever they'd gone, they'd turn up soon enough. All tanned and knackered from too much sex while his wife was at home, going frantic with worry. What a shit. Logan didn't really want to be the one to tell Mrs Cruickshank her perfect husband was probably off on holiday screwing another woman. Maybe he could get a nice, sympathetic WPC to break the news instead.

He got as far as turning the car round before his mobile phone started ringing: DC Rennie calling on behalf of DI Steel – who was obviously still too angry to speak to him in person. Jamie McKinnon was dead.

31

Logan was to collect DC Rennie from FHQ and then go to the prison. Take statements and make sure everything was done by the book. The rain was still hammering down, thrumming on the car roof, as he pulled up outside the back door to the station and called the constable on his mobile to let him know he was waiting. Two minutes later Rennie threw himself into the passenger seat and shivered. 'What a lovely bloody day!' He ran a hand through his hair and flicked the water off into the foot well. 'Here, these are for you.' Rennie handed over a small pile of yellow Post-it notes, each of them marking an individual phone call from Mrs Cruickshank, wanting to know if they'd found her husband yet. She must have called half a dozen times since yesterday. Logan stuffed them in his pocket; she'd just have to wait until they were through at the prison.

Rennie was quiet as they drove down Market Street, past the harbour, but Logan could see him sneaking glances at him out of the corner of his eye. 'Come on then, out with it.'

A blush. 'Sorry, sir, I was just wondering what you'd done to upset DI Steel.'

'Why?'

'Er . . .' Rennie screwed up his face, obviously fighting for some sort of tactful way of putting it. 'She said I was to tell you: "don't fuck this one up, or she'd do the same to you." Swear to God, made me promise: word for word.' He threw another glance in Logan's direction. 'Sorry . . .'

'I see.' God knew why he was surprised – hell hath no fury and all that. 'So tell me about Jamie: what happened?'

'They released him from hospital yesterday morning – went to court on the possession charge and straight back to Craiginches. Found him half an hour ago in the exercise yard. They think it's an overdose.'

'In prison? How the hell did he manage that?'

Rennie shrugged. 'You know what it's like these days, they want it bad enough, they're going to get it.'

'Didn't bring it in from the hospital did he?'

'No: I checked. After we found the drugs up his bum, he wasn't even allowed to take a dump on his own. What a great job that would be, eh? Standing in the corner while some wee scroat has a crap, checking to make sure they don't pick anything out of the bowl and stuff it back where it came from.'

Logan pulled into the prison car park, between a patrol car and a familiar top-of-the-range Mercedes. 'Oh Christ . . .' he said, staring at Isobel's car. Just what he needed, someone else to give him a hard time.

They found her at the furthest corner of the exercise yard, dressed – like everyone else – in a flattering white paper romper suit, hunkered down over the twisted remains of Jamie McKinnon. Looking knackered. The IB had strung together a makeshift lean-to over the body, running lines from one twenty-foot-high wall to the other, draping the blue plastic sheeting over the top. Trying to keep the worst of the rain off Jamie McKinnon's corpse.

He was lying on his side, one arm twisted up behind his back, the other draped across his face. The bandages on his broken fingers were dirty and streaked with vomit. His left knee was up against his chest, right leg pointing due east. 'Right,' said Isobel to an IB technician with a huge digital camera. 'I want everything photographed. Particularly the hands and soles of the feet.' She looked up and saw Logan as he ducked in under the blue plastic lean-to, out of the rain. Scowled. 'When you've done with the pictures, get him back to the morgue.' The photographer got to work, the hard clack of the flash making the raindrops spark as it caught them on their way to the ground. She stood, picked up her bag and started marching for the exit, accompanied by a mountain of muscle in a prison officer's uniform. Probably to ensure she didn't get free and maul one of the inmates.

'Isobel?' said Logan as she tried to walk straight past him.

'Yes?' Staring straight ahead. She really did look terrible: puffy and tired, as if she hadn't slept in a week.

'I need to know what happened.'

She scowled, looked at her watch and then back at Jamie McKinnon's corpse. 'He's dead. Apparently from an overdose, but I'm not confirming that until I do the post mortem. You'll have the preliminary report when it's finished.' Her voice was even more cold and clipped than usual. 'Until then, if you'll excuse me, I have other matters to attend to.' She didn't wait for an answer, just marched off, the paper suit making *zwip-zwop* noises as she disappeared from the compound.

'Aye, aye . . .' said Rennie, 'someone's not gettin' any.' They grabbed a pair of spare SOC suits and clambered into them as the IB team finished off the photos and got ready to bag up the body.

'You want we should hold on a bit?' asked the head technician, water droplets sparkling on his dirt-grey moustache. 'I can't give you long though, all this rain'll play havoc with any trace evidence.' He tucked the body-bag under his armpit and huddled with his colleagues next to the prison wall, keeping out of the downpour.

Logan hunkered down next to Jamie. The

bruises from before had faded slightly, but new ones had taken their place. Whatever was going on in here, Jamie looked like he was on the receiving end of most of it. There was vomit in his hair and jumper, the acrid reek of bile slowly mingling with the stink of fresh urine. 'So,' said Rennie, copying Logan and dropping down next to the body, 'what makes them think it was an overdose?'

'Are you serious?'

Rennie looked up, puzzled. 'What? Is it 'cos he's got a history of drugs and . . .' he trailed off into silence as he saw what Logan was pointing at: a small disposable syringe sticking out of the crook of Jamie's left arm. 'Jesus, that's a bit grim!'

'Er . . . Sergeant?' it was Dirty Moustache again, clutching his empty body-bag as if it was a hot-water bottle. 'We're really going to have to get him back to the morgue now.' Logan left them to it.

Inside the prison, the social worker in charge of Jamie McKinnon's case, along with God knew how many others, was slumped over a desk in the admin wing doodling furious skull-and-cross-bones images on a to-do pad. She was the only person in there. If Logan thought the prison itself was dingy and depressing, it was nothing compared to the in-house social work offices, a converted paint shed with oppressive strip lighting, dirty yellow-grey ceiling tiles, peeling paintwork, and carpet tiles worn down to the fibres. Box files and trays of paperwork lined the walls, filling the space between the high, barred windows and the You Don't Have To Be Mad To Work Here poster. Onto which someone had added the rider Unless You Plan To Stay in blue magic marker. The only concession to life was a cluster of sickly house-plants, their leaves slowly browning as they too succumbed to the atmosphere of doom and neglect. Logan settled down on the other side of the desk and asked her about Jamie McKinnon.

The woman looked tired, bags under the eyes, the end of her long, straight nose tinted straw-berry pink, as if she'd been blowing it for years. 'Wonderful, isn't it? Like I don't have enough bloody paperwork to do!' A sigh. Then she rubbed her face with her hands. 'Sorry, we're short staffed at the moment – as bloody usual – one on mater-nity leave, two off on the stress, one walked out four months ago and we've *still* not hired anyone to replace them!' Logan counted the desks: there were only six.

'So you're pretty much on your own then.'

'Me and sodding Margaret, and she's useless at the best of times.' A loud sniff, followed by fumbling about in a desk drawer for a man-sized paper tissue, and then a lot of wet snorking noises. 'What you want to know?'

'It looks like Jamie's taken an overdose: think he might have done it on purpose?'

Her whole face clouded over. 'He was on suicide watch! OK? We're short staffed. There's only so much—'

'I'm not looking to assign blame: I just want to know if you think it was an accident, or suicide.'

She sighed, sounding tired and depressed. 'He's been having a rough time. Beaten up a lot – don't know why, but a lot of the guys had it in for him. Then there's being accused of murdering his lover, on top of having to deal with her death. And last time we spoke he'd just found out she was pregnant with his kid. He wouldn't stop crying . . .' Shrug. 'So yeah, I think it's likely. What's he got to lose? The love of his life's dead, so's his unborn child, and all he's got to look forward to is getting beaten up in prison every day for the next thirteen to twenty years.'

Logan nodded gloomily. 'What about witnesses? I mean, it's the middle of the day and he's out there in the exercise yard, surely someone must have seen him do it?'

That produced a short, derisory laugh. 'You've got to be kidding me! Witnesses? In this place? You'll be lucky.'

'Well, what about the security cameras then? They—'

'Buggered. Someone was supposed to come fix them last Thursday, but so far: nothing. Only ones working are inside the building, and half of them are screwed.' She shrugged. 'You know what it's like.'

'Starting to.' This was a dead end. Jamie had scored some dope and put himself out of his misery. 'How did he get the drugs?'

'You'd be surprised what you can buy inside. We do everything we can to keep it out, but they're always finding new ways. It's like a pharmacists' cash and carry round here some days.'

Logan sat back in his seat and stared at the ceiling, trying to think of anything else he should be asking. 'Did he have any visitors since he got back from hospital?' Like two large gentlemen from Edinburgh, for example. She didn't know, but she could find out. One quick phone call later and the answer was yes – yesterday evening: Jamie's girlfriend. That made no sense and Logan said so. 'Girlfriend? How can he have a girlfriend? The love of his life's just been beaten to death.'

Luckily the visiting room was one of the few places in the prison where the CCTV cameras still worked. Logan and Rennie sat in the security office, staring at a flickering monitor, looking back in time to yesterday evening. The screen showed an empty room, tables arranged in straight lines, plastic chairs on either side. Logan prodded the fast-forward button, horizontal lines shuddering across the image as the tape whirred on. A prison officer appeared in the corner, as if by magic, and then the first inmate whooshed into view, followed by two more, each choosing a table as far away from the others as possible. The whirring stopped and the picture settled down into normal time. Jamie McKinnon was sitting at the back left, under the poster telling visitors what they weren't allowed to pass across to the prisoners. And then the girlfriend arrived, limping into shot with her back to the camera. But Logan didn't need to see her face to know who it was: black leather jacket, torn jeans, pink spiky hair. Logan stabbed the screen with his finger. 'Suzie McKinnon, Jamie's sister. How come they thought she was his girlfr—' Suzie leaned across the table and slipped a big French kiss into her brother's open mouth. 'Oh. I see.'

'So,' said Rennie, watching as the pair parted, both wiping their mouths on the backs of their sleeves. 'She was slipping him more than just tongue.' A small parcel of drugs, passed from mouth to mouth under the guise of a long, passionate kiss.

Logan nodded. 'Looks like it. Come on, we have to pay her a visit anyway; she's next of kin.'

Suzie McKinnon wasn't in her usual drinking spot with the rest of King Edward's advisors – the rain keeping even the most stalwart monarchist alcoholics indoors – so they tried the address in Ferryhill they'd followed her to last time. The lights were on in the basement flat, shining out into the gloomy afternoon. Suzie was home.

'Right,' said Logan, unfastening his seatbelt. 'Here's the plan: I go inside and knock. Rennie: you wait out front like last time, I don't want her hopping out through the front window and buggering off into the monsoon.' He turned to the family liaison officer they'd picked up during a quick detour back to headquarters, the same nervous young man assigned to Grandma Kennedy. 'You take the garden out back.' The communal door still wasn't locked so Logan let himself in, picking his way down the dark stairs to the basement flat, the glass from a shattered light bulb scrunching underfoot. The McKinnons' front door had taken a beating since he was here last – a large boot print next to the lock, the wood around it buckled and cracked. Logan knocked and it swung open beneath his hand, only stopping when the door chain reached full stretch, the wooden surround was splintered where the lock and deadbolt had been ripped free. A nervous face appeared at the opening, took one look at Logan, then ran for it. Suzie McKinnon. The lounge door slammed: she was going out the front window. He found her outside, struggling with DC Rennie, her pink hair plastered to her head, white make-up starting to run in the heavy rain, as if her face was melting. She sank her teeth into Rennie's arm and he let out an 'Ayabastard!' losing his grip for a moment: just long enough for Suzie to wriggle free and slam a knee into his groin. Rennie went white, but didn't let go, hissing curses between clenched teeth as she writhed and swore.

Logan grabbed her arm before she could inflict any more damage and said, 'Jamie's dead, Suzie.' She froze, staring at him in disbelief while the rain fell all around them. Up close he could see that her make-up had been hiding more than just spots.

As it dissolved in the rain, bruises and scrapes were coming to the surface.

Her mouth worked up and down, until the word 'How?' finally made it out.

'Looks like an overdose. But we won't know for sure until . . .' He stopped, not wanting to go into detail about what Isobel would do to Jamie's body. 'Until later. We won't know until later. Come on, let's go inside.'

The chain was still on the door, so they had to clamber in through the lounge window, treading wet footprints into the tatty settee on their way to the carpet. They stood there in silence for a moment, Suzie chewing on her black-painted fingernails while Rennie limped off to the kitchen under orders to make tea, grumbling non-stop about being kneed in the balls.

'What happened to the front door?'

She frowned, as if his words were coming from a long way off. 'Door? Oh, it . . .' she shrugged, wincing at the motion. 'Ah forgot ma key.' She wouldn't meet his eyes.

'I expect you fell down the stairs too. What with it being dark out there and all.'

Suzie closed her eyes and nodded, tears sparkling over her lashes and falling onto her bruised cheeks. Logan sighed. 'You and I both know that's bullshit. Someone kicked the door in, then did the same to you. And I'll bet you all the tatties in Scotland I know who did it.'

'Did . . . Did he really overdose?'

'Far as we can tell. We're not sure if he did it on purpose or not.'

'Oh God.' She buried her head in her hands, rocking back and forth with silent sobs. 'I killed him!'

Logan watched her cry for a moment. 'Where did you get it from, Suzie?'

But she wasn't listening to him any more. 'Oh God, Jamie . . .' Tugging at her wet pink hair she mourned for her dead brother.

It was ten minutes before anyone remembered the FLO was still standing in the back garden in the rain.

32

They headed back into town, DC Rennie behind the wheel, clutching at his groin every thirty seconds, making sure it was still there. Logan stared morosely out of the window, watching the people and traffic go by. At least the rain was letting up, blue sky breaking through the lowering clouds, the wet tarmac sparkling in the sunshine. Rennie pulled up behind a huge BMW four-by-four and waited for the lights to change. Another flashy motor with a personalized number plate – the city was rife with them, like some sort of disease. Logan frowned. Flashy motor, flashy motor . . . why did that sound familiar?

The lights changed and the four-by-four rumbled away, taking a left onto Springbank Terrace, with Logan staring after it. When the answer wouldn't come he pulled out his phone and checked his messages – just the one from Brian, Isobel's assistant: Jamie McKinnon's post mortem was being delayed until four. Dr

MacAlister wasn't feeling too well. Logan closed his phone, tapping the plastic casing against his chin as he frowned out the window. It wasn't like Isobel to show any sort of weakness: she'd have to be half dead to postpone a post mortem. Four o'clock . . . It was just coming up on two now. 'Right,' he said, stuffing the phone back in his pocket and pulling out the wad of messages from Mrs Cruickshank. 'We've got a couple of hours to kill before they fillet Jamie. I've got a treat for you: we're off to Westhill.'

Westhill was an ever-expanding suburb seven miles west of Aberdeen. It had started off as a collection of pig farms before the developers got their claws into it, and now it sprawled all the way from the main road up the hill, slowly encircling the golf course with pale brick arms. By the time Rennie had negotiated the roundabout by the business park and was heading into Westhill proper the rain was gone and everything shone in the warm sunshine. Half a dozen magpies leapt and chattered in the grass of Denman Park, strutting back and forth like barristers as they drove by. And then it was past a cramped shopping centre, up the hill, and left – making for Westfield Gardens: home to the adulterous Mr Gavin Cruickshank. The house sat three quarters of the way around the cul-de-sac, backing onto Westhill Academy. Out front the garden was pristine, laid out with circular rose beds, the yellow and pink blooms glittering with raindrops caught in the sun; built-in garage; red, part-glazed front door; twee wooden plaque with CRUICKSHANKS' REPOSE carved into it. The lampposts all the way around the street were decorated with bright-yellow, laminated A4 posters: a picture of a huge Labrador, its features grainy and indistinct from the photocopying, and the words: MOPPET'S MISSING!!! The address given was for the house next to Cruickshanks' Repose – an identical building, but not so well kept. The garden was a mess of dandelions and clover, the front door in need of a fresh coat of paint. The garage was lying open, revealing a rusty Fiat nestling amongst piles of old newspapers, paint tins, empty bottles and bits of bicycle. A large chest freezer was the only thing in the whole place that looked as if it still worked. 'So what's the story then?' asked Rennie, locking the car.

Logan pointed at Cruickshanks' Repose. 'Husband's been missing since last Wednesday. Poor cow thinks the next-door neighbour's got something to do with it. Doesn't know darling Gavin's been getting his leg over women all around town – including a pole-dancer with a habit of disappearing off on holiday at a moment's notice.'

'You think he's just buggered off with her?'

Logan dug the postcard from Secret Service out of his pocket and handed it over. 'What do you think?'

Rennie's eyes roved across Hayley's leather-bikinied body. 'Phwoar, not bad! She can dance on my pole any time she—Hey!' Logan had taken the picture back.

'Come on,' he said, as Rennie pouted, 'we might as well go see the next-door neighbour before we tell the wife her husband's a cheating bastard.'

Pressing the doorbell produced a single, dry clunk, so they had to knock. Eventually a swearing silhouette appeared in the door's rippled glass. 'This better not be you fuckin' bob-a-job bastards again . . .' trailing off as the door opened. A crumpled woman in her dressing gown scowled at them. 'Aw, fuck. What is it now?' Her hair was lank with two inches of brown and grey roots showing, hanging around an oval face with puffy bags under the eyes, broken veins spidering across her cheeks and nose. 'I told them at the station: the fuckin' insurance is in the post.'

'We're not here about that, Mrs . . . ?'

Panic flickered across her eyes, swiftly followed by a defiant sneer. 'What you want then?'

'Last Tuesday you were involved in an altercation with Mr Cruickshank from next door.'

'Says who?' She was slowly inching the door shut.

'I want you to tell me about it. Right now. Before I arrest you and drag you down to the station.' Logan flashed her an insincere smile. 'Up to you.'

She closed her eyes and swore. 'OK, OK.' She jammed her hands in her dressing-gown pockets and stomped back into the house, leaving the front door open for them. They followed her through a cluttered hall to the kitchen, where a smeared window looked out on a rectangle of chewed-up grass and dog toys, the borders around the edge a collection of churned mud and weeds. The kitchen was a mess of pizza boxes, clear plastic takeaway containers still swimming with grease, empty tins of lager, dirty washing spilling out of an overflowing laundry basket, and the smell of something festering in the sink.

There was an unopened stack of bills on the table and Logan picked one up. It was addressed to Mrs Clair Pirie, with what looked like FINAL REMINDER just visible through the plastic window. 'Mr Pirie about is he, Clair?'

She snatched the brown envelope from his hands and stuffed it into an already overflowing drawer. 'None of yer damned business. Filthy bastard fucked off years ago.'

'I see.' Logan watched her stab the kettle's 'on' button and pick a teabag from a pile of desiccated brown circles slouching in a saucer. 'Not for us, thanks. So you live here alone?'

'No . . . aye, I mean yes: alone.' Shifty, shifty, shifty. Logan leant back against the working surface and stared at her in silence as the kettle growled and rumbled to a boil. 'OK, OK,' she said at last. 'Jesus . . . My boyfriend used to stay here, OK? We was goin' to put him on the council tax next time. But we split up, OK? Satisfied? Bastard walked out on me.' The dried-up husk of a teabag was hurled into a dirty mug, chased with boiling water.

'Tell us about the people next door, Clair.'

'She's an interferin' cow – puttin' up fuckin' posters about other people's fuckin' dogs, cheeky bitch. And he's an arsehole. Bastard's round here complainin' the whole time. Never fuckin' happy.'

'That why you hit him?'

A small smile flickered over her face, before disappearing once more. 'He started it. Comin' round here and swearing a blue fuckin' streak. No fuckin' manners at all.' She wrenched open the fridge, dragged out a carton of milk and slopped some in on top of the teabag. A horrific stench slithered out into the kitchen, mouldy cheese and the unmistakable sickly-sweet smell of meat *long* past its sell-by date. But Clair didn't seem to notice.

'You hear he's gone missing?'

She froze, the dirty mug to her lips. 'Oh aye?'

'Since Wednesday, day after you assaulted him.' Logan watched her eyes and there was definitely something there. He just didn't know what it was yet. 'Bit of a coincidence, isn't it?'

She shrugged. 'Nothin' to do with me. Probably run off with one of his tarts anyway. Left that soppy cow of a wife. Just fuckin' abandoned her . . .' Clair fished the teabag out of the mug with a fork and hurled it into the dirty sink. 'It's what you fuckin' men do, isn't it?'

*   *   *

Back outside in the sunshine Rennie gasped for air. 'Jesus,' he said, waving a hand in front of his nose. 'What a stink! No' surprised her husband left her. Woman's a bloody slob . . . What?' He looked at Logan who was staring at the front of the house.

'Do me a favour, OK? I want you to get onto Control and have them do a full check: everything they have on Mrs Clair Pirie.'

'Think she's got something to do with Cruickshank going missing?'

'Nope. My money's still on Ibiza, Hayley the pole-dancer and her tiny leather bikini. But she is up to something.'

They went next door to Cruickshanks' Repose. Ailsa appeared, dressed in a blue-and-white-striped apron and rubber gloves, blonde hair tied back. Stunning. Her face went white when she saw Logan standing on her top step. 'Oh, God.' She wrung her yellow-rubber-gloved hands, making them squeak. 'Something's happened!'

Logan tried for a reassuring smile. 'It's OK, Mrs Cruickshank, nothing's happened: we're just here to have a little chat, OK? Can we come in?'

'Oh, of course. I'm sorry . . . Would you like some tea? It's no problem.'

She sat them down in a pristine lounge and went to put the kettle on. As soon as she was out of sight, Rennie leaned over and hissed at Logan, 'OOOH! *Suits you, sir!*'

'Would you grow up! The woman's husband's missing.'

'I know, but Jesus, how the hell do you leave that? She's bloody gorgeous! I would! Would you?'

'Shut up – she'll hear you.'

Rennie looked longingly at the kitchen door. 'Tell you: she could keep the rubber gloves on, I'd—'

'Constable – I'm warning you!'

Rennie stared at the carpet. 'Sorry, sir. Must be the shock of my nadgers still working after Suzie Bloody McKinnon's kneecap vasectomy.' Logan couldn't help smiling.

Ailsa Cruickshank returned bearing a tray topped with mugs of tea and chocolate biscuits. As Rennie helped himself to a Penguin, she perched herself on the edge of the sofa and fidgeted with a cushion. Logan cleared his throat, not looking forward to what was going to come next. 'Er . . .' he said, wondering how he was going to tell her that her darling Gavin was probably off having lots of holiday sex with a pole-dancer. 'I was wondering if you've heard from your husband at all?'

She sighed, deflating slightly. 'No. No I haven't.'

'I see . . .' Go on: tell her. 'Er . . . when you reported your husband missing, did they ask you about other things not being there: his toothbrush, change of clothes, passport. That kind of thing?'

'You don't think he's . . . Gavin wouldn't just leave me without saying anything! He wouldn't.'

Logan bit his lip and nodded. 'OK. Well, just in case, do you think we could take a look?'

Ailsa took them upstairs to the master bedroom, unaware of DC Rennie's eyes locked onto her backside as she climbed up in front of them. The house was decorated in soft shades, everything carefully coordinated. The bed linen matched the curtains, carpet and overstuffed cushions lying on a wicker chair in the corner. In fact the only disorderly part of the room was the huge collection of detective novels – all hers, she explained with an apologetic smile, Gavin didn't like to read. She rummaged about in a chest of drawers, digging out a pair of burgundy EU passports. One hers, one Gavin's. His toothbrush was still in the bathroom. His razor, moisturizer, facial scrub, and hair gel still in the medicine cabinet. But that didn't prove anything. Given the kind of life Gavin Cruickshank led, he probably had identical toiletries in the bathroom of every woman he was shagging. And a lot of people in the oil-service industry had second passports; it helped when you had to get visas organized for contracts in Azerbaijan, or Angola, or Nigeria . . . So all in all this proved nothing, just gave Logan a chance to put off the inevitable and Rennie a chance to stare at her backside as they went from room to room. Back down in the lounge, Logan took a deep breath and told her the bad news. She stood there in stunned silence for almost a minute before the tears started. Logan and Rennie let themselves out.

They sat in the car, Logan swearing softly, Rennie gazing wistfully back at the house. 'You sure I shouldn't just pop back in there and comfort her, sir? Bit of a shoulder to cry on and all . . .' He stopped when he saw the expression on Logan's face. Cleared his throat and started the car. 'Fair enough.'

Logan took one last look over his shoulder, not surprised to see a suspicious pair of piggy eyes staring at him from the house next door. She was definitely up to something.

The morgue at Grampian Police Headquarters had a strange smell of cheese and onion when Logan arrived seven minutes early for Jamie McKinnon's post mortem. The guest of honour was already there, lying flat on his back in the middle of the cutting table, naked as the day he was born. But other than that the place was deserted. There wouldn't be a big turnout for Jamie's farewell performance – after all, this was just another junkie suicide. Because he'd topped himself in prison they'd have to go the whole hog and do a Fatal Accident Enquiry, but it wasn't likely to explode into a public scandal. Jamie's only surviving relative was his sister and as she'd given him the drugs in the first place she was in no position to complain about his death in custody. So today it would just be Logan and DC Rennie in the cheap seats, not so much as a deputy procurator fiscal to keep them company. Though where the hell Rennie had got to was anyone's guess. Isobel slouched through into the cutting room at two minutes to four, not bothering to cover a jaw-cracking yawn. She scrubbed up in the sink without saying hello.

Logan sighed. Might as well make the gesture: 'Rough night last night?'

'Hmmm?' She looked up from drying her hands, face set in the same scowl she was wearing this morning. 'I don't want to talk about it.'

'OK . . .' This was obviously going to be one of those 'fun' post mortems.

'Look if you must know, Colin didn't come home last night.' She pulled a green plastic apron from the roll by the sink and put it on over her surgical get-up. It was long enough to cover the toes of her Wellington boots.

'Oh?' Sounded as if Miller was in for a world of hurt when he got back from work today. 'What was his excuse?'

The scowl grew darker. 'I haven't spoken to him yet.' She threw a tray of surgical instruments down on the trolley next to Jamie's corpse. 'It's four o'clock: where the *hell* is everyone?'

Isobel's assistant Brian was the first one to turn up, full of apologies, closely followed by DC Rennie. Doc Fraser was the last to show: a full eight minutes late and completely unrepentant. He'd been ready at three, he said, something else came up and was it OK if he did his expenses, only he was two months behind and needed the cash. Taking Isobel's silent scowl as a 'yes', he popped his briefcase up on the next cutting table along, spreading out reams of paper and receipts on the shining stainless steel surface.

With an exasperated sigh Isobel started in on the preliminary examination. She narrated her way around the corpse, finding evidence of at least a dozen separate violent incidents. The most recent set of contusions weren't even old enough to bruise properly. It looked as if someone had held Jamie down so someone else could punch him repeatedly in the stomach. There were even little marks around his mouth, probably caused by a hand being clamped over it to stop him from screaming. No wonder the poor sod had killed himself.

And then it was time to open him up, but for once Logan got the feeling Isobel was just going through the motions. She sliced through flesh and tissue in a half-hearted, distracted way, as if there was something else on her mind. Probably what she was going to do to Colin Miller when she got her hands on him. The morgue phone rang while Isobel was lifting out the contents of Jamie's lower abdomen. Brian scampered off and answered it, speaking in hushed tones, telling whoever it was on the other end that the pathologist was in the middle of someone right now, but if they wanted to call back, she'd be done in about an hour. Pause. Then a hand over the mouthpiece as he simpered at Isobel, 'I'm sorry, Dr MacAlister, but there's a phone call for you.'

She stopped, Jamie's liver in her hands, speaking

slowly and carefully through gritted teeth. 'I'm busy: *take a message!*'

Brian's face contorted itself into an ingratiating smile. 'I'm sorry, Doctor, but they say it's urgent.'

Isobel swore under her breath. 'What is it?' Brian hurried over to the cutting table, taking the phone with him, holding it to her ear as she severed the last strip of connective tissue and lifted the liver free. 'Yes, this is Dr MacAlister . . . What? . . . No, you'll have to speak up.' Jamie's liver was dark, dark purple, hanging like a vast slug between her gloved fingers. 'He's what?' Her eyes went wide above her mask. 'Oh my God!' The liver slapped against the tabletop then slithered to the tiled floor at her feet.

Isobel turned and ran out of the sterile area, past the fridges, discarding blood-soiled latex gloves, mask and apron on the way. Logan ran after her, catching up as she charged up the stairs to the rear podium. 'Isobel? Isobel!' She pointed a key fob at her large Mercedes and jumped in behind the wheel, still wearing her blood-smeared green scrubs. Logan grabbed the door handle before she could slam it shut. 'Isobel, wait! What is it?'

'I HAVE TO GO!' She grabbed the door and slammed it shut, flooring the accelerator, leaving twin trails of black rubber on the tarmac.

'Fine,' he muttered to himself as her car raced down the ramp, round the corner and out of sight. 'Be like that then.'

33

Back in the morgue, Doc Fraser was slowly lumbering his way into a set of surgical greens while Brian washed the little bits of grit and fluff off Jamie McKinnon's liver. 'Any idea what that was about?' asked Logan as Brian patted the slab of purple offal dry with green paper towels.

'No idea,' he said, laying the thing in a kidney dish. 'It was the hospital and they said it was urgent, but other than that, nothing.'

'OK, ladies,' said Doc Fraser, snapping on his latex gloves. 'If you don't mind we'll get through this one sharpish. I've still got all those bloody expense forms to fill in.'

The rest of the post mortem went by in a haze, Doc Fraser cutting, hefting, weighing and examining Jamie's innards, taking tissue samples for Brian to preserve in tiny plastic tubes full of formalin. It wasn't long before Brian was stuffing Jamie's organs back where they'd come from, using a well-practised blanket stitch to sew the body back up again.

'Well,' said Doc Fraser, pinging his gloves into a pedal bin like elastic bands. 'I'll have to go through the Ice Maiden's tape before I can give you the full monty, but it looks like your boy here didn't actually die of an overdose. OK, the silly wee bastard shot himself so full of shite there was no way he was going to survive, but it was the diced carrots that killed him.' Logan looked puzzled. 'I'd guess,' said Fraser as Jamie was wheeled past on a gurney, heading for cold storage, 'that he'd been on the wagon for a bit, so the effects of the dose were magnified. Heroin, and lots of it. There's a whole heap of diamorphine still in his bloodstream; your lad snuffed it before his system could absorb it all. Fell unconscious and choked on his own vomit. Classic rock star death.'

Logan nodded sadly. That explained why they'd found the body with the syringe still sticking out of it. Normally a heroin overdose would only kick in a couple of hours after the injection. Then Logan remembered the fresh bruises: the hand clamped over Jamie's mouth, the marks around the wrists where he'd been held down and punched . . . Or maybe just held down, the hand preventing him from screaming for help while someone forced a syringe into his arm, saying, *'No one rats on Malk the Knife!'* He shuddered. That kind of thing would be right up Chib Sutherland's alley. 'Any chance he didn't do it to himself?'

The pathologist paused, halfway out of his

scrubs. 'Don't remember Isobel saying anything about it . . .' He looked thoughtful for a moment before telling Brian to get Jamie back out of the fridges: they had some more slicing and dicing to do.

It took Doc Fraser twelve and a half minutes to determine whether or not the overdose was self-inflicted. There was a cluster of old injection points in the crook of Jamie's arm, the skin rough and pockmarked, and in the middle of them a little black dot ringed with a faint purple halo. Jamie had only been an occasional user, but he would have known better than to ram the needle right through the vein and muscle and into the bone. Doc Fraser dug around with a pair of tweezers, coming out with a sliver of metal that matched the tip of the syringe found with the body. There was only one needle mark, he explained, because the broken needle was only partially withdrawn from the hole, before being pushed into the vein properly. Doc Fraser was embarrassed at having missed it the first time round; he'd thought Isobel had already looked at the injection site, when she'd obviously been saving it for last.

Logan told him not to worry about it and spent the next hour and a half filling in the usual pile of paperwork and online forms that followed a suspicious death, before printing the whole lot out. He was going to sneak up to DI Steel's office and dump it in her in-tray while no one was about.

Avoid the inevitable confrontation. His conscience got the better of him by the time he'd climbed the stairs: Jamie McKinnon had been murdered and, like it or not, Logan owed it to him to set the wheels in motion properly. With a sigh, he stomped his way up to the inspector's incident room. It was bedlam: piles of reports; a queue of uniformed officers waiting to present them; mobile whiteboards with maps of various forests stuck to them, clarted in red and blue pen; phones going; people all talking at once. And sitting at the centre of the tornado was DI Steel. Logan took a deep breath and marched up to the front of the queue, sticking his paperwork under the inspector's nose. She snatched it and skimmed through the first couple of pages, swearing as she read. 'What the hell do you mean *suspected murder*? I thought the wee shite was supposed to have killed himself.'

'Looks like he might have had a little help.'

'Fuck, that's all I bloody need, another sodding murder enquiry.' She screwed up her face, the wrinkles all aligning into a starburst centred on her nose. 'And it's Craiginches! Who the hell's going to talk to us? Might as well interview the bloody pavement! Waste of bloody time . . .' Steel chewed thoughtfully on the inside of her cheek for a bit, then shouted across the room. 'Rennie! Get your arse over here.'

'Yes, ma'am?'

'I have decided to give you a chance to fuck something up all on your ownsome.' She thrust

Logan's report into the constable's hands. 'Read that, then get up to Craiginches and find me whoever killed Jamie McKinnon. I want a written confession and a packet of Embassy Regals on my desk by this time tomorrow.'

A look of fear crawled over DC Rennie's face. 'Ma'am?'

Steel punched him on the shoulder, hard enough to make him wince. 'I have every faith in you. Now bugger off – I've got work to do.' Rennie did what he was told, shaking his head in bewilderment.

'Er . . .' said Logan, knowing this was probably going to get him even further into the inspector's bad books. 'Are you sure that's wise? I mean, he's only a constable and—'

'And you are only a backstabbing arsehole, but I still let you play cops and robbers, don't I?' Logan shut his mouth. Steel hopped off the desk and dug her hands into her pockets, rummaging around until she found a wrinkled packet of fags. 'What's the worst he can do? No one's going to come forward and admit to seeing anything; sure as hell no one's going to confess. So Rennie gets a bit of experience under his belt. He can't screw it up any more than it already is. And let's face it: no one's going to miss a little bastard like Jamie McKinnon anyway.' She saw the disgusted expression on Logan's face and snorted. 'Oh, don't look at me like that – he was a shitebag. Remember Rosie Williams? Maybe McKinnon didn't kill her, but he still beat her up badly enough to make her throw his arse out. And do you *really* think that was the first time he'd had a few pints and laid into her? Check his record: McKinnon liked to get drunk and beat up women. Bastards like that deserve all they get.' Her voice was flat and bitter. 'Now if you'll excuse me, Sergeant, some of us have real police work to do.'

'Backstabbing arsehole . . .' Logan stomped back down the stairs, muttering all the way. DI Steel seemed to have conveniently forgotten that *he* was the one who'd spotted the car with the missing prostitute in it. That if it wasn't for *him*, DI Steel wouldn't even have a suspect in custody . . . Wasn't his fault Insch was on the warpath; if Steel had got her finger out and acted like a proper bloody detective inspector in the first place and actually *told* Insch they had Chib and his mate in custody, this would never have happened. Bloody DI Steel and her personal crusade to grab any glory going.

He stared out of the back door, watching the clouds whip across the pale grey sky. Jackie wouldn't be home until after midnight, so all he had to look forward to tonight was an empty flat, a carry-out and a bottle of wine. Maybe two bottles. It wasn't as if he'd been sticking to the diet anyway. Could always start again next Monday, when things got a little better. But he'd been saying that for the last three months, and they never did . . . It was time to go home.

He got as far as the off-licence before his mobile phone started ringing. Oh Christ, now what?

A depressingly familiar gravelly voice on the other end: *'Where the hell did you disappear off to?'*

Logan groaned. Bloody DI Bloody Steel. 'Shift's over, I'm going home.'

'Don't be daft: more important things in life than beer and nipples. Search team three's just called in, they've found something.'

'Holly McEwan?' They'd found the fourth victim's body.

'No. Suitcase: red, smells like a dead dog in a sauna.' *A pause then some muffled conversation.* 'Get your arse back to the station – we've got a dismembered corpse to go play with.'

34

Garlogie Woods again. Logan pulled the filthy CID car up onto the grass verge about a hundred yards down from the packed lay-by. Steel had spent the trip out brooding and smoking while Logan drove. DC Rennie, however, had cleared himself a little nest in the piles of chip papers and pizza boxes that cluttered the back of the car – the damn thing was *still* filthy from Operation Cinderella – and discovered the foot well to be full of painful, eye-watering pornography. Showing remarkable strength of character, Rennie ignored it, sticking to Logan's report on Jamie McKinnon's murder instead, desperate to get it finished so he could go and start interviewing up at the prison when they were finished here.

The inspector clambered out of the car without a word and squelched her way through the rain-soaked undergrowth back to the lay-by, squeezing past the line of cars and vans parked up on the verge. Everyone and their dog were here: a canine unit sitting in the middle of the churned-up mud, flanked by one of the search team minibuses and what looked like Doc Wilson's car. For once Logan was glad he was working with Steel rather than Insch. Given the inspector's last encounter with the duty doctor, Logan didn't want to be around when those two ran into each other again.

He waited on the grass verge while Rennie rummaged about in the boot, coming out with handfuls of latex gloves and evidence bags which he secreted about his person, making the pockets of his suit bulge. Logan locked the car, before asking Rennie what he was doing out here. 'Thought Steel wanted you to look into Jamie McKinnon's death.'

DC Rennie gave the same nervous smile he'd been wearing back at FHQ. 'The inspector says I have to learn to multi-task. Says she doesn't trust many people to do this one, just you and me, sir.' Logan gave a humourless laugh. 'Trusting' wasn't exactly the word he'd use to describe his relationship with DI Steel right now.

The gate to the dirt track leading into the forest had been jemmied open, a pair of fresh tyre tracks gouged into the dirt leading off up the hill. A uniformed constable examined their warrant cards and waved them through. The track was pitted and slithery with mud; heather bushes grew on either side, their little purple and white spears waving in the breeze as Logan and Rennie picked their way along the verge. Broom grew in dark green profusion to their right, the brown, brittle seed casings rattling in the breeze like a nest of venomous snakes. And on the other side, tall pine trees, the forest floor beneath them carpeted with fallen needles, soaked almost black with the rain, studded with red mushrooms and luminous green ferns. 'You going to this thing tomorrow then?' asked Rennie, as they waded through the wet grass.

'Tomorrow?'

'The funeral? You know, Trevor Maitland?'

Oh shit. Logan winced; he'd forgotten all about it. How the hell was he supposed to stand there and look Maitland's widow in the eye? What was he supposed to say – I'm sorry I screwed up and got your husband killed? Great bloody comfort *that* would be. 'What happened with that search on the Pirie woman?' he asked, changing the subject.

'Eh? Oh, right . . .' Rennie shook his head. 'Jesus, what a munt she was! The Cruickshanks have filed about twenty complaints against her since Christmas: drunken, abusive behaviour mostly. Even tried for an antisocial behaviour order, but no luck so far. Banned for drink driving about three months ago – Mr Cruickshank tipped the local station off – done for assault last year, two counts of possession, but she got off with a warning. Rumours she was involved in some sort of kiddie porn ring, all anonymous complaints, but the Westhill station recognized the voice—'

'Gavin Cruickshank again?'

'Bingo.' They reached the top of the hill and started down the other side, still following the rutted tracks in the mud. 'There's piles more, but basically she's a dirty scumbag and Mr Cruickshank's had it in for her ever since she moved in. Last complaint was made on the Tuesday night when she thumped him one.'

Logan grunted. No wonder Ailsa thought the woman had something to do with her disappearing husband. She certainly would've had a motive. That's if Gavin wasn't screwing a pole-dancer on a foreign beach somewhere, while his poor wife fretted and worried.

'What about Ritchie, the Shore Lane Stalker?'

Rennie shrugged. 'Have to ask the inspector about that. Playing it close to her chest.'

That figured. She wouldn't want to share even the slightest hint of glory . . .

The forest suddenly opened up into a large, waterlogged dip. This was as far as the Identification Bureau van had got. It was abandoned halfway down the track, its rear wheels partially submerged in watery brown slime, the sides covered with fresh sprays of mud. There was a line of blue and white POLICE tape leading off into the trees just up ahead, and Logan and Rennie followed it. Two hundred yards in and they came across the cordon marking the outermost edge of the crime scene. A bored-looking WPC with a clipboard made them change into SOC boiler suits and overshoes before signing them in. The IB had put up a makeshift canopy of blue plastic, stringing it up between the trees on the periphery of the clearing. Smack bang in the middle of this impromptu marquee was a red fabric suitcase, identical to the last one, wedged under the bole of a fallen tree, partially covered by a layer of pine needles and soil, with fern fronds piled on top as camouflage. 'I don't get it,' said Logan, watching as one of the IB team squatted down in front of the case and started delicately clearing off the greenery, needles and dirt into a large evidence pouch. 'Why buy a bright-red suitcase if you're going to hide the damn thing in a forest? I mean, it's always going to stick out like a sore thumb, isn't it? Why not buy a green one, or black? Why red?'

Rennie shrugged. 'Wanted it to be found?'

'Then why take it out into the middle of the bloody woods and hide it under a fallen tree? Why bury it under leaves and stuff?'

A thoughtful pause and then: 'Maybe to make it easy to find, but *look* like it's hard to find, so you'd find it but think it wasn't meant to be found, even though you only really found it because someone wanted it to be found?'

Logan looked at him. 'Did that make sense when it was inside your head? 'Cos it lost something in translation.'

Doc Fraser was already there, his medical bag sitting next to him on a roll of plastic sheeting while he leant against a tree and read the paper, waiting for the IB to finish taking samples, photographs, video, dusting for prints . . . He looked up from the P&J's farming section and smiled. 'What-ho, chaps,' he said in a mock English accent, 'smashing evening for a spot of the old dismembered-corpse routine, don't ya think?'

Logan pointed at the milling throng of IB technicians. 'Any sign of the PF yet?' Doc Fraser shook his head: no one here but us chickens – not even DI Steel, who by rights should have got there before Rennie and Logan. Grumpy Doc Wilson was about somewhere, but given his recently acquired permanent foul mood the pathologist hadn't bothered to make conversation and he'd sodded off into the woods to make some phone calls. There was a crash and a clatter from down the track they'd just walked up and DI Steel emerged, looking a little flustered, hauling at the backside of her boiler suit.

'Call of nature,' she said. 'Don't ask.' The inspector took a quick stroll round the fallen tree, following the IB's little raised path. 'So,' she said to Doc Fraser when she'd made a complete circuit, 'you going to hang about here all day reading the paper, or you planning on actually doing some work?'

The suitcase's lock came off in one piece and was dropped carefully into an evidence bag by a nervous-looking IB techie. 'You know,' said Steel as Doc Fraser gripped the top of the case, 'we're all going to look like a right bunch of idiots if this is a Cocker Spaniel.'

Fraser opened the case.

The smell wasn't a patch on the dismembered Labrador, but it was still strong enough to make them all gag. There, lying in a pool of putrid liquid, was a large, grey-white chunk of meat. Definitely not a Cocker Spaniel. It had the word AILSA tattooed on its chest.

Rennie drove foot flat to the floor, rallying along the country roads making for Westhill while Logan phoned the Wildlife Investigation Officer who'd worked the dog-torso case. Had he spoken to a Mrs Clair Pirie when he was going through the list of missing black Labradors? No, he hadn't, because Mrs Pirie hadn't reported her dog missing. DI Steel sat up front in the passenger seat, a grin stretching her face wide. The Procurator Fiscal had been ecstatic – a search and arrest warrant was being rushed through. Her office promised it would be faxed to the Westhill police station by the time the inspector's team got there. Alpha Two Nine was following on behind, having difficulty keeping up with Rennie's driving.

The PF's office was as good as its word and twelve minutes later Rennie pulled up outside Clair Pirie's house in Westfield Gardens. Alpha Two Nine was parked round the back, on the entrance road to Westhill Academy – just in case. Next door, Cruickshanks' Repose was in darkness, no car in the driveway, no answer when Logan phoned. But the television flickered in Clair Pirie's lounge, making bruise-coloured shadows lurch and sprawl across the wallpaper.

'Right,' said Steel, holding a hand out to Rennie. 'Warrants.' The constable handed over the wad of faxed documents, all duly signed and counter-signed. 'Let's do it.'

Rennie knocked on the front door, forgoing the broken bell, and settled back to wait. Behind him Steel shifted excitedly from foot to foot, like she was a little kid waiting for her turn at the ice-cream van. Eventually, grumbling and swearing, Clair Pirie opened the door, took one look at Rennie standing on her doorstep and slammed it shut again. 'Fuck off!' she shouted through the rippled glass, 'I'm not in.'

Steel shoved Rennie out of the way, squaring up to the closed door. 'Don't be bloody stupid. Open this door now, or I'll have it kicked in.'

'You can't do that!'

'Really?' Steel dragged the warrant out of her pocket and pressed it against the glass. 'Clair Pirie: I have a warrant here to search these premises. You can either . . . Damn!' The large silhouette had disappeared from the glass. Steel grabbed her radio. 'Heads up, people – she's doing a runner!' She slapped Rennie on the shoulder. 'What the hell you standing there for? Break it down!'

DC Rennie slammed his foot into the wood and the door sprang backwards. At the other end of the hall they could see the kitchen window, and through that into the back garden where they had a perfect view of Mrs Pirie's backside as she clambered over the garden fence. Her large rear-end froze at the top and then she dropped back into the ruined flowerbed, shoulders slumped – closely followed by a uniformed constable from Alpha Two Nine.

DI Steel steepled her fingers and grinned. 'Excellent.'

The Identification Bureau van arrived at twenty past nine, having just finished up in Garlogie Woods. Gavin Cruickshank's torso was now on its way back to the morgue. They started in the bathroom: bathtubs being a popular location for the hacking up of dead bodies. People were always so keen to not make a mess. Steel left Mrs Pirie in the tender care of DC Rennie while she and Logan went upstairs to watch the IB team work. Willing them to find something.

The bathroom was a mess: a pile of dirty towels lying in the corner; dusty plastic tampon wrappers lying on the floor by the toilet; slivers of old soap decaying in a little dish attached to the shower. Mildew spread grey tendrils across the corner above the medicine cabinet and limescale turned the off-pink tiles a dirty grey. Very homely. 'Manky cow . . .' Dirty Moustache was kneeling by the side of the bath, working a cotton swab about in the plughole. It came out clarted in pubic hair.

It didn't look as if the bathtub had been used to hack up a body, but when they tested it for blood the thing lit up like a Christmas tree. Little crusts of congealed haemoglobin in the waste pipe, overflow, under the bath's handles, behind the scratched chrome taps.

DI Steel let out a delighted whoop and charged down the stairs to the lounge, where the Pirie woman was fidgeting on a floral-print couch. 'Guess what?' Steel said, leaning over a cluttered coffee table to grin in Clair Pirie's face. 'You're *fucked*!'

DI Steel was determined to interview Clair Pirie on her own. Logan may have identified the body and given them a suspect, but she still wasn't speaking to him. So he had to stay behind with Rennie and keep an eye on things while she went back to FHQ to take all the bloody credit. As usual.

The search team was already going through the attic, so rather than sit about twiddling their thumbs, Logan and Rennie pitched in, starting with the lounge. They found nothing more incriminating than a couple of roaches down the back of the sofa, still smelling faintly of cannabis resin. The IB was still working in the kitchen so Logan pushed through an unlocked internal door into the garage. It took both of them to get the rusty, up-and-over garage door closed, the metal groaning and squealing as they heaved, shutting out the crowd that had begun to gather from the time Steel had driven off with Clair Pirie. The *Evening Express* was the first paper to send a journalist, but they were still blissfully free of television cameras so far. Oddly there was no sign of Colin Miller; he was usually pretty quick off the mark whenever the POLICE tape went up.

Rennie picked his way through a mound of debris piled up against the back wall of the garage, while Logan contemplated the chest freezer. Years of filth and grime had left it a nasty nicotine-stained grey with suspicious brown splodges of rust streaking the surface. It took him two attempts to open the lid, a thick layer of frost and ice cracking and skittering across the garage's concrete floor. Unlike the freezer at Chib's house, this one was packed with mystery meat and long-forgotten packets of sweet corn. He was a third of the way down, fingers burning with cold, when DC Rennie shouted that he'd found something crammed down the back of a pile of old *Daily Mail*s. It was a boning knife with a seven-inch, single-sided blade – scooped near the handle, straight for most of its length and curved at the tip.

Logan pulled out his phone and called Steel, wandering through the house as it rang. It bleeped over to voicemail and he left a message about the knife. That, plus the body and the blood in the bathroom meant there was no way Pirie was ever going to be able to wriggle out of this. Not even Hissing Sid could get her off. Next he tried Jackie's mobile, hoping to spend a couple of minutes not talking about work or bloody soap operas with Rennie. No answer, so he dialled Colin Miller and settled back against the kitchen table, looking out through the French windows at the silent bulk of Westhill Academy – lit up in the darkness by a row of streetlights. The phone rang and rang and rang and rang before a recording of Miller's Glaswegian crackled in Logan's ear, telling him that if he left his name, number and a short message the reporter would get right back to him. 'Colin, it's Logan. Wanted to know if you were still alive after Isobel got her hands on you, you dirty stop-out. I—'

A rectangle of light blossomed in the back garden next door. Ailsa Cruickshank was home. 'Damn.' He hung up. No one had been able to track her down; she didn't know her husband was dead yet. And with DI Steel gone Logan was the senior officer on site.

With a sigh, he headed next door and broke the news as gently as he could, taking a WPC from the search team with him for moral support. Her husband wasn't on some foreign beach with a pole-dancer after all; his torso was lying on a slab in the morgue. Logan didn't know which was worse – discovering your husband was a lying, adulterous bastard, or a dismembered corpse.

35

Back at FHQ the mood was grim but optimistic.
DI Steel hadn't managed to get a confession out
of the Pirie woman yet, but it was only a matter
of time. Half past ten and the rest of the team
were in the pub. Archibald Simpson's sat at the
eastern end of Union Street, a hop, skip and a
stagger away from Force Headquarters, a popular
hangout for off-duty policemen in need of something to take the day away. The Procurator Fiscal
bought the first round, told everyone what a great
job they'd done getting a suspect into custody so
quickly, and that they were going to put Clair Pirie
away for a very, very long time. She raised her
glass and Logan, Rennie and Rachael Tulloch
chinked their drinks off it, self-consciously, trying
to kid on they didn't feel ridiculous. The PF left
after the first one, but her deputy stayed behind,
face covered in a huge smile as she got the second
round in. Then it was Rennie's turn to buy and
the conversation started drifting away from work.

By the time Logan was lurching back from the bar with two lagers and a large gin and tonic, things had started to get a bit fuzzy round the edges – the effect of three pints on an empty stomach and no decent sleep for a fortnight. Back at the table Rachael told a joke about two nuns on holiday in a Mini Metro, fluffing the punch line by giggling too much. Rennie told one about two nuns in a condom factory and Logan thought the deputy PF was going to wet herself. She howled with laughter and slapped Logan's thigh, letting her hand linger there as she wiped the tears from her eyes . . .

He eventually crawled back to the flat just after midnight, dropping his clothes on the hall floor as he stripped off on the way to the toilet. Bleary urination followed by roughly brushed teeth and two pints of water. He staggered into the bedroom, curled up under the duvet and was snoring away within minutes. He didn't even hear Jackie coming in off the back shift half an hour later.

The music was probably supposed to be soothing, but came off more gloomy than anything else – a low-key set of hymns on the church organ as the place slowly filled up with police officers. Sitting up at the back, Logan tried not to look as bloody awful as he felt. Monday morning had arrived on the wings of a hangover, beating in time with his lurching stomach. He'd not been sick yet, but there was still time. Half past eight was *way* too early for a funeral.

Jackie looked up from the order of service as *We Plough the Fields and Scatter* wheezed to a halt. 'Good turnout.' The place was packed – one of the benefits of getting seen off at this ungodly hour was that the night shift were able to attend after knocking off for the day. PC Trevor Maitland had spent a lot of time on the night shift, and the dark, wooden pews in Rubislaw Church were full of his colleagues, friends, family and the man who'd got him shot. A sudden hush as the minister stepped up to the lectern and thanked them all for coming.

The service was every bit as depressing as Logan had expected. His stomach lurched all the way through the eulogies, each one a glowing character reference for the recently deceased. Then the Chief Constable got up and made a speech about how dangerous the life of a police officer was and how brave everyone was who stepped up to that challenge. And how the courage and sacrifice made by their families was every bit as great, while Maitland's widow cried quietly. Then the music started, Whitney Houston warbling her way through *I Will Always Love You* as the funeral directors picked up the floral tributes and piled them carefully on top of the coffin before wheeling it out of the church and into the hearse.

What a great way to start the week.

*   *   *

DI Steel's incident room was charged with excitement when Logan got back to FHQ, dirt under his nails from throwing a handful of earth down onto the polished mahogany casket: yesterday they'd discovered a body in a suitcase AND got a suspect into custody. Today the search teams were back out again, working their way carefully through the Tyrebagger, Garlogie and Hazlehead woods. It was a lot of forest to search, but they were making good progress; the maps pinned to the incident room's walls were covered with crossed-out grid marks. Another two days at most, and they'd be finished. Then they'd start searching the next set of woods on the inspector's list and keep on going until Holly McEwan was lying in one of Isobel's refrigerated drawers.

Someone had pinned up a copy of that morning's *Press and Journal*, the front page screaming SUITCASE TORSO MURDER WOMAN HELD! along with a photo of the police cordon at Garlogie Woods and an inset of DI Steel – the picture apparently taken on one of the rare days when she didn't look as if her hair had been styled by seagulls. According to the story that went with the indecipherable headline, Detective Inspector Roberta Steel had solved one of the most difficult murder cases in Scottish legal history. There was even a quote from Councillor Andrew Marshall, telling the world what a credit DI Steel was to the force and how lucky Aberdeen was to have someone like her about. Logan and Rennie didn't even get a mention.

Grumbling under his breath, Logan slouched across to the admin officer – who told him the inspector was still up in interview room three with the Pirie woman and didn't want to be disturbed. Logan swore. Bloody Detective Bloody Inspector Bloody Steel. He started poking about for something useful to do, but everything seemed to be in hand. Teams were out searching for the missing prostitute's body, Steel was off questioning the torso murderer . . . That left Insch's arsonist, Karl Pearson's torturer and Jamie McKinnon's killer. And Logan was pretty sure he knew who was behind Jamie's 'rock star' ending: Brendan 'Chib' Sutherland. With McKinnon dead the drugs case was too. They had no other witnesses, or evidence. The Procurator Fiscal wasn't going to take it to trial – it just wasn't worth it.

So if they wanted to put Chib away for something it'd have to be Jamie McKinnon's murder. There was bugger all linking him to Karl Pearson – nothing that would stand up in court anyway – but if Logan could prove Chib had ordered McKinnon's death it'd be a different story.

Rennie backed into the incident room with another tray of coffees and a plate of chocolate biscuits. The mug he put down in front of Logan came with a Jammie Dodger and a couple of paracetamol. 'Looked like you could use them,' he explained before settling down at his desk to finish reading Jamie McKinnon's post mortem report – what with all the excitement, and the visit to the pub, there'd been no time to finish it yesterday. Poor sod, thought Logan knocking back the painkillers. Rennie complained about always having to make the coffees, but he still went the whole hog with proper mugs and biscuits every time. He just didn't seem to understand that as long as he kept doing that, DI Steel was going to keep on using him as a tea boy. If Rennie didn't want . . . Logan had a brief moment of epiphany and groaned. *Just like if he kept on solving Steel's cases for her, it was always going to be in her best interests to keep him around.* She'd never give him enough of the credit to let him escape her Screw-Up Squad. All that time he'd spent telling Jackie this was his only way to get away from that manipulative, wrinkly old bag, and he'd just ended up making himself indispensable. 'Bastard.' Insch had pretty much told him the best chance he had of getting out of the Fuck-Up Factory was to work on the arson investigation. But would he listen? No. He had to go busting his hump, day in, day out, so DI Steel could take all the glory.

'Everything OK, sir?'

Logan looked up to see the admin officer frowning at him. 'No it bloody isn't.' He dragged himself out of his seat. 'I'm going out. If anyone wants me, you don't know where I am.'

The admin officer's frown grew confused. 'But I *don't* know where you're . . . Sir?' But Logan was gone.

He signed for a patrol car, not recognizing the

registration number until he got down to the rear podium and beheld the same rubbish-filled mobile tip they'd taken yesterday. If anything, it was even more of a mess now; the whole vehicle stank of stale fast food and cigarette smoke.

A patrol car pulled up as Logan was stuffing chip papers into the wire bin by the door with bad grace. Someone familiar unfolded himself from the back seat: DI Steel's mate from the Drugs Squad, the one with the big hands. He looked up, saw Logan, nodded a greeting then turned to help an old lady out of the car. Graham Kennedy's grandmother, looking shaken. Poor old cow probably had her flat broken into and vandalized again. 'You OK, Mrs Kennedy?' asked Logan, going back for an armful of pizza boxes, the cardboard waxy with cold cheese-grease.

She wouldn't look at him, but Detective Big Hands grinned. 'Not today she isn't. Sweet little old ladies shouldn't run drug rings from their homes, using wee kiddies as mules. Should they, Mrs Kennedy?' No response. 'She had a pair of little boys pushing their wee sister about in a stroller packed with drugs. All nice and innocent looking. Attic was full of hydroponic equipment and a big fuck-off chemistry set – growing cannabis and making PCP. One-woman drug cartel. Weren't you?' The old woman kept her face folded shut, staring at the ground. 'No comment, eh? Well, we'll see if you're more talkative after a full body-cavity search.' He led her in through the back door, followed by the WPC who'd been driving – carrying a large plastic evidence bag with a teddy bear in it, one of the ears chewed almost bald – leaving Logan alone on the rear podium with a pile of fat-saturated cardboard.

'Fuck.' He should have bloody known. Bloody thing had been staring him in the face the whole bloody time! He'd even found a huge bag of the stuff in her fridge, for God's sake! 'Fuck!' He hurled the pizza boxes in the bin and stomped back to the car. All those kiddies hanging around, watching her house, waiting for the police to sod off so they could go about their Telly Tubby drug-running business. 'Fuck!' The bloody chemistry teacher thing. The locked attic. The grandson/drug dealer. It was all there and he didn't put it together. 'FUCK!' Swearing and cursing he mashed the last of the boxes into the bin then took two steps back and kicked it hard enough to buckle the wire frame. Then limped back to the car, pulling out his mobile phone and telling Rennie to get down here pronto: they were going out.

By the time they pulled into the Craiginches car park the sun was blazing, not a cloud in the sky, a faint haze on the horizon as the morning haar burned off. But summer didn't seem to have penetrated the prison walls. There was a man in a filthy boiler suit hunkered down by a radiator in the reception area, banging away at it with a spanner, trying to make it work by a combination of foul language and violence. 'Right,' said Logan when the tired-looking woman behind the desk went off to get a list of all the prisoners who were supposed to be out in the exercise yard when Jamie McKinnon overdosed. 'This is how it's going to work – you lead the interview, I observe. If I want to ask a question I'll step in, but other than that, you're the man, OK?' Logan was going to be the organ grinder, rather than the monkey for a change.

Rennie squared his shoulders and nodded. This was his chance to shine . . .

Four interviews later and they were no nearer getting anyone for McKinnon's death. No one had seen anything. Surprise, surprise. As the fourth inmate trooped out of the door Logan let out a yawn. Much to his surprise, Rennie had turned out to be a pretty competent interviewer; he'd only had to step in twice to get something clarified and that was during the first session – after that the constable had made sure he included Logan's supplementary questions for everyone else.

But they still weren't getting anywhere.

Frustrated Logan checked the list they'd got from the front desk again – twenty-seven people in the exercise yard while someone pinned Jamie McKinnon down, someone else covered his mouth so he couldn't scream and a third rammed a syringe into his arm. How could no one have seen anything?

'Er, sir?' He looked up to see Rennie shifting uncomfortably in his seat. 'Any chance we can take a break? I'm bursting.'

'Good idea: pee and tea break.'

Rennie nodded, resignation on his face. 'Yes sir. Two teas coming up: milk no sugar.' And Logan remembered his own moment of epiphany.

'No, you know what? This time I'll make the tea.'

The staff rest area was a small room, jaundiced by decades of cigarette smoke, the THANK YOU FOR NOT SMOKING sign on the wall modified by someone with a black marker pen so the cigarette in the red circle now looked like a penis, dripping sperm from the end. The word SMOKING had been crossed out and WANKING scrawled in its stead. Classy.

Logan filled the kettle and stuck it on to boil. There were no clean mugs in the cupboard, but someone had hidden a packet of Wagon Wheels behind a collection of yellowing coffee filters, so Logan helped himself to a couple. There was a loud sneeze from the corridor outside and he hurriedly stuffed the biscuits in his pocket as the rec-room door opened. It was the social worker from last time, still looking as if she was dying from a cold. Logan slapped a smile on his face. 'Hi, just looking for some clean mugs,' he said, trying to provide a non-chocolate-biscuit-stealing reason for rummaging about in the cupboards.

'In this place? No chance.' She blew her nose on a tatty grey handkerchief and prodded the rumbling kettle. 'You'll have to wash one.' So Logan did, picking two that didn't look as if they'd recently been used for slopping out and rinsing them under the hot tap.

'Still on your own?' he asked, making small talk while the kettle boiled.

'As sodding usual.' She shook a mountain of instant coffee into a huge mug. '*Margaret* can't come in today. *Margaret*'s got flu.' The coffee was followed by an unhealthy amount of sugar. 'Bloody hangover more sodding like . . .

'So,' she said as they walked back along the corridor, 'you here for anything special?'

'Remember Jamie McKinnon?'

'Christ, how could I forget! Got a sodding Fatal Accident Enquiry to go to for that one.' She scowled and sniffed, putting on a whining voice, '"Why wasn't he more closely supervised? Why was he allowed to commit suicide on the premises? Why was he allowed to get hold of drugs?" Like he filled in a sodding form asking permission!'

'If it's any consolation, we think someone killed him. We're interviewing everyone who was in the exercise yard at the time.'

That produced a laugh. 'Good luck – you'll need it!' They'd reached the interview room. 'Anyway,' she said, 'I've got a pile of reports to get back to. Every bastard in here has to be re-checked for "suicidal tendencies" since Jamie McKinnon.' Another bitter laugh. 'And do I get any sodding credit for doing the work of a whole sodding department on my own? Do I hell!'

Logan grunted, the scowl on his face matching hers. 'Tell me about it,' he said. Bloody Steel and her . . . something occurred to him. 'What about Neil Ritchie? He on suicide watch?'

She looked momentarily puzzled. 'Ritchie . . . ? Oh, the "Shore Lane Stalker". Too bloody right he is, the man's a wreck. One death in custody a week's more than enough.'

A grim smile pulled at Logan's face. DI Steel couldn't get a confession out of Ritchie, but then she couldn't interview her nose for bogies. Now if *he* got Ritchie to cough, they'd have to let him out of the Screw-Up Squad. 'Any chance I could have a word?'

She shrugged. 'Don't see why not. Can't hurt after all.'

No, thought Logan, it couldn't hurt at all.

36

Neil Ritchie looked like shit: hunched over, dark purple bags under his bloodshot eyes, hair wild and unkempt, rocking back and forth in a creaky plastic chair. The noise of an overcrowded prison going about its daily life filtered in through the interview-room walls, while an old cast-iron radiator clunked and rattled impotently in the corner. All being recorded for posterity by the tapes whirring away in the machine. The mug of tea Logan had made for DC Rennie sat in front of the trembling man along with one of the pilfered Wagon Wheels, neither of which he'd touched. 'So,' said Logan, leaning forward in his seat, purposely mirroring Ritchie's posture, 'how you feeling, Neil?'

The man stared fixedly at the tea, watching a thin skin form on the surface. His voice was little more than a whisper. 'They . . . they put me in a cell with a *criminal*. He stabbed someone! He told me he stabbed someone . . .' Neil Ritchie screwed up his face, holding back the tears. '*I don't belong here!* I didn't do anything!'

This was exactly the same trick he'd pulled with DI Steel, protest total innocence and repeat ad nauseam. Logan struggled to keep the sympathetic expression on his face. 'What about Holly McEwan, Neil? They found her hair in your car, on the passenger seat. How did it get there, Neil? Help me understand how it got there and maybe I can help you. Did you give her a lift?'

'No!' The word came out like a moan. 'I never did anything with those women – I promised Suzanne. Never again. Never.'

'But they found her hair in your car, Neil.' Logan settled back in his seat, sipping his lukewarm tea, letting the silence stretch.

On the other side of the desk, Ritchie shuddered. 'I *told* her – the inspector – I told her it must have happened before I got the car!' His eyes locked on Logan's, shining with tears. 'Someone else gave her a lift! It wasn't me . . . it wasn't me . . .'

'Your car's brand new, Neil. The garage delivered it to you by seven pm the night Holly went missing: there's a video of her being driven away in your car five and a half hours later.'

'No! No! It . . . the car wasn't there till the morning! I woke up and it was in the drive, it was supposed to be there on Tuesday night – I had to take the bike to the shops. I was going to complain to the garage, but they left a note and a bottle of champagne . . .'

Lies. Logan sat back in his seat and watched Ritchie rattling on about how he didn't like to complain, like the good, little passive-aggressive monster he was. It was odd to think that this trembling wreck had killed three women. Not to mention beating the crap out of Skanky Agnes Walker. 'What happened to your old car, Neil?' he asked, cutting across Ritchie's incessant whining. He was willing to bet it would be chockablock with forensic evidence. 'When you bought the Audi – what happened to your old car?'

The man looked at him, puzzled. 'I . . . I didn't have one. Not for years. I've been on the bike. I only bought the bloody Audi because Suzanne kept going on about growing up . . .' A sob. 'Oh God, why did I have to listen to her?'

Logan sat and stared at him. Then slowly, and with much consideration, he said, 'Oh, shite.'

Five minutes later Logan charged back to the interview room and told Rennie to drop whatever he was doing. The constable spluttered, pointing at the greasy individual sitting on the other side of the table. 'But I'm in the middle of an interview!'

Logan shook his head. 'Not any more you're not. And anyway,' he said, giving the prisoner a quick once over, 'Dirty Duncan here isn't your man. Wouldn't hurt a fly would you, Dunky?' The man smiled nervously and mumbled apologies, hands busy beneath the table while Logan hurried Rennie out of his seat.

'But—'

'But nothing. Dunky would've been too busy wanking himself blind to see anything. Wouldn't you, Dunky?' Dirty Duncan Dundas nodded coyly, his shoulders quivering as he rubbed at himself under the table. They got out of there before he could finish.

'But I don't understand!' Rennie whined on the way back to the car. 'What's going on?'

'Someone's screwed up big time, that's what's going on.' Logan hooked a thumb over his shoulder, back the way they'd come. 'That brand-new car Neil Ritchie bought? It's the first one he's owned for years; he normally rides a motorcycle, his wife drives a tiny hatchback.'

'So?'

'Skanky Agnes: her flatmate said whoever beat her up was driving a big flashy BMW. That sound like a Renault Clio to you?'

Rennie thought about it. 'Oh fuck.'

'Pretty much what I said.'

'So we're back to square one!'

'No,' Logan grinned again. 'We're not. Not by a *long* chalk.'

Wellington Executive Motors gleamed in the sunshine, the glass-and-chrome building only outshone by the polished, expensive motorcars arranged around it. The same Vivaldi soundtrack greeted them as they pushed through onto the showroom floor, but the saleswoman kept her distance: she'd obviously learned her lesson last time – McRae and Rennie weren't here to spend money.

Mr Robinson, the manager, wasn't pleased to see them back either. He hustled them into his office before any of the paying customers could be put off their purchases. 'What now?' He closed the blinds, hiding the showroom.

'Your staff,' said Logan. 'Do they have access to the cars? Out of hours?'

Mr Robinson licked his lips and said 'em . . .' a couple of times. 'The sales team are encouraged to drive the demonstrator models and study the manuals, so they can answer any questions.' He gave a sickly smile. 'It's all part of Wellington Executive Motors' commitment to—'

'The guy who delivered Neil Ritchie's car . . .' Logan checked his notebook for the name. 'Michael Dunbar – what does he drive?'

'He, em . . .' Round beads of sweat were prickling out on Robinson's shiny forehead. 'I'd have to check.'

'You do that. And while you're at it, I want to know every car he's had in the last two months. And I want to see his personnel records too.' Logan sat in one of the comfortable leather seats reserved for special customers and smiled as the beads of sweat on Mr Robinson's face started dribbling their way down his face and around his jowls. 'And yes, we'd love a cappuccino.'

* * *

According to the company's records, Michael Dunbar had been assigned a different car every week: Lexus, Porsche, Mercedes, but he was driving a silver BMW the week Skanky Agnes was assaulted. 'So,' said Logan, 'where is he today?'

Mr Robinson worried a hand through the strands of hair stretched across his bald crown. 'I just don't see how this can do any good. I mean, there's no way any of my staff—'

'*Where* is he?'

'He, erm . . . called in sick this morning: migraine. Michael suffers from them now and then, ever since the divorce . . . '

Logan scanned through the showroom timesheets for the last fortnight. 'Looks like he called in sick last Wednesday too.' The day after Holly McEwan went missing, presumed dead. 'Another migraine?' Mr Robinson nodded. Logan double checked the sheet: every time a prostitute was abducted and killed, Michael Dunbar called in sick the next day. And today he was off with another migraine. That probably meant another dead body.

The radio is on in the garage, Classic FM playing *Dido's Lament*, Dame Janet Baker making every word hang in the air like a dying jewel. Humming along with the music, he packs away the vacuum cleaner's extendable hose and carries the machine back through into the house, returning it to the cupboard under the stairs. Ever since Tracy . . .

Ever since THE DIVORCE, he has kept the house spotless. Not a thing out of place.

It's a big house – big enough for a husband, a wife and three children. Big enough to feel empty and hollow now that it's just him on his own. With a sigh he lays his forehead against the wall and closes his eyes, sharing the house's emptiness. Its sadness.

In the garage, the music swells to a close and then some crass advert for double-glazing blares out, spoiling the moment. Frowning, he goes back through and turns the radio down.

The car sitting in the middle of the garage is now as clean as the house: a shining, top-of-the-range BMW coupé, silver with black leather and walnut trim. Very stylish, and his for another three days. Then, maybe he'll try a Lexus, something with a lot of storage space? After all, this time it's been a bit of a squeeze. He closes the BMW's boot, making sure the plastic sheeting doesn't get caught in the lock. He'll go for a drive later, somewhere nice and secluded where no one will see him.

He takes one last look at the car before heading back into the house.

The cellar is bigger than it looks. Before THE DIVORCE this room was full of things: forgotten wedding presents, the children's old toys, shoe-boxes full of photographs, bits of furniture Tracy inherited from her parents . . . But not any more. It all went when Tracy did. Now the basement is hollow and dead, swept twice a day, mopped every other day. Cleanliness is important. Cleanliness is always important. After all, one wouldn't want to catch anything.

The doorbell goes and he looks up at the ceiling. Perhaps if he ignores it . . . But the doorbell sounds again, a cold and empty noise in a cold and empty house. He sighs, but does his trousers up. He can always come back. There's no rush.

He climbs back up the stairs to the hall, and locks the cellar door behind him as the doorbell chimes once more. 'All right, all right, I'm coming.' He walks down the hall, pausing to check his reflection in the mirror, putting on his migraine face, just in case it's someone from work, come to see if he needs anything. They're good that way. But when he opens the door – squinting painfully into the afternoon light like his head is splitting open – there's a man he doesn't know standing outside, dressed in a dark grey suit that would benefit from professional cleaning. A man he's sure he's seen somewhere before . . .

'Mr Dunbar?' says the man, with a cold smile, holding up some sort of ID card, 'DS McRae. Mind if we come in?'

37

They found the body in the boot of a spanking-new BMW, in Michael Dunbar's garage. It was a woman, naked, wrapped in clear plastic sheeting, her limbs stiff and cold. Her body battered and bruised. Her head wrapped in a blue plastic freezer bag.

'Christ,' said Rennie, reaching into the open car boot with a gloved hand, prodding the cold, pale skin through the clear plastic. 'She's rock solid . . .'

Logan turned and stared at the muted figure of Michael Dunbar. He was an unassuming-looking man, late twenties to early thirties, in tan chinos and a denim shirt, both ironed to razor-creased perfection. Tidy haircut sitting above a slightly rectangular, clean-shaven face. Killer. 'Well, Mr Dunbar,' said Logan, trying to keep the anger out of his voice. 'Care to explain why you've got a naked woman's corpse in the boot of your car?' Dunbar bit his lip and shook his head. 'I see,' said Logan. 'Well, guess what? Doesn't matter if you want to tell us or not. We've caught you red-handed. Soon as we've finished searching the premises, we're all going down to the station. And you're going to get fingerprinted and DNA-sampled and then the forensic boys are going to tie you to the two other women you've killed.'

'You . . .' Dunbar's dinner-plate eyes slid from Logan's face across to the open boot of the car and its cold, dead contents. 'I . . . I don't want to go. I want to speak to a lawyer.'

'I'll bet you bloody do.' Logan turned round to see DC Rennie, still staring into the car boot, with his mouth hanging open. 'Rennie, get on the phone – I want a duty doctor, pathologist and the PF over here, and I want them here now.' Rennie dragged his eyes from the woman's battered corpse and his mobile from his pocket as Logan marched their suspect out into the hall, where the noisy sounds of a search in progress rattled down from the upstairs rooms. Four uniformed officers from FHQ, turning the place upside down.

A banging at the front door, and a familiar dirty-grey moustache and its owner struggled into the hallway, carrying a large box of equipment. 'Where d'you want us?' Logan told him to start with the body in the garage, then pretended not to notice the line of white-boiler-suited technicians whistling *Heigh-Ho, Heigh-Ho, It's Off To Work We Go* as they trooped through the hall.

When the last grey box had been manhandled out of sight, Logan took a look around the bottom floor, dragging Michael Dunbar with him. Large lounge: festooned with photographs of Dunbar, a woman, and three children – two boys, one girl; spotless carpet and ornament-free mantelpiece. The kitchen was similarly immaculate, big enough to accommodate a breakfast bar and a dining table. Utility room off the kitchen: upright freezer full of ready meals, dishwasher, sink, cupboards. There was one more door leading off the hall, but when Logan tried the handle it was locked. 'Where's this lead?' Dunbar wouldn't meet his eyes. Logan poked him in the chest. 'Give me your keys.'

'You . . . you can't do this! I want a lawyer. You can't come in here and do this. This is my home!'

'Yes I can: I have a warrant.' Rachael Tulloch had rushed it through in record-breaking time. 'Now give me your keys.'

'I . . . I don't feel well, I need to lie down . . .'

'Give me the bloody keys!'

With trembling hands, Dunbar pulled out a gleaming bunch of keys. Logan snatched them, trying one after another in the sturdy Yale lock until the thing went 'click' and the door swung open. A flight of wooden steps disappeared down into the darkness. Logan flicked the light switch and a dim glow filled the area at the bottom of the stairs.

'Rennie!' he shouted back into the garage and the constable came trotting out, still clutching his mobile phone to his ear, telling whoever it was on the other end that they needed the pathologist now, not next week. Logan pushed Dunbar at the constable.

'What you want me to do with him?'

'Buy him dinner and take him dancing. What the hell do you think I want you to do with him? Hold on to him!' Logan turned and headed down the steps, already feeling guilty about snapping at the constable. He stopped, apologized and told Rennie he could come too, just as long as he kept hold of Dunbar and didn't let him accidentally fall down the stairs.

The basement steps were enclosed on either side with plasterboard and rough lengths of timber, thick ribbons of grey wire looping across the ceiling between the exposed joists. And then Logan stepped out into the cellar proper, plastic sheeting scrunching beneath his shoes, and saw what was down there. 'Oh shit.'

Rennie: 'What? What is it?'

Dunbar: 'I really don't feel well! I have to go lie down . . .'

Clear plastic sheeting covered the floor, sparkling in the light from the bare bulb like ripples on the surface of a dark lake. It was all the way up the far wall as well, held in place by reams and reams of silver duct tape. Ensuring the crumpled, naked woman – lying on her back with her legs spread at twenty past six, pale skin covered in purple-yellow bruises, face unrecognizably swollen and bloody, arms tied together above her head, fixed to the wall with a six-inch bolt – left no stains.

She wasn't moving.

A scuffling sound behind him and a sudden intake of breath – that would be Rennie – then Dunbar said again, 'I . . . I'm really not feeling well . . .'

Logan grabbed him by the collar and rushed him backwards, crashing the man against the bare brick wall. 'You sick, twisted piece of shit!' Dunbar's eyes went wide, fear sparking from the edges, and Logan froze. He let go of the man's shirt and backed away. Dunbar wasn't worth it. He wasn't worth it . . . But Logan *seriously* wanted to beat the living hell out of him.

Trembling with the effort, he turned and inched his way across the plastic sheeting, feeling it shift and slither beneath his feet as he picked his way carefully to the battered body, trying not to stand in any evidence. As First Attending Officer it was his responsibility to make sure the victim wasn't in need of medical assistance, even though it was bloody obvious she was dead. Christ, she looked as if she'd been run over by a combine harvester. There wasn't an inch of her that wasn't covered with a bruise or contusion. Maybe it was time for Michael Dunbar to fall down the stairs after all. Grimacing, Logan snapped on a fresh pair of latex gloves and squatted down beside the body, peering at the ruined face, trying to match the battered mess with any of the women he'd seen prowling the red light district, offering a good time in exchange for cold hard cash. Instead of which she'd got a cold hard death at the hands of—

A bubble of blood swelled and popped between her swollen lips. She was still alive!

Interview room four had an unwashed smell about it that seemed to make Michael Dunbar very uncomfortable. He sat on the edge of his seat, obviously trying not to fidget, while Logan made DC Rennie do the tapes and introduction bit. They'd dragged Dunbar back to the station, processed him and got him into an interview room without having to talk to DI Steel: according to Big Gary she was *still* going at it with Clair Pirie and didn't want to be disturbed. This was followed by a leering, 'if you know what I mean . . .' Which meant that technically Logan was still in charge.

'So, Michael, or can I call you Mikey?' said Logan, settling back in his seat.

'Michael. Please. Michael. Not Mikey.'

'OK, Michael it is then.' Logan smiled at him. 'Why don't you tell us all about the two women we found in your house today? You can start with the one who's still alive if you like?'

'I have no idea what you're talking about,' said Dunbar, staring dully at the tape recorder, watching the spindles go round and round behind the glass.

'Don't be stupid, Michael: we found them in your house! You were there remember?'

He took a long, shuddering breath. 'I really don't feel well.'

'Yeah? Well the duty doctor says there's nothing wrong with you. Not like the poor cow we pulled out of your basement – fractured skull, broken arms, legs, ribs, fingers, internal bleeding . . . feel free to jump in any time.'

'She was having an affair.' The words came out in a flat monotone. 'She . . .' He closed his eyes and took a deep breath, holding it in, then letting it out in a long, shivering breath. 'His name was Kevin and he was a chartered accountant. I . . . I come home one evening and they're SCREWING in our bed, while the kids are downstairs watching *Sponge Bob Square Pants* . . . Didn't even know I was there.' A bitter laugh that ended in a tear being wiped away. 'So I got my revenge: went out, picked up some ugly tart down the docks and fucked her. Then I went home and fucked Tracy. Just like *he'd* fucked her . . .'

'But she found out, didn't she?'

Another bitter laugh. 'Three days later my dick starts weeping yellow pus and I'm pissing barbed wire. Course she caught it too. And so did *darling* Kevin.' This time the laugh was more genuine. 'That'll teach the cheating bastard!' Dunbar paused, watching the tape go round in silence. 'She left me. Took the kids and all her stuff and walked out the door . . .'

Logan pulled out a sheaf of photographs, propping one up against the tape recorder directly in front of Dunbar: a naked woman, lying on her back in the middle of a dark alley. 'Tell me about Rosie Williams.' Dunbar moved so he wouldn't have to look at the battered body any more, but Logan stuck another picture in front of him. A naked woman lying on her side on the damp forest floor. 'No? How about Michelle Wood?' Another photograph: wrapped in clear plastic in the boot of a car. 'Or Holly McEwan? No? How about this one?' A battered face, covered in blood, the photograph taken an hour ago while they'd waited for the ambulance to turn up. The final picture was a mugshot from the station's collection: Skanky Agnes Walker, full face and side on. Dunbar stiffened.

Logan tapped the print with his finger. 'She was the first wasn't she?'

'Dirty bitch . . .' they were barely words.

A long silent pause, only broken by the dull whir of the tape machine and someone's shoes squeaking on the linoleum in the corridor outside.

'Tiffany. The one in the cellar. She said her name was Tiffany. Picked her up last night in a shiny new car and took her out to Balmedie beach.' A small smile played around his lips as he relived the memory. 'Paid her to suck my cock and when she was finished – smacked her over the back of the head with a hammer. Bundled her into the boot. Took her home. Dragged her down to the basement and tied her up. Couldn't have timed it better, 'cos you know what?' He leant forward and whispered the words. 'The last one was dead.'

Something cold settled in the pit of Logan's stomach. 'The last one was dead?'

'Dead. Three whole days she lasted for. You see, after I got away with the first couple I thought: what the hell? Why rush it? Why not just take her home: really make her pay for giving me her filthy fucking disease? Take my time. Make her pay for leaving me . . .'

Rennie's face went white. 'Christ on a stick.'

There was more. Now that the floodgates were open, Michael Dunbar wanted to tell them everything. Every last sordid detail of how he beat them, then raped them, then beat them some more. Stamping on their ribs, snapping their arms and legs, making them pay for what they'd done to his marriage and his family and his children and his life. Stripping them naked so there wouldn't be any evidence. Dumping their bodies when they got too cold to play with any more . . .

Out in the corridor afterwards, Logan slouched against the wall, feeling nauseous, while DC Rennie carted Dunbar downstairs to the holding cells. The Shore Lane Stalker was due to appear in court at nine o'clock tomorrow morning, where he'd be refused bail and sent up to Craiginches until it was time to stand trial. And given his full confession and all the forensic evidence, there was no chance of anything other than a guilty verdict. And all done by the book.

With a deep sigh, Logan heaved himself upright, just in time to see DI Steel come thundering down the corridor, her face pinched and furious. 'Where the hell is he?' she demanded, stomping to a halt.

'Who?'

She scowled. 'You bloody well know "who". The bastard you hauled in here without even *consulting* me!'

'You were busy interviewing the Pirie woman—'

'Don't give me that CRAP! You know fine well I would've suspended the fucking interview!' She stabbed him in the chest with a rock-hard, bony finger. 'You interviewed Ritchie without my approval. How bloody dare you!'

Logan squared up to her, drawing himself up to his full height. 'He confessed, OK? Four murders and two attempted. *I* interviewed him because *you* didn't want to be disturbed, and he confessed.'

'What the hell's that got to do with anything? You went behind my back, you—'

'I did my bloody job!'

'Your job is to do whatever I *tell* you to do, you backstabbing, glory-grabbing—'

'Me?' Logan couldn't believe his ears. 'What about you? Remember this morning's P&J? "DI Steel solves one of the most baffling cases in Scottish—"'

'I don't write the press releases, and you know it!' They'd been getting steadily louder, but now her voice dropped to an icy whisper as she dug an envelope out of her jacket pocket and tore it open. 'Know what this is?' she asked, pulling out a sheet of paper. 'It's the letter of commendation I wrote to the Chief Constable for you and Rennie.' She tore it into shreds and threw it in his face. 'Believe me, *Sergeant*: if you ever fuck with me again I will personally screw you over so badly you won't know whether to clutch your dick or cry.' She turned on her heel and stormed off, leaving Logan to pick up the pieces.

38

They were supposed to be celebrating, but Logan wasn't in the mood. His phone had gone off at least half a dozen times, but whenever he dragged it out the display said DI Steel was on the other end – probably wanting to have another go at him – so he let it ring through to voicemail, before giving up and just switching the damn thing off. He was off the clock; if the inspector wanted to shout at him, she could do it during office hours. He felt far too guilty to face her at the moment, especially after spending ten minutes Sellotaping the shredded letter back together again – her praise of Rennie and himself had been embarrassingly effusive.

Half seven and DC Rennie was back from the bar with the drinks: G&T for Rachael; pint of Stella for Logan and himself; vodka Irn-Bru, pint of special and two rum and Cokes for the four members of the search team who'd helped rummage through Michael Dunbar's house.

Rennie launched into an impromptu speech about how great they all were for catching Dunbar before he killed again, finishing it off with a toast to Detective Sergeant Logan McRae, without whom none of this would be possible.

There was a cheer and general clinking of glasses. Rachael was leaning over and telling one of the WPCs how many strings she'd needed to pull in order to get the search and arrest warrant set up so quickly, but how she knew it'd be worth it, as Logan was so damn clever. Two major high-profile crimes solved in as many days: first the Torso in the Suitcase and now the Shore Lane Stalker. Apparently there was nothing he couldn't do.

Doc Fraser turned up in time for the second round. He looked knackered as he knocked a huge bite out of his Guinness, sighed and wiped the white foam moustache off his top lip. 'Christ, I needed that.'

'Rough day?'

Doc Fraser nodded and took another deep gulp. 'You don't know the half of it. With Isobel out of the picture I've got to do the whole lot myself. And you know what it's like just now: bloody dead bodies all over the place. The amount of junkies I've sliced up this week . . .' Sigh. 'Oh, and before I forget, that stinking torso you lumbered me with yesterday: same stab wounds and stomach full of antidepressants as your rotting dog carcass.' He sat back, frowning. 'Come to think of it, every rotten, suppurating corpse I've hacked up in the last six months has been one of yours, did you know that? You're now officially off the morgue Christmas-card list.'

'Ah, you love it really.' Logan smiled. 'So how come you're doing all the post mortems? Where's Isobel?'

The pathologist shrugged and polished off the last of his pint. 'No idea: didn't come in today. Tried phoning her, but no reply. Mind you, she's been acting like a rabid futtrit for weeks now, maybe the boys from Cornhill finally came and carted her away? Gave her a nice padded cell and all the crayons she can eat.'

The mood started to sour when someone from the Drugs Squad turned up and told them how DI Steel had caught the *real* Shore Lane Stalker! Rennie surged to his feet, demanding to know who the hell said DI Steel caught anyone. 'It was us!' he said, slapping his chest. 'We caught the bastard, not her! She wasn't even there!' Logan just groaned. He hadn't got around to telling Rennie about the letter of commendation yet.

The fourth round was Logan's. He lurched back to the table bearing a tray full of glasses and snacks: crisps for the normal people, pork scratchings for Doc Fraser. He was handing out the drinks when someone swore, grabbed him by the sleeve and pointed up at the television hanging from the ceiling in the corner. DI Steel stared down at him from the screen, a serious expression on her face as she said something to camera, the words inaudible in the noisy pub. Her craggy face was illuminated by the staccato flash of cameras, then she sat down and the picture cut to the Chief Constable who made some sort of speech. And then it was stock shots of Shore Lane and pictures of the victims before Michael Dunbar had got his fists on them.

Logan closed his eyes and swore. He'd royally screwed up any chance he had of getting credit for solving the Suitcase Torso Murder and Steel wasn't likely to give him any for the Shore Lane Stalker either, not after their shouting match in the hallway. It was time for some serious drinking.

Logan lurched out of the taxi and paused, not falling forward, not falling backward, but teetering between the two as the rusty Ford did a three-pointer in the crowded street and slunk off into the night. With a frown he turned and watched the back of the car disappear round the corner and out of sight. Arse. He'd meant to ask it to wait for him. Taking a deep breath he tucked his shirt back into his trousers and strode purpose-fully towards Dr Isobel MacAlister's front door. Miller used to have a flat in this part of town, but he'd sold it and moved in with the Ice Maiden instead. 'May they have many, many happy years together,' Logan told the huge rhododendron bush lurking in the evening light, dark green leaves glit-tering like burnished liver as the sun began its slow slither towards night. He leaned on the bell, and a deeply conservative *biiiiiing-bonnnnnnng* sounded from the other side of the frosted glass. This was a fancy neighbourhood: Rubislaw Den, money territory. Four-storey granite buildings worth a not-so-small fortune, some of which had been in the family for generations. Lawyers, accountants, bigwigs in the oil industry. People who had four foreign holidays a year and sent their children to private schools. Logan leaned on the bell again.

The light was on above the door. They had to be in.

He squatted down to peer through the letterbox and tipped over onto his backside, scrabbling upright in time to see a shadow loom through the glass on either side of the door. A nervous voice came through the wood. 'Who is it?'

'Isobel? It's me,' said Logan, before thinking about it and adding, 'Logan.' After all, just because they'd shared an attempted murderer and a bed for seven months, there was no reason to expect her to remember who he was.

The door didn't open. 'Are you alone?'

'Am I alone?' Logan took a pace back and nearly fell off the top step. 'Well, I'm still living with WPC Watson, but I think the new deputy PF likes me as well . . .' He grinned. Two women. Tee-hee. 'Can Colin come out to play?'

The door cracked open an inch and a worried face peered out at him. Isobel looked terrible: pale, drawn, deep purple bags under her eyes, lines creasing the skin between her eyebrows and down the sides of her mouth. As if she'd aged a dozen years since last week. 'You're drunk.'

Logan saluted her. 'And you fiddle with dead people for money. But I can respect that. Where's Colin?'

'You don't know?'

'Don't know what?'

Colin Miller was in bed, curled in around himself, grey and shivering, his hands wrapped in white bandages. Logan took one look at Miller's huddled form and suddenly got a lot more sober. 'What the hell happened to you?'

Miller looked up from the bed and stared at him. The reporter's face was swollen and bruised, dark purple tinged with green spreading out from his left cheek, another across his chin, his nose squinter than it had been a couple of days ago. 'Me? What happened to me? I'll tell you what fuckin' happened to me: YOU FUCKIN' HAPPENED!'

Logan flinched back. 'But . . . I didn't do anything!'

'Had to play the big detective, didn't you? Had to push your fuckin' nose in where it didn't belong!' He was half out of bed now, struggling not to use his bandaged hands. 'He recognized you, you stupid prick. You fucked about with him in the pub, even though I told you not to, *and he fuckin' recognized you*!' Miller's naked feet sank into the deep, blue carpet as he lurched towards Logan, holding up his hands. 'Then you arrested him and he knew I'd screwed him over! 'Cos *there you fuckin' were!*'

'Colin, I—'

'HE TOOK MY FUCKIN' FINGERS!' The reporter was crying now, face scarlet beneath the bruises, spittle flying from his twisted mouth, exposing cracked and missing teeth. 'My fingers . . .' Miller buried his head in his stiff, bandaged hands and sobbed. 'My fingers . . .'

They sat in the kitchen, an open bottle of Bowmore sitting on the tabletop along with three glasses, even though Colin wasn't there. Dying sunlight drifted in through the kitchen window, painting the varnished wood with amber, the shadows slipping from pale violet to deep blue as the sun set. Isobel was slumped in a chair on the opposite side of the table, clutching her emptied glass as Logan slugged in another stiff measure of malt whisky. But he was sticking to water. 'What happened?'

Isobel took a deep drink, shuddering as the neat spirit went down. 'He says they grabbed him outside the house. Bundled him into a car and took him out into the woods somewhere. Tied him to a chair and hacked off his fingers, one joint at a time, with a pair of poultry shears.' Her voice was low, matter of fact, as if she was speaking for the benefit of the tape recorder at a post mortem.

'Left hand: little finger, distal, middle and proximal phalanx; ring finger, distal and middle. Right hand: distal phalanx from the little finger, all bones from the ring finger. Each finger severed at the interphalangeal joints. One bone at a time.' She took another long swig, nearly emptying the glass. 'They . . . they left him in a lay-by. Dialled for an ambulance using his mobile phone and left him there.' She shuddered. 'The surgeons managed to reattach three sections. They don't know if they'll take or not.'

Logan slopped another huge whisky into her glass. 'I'm sorry.' Miller was right: this was all his fault.

She looked up at him, as if seeing him for the first time, then stood and crossed to the fridge, coming back with a blue plastic container, placing it down on the table between them. Gingerly Logan popped off the lid and frowned at the contents: small grey-white tubes, like albino chipolata sausages. Then he recognized a fingernail on the end of one.

'Jesus!'

Isobel didn't move. 'He threw up under the anaesthetic.'

'Threw . . . ? He'd eaten them?' Silence. Logan put the lid back on the box. 'Isobel, I never meant for this to happen, I—'

'No? Well guess what: it did.' The last of the sun disappeared behind a wall of granite and the kitchen settled into awkward twilight. 'I want you to find them and I want you to hurt them. Understand?'

'Will Colin testify?'

'They said if he talks to the police they'll come back and finish the job.' She poured herself another drink, her hand trembling, spilling Bowmore on the tabletop. 'You don't involve him. You find them and you hurt them!'

'But—'

'He's your friend! You owe him. You owe me.'

Logan didn't take a taxi back into town. Instead he walked through the gathering dusk, brooding. Colin Miller had lost nearly half his fingers because of him. The reporter was right: he just couldn't keep his nose out. Couldn't leave Miller alone with Chib in the pub, had to know what was going on. Drunken singing came from up ahead and a party of under-dressed girlies lurched out of the Windmill Inn, belting out something unrecognizable at the top of their lungs, hugging lampposts, wolf-whistling at the passing cars.

What the hell was he supposed to do about Chib and his gimp? 'Find them and hurt them.' Yeah, easy for Isobel to say, but he was a police officer. It wasn't as if he could just roll up unannounced and shoot them – this was Aberdeen, not New York. If Colin Miller wasn't prepared to testify, there wasn't much Logan *could* do . . .

Not unless he actually caught them doing something. Even then Isobel wouldn't be satisfied: she didn't want justice, she wanted revenge. Well, she'd just have to settle for what she could get. He pulled out his mobile and turned it back on again: another three messages, all from DI Steel. Ignoring them, Logan started dialling.

39

'Are you sure we should be doing this?' asked Jackie for what felt like the millionth time in the last half hour. The car was cold and uncomfortable, sitting in a small pool of darkness between two lampposts on the quiet residential road. Once more Logan said no, he wasn't, and went back to staring through the windscreen at Brendan 'Chib' Sutherland's house. An unofficial stakeout in a purloined CID pool car? Of course they shouldn't be doing it. Especially as Jackie was technically still on duty for the next thirty-two minutes.

A faint groan came from the back seat and DC Rennie sat up, clutching his head. 'How you feeling?' asked Logan, looking at the constable's green face in the rear-view mirror.

'Like shite . . .' He closed one eye and squinted at the house opposite. 'Where the hell's Steve got to?'

Jackie half turned in her seat. 'Give him a break, OK? He's not the one been out getting pished.'

'Zeesh, who rattled your bumhole?'

Logan gritted his teeth. 'Will you two shut up?' He scowled into the rear-view mirror and Rennie held his hands up in surrender. Silence settled back into the filthy Vauxhall: Jackie sulking, Rennie rummaging about in the rubbish tip that was the back seat, coming up with one of Councillor Marshall's pornographic magazines. He flipped through it in the dim yellow glow of a nearby streetlamp, with an amused expression on his face.

Logan turned round and snatched the thing off Rennie, getting a 'Hey, I was reading that!' for his pains.

'Where the hell did you get this?'

Rennie shrugged. 'It was back here, under all the empty Burger King and KFC boxes.' Logan shook his head and tossed the magazine back to the constable. This was ridiculous: it wasn't even the same car they'd had on the stakeout. It looked like Councillor Marshall's porn collection was doing the rounds all over Aberdeen Command Division – police men and women from Stonehaven to Fraserburgh giggling their way through the man's anal fetish. Made you proud.

'You realize I have to go sign out at midnight, don't you?' said Jackie, peering over her shoulder at Rennie's magazine.

'Tell you what, soon as PC Jacobs gets here you can both go back to the station, sign out, then come back. OK?'

461

'What you going to do if Sutherland leaves the house while we're away?'

'Follow him.'

Jackie snorted. 'You can't follow him: you've been drinking. So has Captain Caveman here.'

'Maybe we'll get lucky and . . . oh-ho: company.' A pair of headlights cruised up the street towards them, pulling up on the other side of the road. A pause, then the lights clicked off. No sign of movement from Chib's house. A figure got out of the manky old Fiat – PC Steve Jacobs, still wearing his uniform – arms full of takeaway. He clambered into the back beside Rennie.

'Evenin' all,' he intoned, popping the cardboard lid off a huge bucket of chicken. 'I got some aspirins, one of them bargain family things and— Hey, wait your turn!' Rennie was already helping himself. 'Did the inspector get hold of you?' asked Steve, handing Logan a bag of chips. 'She said it was urgent: something about a press conference?'

'We saw it in the pub,' said Rennie through a mouthful of chicken. 'Cheeky cow taking all the credit.' Logan blushed in the darkness and kept his mouth shut. Silence returned to the car as they ate, munching and slurping the only noises, while a huge bottle of Pepsi was passed back and forth. One by one they piled the empty wrappers, napkins and bones back into the bucket, then PC Steve stuffed it down at his feet along with all the other rubbish.

'Now what?' asked Rennie, washing down a couple of Steve's aspirins with greasy Pepsi.

Jackie checked her watch. 'Now we have to go sign out.'

'It's OK,' said Steve, 'I got Big Gary to do it for us. Cost me three Mars Bars, but we're free for the night.'

They spent a while playing Spits-or-Swallows, Logan steering well clear of the game; it just made him think of Colin's fingers. Then came a wide-ranging philosophical discussion on thongs versus big pants and after that Rennie's extended monologue on *EastEnders'* villains, past and present. With Steve throwing in the occasional helpful discussion topic like, 'Who'd win in a nude mud-wrestling match: Marge Simpson or Wilma Flintstone?' which kicked off yet another round of Spits-or-Swallows. Betty Rubble apparently spits. But eventually silence and boredom descended again.

Half past one and Chib's lounge was plunged into darkness. Logan stretched in his seat, feeling his back pop and twinge, complaining about sitting here for the last two and a bit hours. His alcohol buzz was long gone, leaving behind a headache and heartburn. The sound of gentle snoring was coming from the back seat, but up front Jackie squinted at Councillor Marshall's magazine, twisting and turning the page to catch as much of the faint sulphurous street lighting as possible. 'You know,' said Logan as the upstairs light flickered on in the house they were watching. 'Maybe this isn't such a good idea after all.'

Jackie looked up from what *had* to be a faked photograph. 'Thought you said it was the only way we'd get anything on Chib and his mate?'

Logan shrugged, head resting against the misty passenger window. 'I don't know.' Sigh. 'To be honest I don't know anything any more . . .' He took a deep breath and told her about Colin Miller and what Isobel said had happened. And how it was all his fault.

'Oh come on, you've *got* to be kidding me!' She threw a glance into the back seat – where Rennie and Steve were curled up like a pair of gangly spaniels, sleeping peacefully – and lowered her voice to a soft hiss. 'How could it be *your* fault? You didn't hack Miller's fingers off, did you? No.' She reached out and took hold of his hand. 'You're a good cop, Logan. You caught Dunbar and that Pirie woman – that old cow Steel would have fucked those cases up like she fucks up everything else. What happened to Miller was just bad luck.' When he didn't say anything she gave his hand a squeeze. 'Tell you what, let's call it a night: tomorrow we go speak to Insch and get a surveillance op set up. That wrinkly-faced bitch might not give credit where it's due, but Insch will. Solve the Karl Pearson thing and he'll get you out of Steel's team like that.' She snapped her fingers and the snores from the back seat came to an abrupt, snorking halt.

A bleary-eyed PC Steve poked his head through to the front and asked what was going on. Logan was just about to tell him they were going home when the light clicked on above Chib's front door and a shadowy figure hurried out into the night, carrying a holdall. 'Heads up,' said Logan, 'something's happening . . .' He squinted, wishing he'd got Steve to lift a pair of night-vision goggles. The figure passed beneath a streetlight: black coat, black jeans, black woolly hat, long black hair and moustache. Chib's mate – the Gimp – walked down to the far end of the street, turning right onto Countesswells Avenue.

'OK!' Jackie sounded excited to be doing something for a change. 'Buckle up, people!'

Logan stopped her before she could turn the key. 'We can't. What about Chib?'

'What about him? The Gimp is on the go, his mate isn't. We have to get cracking or we'll lose him!'

'OK, OK . . .' Logan screwed his face up, running the different scenarios quickly through his head. 'You take Rennie and follow him, Steve and I stay behind and keep an eye on the house.'

It was Jackie's turn to frown. 'How come I get Rennie? Why can't I take Steve?'

'Because Rennie and I've been drinking, remember? Can't drive.'

'Then *you* come with me.'

'And leave these two in charge of the house? I'd kinda like at least one sensible person in each team, if it's OK with you.'

PC Steve's face fell. 'Hey, I heard that!'

'No offence.' Logan eased his door open and slipped out into the night. 'Now get your arse in gear.' Ten seconds later they were huddled in the shadows watching Jackie drive away in pursuit of Chib's pet Gimp, with Rennie rolling about blearily in the back seat.

'Er . . . sir, do you really think they should be going after the child molester on their own?' asked Steve as they sneaked back to his car.

'Relax, he's probably just off for a wank in a playground or something. Anyway,' Logan pointed at the house, where a shadow moved behind the upstairs window, 'it's the bastard up there you've got to worry about.' According to Colin Miller anyway.

The night was dark and quiet, just the way he liked it. Tonight was going to be a special night, one to put in the diary, a red-letter day. Giggling softly, he crossed over the road, picking up the pace as he nipped around the playing fields, enjoying the feeling of light and shadow between the lampposts. Airyhall Avenue was lined with attractive family homes: mother, father, two point four children. Happy, happy families, all snug in bed, dreaming their happy family dreams and waiting for another beautiful family day to dawn. Despite the chill his armpits were already beginning to feel sticky with sweat, and he shifted the heavy holdall from one hand to the other. Tonight was going to be fun; mixing business with pleasure always was. And this time Brendan wouldn't be angry with him. No more black eyes. Anyway, they were going to be leaving Aberdeen soon, heading back home to Edinburgh. He smiled at the thought. The weather up here was too unpredictable: one minute it was blazing sunshine, the next it was hammering with rain, sometimes both at the same time.

At the bottom of the Avenue he stopped to get his bearings, his heart quickening as he saw the sign on the other side of the road: AIRYHALL CHILDREN'S HOME. He'd come too far, shouldn't have come down this road. Should have stuck to the road he was on . . . the home was smaller than the one he'd gone to, where THE MAN had been, the man Brendan had stabbed for him, but that didn't make it any less frightening.

Shivering slightly, he turned and walked the other way, heading back towards the city centre, getting as far away from the place as possible. Only once did he look back over his shoulder at the bulky home and its slumbering, silent inhabitants.

It took ten minutes to walk up past the cemetery on Springfield Road – whistling the *Simpsons* theme tune from the moment he saw the sign – right, onto Seafield Road, and all the way along to the roundabout on Anderson Drive. He stopped beneath a streetlight, setting the holdall down on the grass verge. Why did he have to pack so much stuff? He dug out Brendan's directions – a little map, with a smiley stick figure following the arrows towards a big skull and crossbones surrounded by flames. The house they'd trashed because the old lady wasn't in. Tonight she wouldn't be so lucky.

A siren's wail broke through the quiet rumble of midnight traffic and his heart stopped. A white patrol car roared past, blue lights flashing, taking the roundabout without slowing down and speeding off into the night. Not looking for him.

With a broad smile he picked up the holdall and, looking both ways, crossed the road and hurried towards the centre of town.

'So,' said Rennie, scrambling over from the back seat, nearly standing on Jackie's broken arm twice as she fought with the gear stick. 'You think he's up to something?'

'Get your arse out of my face and sit down!' Jackie snapped. 'Jesus, I would have stopped the car, OK? You just had to ask.'

'Didn't want you to lose him.'

'How the hell am I going to lose him? He's on foot – what's he going to do, outrun us?'

'OK, OK, bloody hell, I'm sorry.' He snapped his seatbelt on and scowled out the windscreen at the figure two hundred yards ahead of them, struggling along the pavement with a heavy-looking holdall over one shoulder. 'You know, ever since you broke your arm, you've been a right cow.'

'*I* didn't break my arm, OK? *Someone else* broke it.'

'Same thing: you've still been fucking horrible.'

She opened her mouth, closed it again, sniffed and shrugged. To be brutally honest, he was probably right. 'Anyway,' she said at last, 'of course he's up to something. We wouldn't be following him if he wasn't up to something.' She drifted the car to a halt at the side of the road and killed the lights, letting their man get a little distance between them.

'So what d'you think he's up to then? Dressed in black, holdall: think he's off on the blag?'

'Nah – the bag's too heavy for that, wouldn't be able to cart anything away afterwards. Making some sort of drugs run? Dropping the stuff off at his resellers?' When she thought that Chib's mate was far enough down the road to not notice the car following him, Jackie turned the headlights back on and pulled out into the quiet road, driving slowly past the playing fields and across the roundabout into Union Grove.

'You know,' said Rennie, 'they did an old lady down here today. She was using little kids as runners. PCP and cannabis and crack and all sorts.'

'Yeah? Well, maybe our boy's looking to take up where she left off.'

Rennie grinned. 'Extra, extra, read all about it: Off-Duty Police Foil Edinburgh Drugs Baron!'

Jackie smiled back at him. 'I can live with that.'

40

The Gimp stopped halfway down Union Grove outside a grubby-looking tenement and scanned the street, making sure no one was watching him. Jackie turned the radio on, cranking up the volume until it was nearly painful – some late-night DJ on Radio One pounding out dance music into the early morning hours, making the car throb – and drove straight past, eyes forward, not paying any attention to the man with the bag full of drugs. It seemed to work: Rennie twisted and slouched, keeping an eye on the Gimp in the passenger-side wing mirror as the man pulled a key out of his pocket and let himself into the building. Rennie slapped the dashboard. 'He's in!'

'Good.' Jackie killed the radio and swung the car around, driving slowly back towards the tenement, settling for a parking space a couple of doors down. They sat in the dark, watching the front of the building.

'Now what?'

'Now we wait.' Silence settled on the car, punctuated by Rennie humming the theme tune to *Emmerdale*. 'Er . . . Jackie,' he said, when he'd finished. 'Should we not be catching him with the stuff on him? I mean, if he's not got the drugs, how do we arrest him for it?'

Jackie scrunched up her face and swore. Rennie was right. She opened her door and stepped out into the quiet, night-shrouded street, looking very conspicuous in her Grampian Police uniform. 'Well, come on then: what you waiting for?'

The building was in darkness, not even a hallway light showing through the glass above the grimy communal front door. Not that much of a surprise: after all it was going on for two in the morning, everyone would be in their bed, asleep. Except for the Gimp and whoever it was he was meeting. Jackie frowned up at the filthy granite. 'That woman who was done for the drugs: you think this is the same building?' Rennie just shrugged, so she clicked on the radio strapped to her shoulder and asked Control for an address check on the old woman arrested for running a pre-school drugs cartel. A familiar voice crackled out of the speaker and Jackie cranked down the volume, trying not to alert the Gimp. It was Sergeant Eric Mitchell, asking why she wanted to know and how come she was using a police radio: wasn't she supposed to be off duty? 'Aye, well . . .' said Jackie, trying to think of a diplomatic lie. 'I was giving DC Rennie a lift home when we saw a suspicious individual entering an address on Union Grove.' It came out sounding as if she was giving evidence in a shoplifting court case, but it was too late to turn back now. 'I wanted to know if this was the same address, as I recognized the individual as someone who has previously been arrested on suspicion of drug dealing.'

'Have you been practising that?' asked the voice on the other end of the radio. *''Cos it needs some bloody work.'*

'Look: he's a dodgy character, he's got a huge holdall with him and we think it's full of drugs. Now you going to give me that address or not?' It took a minute, but eventually Sergeant Mitchell confirmed that it was the same building they were now standing outside. No way that was a coincidence.

'You want me to send backup?'

'No, we got this one. Just get the letters of commendation ready, OK?'

Sergeant Mitchell said he'd see what he could do.

The building's front door wasn't locked – the Gimp had left it on the snib – so they pushed through into the building's tiny airlock lobby, their shoes scuffing on the coconut matting. It was dark in here, getting even darker as Rennie eased the door closed. Now the only light came second-hand through the rippled glass above the door, the streetlight's yellow glow doing little to lighten the gloom. A second wooden door formed the far side

472

of the airlock, and on the other side of that was nothing but darkness. Something brushed her hair and Jackie nearly yelled, before realizing it was Rennie's hand, fumbling about. 'What the hell are you doing?' she hissed.

'Looking for a light switch,' he whispered back.

'Are you fucking mental? Do you want everyone to know we're here?'

'I can't see a bloody thing . . .'

'Then shut your cakehole and *listen*!'

Silence. Then slowly, a low puffing and the occasional grunt became audible from somewhere above. Jackie grabbed Rennie's shoulder and inched forward to the stairs. They crept their way up the first flight, pausing at the bend, where a large stained-glass window let in a faint smear of light. It wasn't much, but it was better than nothing. Jackie looked up, trying to judge where the noise was coming from and saw it: torchlight at the very top of the stairs, the outline of a man, hunched over, doing something suspicious.

She crept forward again, almost getting to the middle floor when the banister creaked beneath her hand. The grunting from above stopped. Now the only sound was the blood whumping in her ears. Then the torch's beam brushed the stairs behind them and swept upwards, catching Rennie full in the face. Someone said 'Fuck!' then all hell broke loose.

A glass bottle smashed against the stairs above their heads, showering the wall with what smelled like petrol. Jackie took a deep breath and bellowed at the top of her lungs: 'POLICE! HOLD IT RIGHT THERE!' then had to jump out of the way as another bottle crashed into the banister, spewing hydrocarbons across the stairs and carpet.

Rennie cried out in pain and stumbled into her in the dark, sending them both crashing onto the landing. And then the stairs juddered: the Gimp thundering down towards them. Jackie struggled to stand, but Rennie was sprawled on top of her, swearing a blue streak. She slapped at him, shouting, 'Get off me you moron!'

Thud, thud, thud and the Gimp was on the middle floor, running past at full tilt. Jackie flailed a leg out, her boot connecting with a kneecap. A grunt of pain, swiftly drowned out by the crash, thud, crack of the Gimp tumbling head-first down the stairs.

'Move!' Jackie slapped Rennie again and he lurched off her, letting loose another agonized yelp and a fresh bout of foul language. She scrabbled to her feet and threw herself down the stairs, aiming for the rounded, bulky shape silhouetted against the landing window. She slammed into him just as he was getting to his feet, sending them both careering into the corner with a clatter of glass bottles. Bang – hot yellow fireworks burst across Jackie's vision as her head bounced off the wall. She staggered back, ears ringing, and slipped on the top step, collapsing against the banister as the Gimp lurched to his feet.

Jackie lashed out randomly with a foot and missed, but the Gimp didn't: a heavy boot connected with her ribs, lifting her clean off the floor, sending her crashing back into the wood-work. Oh Christ that hurt! She tensed, ready for the next kick, but it didn't come: the Gimp was making a run for it.

Harsh light, as if someone had turned on the sun, stinging her eyes, making everything leap painfully into focus. She squinted up to see Rennie leaning against the wall of the first-floor landing, one blood-soaked hand holding on to the light switch, still swearing for all he was worth.

More thudding down the stairs: the Gimp was nearly at the bottom. Jackie struggled upright, then ducked as another bottle exploded against the wall beside her, sending petrol everywhere. 'BASTARD!' She charged, stopping dead when she saw what the Gimp had in his hands: a Zippo lighter. Her hair was full of fucking petrol!

Blood oozed from a gash in the Gimp's forehead, running down the side of his nose and into his moustache. He grinned. Then set the world on fire.

'Christ I'm bored.' PC Steve slumped forward in the driver's seat of his scabby Fiat. Arms crossed over the top of the steering wheel, he let out a theatrical sigh, then said, 'Spits-or-Swallows?' Logan said no. 'If-You-Had-to-or-Die?' Another no. 'Shoot-Shag-or-Marry?'

'*No*. I don't want to play anything, OK?'

'Only trying to pass the time . . .' They sat in silence for a whole two minutes before the constable came out with, 'Did you hear about Karen's boyfriend?'

Logan frowned. 'Who the hell is Karen?'

'You know, Karen Buchan? WPC? 'Bout so tall? She was with me when we found Rosie Williams?'

The frown turned into a scowl. 'Oh . . . *her.*'

'Aye, well.' Steve leaned over and dropped his voice into a conspiratorial whisper, even though there were only the two of them in the car and the rest of the street was deserted. 'Rumour has it her bloke – PC Robert Taylor to you and me – has been playing "non-league fixtures", if you know what I mean.'

A small bout of schadenfreude made Logan smile. 'Serves her right.'

'Yeah, she is a bit of a cow. Anyway, he's been seen down the docks doing it! Actually doing it! Can you believe it? I said to Jackie, I said . . .' There was more, but Logan tuned it out, staring through the window at the dark, silent house. It was nice of everyone to help out, but basically, this was a monumental waste of time. Another half hour and he was calling it quits. Tomorrow he'd talk to Insch and— The light above Chib's front door blossomed into life.

'. . . and then she's like all, "could he *be* any balder?" and I said—' Steve was still babbling away to himself so Logan jabbed him one in the ribs. 'Ow! What was that for?'

'Something's up.' He pointed at the house where Chib Sutherland was hurrying out of the front door, a mobile phone clamped to his ear. He went straight to the silver Mercedes sitting outside and jumped in behind the wheel. The car roared out of the driveway, speeding away from the house. Cursing, PC Steve coaxed his grubby Fiat into life and hurried after Chib, trying not to make it too obvious he was following him.

'What d'you think's got into him?' asked Steve, as Chib jumped the red lights on Springfield Road.

'No idea . . .' But whatever it was, it wasn't going to be good.

Blue flames raced up the stairs, leaping from step to step on the petrol-soaked carpet. Jackie turned and ran, trying to stay ahead of the blaze. The wall behind her burst into flickering yellow where the last petrol bomb had hit, tendrils of black smoke curling around the next flight of stairs, spiralling upwards to the ceiling. She slithered to a halt on the first-floor landing where Rennie was banging on the door to the nearest flat and shouting, 'Open up for God's sake!'

'Kick it in!' yelled Jackie. Rennie took two steps back and slammed his boot into the wood: the whole frame juddered, but the door stayed shut. 'Again!' This time the door exploded inwards, taking half the surround with it. A sudden blast of heat from upstairs and the paint began to blister on the underside of the landing, drips of molten carpet oozing down from above. Smoke was rapidly filling the stairwell – thick, black, lung-searing clouds that reeked of petrol and burning nylon. They charged into the flat. Inside someone was screaming the word 'burglars' over and over again. And then the smoke detector picked up on the inferno and added its shrill bleeping to the shouting and swearing and the roar of the flames.

Jackie snatched the radio off her shoulder and yelled for a fire engine and ambulances, following Rennie through the nearest door. The screaming became an incoherent shriek. A double bedroom: old woman in bed, clutching the blanket to her chest, teeth on the bedside cabinet next to her; old man already on his feet, wrinkled willy poking out the front of his stripy pyjamas, brandishing a walking cane, snarling.

Rennie slammed the bedroom door closed. 'We're the police, you silly bugger! Is there anyone else in the house?' The old man lowered his makeshift cudgel and shook his head. 'What about next door?'

'Mr and Mrs Scott.' He coughed; smoke was already beginning to find its way into the bedroom. 'They have a young daughter and a dog . . .'

Rennie swore. 'I want you to get that window open!' he said, pointing. 'Chuck the mattress out and lower your wife and yourself down. WPC Watson will help you.' He turned – catching Jackie's eye as she rattled off a description of their attacker to Control, telling them to pick the bastard up and kick the shit out of him – then Rennie wrenched the bedroom door open and charged out into the hall, slamming it shut behind him.

Jackie didn't figure out what he was up to till it was too late. 'Rennie! Rennie, you daft bastard!' They were out of time: just have to hope he knew what he was doing. She joined the old man at the painted-shut window, yanking and hauling on the frame until it creaked open like an arthritic joint. The double mattress tumbled out, spinning as it fell, leaving the duvet caught on a little oval satellite dish. The old man peered out uncertainly at the rectangle of foam and springs. Even if it was just a first-floor flat, it was still a *long* way down. Jackie grabbed him by the arm and shoved him towards the open window. 'Come on: you have to go first. I'll lower your wife, you catch her, OK?' She was having to shout now, the roar of the fire drowning out everything but the incessant squealing of the smoke detector. He hesitated and she cast another glance over the lip of the window to the crumpled remains of a mattress fifteen feet below. 'There's nothing to worry about,' she lied, 'you'll be fine!'

'Don't bloody patronize me . . .' Gingerly he inched out of the window, lowering himself as far as possible before plummeting the last eight feet onto the mattress, landing in a tangle of limbs and foul language. The old woman was a lot more nervous, and a lot heavier, but Jackie still managed to force her out the window, even if she did come close to crushing her husband when she crashed down on top of him.

Something burst inside the building, making the bedroom door rattle. From outside came the faint wail of sirens. Jackie took a deep breath and jumped.

41

Brendan 'Chib' Sutherland's driving became a lot less erratic when he hit Union Grove. The silver Mercedes slowed until it was well below the speed limit, almost as if the driver was looking for something. PC Steve slowed down as well, keeping the distance between the two cars constant. A siren was sounding from somewhere up ahead. Then they saw the orange glow in the sky. Something was burning.

The Mercedes jerked to a halt in the middle of the road and a figure lurched out from the pavement, bent over, limping, a sagging holdall in his hands. He clambered into the car, there was a short pause, and then Chib drove off. 'Damn . . .' Logan dug out his mobile and dialled Jackie's number. Worried. She'd been following the Gimp and now there he was, looking as if he'd been in a fight, and there was no sign of either Jackie or Rennie. 'Come on, pick up the bloody phone!' Twelve rings later it cut to voicemail and he cursed, hung up and hit redial.

Steve was still on Chib's tail, following him up Union Grove towards the junction with Holburn Street. 'Holy shite!' He stared agog out of the windscreen: up ahead flames leapt from a tenement rooftop, neon-yellow sparks spiralling into the night, a pall of thick, black smoke spreading like a bruise across the sky – the top two floors were ablaze. Chib drove calmly past.

Logan swore again as Jackie's recorded message told him she was just too damn special to come to the phone right now, so leave a message. Hang up. Redial. He grabbed the radio off PC Steve's shoulder, clicked it on and demanded to be put through to WPC Watson, only to be told to wait his turn: she'd called in from a serious fire and wasn't answering her radio any more. Logan shouted, 'Stop the car!' and PC Steve slammed on the brakes. Logan wrenched open the door and sprinted towards the burning building, shouting for Jackie at the top of his lungs. The howl of sirens was getting stronger.

A small knot of people were gathered around a fallen figure on the pavement, one of them performing CPR, while others cried and moaned.

'JACKIE?'

A grubby, soot-stained face looked up at him. It was DC Rennie; he was the one doing the mouth-to-mouth. The victim was a middle-aged woman in an oversize Aberdeen University T-shirt, the fabric riding up to show off a pair of grey pants and a mealie-pudding stomach. 'Over there,' he said, pointing to a figure hunched by the front of the building, while embers fell from the sky like incandescent snow.

'Jackie?'

She was bent over the still body of a golden retriever lying on its side with a pool of something dark oozing slowly out of its head, gently stroking its fur. A spark drifted down, landing on the dog's flank, producing the bitter smell of burning hair. Logan dropped down beside her, gently touching her arm. 'Jackie? Are you OK?' Her face was filthy, and so was her once-white uniform shirt. She didn't look up at him, just brushed the smouldering ember away.

'He wriggled when Rennie was lowering him out of the window,' was all she said. A newish-looking double mattress lay on the ground less than two feet away.

'Come on,' he said, helping her to her feet. 'It's not safe.'

She gazed back at the dog as he led her out to the pavement, only snapping back to earth when Alpha Three Six screeched to a halt right in front of her. A huge neon-orange fire engine was next, disgorging its occupants and reams of equipment out into the road, the braying honk of another engine not far behind. 'He got away!' she shouted over the din. 'It was Chib's mate. He covered the whole place in petrol!' A fireman charged past, spooling out a length of hose behind him. 'He got away!'

'I know: Chib picked him up. We were following him and—'

'You can't let him get away! The bastards'll do a runner!' She grabbed him by the collar and dragged him towards PC Steve's fusty old Fiat, abandoning Rennie to deal with the fire scene. 'You,' she shouted, jumping in beside Steve while Logan clambered into the back. 'Drive!'

Steve put his foot down and the car raced to the end of the street, passing an ambulance going just as fast the other way. 'Left or right?' Logan had no idea and said so. 'OK,' said Steve, squinting in concentration. 'Right . . .' He raced out into the box junction, heading down Holburn Street. A pair of red tail-lights glowed in the distance; no sign of any other vehicle. Steve put his foot down. The Mercedes was almost at the Garthdee round-about, doing a sensible thirty miles an hour, when they caught up with it. Steve sped past on the wrong side of the road – the Fiat's ancient engine sounding like an angry hairdryer – and slammed on the brakes. The car squealed round in a fair-ground pirouette, stopping sideways-on as the Mercedes screeched and juddered to a halt, its ABS kicking in, leaving Morse-code trails of rubber behind. Jackie was first out of the car, with Logan and Steve close behind. She swung her truncheon like a baseball bat at the windscreen, shattering a vast spider's web into the glass. She was reaching back for another swing when the passenger door exploded open and the Gimp leapt out. There was

484

something in his hands – Logan got as far as shouting, 'GUN!' before a harsh crack rang out and PC Steve went down like he'd been hit by a bus. Screaming.

Logan and Jackie hit the deck. Another shot dug a hole out of the tarmac by Logan's leg and he scrabbled backwards, getting the tiny Fiat between him and the shooter. Another shot clanged into the bonnet and a fourth into the bodywork, all punctuated by PC Steve's high-pitched wailing. A squeal of rubber and the Merc shot backwards, paused and roared forwards, sending up a cloud of grey smoke, nearly flattening Jackie on the way past. A final bark from the gun, forcing Logan to scramble out of the way, and the car was gone. Its brake lights flashed hard on and it slithered sideways into the Garthdee roundabout, rear alloy wheels bouncing off the barrier in a flurry of sparks, before the Mercedes fishtailed out onto the Bridge of Dee and raced away into the night.

PC Steve was lying on his back in the middle of the road, already white as a sheet, a huge dark stain spreading out from the right side of his chest, blood bubbles popping and frothing from between his lips. Jackie ran over to him, peered at the hole in his chest, swore silently, then leaned on it hard: trying to staunch the bleeding. Logan called for an ambulance. If they were lucky he'd still be alive by the time it got here.

Jackie looked up from Steve's pale face. 'What

the fuck just happened?' The constable's screaming had died away to shallow, gasping pants, each one bringing up more blood to spill down his chin.

Logan knelt down next to Jackie. 'How is he?'

She stared at him, dark red soaking its way up her sleeve. 'How the hell do you think he is?' Steve moaned and a cascade of blood rolled down the sides of his face. She tried to wipe the worst of it off, but more kept coming.

'Come on, Steve: don't you dare fucking die on me! If you leave me stuck with that bastard Simon Rennie, I'll kill you!'

'Did you . . .' Logan drifted to a halt then swore. 'What?'

'I just figured it out. All of this: it's a turf war. Malk the Knife making his play for Aberdeen. He sends Chib up here to break into the local market – they find out Karl Pearson's a dealer so they grab him and torture the poor bastard until he gives up his mates. Then the Gimp burns them alive. Same with Kennedy's Grandmother.' He pointed up Holborn Street where the sky glowed a fiery orange. 'They try to scare her off, but it doesn't work, so she's next. Christ knows where the second house fits in – maybe they're in on the deal, so they get burnt too. Chib and his mate have been getting rid of the competition.' He pulled out his mobile and called Control, telling them to get a couple of patrol cars down here pronto.

Jackie shifted her grip on Steve's heaving chest,

trying to find purchase on the blood-slicked fabric. 'Where the hell's that ambulance?'

'They'll be here soon. Everything will be OK,' he lied, trying to sound confident – this whole thing was a complete fucking disaster.

'How's he doing?'

'You're doing great, aren't you, Steve?' The jollity was as forced as the smile. Steve just shuddered and bled.

The wailing cry of an ambulance made Logan's head snap round. 'About bloody time!' He grabbed one of Steve's cold, blood-soaked, trembling hands. 'Come on, not long now: you'll be fine.' But Steve's eyes were unfocused and his breathing was becoming more laboured and painful. The bloody froth wasn't just coming out of his mouth any more: it was bubbling out between Jackie's fingers.

42

The ambulance's cold blue light swept the tarmac, reflecting back off the windows of parked cars and houses lining the bottom end of Holburn Street. Curtains had been twitching ever since the first shot rang out, but now the residents stood with them fully open, silhouetted against their bedroom lights, staring down at the car and the ambulance and the dying policeman.

Jackie sat on the bonnet of the bullet-pock-marked Fiat, slapping a paramedic's hand away as he waved a finger back and forth in front of her face, trying to figure out if she had concussion or not. 'I'm fine! Leave me the fuck alone.'

Steve was being hurriedly strapped into a stretcher, drips going into his arm, oxygen mask on his face, a huge wad of compression bandages sticking up from his chest. They hefted him into the back of the ambulance, then the doors slammed shut, the siren yowled into life and the driver put his foot down, taking the quickest route to Aberdeen Royal Infirmary.

Logan was still on the phone to FHQ, getting them to set up roadblocks on every road south from Aberdeen. Chib would ditch the car first chance he got – a silver Mercedes with a smashed front windscreen was hardly inconspicuous – so the teams were to look for two tall men with Edinburgh accents, one with short blond hair, the other with long dark hair and a moustache. Both to be considered armed and *extremely* dangerous. That done he hung up and dialled DI Insch's number – not wanting to face Steel right now. He wanted backup from someone that actually trusted him.

'Any luck?' asked Jackie as Logan finished the call.

'Not happy about being woken up at half two in the morning, but he's on his way.' Logan rubbed at his face with tired hands. The adrenaline rush of being shot at was ebbing away, leaving him exhausted and feeling sick. 'He's going to call the Chief Constable and let him know about Steve.' God it was going to be a mess: another policeman shot on the streets of Aberdeen – there would have to be press conferences, briefings, meetings, updates, more meetings . . . none of which would help PC Steve Jacobs. 'What did the ambulance crew say?'

'Not much. Lot of swearing . . .' She hung her head and sighed. 'Bastard.'

Logan had to agree. 'What we need to . . .' He

drifted to a halt, as a fresh siren cut through the night. 'Here we go.' Alpha Two Seven pulled up on the other side of the road and a pair of uniformed constables clambered out, wanting to know what had happened. They stared in silence at the blood slick on the tarmac, while Logan brought them up to speed then ordered them to seal off the street and call for an IB team. The whole scene would need to be bagged and tagged.

News was travelling fast. Another three patrol cars arrived in as many minutes, the police men and women looking pale and shocked as they heard about PC Steve. All except for WPC Buchan who wore a superior 'I told you so' expression, muttering to anyone who'd listen that this was just like what happened to PC Maitland and wasn't it a HUGE coincidence that DS McRae was in charge both times? But Logan was too tired and too pissed off not to bite: 'You! Get your arse over here NOW!'

WPC Buchan straightened up and marched across the road, standing in close with cold, ugly eyes. 'Yes . . . *Sergeant?*'

Logan prodded her in the shoulder, speaking through gritted teeth. 'You got something to say? Have you, Constable? Come on then, let's hear it! Nice and loud so everyone can hear what *you've got to say.*' She stared up at him, her whole face tightening around her scrunched-up mouth. Logan let the pause grow before lowering his voice to a growl. 'Just because your boyfriend is screwing around behind your back you *will not* take your shit out on me. Understand?'

She went bright red. 'That's got nothing . . . he's not . . . I—'

'Steve Jacobs is my friend and I've got enough to worry about trying to catch the bastard that shot him without having to deal with YOU!'

'But I—'

'Get your arse back in that patrol car and keep it there.'

WPC Buchan spun around, looking for support, but suddenly everyone was busy doing something else, anything else. She turned back to find Logan looming over her. 'I am *ordering* you off my crime scene, Constable. You can expect a written complaint about your behaviour and attitude.' He leaned forward so their faces were almost touching. 'Now get out of my sight.'

'What do you mean there's no sign of them? There has to be!' Logan marched back and forth across the road, not paying any attention to his surroundings, forcing the IB team to scuttle around him as they photographed ejected shell casings and bloodstains. 'Are they stopping every car?' The harassed woman on the other end of the phone said yes they were, and searching every boot too because, believe it or not, they had actually done this kind of thing before! Logan apologized and hung up. They were getting nowhere fast. Every major road was blocked, and most of the little side routes too. Not an easy task in farming country where minor roads criss-crossed the landscape, knitting tiny clusters of farm and residential buildings together. There were hundreds of possible routes south, as long as you knew where you were going. But the chances of a big-city Edinburgh boy like Chib being familiar with the road layout of Lower Deeside were slim. He would be a dual carriageway kind of guy.

'Where the hell are they?' Logan stopped pacing and stood looking down at Jackie – curled up in the passenger seat of an empty patrol car, mouth open, snoring softly. She was filthy, her face black with soot, smears of Steve's blood on her cheeks, more on her uniform, an egg-sized lump above her left eye where she'd banged her head on the wall. Logan sighed: there wasn't anything else they could do tonight. The roadblocks would either catch Chib and his mate or they wouldn't. And if they made it as far as Edinburgh, Lothian and Borders Police would pick the pair of them up and return them to Aberdeen for questioning and trial. Chib had screwed up big time: he'd been involved in the shooting of a police officer and left witnesses. Not even Malk the Knife could make that disappear.

'What the hell happened?' Chib was shouting, gripping the steering wheel in both hands, trembling with rage. 'I give you one simple *fucking* task . . .' He let go of the wheel and slapped the cowering figure in the passenger seat who squealed in pain. 'Where the fuck did the police come from?'

'I don't know, I don't know!' Greg wrapped his arms around his head, crying, but Chib hit him again anyway, knowing he'd feel bad about it afterwards. He always did. Swearing, he dragged the van into a quiet-looking cul-de-sac and killed the engine, sitting in furious silence as it pinged and clunked. He'd really loved that Mercedes, but by now it was little more than a burning hulk, abandoned and torched on a dirt track on the South Deeside Road.

Gritting his teeth, Chib took a deep, deep breath and counted to ten. This wasn't Greg's fault . . . 'OK,' he said at last. 'I'm sorry I hit you. That was wrong of me. I was upset, but I shouldn't have taken it out on you.' He reached over and patted his passenger on the arm. 'Now, can you tell me what happened?'

Greg shifted in his seat, wiping his runny nose on the back of his sleeve. 'I was . . . I was in the house and everything was going great: I did the old woman's front door with the screws and I poured in the petrol and I heard something on the stairs! There was two of them and they shouted at me and I tried to get away, but one of them hit me in the knee and it really hurt and she was all over me and hitting and kicking and biting and I kicked her back and ran away and set fire to the stairs and ran outside and called you . . .'

Chib patted him on the knee. 'You did good, Greg, you did good.' And Greg's whole face lit up, happy that Chib wasn't angry at him any more. 'How did they know you were there? Did they follow you to the building?'

'I looked! I did! But there wasn't anyone I could see.'

Chib scowled. It was that bastard DS McRae again – he'd recognized him jumping out of the car, just before that grubby bitch broke the Merc's windscreen. Bloody DS McRae. A small smile fluttered across his lips. The police would expect him to go south: get out of Aberdeen and back to his home turf as quickly as possible. But instead they were going to head north, go up round Inverness then down the west coast, past Oban, through Glasgow and back to Edinburgh. If he put his foot down they could be back home before the pubs shut tomorrow. But there was something he wanted to do first.

Get even.

43

DI Insch turned up looking like someone had dragged him out of bed at half two in the morning. He listened in silence as Logan took him through everything from the time Jackie called the fire in, to the current status of the roadblocks. Insch popped a Liquorice Allsort in his mouth and chewed thoughtfully, the IB spotlights shining off his huge, bald head. 'Right,' he said at last. 'Bugger off home out of it.' He pointed at Jackie snoozing away in the front of the patrol car. 'And take Rip Van Winkle with you. We'll meet again at twelve hundred hours tomorrow. There'll need to be an enquiry into the shooting.' Another Allsort disappeared. 'They're going to want to know what you were all doing out here.'

Logan blushed. 'Ah, yes, well, you see—'

Insch stopped him with a hand, face cold and impassive. 'No. I don't want to know. But you'd better pray all your stories fit together. Maitland was shot in the line of duty: but if this was some half-arsed unofficial operation, you're screwed.'

A patrol car dropped them off in Union Grove so they could take the pool car Jackie had been driving back to the station. There wasn't much left of Grandma Kennedy's building: the top two floors were a write-off, just a hollow shell of granite and blackened timbers, the roof partially collapsed. Getting arrested for drug dealing was probably the luckiest break the old lady ever had, otherwise she'd be dead by now.

Logan clambered in behind the steering wheel, but Jackie told him to shift his backside over. He wasn't getting to drive. 'But it was ages ago, I—'

'I don't care. Last thing we need is you getting done for drink driving. We're in enough trouble as it is.' She started the car and struggled into her seatbelt, wincing as she twisted to clip the buckle into place. 'Did Insch know you'd been on the piss?'

'Don't think so . . . Least, he didn't say anything.'

'Good.' She pulled out into the road, heading back towards the flat. 'What did you tell him?'

'Everything . . . Well, everything except for Colin's fingers and the fact we were staking out Chib's house without any sort of official sanction. Didn't think that would go down too well.'

Jackie groaned and swung the car onto Holburn Street. 'Why the hell did we let you talk us into this?'

Logan sank down in his seat. 'Thanks,' he said, 'I don't actually feel bad enough already.' He clicked on the police radio, looking to pick up any news from the roadblocks, or an update on Steve. Nothing. He pulled out his phone and called A&E. Constable Jacobs was in surgery and his condition was critical. They'd know more in a few hours.

Logan let his head rest against the cool glass of the passenger-side window. What a great day: in the morning he'd gone to the funeral of someone he'd got shot; in the afternoon he'd caught a serial killer; in the evening someone else had taken all the credit for it; and now he'd presided over yet another shooting. What a great, great, great, great, day. Not to mention finding out he'd been responsible for a friend getting their fingers hacked off. No wonder he was part of DI Steel's Screw-Up Squad: it was where he belonged. Speaking of which, he might as well get it over with . . . He pulled out his phone and called up DI Steel's messages, feeling more and more depressed as they played. *'Logan, where the hell are you? Press conference in half an hour – be there!'* Beeeeeeep. *'It's me again – what, are you sulking? Come on, get your arse in gear, the CC wants you to give a speech, or some fuckin' thing.'* Beeeeeeep. *'Ten minutes – where are you? Look, I forgive you, OK? Now get back here!'* Beeeeeeep. *'Jesus, Logan: why do you have to be so high fucking maintenance? Come on!'* Beeeeeeep. And on and on. The last one was a curt *'You'd better have a bloody good excuse for not turning up!'* Far from stealing all the glory, she'd actually been trying to give him his moment in the spotlight. 'Wonderful.' He deleted all the messages. It was too late now anyway, he'd screwed that up, just like he'd screwed up everything else.

He still had no idea what to do about Miller. With Chib on the run Isobel would be on Logan's back the whole time: nipping his head about how he was supposed to have done something, and why had no one caught them yet, and what if they came back, and . . . Logan screwed up his face and swore and swore and swore. 'Turn the car round!'

'What?' Jackie pointed at the junction in front of them. 'We're nearly home.'

'Turn it round!'

She gave a theatrical sigh and hauled the car around, doing a U-turn on Union Street. 'Where to, o great and wise master?'

'What if Chib's not on his way south? What if he's got unfinished business?'

Now it was Jackie's turn to swear. 'Colin Miller's fingers.'

'Exactly. Chib knows we're on to him, he's going to think it's Miller's fault.'

She floored the accelerator, tearing down Union Street, ignoring the red lights on Union Terrace and the amber outside the Music Hall, deserted streets and shops flashing by on either side. 'You going to call for backup or what?'

Logan braced himself as Jackie bounced the car through the Y-junction at the top of Holburn Street, following the road round onto Albyn Place. 'What if I'm wrong?'

'Then you look like an arse. What if you're right?'

'Miller doesn't want anyone to know about his fingers, he—'

'Tough shit. Steve doesn't want to be lying in hospital with a bullet in him! That Weegie bastard held his hands up earlier we'd have Chib in custody days ago, instead of getting our arses shot off!'

She was right. Logan pulled out his phone and made the call – closing his eyes as Jackie rallied the car around the Queen Victoria roundabout – only to be told no one was available: everyone they had spare was manning roadblocks. Logan swore, hung up and dialled DI Insch's mobile. 'You do know he's going to fire me for this, don't you?' he asked while the phone rang. 'Inspector? It's Logan – I need some backup.'

'*Backup? What the hell do you need backup for?*' Logan told him about Miller's fingers and Chib's threat to return if he was caught talking to the police again. '*You think he's daft enough to go back there? You mad? He'll be scooting it down the road with his tail between his legs!*'

'What if he's not?'

Grumbling, Insch said he'd see what he could do and hung up. Jackie slowed the car to a more normal speed and turned off onto Forest Road, the entrance to Aberdeen's moneyed district. 'Well?' she asked.

'Maybe.'

'Maybe? What sort of answer is that?'

'The one I got, OK?' He pointed at the entrance to Rubislaw Den North. 'You want to go left here then on round the corner.'

The street was silent. Little flecks of light danced across the pavements, sodium-yellow streetlight dappled through the swaying leaves of huge, mature beech trees. The house was up ahead, as dark and silent as the rest of the street. Logan tapped on the passenger window. 'Pull in here.'

Jackie squeezed the car in between a grubby blue Transit Van and a soft-top Porsche. 'Right,' she said, creaking on the handbrake, 'what's the plan?'

'Sneak up, have a look about. If nothing's happening we come back and wait in the car.'

'Great. Just what I need: *more* hours cooped up in this bloody heap.'

They stepped out into the night, picking their way past the filthy van. Logan stopped, turned, frowned and asked Jackie if it looked familiar to her. 'You kidding?' she said, turning her back on it. 'Looks like every other crappy Transit in the whole city. I thought we were in a hurry?'

Logan marched up the path to Isobel's house, cupping his hands against the drawing-room window and peering through into the darkened room. Nothing. The lounge was the same. There was no way to get around to the back of the house.

'Now what?' asked Jackie.

'Could always try the bell I suppose.' Logan pressed the button and the familiar *biiiiiing-bonnnnnnng* rang out from deep inside. They settled back to wait, and wait and – Logan tried the bell again. Both cars were in the drive: they *had* to be in, it was half past three in the morning!

Jackie peered through the letterbox. 'Like a graveyard in there.'

'Is it just me,' said Logan, 'or are you starting to get a bad feeling about this?'

'Maybe they've both passed out? You said Doc MacAlister was getting laid into the whisky when you were here – Miller'll be on painkillers . . .'

Logan stood back, gazing up at the dark house. 'What's the worst that can happen if we go in there and nothing's wrong?'

'You get your bollocks chewed off for breaking and entering.'

'Not if we've got a key . . .' He tipped up the small pot of pansies growing beside the door and rummaged about in the shadows beneath it, coming up with nothing but dirt and a worm. He tried the other side. Nothing. 'Damn, she used to keep a spare key out here.'

'Under a flowerpot by the door? Why not just put a big sign in the front garden saying, *I'm stupid: please rob me*?'

'You got a torch on you?' Jackie did; after all

she was still wearing her uniform, drenched in sweat and blood, the faint, lingering whiff of petrol just discernible under the smoky stench of burning building. She was in the middle of handing it over when a light blossomed in the hall, glowing through the glass panes surrounding the door.

''Bout bloody time,' said Jackie under her breath as the deadbolt clicked back, the chain rattled and the door opened wide.

Isobel peered out at them. She looked a mess, hair flat on one side and sticking up all over the place on the other. Bloodshot eyes, a fresh graze on her left cheek. She was wearing baby-blue pyjamas with penguins on them – very appropriate. 'What do you want?' The words wreathed in whisky fumes.

Logan stepped up to the door. 'Isobel, are you OK? What happened to your cheek?'

A hand fluttered up to the graze and she tried for a smile; it didn't work. 'I may have . . . fallen over on the way to be sick.' She stepped back and then held out a hand to him. 'Come in, come in, you and your lovely wife Daphne.' She swung a finger round to point at WPC Watson. 'I've got some Pernod somewhere, I know you both love that.'

Logan opened his mouth to say, 'You *know* I hate Pernod!' but she was already weaving her way back up the hall.

'Daphne?' hissed Jackie. Logan shrugged, Isobel must be more plastered than he'd thought. But then she'd never been much of a drinker. They followed her into the house and through to the kitchen at the rear. All the lights were on and there, in front of the breakfast bar, naked and strapped to a kitchen chair, was Colin, a bondage gag stretching his jaws wide, blood running freely from his chest, marking the place where his left nipple used to be.

A noise behind them in the hall; Logan spun around and found himself looking down the barrel of a gun. It was the Gimp, one side of his face covered in dried blood. He motioned Logan through the door and into the kitchen proper.

'DS McRae,' said a familiar Edinburgh accent as the door was closed behind them. 'What a pleasant surprise.'

44

Chib sauntered over to stand beside Colin Miller. The reporter was pale and sweaty, shivering and moaning behind the gag. Chib pulled out a pair of bull-nosed pliers, the rubber grips dark against his latex surgical gloves. 'Now then,' he said, all pleasant smiles as Colin started to cry, 'DS McRae, I'd like you and . . . I'm sorry, darling, but I don't know your name.' Jackie just gazed in horror at the gun in the Gimp's hands. 'No? Cat got your tongue? Doesn't matter: I'd like you both to sit down, nice and quietly, and we'll have a chat about what's going to happen next. OK?'

The Gimp pointed to an empty chair at the kitchen table and Logan sank reluctantly down into it, trying not to flinch as the gun was jabbed into his ear and Isobel was told to secure his hands to the seat with some of the cable ties on the breakfast bar. She put them on nice and loose, leaving Logan plenty of room to escape. But the Gimp grabbed the end and yanked on the plastic, pulling the catches so tight that Logan hissed in pain.

Jackie staggered back into the corner by the wine rack, hands up to her mouth, tears in her eyes, whimpering 'Oh, God no. Oh, God no. Oh, God no' over and over again.

'Let's get started,' said Chib, dragging Colin's left arm up, twisting it and forcing the wrist back so it was locked in place. The bandages on Colin's hands were missing, exposing raw lumps of flesh stitched together over the swollen, bruise-covered stumps. The joins where two segments of finger had been reattached were clearly visible, the stitches puckering the inflamed skin. Chib levered open the pliers and clamped them around one of the restored joints. 'Just so we all know we're not playing games here . . .' He grunted and twisted, yanking the length of finger away from Colin's hand, ripping the stitches free. Fresh blood welled up in the ragged hole and, behind the gag, Colin screamed. Smiling, Chib crossed the kitchen to the pedal bin, stepped on the lever, and dropped the chunk of finger in amongst the eggshells. 'These are the easy ones, it gets a lot more messy when we have to go in with the shears.'

Isobel sat at the kitchen table next to Logan, eyes glazed, face pale as marble, tears running down her cheeks as the Gimp fixed her hands to the seat, just like Logan's.

'Now, that was just one little bit of finger. Colin still has oh, four whole fingers, two thumbs, all those stumps . . .' Chib's lips moved as he did the arithmetic. 'Twenty-three bits left! God, we could be here for *hours*, couldn't we?'

Logan tried to keep his voice calm and even, almost managing it. 'This isn't going to achieve anything, Chib, why d—'

'No: it's Brendan, not "Chib": BRENDAN.' Chib nodded and something hard clattered into the side of Logan's head, pain slicing across his scalp as blood oozed down the side of his face. '"Chib" is such a childish nickname, don't you think?' He straightened his tie and put on his calm smile again. 'Contrary to popular belief, torture and senseless violence *do* achieve things. You see, once we're done here, they'll discover what's left of your bodies and know not to fuck with us. It'll keep the junkies and pushers and whores in line. Fear is a great motivator.'

'That how you keep your Gimp in line, is it?' said Logan through gritted teeth. 'Beat him every now and then? Teach him the error of his child-molesting ways?'

'HE IS NOT A CHILD MOLESTER!' Chib lunged forwards, ramming a fist into Logan's face, snapping his head back, making the darkness roar. 'Understand? *I will not fucking tell you again!*'

Logan rocked forwards in his seat, blood spiralling from his mouth, the edges of the room lurching in time to the hammering in his skull. Maybe getting Chib mad wasn't such a good idea after all. The Edinburgh thug grabbed a handful of Logan's hair, dragging his head up, shouting in his face, 'You want to meet a child molester? Try growing up in a fucking children's home! Try spending six years in borstal!'

Huddled in the corner by the Shiraz and Zinfandel, Jackie sobbed, her cries getting louder and louder, blending into one long incoherent stream. 'Ohgodnoohgodnoohgodnoohgodno . . .' Her knees were drawn up to her chest, her broken arm covering her face, the plaster cast almost unrecognizable under the layers of soot and PC Steve's blood.

'Oh for goodness' sake . . .' Chib turned his back on her in disgust. 'Greg, please do something about that dreadful racket!'

The word 'No!' burbled from Logan's split lips, as the Gimp advanced, raising the gun like a cudgel, looking to crack her head open. And that's when WPC Watson punched him full strength in the balls. The Gimp opened his mouth to suck in a tortured breath, but Jackie's feet lashed out, catching him in the knee, sending him crashing to the kitchen floor. Snarling, she leapt on him, smashing her plaster cast into his face again and again and again. Chib screamed and leapt for her, but Jackie was too quick, rolling clear as the larger man clattered into the wine rack, sending bottles flying. Then she was on her feet, the gun in her right hand, the plaster on her left arm cracked and flaking, splattered with a patina of fresh, bright-red blood. The Gimp wasn't moving.

The whole thing had taken less than four seconds.

She smiled, all traces of hysteria gone. 'Women, eh? Can't trust them an inch.'

Chib licked his lips, looking from the barrel of the gun to the splayed, bloody figure of his friend. 'Greg?'

'On the ground – hands behind your head, legs crossed.'

Chib crawled to his knees and inched forward, placing a hand on his friend's motionless body. 'Greg, are you OK?'

'I said, hands behind your head!'

'We need to get an ambulance! He's not breathing!'

'Good!' She aimed a kick at the Gimp's leg. 'Bastard shot my friend!'

Logan spat out a mouthful of blood and winced. 'Jackie, we have to get him an ambulance.'

'Yeah? Why?' She turned on him, face creased and angry. 'Why should this piece of shit live when Steve's going to die?'

'Why should either of them live?' It was Isobel, her voice cracking on the words. 'Look what they've done! You arrest them – then what?' She was getting louder. 'They go to trial, maybe get fourteen years? Out in seven for good behaviour, less with time served! You think the bastards won't come back? Kill them!'

Logan turned and stared aghast. 'You can't just kill them – they're not bloody animals, they're human beings!'

'No they're not.' Jackie placed her boot in the small of Chib's back and shoved, sending him sprawling across the body on the floor. She held up the gun, examining the mechanism, then racked a round into the chamber.

'JACKIE, NO!'

'Greg?' Chib was back on his knees. 'Come on, Greg, breathe!'

'Do it!' Isobel was wheedling now, her face contorted and ugly. 'No one will ever find out. Colin knows someone with a pig farm – we can get rid of the bodies! *They'll come back if you don't!*'

'JACKIE!'

She placed the gun to the back of Chib's head.

45

Two days later.

'How much of this is true?' asked Insch, tossing Logan's report back across the desk. Fifteen pages of lies and half-truths, printed out this morning when he'd got back from the hospital. Outside the inspector's window morning sunshine caressed the city, making the monolithic glass tombstone of St Nicholas House sparkle and gleam as summer put in a farewell appearance. From now on the weather forecast was doom and gloom. Thank you Aberdeen, and goodnight . . .

'All of it. Every last word.'

Insch just looked at him, letting the silence grow, waiting for Logan to step in and fill the void with something incriminating. Logan kept his swollen mouth shut. Two days on and Chib's fist was still making its presence felt. 'Fine,' said the inspector at last. 'You'll be interested to know that the lab's come back on the bullet they dug out of

PC Jacobs – believe it or not, it matches the one they found in PC Maitland. Same rifling marks. Same shooter.'

Same shooter? Logan closed his eyes and groaned. 'The van.'

Insch stopped and stared at him. 'What van?'

'Outside Miller's house: grubby blue Transit. It was the same van that turned up at the warehouse when Maitland was shot. I *knew* I recognized it!' He swore and stared up at the ceiling. There never had been any stolen property in that warehouse; it was Chib's drugs distribution point. Miller said Graham Kennedy was the one who'd tipped him off about the place being full of nicked electrical goods, but Kennedy just wanted the police to get rid of the competition for him. Turn up, find the drugs, arrest the new boys from Edinburgh. Fine if it had worked, but it hadn't: Chib and his pals got away. Then they returned the compliment, only Chib didn't piss around with anonymous tip-offs, he went straight in with the abduction, torture and mass murder. Gotta love someone who takes their work seriously. Logan swore again.

'You OK, Sergeant?'

'Not really, sir, no.'

Insch nodded and creaked his massive frame out of his chair, scrunching up an empty Jelly Babies packet and tossing it into the bin. 'Come on, Fatal Accident Enquiry's not till half four, I'll stand you a bacon buttie and a cup of tea.'

Logan's stomach churned. 'No, thanks, but I'm not really in the mood for bacon.' All he could think about were Miller's friend and his pigs. 'If you don't mind, I've got something I need to take care of.'

He picked up a pool car and went looking for someone in uniform to take with him. WPC Buchan was standing by the back door, smoking a cigarette and chewing at her nails. She looked as if she hadn't slept a wink since he'd ordered her off his crime scene two days ago. 'It's half ten, how come you're still on?' he asked and she flinched. 'Thought night shift finished at seven.'

She looked at the ground beneath her feet and shrugged. 'Put in for a green shift. Couldn't just go home and wait for Professional Standards to call. Climbing the walls . . .'

'Come on,' he said, tossing her the keys. 'You're driving.' They made it as far as Hazlehead before she cracked and asked him when he was going to file his complaint against her.

'You know you've been behaving like a complete arsehole, don't you?' said Logan as the tower blocks drifted past and the countryside opened out on either side of the car. Her back stiffened, but she kept her mouth shut. 'If I could go back,' he said, 'and fix things so Maitland and Steve didn't get shot, I would. I never wanted it to turn out like this.' The road up to the crematorium went past on the left, the building hidden behind a hill and a stand of trees. Logan sighed.

'I'm not putting in a complaint. I'm giving you another chance.'

She squinted at him from the corner of her eye. 'Why?' Suspicious.

'Because . . .' Pause. 'Because everyone needs a second chance.' Or in Logan's case a third and fourth. Things still weren't back to normal with DI Steel – this morning's headline in the P&J hadn't helped any . . .

Silence settled back into the car again. It stayed there until the Kingswells roundabout had been and gone. Now it was just fields and the occasional house until Westhill, the grass shining emerald green in the sunshine. That was one of the great things about Aberdeen: no matter where you lived, the countryside was never more than fifteen minutes away. Except during rush-hour. 'I . . .' WPC Buchan cleared her throat. 'First I thought he was just having an affair, but . . .' Deep breath, the words coming out in a rush. 'But I think he's been sleeping with the women down the docks. The . . . prostitutes. Letting them off with cautions if they—'

Logan held up a hand. 'It's OK, you don't have to tell me.' He'd already guessed: that was why Michelle Wood and Kylie didn't have criminal records, and why the Lithuanian schoolgirl had offered to do him for free – because he was a policeman.

'I kicked the bastard out.'

'Good.'

*   *   *

513

Ailsa stood at the kitchen window, watching the children playing in the schoolyard: the younger ones running around like mad things, the older, cooler kids kicking back on the grass, soaking up the sun. The horrible woman from next door had been remanded without bail. That's what the papers said this morning. Remanded without bail: charged with the gruesome murder of Gavin Cruickshank. There was even a small picture of her ugly, hate-filled face staring out of the *Press and Journal*'s front page as they led her from the court building. Of course Gavin's death wasn't as *important* as some local sex scandal – Gavin only merited three short columns at the bottom of the page, but it was enough to let everyone know what a bitch Clair Pirie, neighbour-from-hell, had been. Ailsa took a deep shuddering breath. Oh God: she was finally gone.

The children blurred and she blinked back tears, biting her bottom lip. She wasn't going to cry, she wasn't going to – a sob escaped. A low, keening noise, full of pain. Gavin . . .

She stood at the kitchen sink and cried, mourning her marriage and her husband, while the children played. Children they would never have together.

Clutching the edge of the sink she lurched forward and was sick, splattering the spotless, stainless steel with Fruit 'n Fibre, retching up mouthful after mouthful until there was nothing left.

She was upstairs in the bathroom, washing her face, when the doorbell went. Probably the press again. Reporters had been ringing her phone day and night, banging on her door, wanting to get their grubby little hands on the story of a grieving widow. As if there wasn't already enough pain and misery without rubbing a little more salt in the wound. *'Mrs Cruickshank, is it true your husband was having an affair?' 'Mrs Cruickshank, have they found your husband's head yet?' 'Mrs Cruickshank, how does it feel to know your next-door neighbour dismembered the man you loved?'*

The doorbell again, this time accompanied by a voice. 'Mrs Cruickshank, it's DS McRae. Can you open up please?'

She swirled some toothpaste round her mouth – gargling and swallowing the foam, coating the bitter taste of bile with a thin veneer of mint – then hurried downstairs and opened the door.

DS McRae stood on the top step, with a plain-looking WPC. 'Can we come in?'

Logan followed her through to the kitchen where the window hung wide open, the sound of playing children drifting in from the school across the road, the harsh stench of floral air freshener masking the acid smell of vomit. There was a copy of that morning's P&J on the table, the front page dominated by the words Councillor Had Sex With 13-Year-Old Prostitute! Not one of Colin Miller's catchier headlines, but it was difficult to type when you were missing half of your fingers. He skimmed the article while Ailsa Cruickshank made tea. There was no mention of the Chief Greenbelt Development Planner, or McLennan Homes, and the whole thing was attributed to 'a detective inspector on the vice squad, who wishes to remain anonymous . . .' but it was still enough to get Councillor Marshall suspended from the council and investigated by Grampian Police. DI Steel was spitting nails.

Three delicate china mugs clinked down onto the table, accompanied by a plate of chocolate digestives. Ailsa settled into one of the chairs and looked expectantly at Logan.

'Mrs Cruickshank,' he said, wondering how best to phrase this, 'there's something that's been bothering me for the last couple of days . . .'

'Yes?'

'Your husband's remains were found to contain large amounts of antidepressants.'

She looked confused. 'But Gavin wasn't depressed – he would've told me! I'd have noticed.'

'So the question remains: how did he end up with all those pills in him?'

Ailsa prodded Clair Pirie's photo on the bottom of the P&J's front page. 'Maybe, she forced him to eat them? Crushed them up and mixed them in something?'

'You like crime fiction, don't you, Mrs Cruickshank? You showed us your collection first time I was here, remember? Do you like that bit

516

at the end of the book, where the detective finally sorts through all the lies and unmasks the real killer?'

'I . . . I don't understand.' She put her mug down. 'What's this all about?'

Logan looked her straight in the eye. 'We know.'

She sat on the other side of the table, her face suddenly pale, and stared at him as time stretched like chewing gum. She opened her mouth and closed it, swallowed and tried again. 'I don't know what you're talking about.'

'Why use a bright-red suitcase if you're going to hide it in the woods? Unless you actually *want* it to be found. Why dismember a body but leave a huge tattoo with the victim's wife's name on it? Even if I hadn't seen that photo of him with the Hooters girls, we'd have run a search through the database and your name would've popped up on Gavin's missing person report. Gavin, who just happens to be having three separate affairs. And lo and behold your next-door neighbour, who you've been trying to get rid of for years, leaves her garage door open the whole time, with the connecting door unlocked, and spends a huge chunk of her life passed out in the back garden. How hard would it be to nip round there, smear some of Gavin's blood round the bathtub and stash the knife in the garage?'

'This is ridiculous.'

'Is it? You get rid of your cheating husband *and* the bitch next door all in one fell swoop.' Logan smiled. 'But the pills were a mistake: you should've just clobbered him over the back of the head. How was Pirie supposed to get him to eat half a bottle of antidepressants? Bake him an "I'm sorry I smashed you in the face" cake?'

'He phoned his office—'

'Text message. He didn't need to be alive for you to send it from his phone. And Hayley didn't go away on holiday either, did she? You killed her and hid the body somewhere, but it'll turn up eventually, they usually do.'

Ailsa stood, the chair scraping back across the tiles. 'I want to speak to my lawyer.'

Logan shook his head. 'You read too many detective novels, Mrs Cruickshank. This is Scotland: you get a lawyer when we say so, not before.'

The Fatal Accident Enquiry was adjourned for the evening at half six, to reconvene at eight the following morning. Jackie was waiting for Logan as he slouched out of the conference room. Her broken arm was back in a brand-new case of plaster – shockingly clean after the filthy mess the last one had been in when they'd finally cut it off at the hospital in the early hours of Tuesday morning. 'Well?' she asked. 'What did they say?'

Logan forced a smile. 'PC Maitland died in the line of duty due to unforeseeable events. We're getting together for a lessons learned thing tomorrow.'

'You see? I told you it'd be OK.' Taking a quick check up and down the corridor to make sure no one was watching, she reached up and kissed him hard.

'Ow!' Logan flinched back, one hand going to his swollen top lip. 'Take it easy: loose tooth, remember.'

'Oh shut up, you big baby.' She enfolded him in a long, warm kiss. 'Come on,' she said, when they finally broke for air, 'I promised Steve we'd bring him some Kendal Mint Cake and a pornographic jigsaw.'

'Jackie?' said Logan as they walked down the stairs. 'Would you really have shot him? Chib – could you really have done it?'

Jackie just smiled. 'Oh *hell* yes.'